Red and White

Kenneth Weene

Red and White

This is a work of fiction. Any resemblance to actual persons, living or dead, is purely coincidental.

ISBN 13: 9781732723771

Library of Congress Control Number: 2019944497

Cover Photos: Richard Lee, Unsplash

Cover design © by All Things That Matter Press
Published in 2019 by All Things That Matter Press

This is a work is based upon some true events, however, it has been fictionalized and all persons appearing in this work are fictitious. Any resemblance to actual persons, living or dead, is purely coincidental.

This story is dedicated to a man whom I never met, indeed one who died many years before I was born. While it is recorded in history, Plenty Horses is not a name many would know. In fact, I didn't know of him when I started writing Red and White. I only learned of him when I was researching the Drexel Mission Massacre, which occurred just after the killing fields of Wounded Knee.

Whilst I had not known of Plenty Horses, he must have known of me. For I have no doubt that it is he who has used me to tell the story of Lonely Cricket. I am not a great believer in channeling and otherworldly muses, but I have no question that the Sioux warrior Plenty Horses has spoken to me and through me to the world.

Of course, it is not only Plenty Horses but the thousands upon thousands of Native American youngsters who were taken off to the White Man's Indian Schools who deserve our remembrance. And, it is not just those who died at places like Wounded Knee and the Drexel Mission who deserve our sense of injustice, for so many Native Americans have suffered dearly at the hands of the Euro-Americans who swept over the continent.

This is, of course, a work of fiction. I have attempted to capture a sense of what transpired in this country and to celebrate something of the depth and flavor of Native American traditions while creating so much from the whole cloth of my imagination. I can only hope that what I have created does justice to the world it would mirror.

So, with a last nod of appreciation to Plenty Horses, I give you

Red and White

Foreword

Note to the Reader on the Stories, Accents, and Italics

There are many stories told within the larger story that is this novel. Most of those stories, which I have created, are attributed to Native American communities. They have been set off using ΩΩΩΩΩ above and beneath them. Because they are intended as translation from the native tongues, these stories are told with appropriate grammar. Similarly, when Native American characters are talking to one another and using their own languages, the English reflects proper grammar.

However, when Native American characters are speaking English, I have tried to stay true to how that speech would have sounded.

In those places where Native Americans are speaking their own language in the body of the text, I have used italics. I also used italics to set off a letter written by one of the Indian characters in English.

I have avoided using italics for thoughts or interior dialog. Also, after some discussion, it was decided to not italicize Native American words because they are not considered a "foreign language."

Since this story is set in the second half of the nineteenth century, I have endeavored to use the accents and slang of that period when white and Black characters are speaking. It is not my intent to offend, only to be honest in my writing.

Note on Native American Names and Characters

Some earlier readers of Red and White have found it difficult to keep track of the Native American characters and their names. I liken it to the difficulty I have when reading Russian novels; those names just don't sound like anything I know. Of course, when we meet Native Americans today, they use names that sound just like ours, an Anglo or Spanish sounding first name and a family name which may sound like that of a Euro-American or may be derived from a Native American word. However, the vast majority of Native Americans also have another name in their own language tradition. That name can typically be translated into English just as my first name Kenneth originally meant handsome; of course, that was centuries ago in Gaelic.

Because my characters' names are much more immediate and integrated into the individual's life, I have chosen to translate them directly into English as was the custom when the action of this book takes place, for example Sitting Bull and Crazy Horse. There are a few exceptions in which names can't be translated. Two of the characters have names that begin with Y: Yquili Sparrow and Sparrow Yenri. The Y sound in both is like the Y in yeah. Both names are derived from early French influence. This influence, through intermarriage by French friars who came to North America as missionaries and stayed as husbands and fathers, is part of Ho-Chunk history and the names which were presumably derived from the common French names Jacqueline and Henri have survived in the tribe. I deliberately used Sparrow with both to help cement the idea of that common French ancestry even though the two characters are not related.

While among some tribes there is a tradition of naming children with an operational surname such as "Harold son of Joseph," which, by the way, is also a Jewish tradition, I have opted to go with the more common practice that each person receives a unique name. As the reader quickly learns, those names can be based on stories. So, for example, Lonely Cricket is named for Child of Cricket whose death was marked by the introduction of tobacco. Similarly, Lonely Cricket's younger brother, Many Fish, is named after the recounting of a story. Since Many Fish is born in Nebraska, it may seem strange to emphasize fish. That is deliberate on my part because the Ho-Chunk were originally from the Great Lakes area. Today, the tribe is divided between two areas, Wisconsin and Nebraska. As with so many aspects of Native American life, that division was imposed from Washington. Originally, the tribe was to be forced into the plains and away from their traditional way of life. Some of the Ho-Chunk returned to their historical home and resisted this resettlement.

The history of America's native populations is the story of the Euro-American's constant attempts to destroy the native cultures and traditions. The Indian Schools were one such attempt. The first of those Indian schools was in Carlisle, Pennsylvania. It was the school to which Lonely Cricket was sent, as was Plenty Horses, who is the muse behind this book. At those schools, the speaking of native tongues was prohibited, and the children were given European names, primarily Biblical ones. Just two ways in which the schools worked "kill the Indian in order to save the man."

Major Richard Henry Pratt was not a cruel man. His own relationship with the Native Americans at the school, and especially the Apache who had been placed under his control in Florida where they had been removed from their native land and bands, was at worst paternalistic. Whatever Pratt's intentions, the Indian School system he pioneered became a place of great suffering and death. The young Native Americans did not give in easily to the White Man's attempt to assimilate them. Despite the school rules, many of the young students struggled to retain their identities.

One of the major conflict areas between Indians and Euro-Americans was religion. In large part this was due to the missionary zeal of the Whites. They saw Native religions as polytheistic and pagan and probably many Whites honestly believed they were saving the souls of Indians by forcing Christianity upon them.

Of course, there were differences in theology among the tribes of North America. The native religion I have tried to present is rather simplistic. It is, as is the Judeo-Christian religious tradition, based on myths and traditions. In the Native American worldview as I understand it, there is a creator god, Ma-Ona, who has created not only an orderly world in which we live but also a spirit world that surrounds us. It is the connection between our world and that spirit world that gives traditional Native American theology so much depth.

Of course, that connection was an anathema to the White missionaries who would never believe in a "Trickster" sent to test people but who were perfectly content with the idea of angels doing the same. Today, many of Euro-America descent are much more comfortable with the Native American notion of the cosmos. However, during the late nineteenth century, the time frame of this novel, such acceptance and sense of integration was not to be found. Even when the Native Americans looked for a way to join their traditional beliefs and Christianity, the White man rejected them, which led to the condemnation and annihilation of the Ghost Dancers.

So, who are the Native American characters in this story? The largest number of continuing characters appear in Chapter Two. Below is a brief list designed to give a sense of the relationships among those characters.

Lonely Cricket is the main character of the novel. His parents are Lame Bear and Yquili Sparrow. His older sister is Happy Turtle and his baby brother Many Fish. Small Deer is a young man who is in love with Happy Turtle.

Shadow Fox is an adolescent who teases Lonely Cricket. His younger brother Sparrow Yenri is about the same age as Lonely Cricket and they are friends. Their father is Talking Mountain Sparrow Yenri and Lonely Cricket have a mutual friend, Twisted Rock; but that boy will join in with Shadow Fox to tease Lonely Cricket.

There are three leaders in this community. Dreaming Woman knows the way of medicine and of birthing babies. Sadly, most studies of Native Americans fail to reflect the crucial role that women have played in keeping tribal knowledge and traditions alive. Falling Cloud is a sacred clown, an Heyoka. The role of the Heyoka is pivotal in not only keeping traditions alive but also in defining what is and is not acceptable. Finally, Falling Cloud is the more traditionally known Medicine Man or chief that Euro-Americans expect to find among Indian tribes. As with any gathering, there are other more random members of the community present. Charging Buffalo and One Tree represent the range of the community and its opinions.

Just to clarify, the animals are also given names, but those names are simple and descriptive such as Great Horse or Stubborn Mule.

Since they are central not only in Chapter Two but in the flow of the book, I will mention the Whites who appear in that chapter. The Cook family have come from the East and have taken title to the land adjoining that assigned to Lame Bear and his family. Harry Cook and Lame Bear have developed not only a working relationship but a friendship. Harry's wife, Leah, is a kind-hearted soul, but it is the Cook's only child, Sapphira who is Lonely Cricket's best friend. Harry Cook's nephew Nathan has just come to live with the Cooks. In fact, this is when Lame Bear first meets this young man.

Also, in Chapter Two there is one of the short legend stories that are integrated into the book. The hero of that story is Young Wolf. As with all these stories, the named characters, and there are typically only one or two, are only found in that story and therefore the names stand alone without relationship to other characters in the book.

Occasionally, I have also added Indian names for natural phenomena, which are ordinarily personified, such as the moon. I have tried to place those names, such as Huhawira, in context so that the reader can gather their meanings in the flow of the book.

I think this note a sufficient introduction to help readers get into the flow of Red and White. I greatly appreciate the Beta readers who suggested it.

Part One ~ Of These Roots

Chapter 1 ~ The Coming

ΩΩΩΩΩ

On the third day of the Moon of Young Elk, a stranger stood outside the circle of lodges of The People and called out, "People, bid me enter for I have brought you a great gift." Three times he said this as was the custom, and he stood outside the circle of the lodges as was also the custom, and he waited for a response.

The oldest son of Great Owl, who was then chief, was sent to ask the stranger his name, his tribe, his clan, and his business.

The stranger responded, "I am Walker of Miles from among The Strong People. In my tribe we do not speak of clans, for they are sacred, but I am allowed to tell you that I am not of the sky, the land, or the water."

At those words, the young man ran from the stranger in fear, for if he was not from the sky, the earth, or the water, he must be from a clan of the spirit world and the stranger surely brought death.

The stranger, seeing the man run in fear, called after him, "Do not be afraid. I have brought a precious gift to your people. "The sound of his voice gave wings to the young man's feet, for what man is not afraid of the spirit world? What heart does not tremble at the thought of death when he comes to a camp and asks entry?

Yet, there he was, this Walker of Miles, and he was obeying the etiquette of The People. He was not rudely entering the camp. He was not carrying his weapons in his hands ready for use, but upon his back as befits a guest who has only good intention. He had even repeated his request three times, and now he was doing so again: "I am Walker of Miles of The Strong People. Bid me enter for I have brought you a great gift." The stranger repeated his words twice more.

Great Owl, having heard his eldest son tell of the stranger, sent his middle son to ask the nature of the gift which he brought.

When the middle son approached, the stranger said again, "I am Walker of Miles of The Strong People, bid me enter for I have brought you a great gift."

"What is this gift you have brought?" the youth asked.

"I cannot tell you, for it is magic and can only be shared once the ritual has been performed."

When the middle son learned that the stranger carried magic, he, too, was afraid. He ran in terror back to his father.

Great Owl instructed his youngest son, Child of Cricket, "Ask this Walker of Miles if his magic is for good or evil."

The boy, who was not yet of age to hunt but who knew no fear, did as he was instructed. "Walker of Miles," he called as he strode across the dancing circle, which is the heart of each village. The dancing circle was framed by the lodges of the people and was itself centered on the fire pit where game was roasted for all and around which the dances of war and peace, birth and death, propitiation of the gods and thanks for good fortune took place.

Without thought of the sacred space around the fire pit, the section in which only the chiefs of the tribe, the makers of medicine, and those chosen to prepare the feasts are permitted, Child of Cricket strode across the open ground towards the stranger. Then he stopped in the sacred circle and shouted, "Walker of Miles, is the magic you bring for good or for evil?"

"It is greater than good or evil," the man replied in a voice as loud as the thunder.

His eldest brother, hiding within their father's lodge, yelled, "Run, Child of Cricket; this stranger must be a shaman of great power. Run for your life."

His middle brother, who cowered behind his mother's cooking fire, also yelled, "Hide, Child of Cricket; the stranger is dangerous. He will destroy you."

The boy, knowing nothing of fear, picked up a stone and threw it at the shaman. "Go away! I know you must be a trickster, for there is nothing greater than good, nothing except bravery, and The People have great courage." He picked up another stone to throw, but the stranger backed away from the circle of lodges.

The boy dropped the stone and turned to go back to his father. As he did so, Walker of Miles reached for his bow and for an arrow from his quiver. With quick aim, he shot the youngster in the back. Child of Cricket fell to the ground.

Before The People could react, before Great Owl could seize his own bow and go to kill him, the stranger was gone. He had disappeared into the world of magic and spirits.

The People mourned the death of Child of Cricket. They buried him in the midst of their lodges, within the sacred circle that surrounded the fire pit, in the place where he had fallen.

Three days later, when it was time to hold the feast of mourning, when Great Owl and his two remaining sons had killed an elk and when it had been dressed and placed to roast on the fire, the middle brother noticed that a plant had grown where Child of Cricket had been buried. He took a leaf from the plant and smelled it.

"Look," he exclaimed to his older brother, "a plant we do not know has grown from our brother's body."

The older brother, too, smelled the leaf. "We should throw this leaf into the cooking fire so its smoke can touch the elk, for this is a plant of great fragrance."

The brothers did as he suggested, and the smoke from the leaf covered the elk.

Other members of the tribe smelled the great odor and came to investigate. The village's maker of medicine smelled the smoke and announced, "The gods must have loved Child of Cricket, for they have turned him into this wondrous plant."

Thus, was the first tobacco given to The People, and its smoke is considered greater than good or evil, for it is the scent of courage. So it is when a cricket enters a lodge and spends the night serenading those who sleep, the next day there must be a feast and a smoking of the sacred pipe.

ΩΩΩΩΩ

When the story was finished, Lame Bear rose from his son's sleeping spot. He began preparing for the night, making sure that the flaps of the teepee were properly closed, that the fire would last until dawn and would not leave them to the cold night, that the smoke would find its way out of the teepee to join the spirits outside.

His son tried to watch him, to study Lame Bear's every move, but the boy's raven-black eyes grew heavy. Settling into his blankets, Lonely Cricket slept. He did not see his father—his strong naked body wrapped only in a buffalo robe decorated with black eagles and blue bears—leave the teepee to sit on the cold ground. He did not hear his father's prayers that the Great Spirit allow his coming child to leave the world of spirits and to enter the world of the people.

***

Three days earlier, Yquili Sparrow had told her husband Lame Bear and her oldest son Lonely Cricket to leave the house. Soon the baby would arrive—childbirth was work for women; no man should be in the pregnant woman's lodge. They had loaded the deerskin teepee, their bedrolls, and other supplies on Great Horse, and moved to their neighbor's land.

The White Man, Cook, had offered the use of his barn. "There's plenty of room in the loft, Bear."

"That not Ho-Chunk way," Lame Bear responded.

"Suit yourself, my friend. Plenty of room for that teepee of yours on the upper pasture."

It had been difficult honoring the tradition. Trudging back and forth. Chores to be done, animals tended, but they stayed far from the house and out of sight of Yquili Sparrow and of Lonely Cricket's older sister Happy Turtle.

Lonely Cricket missed his sister even more than his mother. Oldest Sister had always taken care of him. As long as he could remember, it was she who had made sure he had good things to eat, that his clothing was mended, that his moccasins were sewed tight against the snow. It had been Happy Turtle who had first taught him the songs of the Ho-Chunk and who had played with him.

Still, he was proud to be spending these nights with Lame Bear, for it meant that he was seen as a man.

As hard as it was to have to walk back to the Cook's land before eating or drinking, there was some compensation. For one, Leah Cook insisted on feeding them. She was a good cook, and Lonely Cricket loved the hot, crusty bread she baked. It was not like the bread of the Ho-Chunk, the bread which Yquili Sparrow baked on a hot stone, but it was good bread with crust that crunched between his teeth

Each evening, Sapphira, her undisciplined milkweed-orange hair tucked carelessly into her bonnet so that protruding wisps caught the day's last light, would bring a loaf of her mother's bread tucked under her arm. "You have to take it," she had told Lame Bear the first day. "Momma would be right hurt if you didn't."

Lame Bear grunted, and she had handed the bread to Lonely Cricket.

Sapphira Cook was Lonely Cricket's best friend and playmate. Not that there was much time for play in their lives. Lonely Cricket knew that in the old land he would not be playing with a girl, that he would spend his time with other boys; but that was not so easy here, in this place the White Men called Nebraska. Here, the Ho-Chunk lived separate from one another, on land that was allotted to each family. Here, they did not hunt and fish but farmed and raised animals. Here, they had white neighbors and even friends. Harry Cook was his father's friend. The two men worked together, plowing one's fields and then the other's. The heavy iron plow belonged to Mr. Cook; the mule to Lame Bear; the work to both men. If they didn't always understand the other's language, the two men shared the language of hard work. And he, Lonely Cricket, shared the world of childhood and laughter with Mr. Cook's daughter.

"So, Bear, you want a boy or a girl?" Harry Cook asked one day as they built trellises for the spring gardens. He placed one hand on Lonely

Cricket's head when he said boy and another on Sapphira's when he said girl.

"No matter," Lame Bear answered.

Mr. Cook nodded and went back to cutting strips of wood. Lonely Cricket didn't believe his father. He knew that Lame Bear wanted another son. One night he had overheard his parents' murmured words. He shared their hope; it would be good to have a brother with whom he could play and whom he could teach. He would teach his brother the ways of the animals. Of all the chores of the farm, Lonely Cricket most loved working with the horse, the mule, and the cows.

Lonely Cricket also knew that one did not say such things aloud where tricksters might hear. Better to keep hopes and wishes close to the heart.

Now it was time to eat some of the bread Sapphira had brought the night before—to eat and to walk across the fields to their barn where the animals waited. He would help feed Great Horse and Stubborn Mule. He would feed chickens and after Lame Bear had milked the two cows, he would drive them to their small pasture where his father would bring them hay.

If the baby were not so ready to enter this world, Yquili Sparrow and Happy Turtle would do the milking; but this was not a time for men and women to be near one another. So Lame Bear would fill the pail with milk and leave it by the cabin door.

Lonely Cricket shivered as he rose from his warm bedding. Lame Bear was not yet awake. The boy opened the teepee flaps. Across the field he saw his sister running towards them. He waved and Happy Turtle waved her arms in the air—a good sign, the baby must have come.

Chapter 2 ~ Many Fish

When it was time, Yquili Sparrow had not cried out. Grimacing against the pain, she nodded to Dreaming Woman.

"Heat water," the midwife had instructed Happy Turtle. Her ancient voice rasped against the morning cold.

"Yes, Oldest Sister," the girl responded. She rushed outside to the pump. The cold wind surrounded her. Her breath came in white clouds.

By the time the water had heated, the baby was nestled on his mother's chest. Yquili Sparrow took the midwife's knife and cut the cord. Carefully, she tied it and handed her new son to the older woman who would cleanse him with water and cloths and, more importantly, with prayers of welcome. Those prayers would thank the Great Spirit, but they would end in admonition; the Trickster would be told to stay far from this new child of the Ho-Chunk.

Dreaming Woman held the child aloft in her bird-talon hands as she prayed. She took corn pollen from a pouch tied to her waist and sprinkled it on the baby's head. She took a pinch of tobacco from a second pouch, and, praying once more, the midwife opened the door of the heavy metal stove and threw the tobacco into the fire. The flame flared for a moment and illuminated the faded copper of the midwife's skin.

Her work was almost done.

Meanwhile, Yquili Sparrow had taken the umbilical cord and carefully coiled it. She took a small pouch, much like Dreaming Woman's tobacco pouch, and tucked the cord inside. She sewed the pouch closed and gestured to Happy Turtle, who brought an eagle feather to her mother. The feather was attached to the small pouch; then—with a prayer to *Isanaklesh* for her protection—the pouch was attached to the cradleboard.

It was now safe for Little Brother, as the baby would be known until his naming ceremony, to be placed on the cradleboard.

"On your way, Lazy Girl," Dreaming Woman instructed. Happy Turtle pulled her gray-striped blanket tight as she ran from the door to summon her father and brother.

The afterbirth gathered in a pail; the midwife took time to make sure that everything was ready for men to enter the cabin. When she was sure that all had been done, she laid the baby near the stove and said her farewell. "May your home be filled with game and your heart with happiness."

Wrapping her thin frame against the cold, Dreaming Woman opened the door. She would bury the afterbirth in Yquili Sparrow's garden so the Corn Mother would know the boy was welcome.

***

Lame Bear strode quickly across the fields; Lonely Cricket and Happy Turtle could hardly keep up. So quickly did their father move, so intent were the two children on keeping up with him, that they almost crashed against him when he suddenly stopped a hundred of his broad paces from the cabin.

"What is it, Father?" Lonely Cricket asked.

Lame Bear didn't answer. "Happy Turtle," he instructed pointing towards the garden and Dreaming Woman, "tell Older Sister that I thank her for the assistance she has given and for the prayers she has offered. Tell her that I shall welcome her at Little Brother's naming."

The girl moved towards the cabin and the older woman, who was filling a hole at the edge of the garden. Lonely Cricket followed his sister until his father took him by the shoulder. "It is not for a man," Lame Bear said. "There are mysteries into which we must not inquire, just as there are ways of men that your mother and sister will never know."

Lonely Cricket was proud to know that his father had called him a man. He was proud to realize he would someday learn the things a man must understand.

***

The man whooped and danced—his legs flying in all directions. The bells attached to his ankles and wrists clinked and tinkled without discernable rhythm. His song was not of the words of the Ho-Chunk nor of those of the White Man.

Falling Cloud was surrounded. Most of the crowd were children who laughed at his antics and called out at him as he shook his pendulant breasts. The old man was used to such jeers and taunts; he was, in fact, the jester, the clown, the entertainer. There were those who thought him a fool, but he was always welcome. At every celebration, at every ritual, Falling Cloud played his part, whirling and jerking until exhausted he would fall to the ground in a heap.

Sometimes the children would pick up stones or clods of dirt to throw at him, but the older people of the tribe would stop them. "Do you not know that clowns are sacred?" they would ask. "They bring good luck and keep the Trickster from doing us harm."

So, it was that Falling Cloud was welcomed this day. As the dust rose from his steps and as his mismatched clothes—some for a man and some for a woman—flew about in the same disarray as his dance. The people waited for him to stop. While Falling Cloud whirled and danced and the children shouted and laughed, the older adults talked among themselves. The young adults, who were no longer children but who were not old enough to be married, preened and made sly comments and looked to see who might be admiring them.

When the jester had finished his dance, Tall Grass stood in the middle of the crowd. He took the baby from Lame Bear and held him for all to see. Then, cradling the infant in his arms, the old man began to tell a story. He spoke slowly, gazing only into the child's eyes. To Lonely Cricket it seemed as if the medicine man and the baby had been transported to some separate place far from the throng of Ho-Chunk who had come for his brother's naming celebration.

ΩΩΩΩΩ

There were three boys who wanted to go fishing. They took their fishing spears, some pemmican in case they became hungry, and long thongs on which they would hang the many fish they were sure they would bring back for the village.

The boys were excited at the thought of an adventure. They were even more excited at the thought of the welcome they'd receive when they returned with long lines of fish, enough for a great feast.

Young Wolf, who had suggested they go fishing, led the way. The other boys trailed him across a field and into the woods. They followed the path to the brook where their fathers had taught them how to fish, how to carefully stand silent on the rocks and to avoid casting a shadow which might alarm the trout or pickerel that gathered in the eddies to feed.

When the boys found a good place, they lay down their small bundles. Each took off his moccasins, his pants, and his shirt so his clothing would not get wet if he slipped on a wet rock. Then they took their positions and waited.

No fish came. One of the boys said, "I am tired of waiting. Why don't we take a break and eat some of our pemmican?" The third boy agreed, but Young Wolf kept his vigil on the rocks.

While his friends were eating, Young Wolf saw a large trout making his way up the current towards his rock. He readied his spear and held very still. When the fish came into range, Young Wolf cast his spear; but the fish had disappeared. As the disappointed boy pulled the thong that connected the spear to his wrist, he lost his footing and slipped into the water.

The trout reappeared and jumped before the boy's startled eyes.

"Ha, you got me, you Trickster," Young Wolf said.

The trout jumped again and splashed back into the water. The boy laughed.

When Young Wolf laughed, a stranger came out of the bushes. "You are all wet," the stranger said to the boy.

"Yes, the fish got the better of me today."

"Would you like to catch many fish?" the stranger asked. "I know a place where there are so many that your arms will grow weary from spearing them."

The boy was happy at the suggestion. His eyes filled with dreams of the many fish he and his friends would bring home to their village.

"Yes," he said to the stranger, "my friends and I will go with you to this fishing place."

"It will take time and there is danger," the stranger said. "You will have to be patient and brave to go with me."

Young Wolf went to his two friends and told them about the stranger and the wonderful fishing place he knew. The boy who had said, "I am tired of waiting," did not want to go. "I know that I am not patient," he said. "This is not a journey for me. I will go back to the village."

As the boy left, Young Wolf said to him, "Leave your thongs with us so we can use them to help bring back all the fish we are sure to spear." So, the boy gave Young Wolf the long thongs and then headed back to the village.

Then Young Wolf and the other boy followed the stranger along a path they had never seen. They came to a steep place where they would have to climb. It was very dangerous, and the other boy stopped. "I am not brave enough for this," he said. "I will return to our village."

As the boy left, Young Wolf said to him, "Leave your thongs with me so that I can use them to help bring back all the fish I am sure to spear." So, the boy gave Young Wolf the long thongs and then headed back to the village.

When the two boys returned to the village, the men asked where they had been. When they told their story, one of the medicine men said, "I think that Young Wolf has gone off with the Trickster; we must go after him."

A war party was mounted, and the two boys showed the way. When they came to the steep place, two of the bravest men climbed to the top. There they found a great stream in which there were many fish. Next to the stream they found Young Wolf's moccasins and his clothing, but he was nowhere to be found.

Near the boy's clothes lay the long thongs of buckskin the three boys had taken with them, the ones on which they had planned to string their fish. The thongs had been woven into a net, which was stretched across the stream. In the middle of the net there was a large trout ensnared, large enough to feed three men. That was how our people learned to use nets to catch fish.

Young Wolf would never return, but he had indeed found a way to feed the people with many fish. And that, Many Fish, is the story I tell for your naming celebration.

ΩΩΩΩΩ

Tall Grass held the child up once more for all to see before he handed him back to Lame Bear. Many Fish started to cry, and Lame Bear gave him to Yquili Sparrow, who took the baby to her breast. Soon he was sucking and quiet.

People had come for the ceremony. They had brought gifts for the new member of their tribe and food to be shared. They milled about, taking time to look at the gifts, talking, and sharing news and opinions.

"Will there be enough rain this year?" One Tree asked. A knot of men was soon discussing the crops and how they would fare. Charging Buffalo asked, "Will the White Man give us more land for our children?"

"You don't need to worry," Charging Buffalo," One Tree replied. "You are such a good hunter you will not need land on which to grow crops. Your wife will trade venison and elk for the three sisters."

The other men laughed good-naturedly for they knew that Charging Buffalo was not yet married and that every night he prayed to Mother Earth to give him a wife. Those with daughters laughed even harder because they knew that the young women of the tribe often prayed that Father Earth would grant them such a handsome husband.

"Will the White Men kill all the deer? If they do, where will we get buckskin or will we have to buy their cloth at the trading post?" The woman who asked this was already wearing the White Man's clothes, a long calico dress. It didn't fit her. Lonely Cricket thought she looked like a sack of squash. For a moment he wanted to laugh, but the thought of laughing at another person made him feel sad.

Small Deer stood to one side watching Happy Turtle as she carried her baby brother about the yard, introducing him to each person, and waiting as each in turn welcomed him to the tribe.

"May you defeat your enemies, Many Fish," said one of the men.

"May your teepee be filled with children, Many Fish," wished one of the women.

"May your hunt always find its prey, Many Fish," was another benediction.

Finally, Happy Turtle approached Small Deer. As she approached, he pulled two pair of rabbit fur moccasins from the pouch he carried over his shoulder. One pair was tiny, fit for a baby. The second pair was larger and decorated with ribbons of bright color. "These are for you, Many Fish," he said holding out the smaller pair, "May you run as quickly as the rabbit."

Then he handed the second pair of moccasins to Happy Turtle. "I made these are for you, Older Sister, that you might be able to keep up with Many Fish."

Their hands touched for a moment as Happy Turtle accepted the gifts. At the contact, the young man blushed.

"These are beautiful, Small Deer. Many Fish and I thank you. Your hunt must have been good that you found such fine rabbits."

The young man mumbled and backed away.

Happy Turtle had often seen Small Deer watching her. She knew he wished for her to someday be his wife, and Happy Turtle found that idea to be good. But she also knew that Lame Bear and Yquili Sparrow had doubts.

Many members of the Ho-Chunk had reservations about Small Deer. It was rumored that he was a shapeshifter, a coyote in disguise, a child of the Trickster. "How else," it was asked," does he always find so many rabbits with which to make moccasins?"

People were even more bothered that Small Deer made those moccasins himself. "That is woman's work," was the frequent comment.

"Is he of two-spirits?" some asked. "Will he foretell the future?"

Nobody spoke of these things to Small Deer or to his family, but they were often said.

***

Lonely Cricket moved towards Tall Grass and waited for the heavy-set medicine man to stop talking with Lame Bear. The boy wanted to listen, to hear what his father was saying, but he knew that would be wrong. When Lame Bear wanted to tell him, that would be when he would hear the words.

When his father went to talk to some of the other men, Lonely Cricket snapped his tongue against the roof of his mouth to make a sound, just loud enough so that Tall Grass could hear him. If the medicine man was willing to answer his questions, then he could ask.

Tall Grass was dressed in ceremonial robes that pulled tight across his great shoulders. He wore the skin of a buffalo and around his neck hung many beads. The medicine man's hair had grayed with age, but it was still shiny. From one side three feathers hung; Lonely Cricket knew one was the feather of a great hawk, the hunter of the skies. The second a feather from an eagle, the bird of courage. And the third was the banded feather of a horned owl, the messenger of the Great Spirit. Other Ho-Chunk could wear the feather of a hawk or an eagle, but only a medicine man could wear an owl's plumage.

"You have a question, Lonely Cricket?" the medicine man asked.

"My brother's name," the boy began, "it seems strange. Where would our people find such a place? My father and the other men worry about enough rain for the crops, and you talked of a great stream."

The man put his right hand on the boy's shoulder. "You have forgotten two things, Lonely Cricket. First, it is not I who gives your brother his name; it is the Great Spirit and the Earth Mother who speak through me."

Lonely Cricket hung his head in embarrassment that he needed to be so reminded. He tried to turn away. Tall Grass held him in place.

"Secondly," the medicine man continued, "our people have not always lived here. We are in this place because many of us have been driven from our homes by the White Men. They have agreed to let us live here. Perhaps they will not change their words once again. But not all the Ho-Chunk live in this place. Many have found their way back to the land of lakes and of sacred mounds, to the land that is called Wisconsin.

"Perhaps the Great Spirit had those Ho-Chunk in His mind when he spoke this story through me. Perhaps the Earth Mother means for your brother to go to Wisconsin to live. Or ..."

The boy looked up and waited for the Medicine Man to continue. He could see the darkness in Tall Grass's eyes.

"Perhaps your brother is meant to gather another kind of fish. We cannot know." The old man's voice trailed off as he spoke.

They stood in a frozen tableau for a moment. Then Tall Grass spoke again. "The other boys are playing. You should join them." He patted Lonely Cricket's shoulder.

"Thank you, Uncle," the boy said and moved towards the group of boys who were pushing and shoving one another near the barn.

Shadow Fox was organizing a race. The biggest of the Ho-Chunk boys who lived nearby, Shadow Fox, was always trying to prove that he was the quickest and the strongest. Lonely Cricket knew that the other boys didn't like Shadow Fox. They all wanted the bigger boy to stop acting as if he were the chief. They hated the way Shadow Fox cheated at their games. It was his foot that would trip another runner, his shoulder that would butt into somebody's side, and his hands that would grab another boy's wrist and twist. Shadow Fox was old enough to join the young men, the ones who like Charging Buffalo practiced archery and other games of hunting and war, the ones who looked forward to having their own allotments of land and building their own homes. He was old enough to join their discussions of the girls and those they wished to marry and old enough to take part in the tribal ceremonies and discussion.

Shadow Fox was old enough, but he avoided joining the older group; with them he would be the small one, the one who could be pushed around. No, he was going to stay with the boys he could bully.

Sparrow Yenri was almost three years younger than Shadow Fox. Though they were brothers, the two boys could not have been more unalike. All the others liked Sparrow Yenri even though he was one of the smallest and slowest of the boys. If his brother always wore a frown, Sparrow Yenri had a bright and friendly smile. No matter how badly his big brother picked on him, Sparrow Yenri never complained. No matter how hard the older boy hit him or twisted his arm, Sparrow Yenri never cried out or ran to their father.

There was only one time that Shadow Fox stopped tormenting his little brother. That was when Lonely Cricket was around. The bully never explained his animosity, but he never let an opportunity to tease, hit, or trip Lonely Cricket pass him by.

"Here comes the stupid grasshopper," Shadow Fox exclaimed when he saw Lonely Cricket approaching.

Such teasing bothered Lonely Cricket even though he knew that only Twisted Rock would join in. The other boys would say nothing, but he knew they didn't like the way Shadow Fox treated him.

There were two things that Shadow Fox would say about him that upset Lonely Cricket. The worst thing was that they were true.

His hair did not hang straight like the other boys. It did not touch his shoulders no matter how long it grew. Instead, it curled into a nest fit for a swallow. "Bird Head," the older boy would call him, and the label always made Lonely Cricket cringe.

Even worse for Lonely Cricket was being called "Ghost Boy." It was true that his skin was lighter than the other boys. It was also true that in the summer when he worked in the fields with his father and Mr. Cook, Lonely Cricket's skin would turn red and painful. When Shadow Fox saw him burned and suffering, he would call Lonely Cricket "Fire Child" and laugh at the younger boy's doubled discomfort.

That his skin and hair were different from the other boys filled Lonely Cricket with shame, but he tried not to show it. When Happy

Turtle had heard Shadow Fox calling her brother names and had heard Twisted Rock join in, she had told her brother that they were fools.

"Someday, when you are older and are looking for a wife, the women will want to have children with you. But those two, who will want them?" Then she laughed, and Lonely Cricket laughed with her.

On the day of Many Fish's naming, Happy Turtle heard Shadow Fox once again taunting her brother. "Remember the story our mother has told you," Happy Turtle reminded.

"The story of her grandfather's father's father and father of her mother's grandmother?" the boy asked.

"Yes, of the White men who came among the Ho-Chunk many years ago, the ones who did not speak as the Cook family and the other White men we meet. Of the White men who came to trade for furs when we all lived by the water Winnebago.

"And of those who came wearing brown dresses and covered their heads." Happy Turtle smiled at the thought of these strange men.

"The ones who taught of a great god which they carried around their necks," Lonely Cricket added, laughing at the idea. "What a funny notion of a spirit," Happy Turtle agreed. "It was one of the men in the long dress who became the husband of Yquili Sparrow's grandmother's mother's mother."

"That was many years ago," Lonely Cricket said. "I wonder if he could do the dance of marriage wearing his brown dress."

Happy Turtle laughed. "Yes, I wonder. But our mother says that you look like that man." She pointed her finger at the other boys. "And he was also the ancestor of Shadow Fox and Sparrow Yenri."

"But they do not look like me."

No, they are not that lucky," Happy Turtle said. "Sparrow Yenri is not so bad, but Shadow Fox is so ugly that he does not want to become a man. He knows that no woman will want to share her sleeping mat with him. So, you can play with him and the other boys and know that their words are of jealousy."

His sister's words helped to heal Lonely Cricket's painful feelings.

Still, on this the day of his brother's naming, the boy thought, "That will be some day, but today I must listen to Shadow Fox's words." He would play with the other boys and he would put up with the older boy's taunts.

That night, he would lie on his sleeping mat and again try to remember what his sister had said.

***

The animals were in the barn, out of the way of the people who were celebrating the naming of Many Fish. Lonely Cricket knew the cows and Great Horse would be unhappy because it was a beautiful day—a day on which cows and horses would want to eat their fill of grass. Stubborn Mule was always unhappy, today the beast had good reason.

Lonely Cricket and Happy Turtle did not mind leaving the others to take care of the animals. There would be more time for games and for feasting, but for now, hay and water had to be provided and one of the cows had a small wound, perhaps from the nettle bushes that grew near the depression where water gathered in the rainy days.

"Bear, why do you let that bush grow?" Mr. Cook had asked Lame Bear more than once. "It ain't good for nothin' 'cept scratching the stock and if they eat it, they're more'n likely to get the colic."

"Every plant has reason just as person," Lame Bear would answer. "That I not know what Great Spirit plan for nettle not mean He has not planned. Only mean I not wise. Dreaming Woman uses leaves from nettle cure sick. After corn harvested, on night when moon hide, she take leaves. All during moons of cold and snow, she dry in home. When flowers poke once more through snow, she brew tea."

Harry Cook would harrumph the way he always did when he did not understand the Ho-Chunk ways and go back to his work. He knew better than to argue with his Indian friend.

Lonely Cricket carefully applied salve to the cow's injury. He was not sure what was in the smelly pot that Mr. Cook had given his father, but it did seem to be working. The wound was no longer red, and the animal did not pull away when Lonely Cricket's finger touched the sore. He did as Mr. Cook had explained to them—rubbing the salve into the animal's hide with gentle care.

When he was through with the cow, Lonely Cricket took two large handfuls of hay and went into Great Horse's stall. This hay was not for eating; the boy massaged it against one immense side of the animal first and then against the other. The horse swung his tail and whinnied in delight.

"See how good your older brother is with Great Horse," Happy Turtle said to Many Fish as she took the baby's cradleboard from her back and held him in her arms.

Lonely Cricket moved around to the horse's chest. As he rubbed the straw against the enormous brown breast, the horse nuzzled at him. The boy had to brace himself against the power of the beast's affection.

"Someday," Happy Turtle cooed, "Lonely Cricket will teach you how to care for the animals."

Lonely Cricket smiled and turned away in his pride. "You are very fortunate, Many Fish," the boy said, "to have such a good older sister.

She will carry you on her back until you can walk. She will find for you the best treats in the cooking pot. She will always be there to help."

It was Happy Turtle's turn to hide the pride in her face.

At first Lonely Cricket was not aware of the change, then he sensed it—something was not right. Before there had been talking and singing and the sounds of happiness, now there was quiet. What had happened, he could not imagine. He hurried through the rest of his chores.

Happy Turtle, too, sensed the difference in the sounds coming from the celebration. She, however, was pretty sure of what had changed. She could imagine the Cooks striding across the fields towards their home. They would, Happy Turtle knew, be carrying baskets of White Man's food to add to the feast. Leah Cook, short and plump, looking like a cheery mushroom dressed in blue-checked gingham, would have the quilt that she had been working on—the one that could only be for a small boy. Sapphira, too, had been working on a present. Happy Turtle did not know what it was, but she knew that their young neighbor would have put her all into the gift.

Yes, the Cooks would bring the best they could and the best friendship they could offer, but Happy Turtle knew that many of the Ho-Chunk would not want them or any White people around—not during normal times and certainly not for a celebration. She knew that her father and Harry Cook were good neighbors and friends, but many of the Ho-Chunk wanted nothing to do with the White Man.

Talking Mountain, the father of Shadow Fox and Sparrow Yenri, often complained that the white men whose allotments were near his had been given the best land while he and his family had been given barren ground. Even the women and little children knew that Talking Mountain blamed the White Man for everything that went wrong. Everyone knew that Talking Mountain wanted to lead an uprising against the White Men, that he spoke often of the Sioux—of Sitting Bull and of Crazy Horse, of the Little Big Horn and the death of Custer.

Happy Turtle knew that Talking Mountain was the Ho-Chunk who spoke most loudly against the Whites, but she also knew that many other members of the tribe felt the same way. She was proud that her father and Mr. Cook were good friends and neighbors. However, she knew that many of her people were suspicious of Lame Bear. She had heard them say, "He is not really one of our people." Happy Turtle knew that her father was a good man and that he would not have befriended his White neighbor if Harry Cook had not also been a good man.

"If we must live on these allotted patches of land that touch one another, should not our hearts also touch?" Lame Bear had explained. "Does the storm that crosses my neighbor's field not batter at my teepee as well? Does the drought that dries up my crops not colic his cows and take his chickens?

"We have no choice. Perhaps it is the will of the White leaders in Washington, perhaps it is the will of the Great Father in the sky, perhaps it is just the way things have happened, but we are now neighbors. Is it not better to also be friends?"

Lame Bear had said these things, and many of the Ho-Chunk had nodded in agreement. Still Happy Turtle knew that the sudden and disturbing quiet meant that the Cooks had come to join the celebration.

***

When the children exited the barn, Huhawira had already come out even though the sun had not yet gone to bed. Not quite full, she hung like an ornament in the sky. Lonely Cricket knew that such an afternoon moon promised a happy night. Why this was he did not know. Some day he would ask Tall Grass or, perhaps, it was a story to hear from Dreaming Woman.

At this moment, however, the afternoon had lost all happiness. Instead of a celebration, the yard of their home was filled with tension. Suddenly, children had stopped playing, women had stopped their talking, the men had stopped eating and smoking; families had knotted together as if waiting for something terrible to happen. Even Falling Cloud had stopped his antics. He squatted against the post where—when there had been great work done—Lonely Cricket would tether Great Horse to rub his flanks with burlap.

Harry Cook was walking across the field. He held out his arms as if to show that he carried no weapons. His wife and daughter hung behind him. A young White Man, whom Lonely Cricket did not know, shuffled his feet as if not knowing whether to push forward with Mr. Cook or to hold back as well.

"If we ain't wanted, Lame Bear, me and the misses will leave, but we sure hope you and your family will accept some food and a couple of gifts for the baby. By the way, you give that kid a name yet?" Mr. Cook spoke slowly. He kept his voice even—not the way he ordinarily spoke. Lonely Cricket understood that their neighbor was trying to let the other Ho-Chunk know that he meant no harm.

Lame Bear moved forward and held out his right hand in the White Man's way. Harry Cook put down the basket he was carrying, and the two men shook hands. Then Lonely Cricket's father spoke. "Welcome, Harry Cook, my neighbor and friend and welcome to your family." He said this in the White Man's language and then again in the language of the Ho-Chunk.

There was some stirring and murmuring among the people, but nobody said anything to argue with Lame Bear's way.

"Come on, come on!" Harry Cook waved his wife and daughter forward. The young White Man came with them. "This here's my sister's boy, Nathan. He's staying with us a spell. Reckon we can use another pair of hands, Lame Bear?"

The young man slouched forward. Not sure what else to do, he stuck his hands deep into his pockets.

Lame Bear looked at this Nathan carefully as if he were studying a horse for buying. "If he your family, he welcome in my home." He held out his hand to the younger man, who took it reluctantly, pulling back almost in the same motion.

By this time, Sapphira had come up besides Lonely Cricket and Happy Turtle. "So, this is your little brother." She cooed as she touched the baby's chin. "What is his name?"

"Many Fish," they answered in unison, which set them to laughing.

The baby suddenly burped and then he, too, began to laugh in the gurgling way of infants. Then it was Sapphira's turn to join the laughter. In the midst of such childish merriment, the tension of the moment dissolved.

As the White Man's food was added to the feast and the baby's new quilt admired, as Sapphira, somewhat embarrassed, quietly offered the hand-made rattle, which was her gift for Many Fish, some of the Ho-Chunk quietly left. Some made excuses about the time needed to return to their homes. Some said nothing. Among those who said nothing were Talking Mountain and Shadow Fox.

Sparrow Yenri did not want to leave, but he did not argue with his father. He did, however, say something to Lonely Cricket before he followed his father and older brother. "This is a nice party. I wish my father were …." Not knowing how to finish the sentence, the boy nodded once and walked away.

Happy Turtle touched her brother on the arm. "We should be happy that our father is not like Talking Mountain."

Lonely Cricket nodded his agreement. Meanwhile, Sapphira and Leah Cook were busy fussing at Many Fish, who was now in Mrs. Cook's arms. "What a cute baby," they said over and over as they gently poked and brushed his soft skin.

Many Fish cooed back at them and waved his new rattle. It was made from the same bright fabrics as his new quilt. Lonely Cricket recognized some of the scraps of cloth. They were from clothes he had seen the Cooks wear—a shirt too worn for mending, a dress outgrown—even an old blanket he'd helped Mrs. Cook beat clean just that spring. Now they would keep his little brother warm and provide him with a plaything.

For a moment, the baby waved his rattle and cocked his head to hear the castanet of beans. A few minutes later, and he was fast asleep—the toy still clutched in his tiny hands.

Chapter 3 ~ Education

When the harvest was over, the crops stored, and the canning well begun, Pastor Ludlow traveled a circuit of the farms in his parish. An old horse, no longer strong enough for plowing, pulled the preacher's buggy. Perched on the jouncing wooden seat, the emaciated, unsmiling man of God looked ready to meet his maker. Next to him sat a woman who reminded Lonely Cricket of a bird.

"Two old crows," he would describe them that evening to Happy Turtle, "Two old crows dressed in black." For the moment, however, he said only, "Can help?"

"Your Pa about, boy?" The preacher took in the shirtless, barefoot, overall-clad boy with a dismissive glance.

"In barn. Cow have calf." The boy hurried towards the house, where Mrs. Cook and Sapphira were working on laying up a winter's supply of beans and squash.

The old man climbed down. "Boy, you hold this horse," he called; but Lonely Cricket paid no heed; farm work came before manners—even before this strange White Man crow.

"See what I mean, Mrs. Cole," the preacher said to the woman. "The children 'round here need some educatin'."

The woman said nothing. This was the third farm they had visited already this day, and John Ludlow had preached the same lesson at each. The children needed an education, and she was to teach them with a Bible in one hand and a hickory switch in the other.

"I'll tie Bartholomew up and help you down." He led the horse toward a hitching post. By the time the buggy was secured, and the woman helped to the ground, Lonely Cricket was rushing back with a pot; steam was rising from it into the brisk fall day. "Boy," the preacher called out, "you got a name?"

"Lonely Cricket. No talk. Mrs. Cook in house." The boy had hardly stopped and in a moment, he was inside the barn.

"Yes," the man harrumphed as if it were important for him to have the last word, "you take care of that calf, and I'll speak to your mother."

"No respect at all," he muttered to his companion.

"But that boy's an Indian," Mrs. Cole whispered. "I thought you said we were only looking for White children. Surely, you don't expect me to teach wild Indians.

Ludlow laughed. "Of course not, Indians ain't got no brain for learning. Imagine one of them trying to read. But according to the sheriff this place belongs to Harry Cook, and that ain't no Indian name. Boy must be hired help."

"Well, just so long as everybody understands. I won't have any savages in my school."

"No, indeed, Mrs. Cole, no indeed. Although the way children in these parts are raised, they might as well be heathens, but I'm sure you'll learn them proper."

With a determined gait, he moved towards the house. The woman tried to keep up. Behind her, the horse leaned his flank against the hitching post. It was only mid-morning and the animal was already tired.

***

Nathan Wainright's dun horse wasn't much to look at and was less to ride. Still, Maggie, as Sapphira insisted the gelding be called, carried Nathan and Sapphira to and from Mrs. Cole's one-room school each day. Little Cricket quietly watched them from the garden or the barn wherever he was working. He wished that he, too, could be learning the mysteries of books and numbers, but it was not allowed. "Indians ain't allowed in school," the preacher had said and that had been that.

At least Lonely Cricket had the satisfaction of learning a man's skills. He was particularly happy and skillful working with animals, and he was proud when—during the second week of school—Nathan asked if he could care for Maggie in their barn.

Lonely Cricket watched them ride across the back pasture on their way to the Cook's house. He had felt badly for the horse. Nathan had been riding hard, and Lonely Cricket could see the animal was faltering. He had finished picking another basket of beans when he heard Nathan call. "Hey, boy." Then, "Howdy, Lame Bear, nice day."

The discussion had been short. "I'll give the boy ten cents a week fer taking care, and my uncle will give you something' fer the feed," the younger man offered.

"Friend no pay," Lame Bear replied.

Much as he wanted some of the White Man's money in his pocket, Lonely Cricket echoed, "No pay. We friends."

The young man had smiled and nodded. "Well, don't that beat all. Now I see why Uncle Harry's so big on you. Not many White Men know how to be friends like that."

Nathan handed the reins to Lonely Cricket and shuffled off, leaving the pigeon-toed dun saddled and sweaty. "Me and Sapphira'll be over right after breakfast," he added over his shoulder. "You have him ready.

She likes getting' to school early. Says she wants to be a teacher herself, so she helps that old prune every chance she gets."

"Horse ready," Lonely Cricket answered. To himself he added, "First, this horse needs be walked, rubbed, then food."

Gently, the boy pulled the horse's reins, but Maggie didn't move. Turning back, Lonely Cricket stood for a moment and placed one hand softly on the animal's muzzle. At First Maggie pulled back, but he repeated this exercise until the gelding no longer shied at his hand. Then he rubbed gently until the horse was calmer. Finally, the boy moved closer so that his mouth and the horse's nose touched. He blew gently into the gelding's nostrils. Maggie snorted but did not pull back.

Again, the boy gently pulled on the reins. This time the horse nickered and easily followed him around the yard. They walked until the dun was no longer sweating.

Each weekday morning, Lonely Cricket would have the horse ready. Sapphira would always thank him when she and her cousin arrived for their ride to the school. It was a four-mile ride, and she was glad that she, unlike some of her schoolmates who lived such a distance, didn't have to walk. A while later, Nathan would bring the horse back, sweaty and hard-ridden. The boy would stop what he was doing and take care of the animal.

The same routine would be repeated in reverse each afternoon. Lonely Cricket did what he could for the horse, but he grew to dislike the rider, who showed neither thanks for him nor appreciation for his mount.

***

Lonely Cricket was glad that Sapphira liked going to school. He wanted his friend to be happy. But he was also sad that they didn't have more time to spend together. At least, there were Saturdays when they would share tasks such as caring for the animals, picking the late season vegetables, and helping their mothers repair clothes. There was always work that needed doing.

Sunday afternoons were even better. Often Sapphira would invite Lonely Cricket and Happy Turtle to come to her family's cabin where they could play school. She would show them the letters of the White Man's books and teach them how to draw them and how to make their sounds. Numbers, too. The two Ho-Chunk children did not learn much, but they were happy with what there was.

It was even more fun when Sapphira would read stories from the *McGuffey Reader*, which Mrs. Cole allowed her to take home. This was a privilege granted only to Sapphira, who was the best student in the school. With great difficulty, the girl would read passages from the *Bible,* scenes from Shakespeare, and poetry and essays by famous Americans. Sometimes she would need her mother's assistance, for Leah Cook had, unlike most women or even her husband Harry, gone to school. That had been in a faraway place called New Hampshire.

Sometimes, when supper was in the oven and she had a moment to rest, Mrs. Cook would tell the children about her life in New Hampshire. Other times, she'd tell them stories that she had heard as a girl—stories her father's father had told her, the ones he had heard growing up in another country even farther away, a country called Scotland, which was across a great water from New Hampshire.

The children would beg Leah to tell those tales, especially the story of Princess Meghan.

"It was long ago in a country far across the sea that there was a king whose daughter was Princess Meghan. She was very rich and powerful, for she was a princess. And, as was right for such royal folk, she was very beautiful. But what made her most famous, most adored, most wanted by men to be their wife, was her singing.

"When Meghan sang people stopped what they were doing to gather around. The blacksmith would stop his hammering and let his forge go cold. The milkmaid would stop her milking, and the cows would not complain for they, too, would be listening to Meghan's song. Why, even the birds would come close to enjoy the serenade.

"Meghan's fame grew and spread. Suitors came and offered tribute. Kings and potentates, princes and wealthy merchants, troubadours and poets: they came from all corners of the world. Time and again her father, King Michael, was tempted to give her hand for some of the jewels and chests of gold were magnificent. Time and again, the king was almost won over, for some of the poems and songs that were sung in Meghan's praise pleased him greatly.

"Time and again a suitor would present himself at court, and the king would be tempted. He would call Meghan to his side and say, "I have found you a fine husband. What do you say?"

"Each time she would find some reason to turn the fine suitor away. If she could find no other flaw, she would ask them to sing with her. "We will sing a duet," she would instruct and call the court musician to play for them.

"The suitors, very complimented, would start to sing, but having come from far and wide, they had not heard Meghan sing before. As soon as those wonderful sounds left her mouth, the suitors would stop in wonder and just stare. Which, of course, disqualified them at once. After all, who wants to sing duets with a mute?

"You see, Meghan wanted no part of any of these great suitors. She was in love with a stable hand, a lowly stable hand named Jack. He loved her as well, but Jack knew the king would never give his daughter's hand to someone with so little to offer. And Meghan, too, knew that they could never wed, not even though they loved to sing duets." At this point, Mrs. Cook would drop her voice to a whisper, so the children strained to hear.

"You see, other people did not know this, for Jack was, after all, only a stable hand, but his voice was as beautiful as Meghan's. Oh, the horses in the stable knew, for they often heard the young couple singing in the privacy of a stall. The cows in the pasture knew, for they often heard them singing far from town in the fields. The birds in the trees knew, as well, for they often heard Meghan and Jack sing by the brook that wandered through the King's great forest. But not one pair of human ears had heard them."

At this point, Leah Cook would raise her voice to its normal level.

"Finally, one of the suitors, a prince named Eric, decided to take by force what he could not win by suit. He made war on Michael's kingdom and having won, he took Meghan back to his own land."

Each time she told the tale Leah Cook would stop and wait for Sapphira's question: "What happened then? Did they live happily ever after?"

"Prince Eric wanted them to," Leah Cook would continue. "He tried very hard. He bought Meghan beautiful clothes and had the finest women from all his lands come to wait on her. There were great dogs and fast horses. Fabulous gardens filled with rare flowers and animals from other lands.

"But no, they were not happy. Meghan could never forget that she was his captive. She never sang again. Worse, she died very young. That is the nature of birds and men. When we are taken from that which we love, we can no longer sing but only mourn and pass. God made us to celebrate life, to share joy with those we love. What else matters?"

Then Leah Cook would stand up, smooth out her apron, and announce, "It is time for me to get back to work or there will be no supper on the table this evening."

As she busied herself with the tasks at hand, Mrs. Cook would sing—most often hymns since it was the Sabbath but sometimes little dances and tunes she had also learned from her grandfather in that far off place called New Hampshire.

***

The mid-morning was crisp, perhaps even a bit chilly for the last of the squash. Dressed lightly, the two stooping children shivered as they gathered a pile of the orange vegetables. Many Fish, who was well swaddled on his cradleboard, cooed in satisfaction and played with his rattle. That toy was seldom out of his hand or mouth. Frayed and filthy, it is still the baby's treasure.

"Is this enough?" Lonely Cricket asked.

"A few more," replied his sister. "After we bring these into Mother, we'll pick some apples."

"I'll have to climb the trees." The youngster spoke proudly.

Happy Turtle laughed. "You are such a boy."

Lonely Cricket picked up a small piece of squash vine and threw it at his sister, which only made her laugh the more. "See what I mean," she said as she picked up her own piece of vine and threw it at him. "Boys always think they are better." She laughed yet again.

"Hey, boy," Nathan Wainright shouted. He was tying Maggie to the hitching post. "You take care of this damned horse!"

Lonely Cricket stood up, brushed off his hands, and walked towards the barn.

"Hurry on over here," the man yelled.

Lonely Cricket did not alter his pace. During the weeks he had been taking care of Maggie, the White Man had not once thanked him nor offered any assistance. Lonely Cricket did not like Mr. Cook's sister's son, and he was certainly not going to hurry when Nathan Wainright called.

As he approached, Lonely Cricket saw that Wainright was dressed differently. Usually the man wore a farmer's clothes, nothing fancy but hardwearing. For some reason, today he was dressed special. He wore shiny blue pants and a shirt that looked store-bought, soft to touch. His jacket was good enough to wear into town, and his boots had been cleaned.

"This horse seems to be favoring her right front," Nathan Wainright said in a loud voice—far too loud for the distance that remained between them. "You take good care of her. See what you can do. I can't have her going lame."

Lonely Cricket didn't answer. He walked over to Maggie's head and lightly rubber her muzzle. Then moving slowly as to not upset the horse, he felt up and down the shoulder and leg in question. Next, he untied her and led her a few steps. Then, pushing against her great chest, he watched her leg as she took a few steps back. The boy saw nothing wrong, but he knew the White Man would be angered if questioned.

"I take care of horse."

"Yeah, you do that," Wainright snarled as he strode away.

Lonely Cricket was surprised that the White Man didn't walk towards his uncle's farm. Instead, he walked headed towards the garden where Happy Turtle was crouching next to the baby. As Maggie followed Lonely Cricket into the barn, Wainright was reaching down. Lonely Cricket didn't see that the White Man had not reached down to touch the cooing baby but rather to caress Happy Turtle's hair. He did not hear his sister's gasp of surprise nor Many Fish's cries.

By the time Lonely Cricket had taken out the strips of cloth that would be used for such a purpose, wet them in the bucket that Great Horse had already half emptied, and wound them around Maggie's leg, Happy Turtle had collected herself, taken Many Fish from his cradleboard, and held him as a shield against her chest.

"You sure are a pretty gal," Nathan Wainright was saying, but Lonely Cricket, who was just exiting the barn, could not hear the words nor his sister's reply.

"Horse fine. Ride this afternoon," the boy announced loudly as he walked towards them.

"You sure on that?"

"Yes. Horse leg good."

Nathan Wainright said nothing as he strode across the field towards his uncle's house.

"I don't like that man, Oldest Brother," Happy Turtle said as she rocked the baby in her arms.

"There was nothing wrong with horse," Lonely Cricket muttered.

Many Fish had dropped his rattle. Lonely Cricket picked up the toy. He poked his own index finger into the baby's hand. Many Fish closed his tiny fingers around it and smiled. Smiling in response, Lonely Cricket withdrew his finger and gently placed the rattle in his brother's hand.

Chapter 4 ~ Fast

When the moon of The Birds Come Home arrived, Lame Bear called Lonely Cricket to him. "It is time for you to fast, to become a man, to hear the message of the Great Spirit—the message which will reveal your fate and say what is your duty as a Ho-Chunk. This evening you will leave this house and you will fast and pray through the night. When the sun finds you in the morning, you will go to the house of Tall Grass. There you will learn what he will teach and in return you will do as he bids.

"Each night after that you will sleep on the ground and under the watch of the moon. You will not eat again until the Great Spirit has sent you a vision. Do you understand what I have told you?"

"Yes, Father," the boy answered; "It is a good thing to become a man."

Lonely Cricket's chest puffed with pride and he feared his father would see and disapprove of his self-importance. He wanted to leave, to go back to his chores, but Lonely Cricket had a question. "Will Happy Turtle take care of the animals in my absence?"

"Do not worry about the animals, they will be cared for." Lame Bear laughed and took his son's right wrist in both his own hands. "Two other boys will be fasting with you. Sparrow Yenri, son of Talking Mountain will fast; and Twisted Rock, whose father is Morning Spring. I know that you are friends with these boys, and it is good that you should have companions in your fast. However, do not let them mislead you. It is good that they have you with them, but do not give them false advice. Each man must find his own vision."

Lonely Cricket thanked his father for having given him life and the strength to face this time of fasting. "You are a good son," Lame Bear replied. Then, Lonely Cricket went to Yquili Sparrow and thanked her for raising him to become a man. "You have grown strong," Yquili Sparrow answered.

Next, he went to his sister and baby brother. He spoke of his pride and his hope that he would not give in to temptation but would fast until he had a vision from the Great Spirit.

"You are a good brother," Happy Turtle told him in response. "I know that you will see a true vision."

Many Fish said nothing.

Little Cricket turned away. It was his intention to spend some time with the animals for he would not be there to bed them down that evening.

"Wait," Happy Turtle exclaimed. "I have something special for you." She handed him a small stuffed turtle. She had made it herself in the method that Sapphira Cook had used to make the rattle of Many Fish. It was made from scraps of cloth and was of many colors. "I made this knowing that you would soon become a man. This turtle will remind you of your sister and her love for you. When you are hungry and weary, you can take it from your waistband and know that I have faith in you. When you feel lost and fear that the Great Spirit will not visit you, you can hold it in your hand and remember my love for you."

Lonely Cricket looked at the small object. Hints of tears glistened in his eyes as he thanked his sister. "I will keep this always." He turned to leave afraid that those tears would escape if he stayed longer. As he walked towards the pasture where Great Horse, Stubborn Mule, the two cows, and especially Maggie were contenting themselves with the early shoots of grass, he tucked the figure into the waist of his pants and realized that his sister was a true friend.

Lonely Cricket wondered if Sparrow Yenri and Twisted Rock were as proud as he that their fathers had decided they were ready for the fast. He knew he would meet them by the creek where it curved about the great rock outcropping. That was the gathering place of boys from the tribe and of the White boys as well. It was a good place for adventures to begin. As nervous as he felt about the fast, he was also excited to share this new experience with his friends, especially with Sparrow Yenri.

***

That evening, when it was time to eat, Yquili Sparrow did not hand Lonely Cricket a bowl. Nor did she embrace him or show endearment. Instead she held out her hands. In one was a piece of charcoal and in the other a piece of cornbread.

The boy knew the charcoal was to mark his face for the test ahead. It would symbolize that he was without a family, that he had no home to which he belonged. That he took willingly. He would paint his face later when he and the others were at the creek.

He would wash away the charcoal when the Great Spirit had given him his vision, for then he would be ready to be a man, to live among his people, to again have a rightful place.

The bread was tempting, a snack to help him get through the first night. He was already hungry. He had not eaten since the sun had been high in the sky and the shadows of things had been very short. He reached out for the bread, but then decided against it. That was not the way to begin a fast—not the way to approach the Great Spirit. He would not start by cheating even if his mother was giving permission.

Withdrawing his hand, he thanked his mother for the charcoal and for the offered bread. "It is not good that I accept temptation so easily, Mother. I must earn the right to again eat the bread of the Ho-Chunk."

Yquili Sparrow nodded her head and turned from him. Lonely Cricket could not see the smile of satisfaction on his mother's face. That evening she would whisper to Lame Bear and tell him that Lonely Cricket was sure to become a fine man. Happy Turtle would hear her mother's words and would know they were true. There would be tears of love in her eyes as she thought of Lonely Cricket holding the small cloth turtle that she had made for him.

"I wonder if he will recognize the bits of cloth and why I chose them?" the girl asked herself. Each scrap had a history, some he might remember and others that she was sure he would not. She thought of one small piece that had come from the dress she had worn the day they had first met the Cooks.

She had been a little girl—her brother a toddler. These new neighbors, White Men, people whose language she did not know, had arrived in a great wagon. Behind them trailed a cow on a long rope. As soon as Harry Cook had pulled the wagon to a stop, the cow had put her head down to graze. Finding no grass at her feet, she lowed forlornly.

Lame Bear, not bothering with the man who was climbing down from the wagon, untied the animal and took her to the trough where she took a long cool drink. Next, he tied her to the apple tree that was not yet ready to give fruit. Harry Cook had watched Lame Bear care for his cow, and he had realized that this Indian was going to be a good neighbor.

He had turned back into the wagon to help his little girl and his wife to the ground. "Leah," he had said, "I reckon these good folks are going to be our new neighbors."

Happy Turtle had not understood the words of the White Man, but she could feel their meaning. Taking Lonely Cricket in tow, she had approached the little girl, who clutched a doll to her breast.

Happy Turtle had put her hand on her breast and said her name. She repeated it twice. Then she put her hand on Lonely Cricket's head and spoke his name.

Next, she had pointed at the little girl, who stood mute. Repeating the pantomime, Happy Turtle tried again. This time, instead of pointing at the girl, she pointed at the doll.

Sapphira's eyes had brightened. "That's Maggie."

Happy Turtle had held out her hands. At first Sapphira had hesitated, but she handed the older girl the doll.

"Welcome, Maggie," Happy Turtle had said, and she handed the precious toy back.

"I'm Sapphira Cook."

"Welcome to you, too, Sapphira Cook."

Lonely Cricket moved closer to the girls. "Welcome, Sapphira Cook," he had said in his toddler's high-pitched voice.

Happy Turtle remembered that moment and how her mother had gone into their cabin and brought out bread and water for these White people whose language they could not understand but whose actions spoke of friendship to come.

She fell asleep wondering if the Cooks would understand why her brother was fasting and trying to imagine what Lonely Cricket would learn on his fast.

***

The three boys met as the sliver of moon was first appearing. Each had brought charcoal from the cooking fire in his family's home. They decorated their faces and their torsos with lightening and thunderbirds, with the likenesses of animals, of birds, and of fish.

Excited in the way of young boys, they laughed and poked as they helped one another draw the sacred charcoal figures.

When they had finished, they wrapped themselves in their blankets because the night was chilled, and they wore no shirts. At first leaning against the trees and then—as the moon traversed the sky—lying on the ground, the boys talked. They talked of the times they had shared. They talked of things they had heard discussed by their parents: a chief called Sitting Bull and a great leader from the Oglala Lakota called Crazy Horse and of a place called The Little Bighorn. The boys wondered about these things they could not understand. They wondered if the Ho-Chunk would be able to live in peace with their White neighbors or would they, too, fight great battles.

Sparrow Yenri spoke of his father's enmity towards the White Man. He spoke of how the Ho-Chunk had once been a great people and now had to live on strips of land surrounded by these strangers. Twisted Rock muttered his agreement.

Lonely Cricket did not respond, but he thought of the Cooks and how his father and Mr. Cook had become friends. "I would not fight such friends," he thought, but he did not argue with the others.

As The Hunter chased the fleeing buffalo across the sky, the boys fell asleep.

When the sun found them, the three boys were asleep, their bodies curled against the cold and their stomachs hungry for the breakfast they would not eat.

***

The next morning, the three boys were still excited by the thought of their adventure. Even though hunger was beginning to gnaw at their stomachs and even though they had slept fitfully in the chill spring night, the adventure of manhood beckoned. They left their blankets in a pile and set off to find Tall Grass. From him they would learn the way of their people. They chatted eagerly as they trotted across the fields to find the Medicine Man.

When the boys arrived at his cabin, Tall Grass told them to sit and to listen. He told them to listen to the sounds of the earth, to the call of the morning birds, and to the stillness of the wind.

Obediently, they sat as he prescribed—their legs crossed, their hands resting palms-up on their knees, their backs straight, their eyes closed, and their heads still with gazes straight.

Tall Grass waited until he knew his students were ready to hear.

Then he told them of the creation of the world.

ΩΩΩΩΩ

Ma-Ona, The Great Spirit was weary, but there was no place for him to rest, for he had not yet created the world. "I need a place to sit," he declared and with that the great tortoise we call the earth was created. And Ma-Ona sat on the world and took his rest. He lay on the ground and slept.

When The Creator woke, he wondered what he had made, for he could not see—there was not yet the light of the sun or of the moon or even of the stars. "I need light," he declared and with that the sun rose and began its journey through the sky. And the Great Spirit sat on the world and he examined what he had made.

"This is a good place that I have made," Ma-Ona said, "but it is barren. There is little for me to see. I need to fill this world with plants and animals that I can watch them." And with that the grass and the trees, the flowers, and all manner of plants appeared. Then animals appeared and began to graze and to hunt and to procreate. And the Great Spirit sat on a high place on the world and he watched what he had created.

When the sun set, the Great Spirit was still watching and he did not want the darkness, so he created the moon and the stars in order that he could see more. And he watched the goings and the comings of the world and Ma-Ona was happy.

Still, the Great Spirit was not completely happy. There was thirst in the world he had created. So, the Creator said, "We need water in this world that I have created, or the plants and the animals will surely die." And with that there were rivers and lakes. And Ma-Ona was happy.

So great was the world that he could not watch it all in the same moment. The Great Spirit wondered, "What is happening when I am not watching and what is happening under the water where the light of the sun does not reach?" And with that the eagle appeared in the sky and the other birds, too, that they could report to the Great Spirit of what had happened. And in the lakes and the rivers the fish came to be so that they, too, could tell the Great Spirit what had transpired.

"This is a good place that I have created," said Ma-Ona. "I shall create man so that he can enjoy the wonderful place that I have created." And with that were the Ho-Chunk created. And the Great Spirit knew we would care for the great tortoise and all the plants and the animals that he had created. That was to be our duty in this world, to take care of it and of the things that lived upon it.

And Ma-Ona sent dreams and messengers and owls that the Ho-Chunk might know his will.

And the Great Spirit was watching, and he knew that what he had created was good. So it was that the world was created and so it was that we, the Ho-Chunk, must care for it. And when we do so, the Great Spirit is happy, and he gives us good hunting and good fishing and he makes the plants grow for our food.

ΩΩΩΩΩ

When Tall Grass was finished, the boys thanked him for teaching them the way of the Ho-Chunk. "What would you have me do in return?" each boy asked, for they knew it was their duty to repay the medicine man for his teaching.

Tall Grass told Sparrow Yenri to sweep out his house and to wash what needed to be washed. "Do not touch any of the sacred objects," he commanded, "but remove the winter's dirt from that which is not sacred. Do you know how to sweep and to wash?"

"I have helped my mother in our home," the boy answered and went off happily knowing that Tall Grass took good care of his home and there would be little cleaning to do.

Twisted Rock was told to weed the garden where the three sisters had been planted. "You know what is corn, what is bean, and what is squash, do you not?" the Medicine Man asked.

"I have helped my father in our garden," the boy answered and went off happily knowing that Twisted Rock was an excellent gardener and that there would be few weeds to pull.

Then the Medicine Man turned to Lonely Cricket. "To you I give the care of my animals, my cow and especially my horse. Give them some grain because the grass is not yet well grown. Then take them to pasture. Once they are gone from the barn, clean their stalls and replace the straw. I know from your father Lame Bear that you know how to do these tasks."

"I will do as you instruct," Lonely Cricket answered. He knew he faced a difficult job of work, for animals needed much care. He went off happily knowing that Twisted Rock had trusted him with such responsibility.

***

It was late in the afternoon, and the shadows had grown long before Lonely Cricket had finished his work. Perhaps he could have left earlier, but he wanted to give Tall Grass's fine pinto a good rubdown before leaving him in his stall. The horse had whinnied and nibbled at him with pleasure just as Great Horse sometimes did, and Lonely Cricket was happy that he had taken extra time with the animal.

He was the last of the three boys to return to the bend in the creek. When he arrived, he was surprised to see Shadow Fox leaning against a tree and talking to the others.

"So, Ghost Boy," the older boy shouted as soon as he saw Lonely Cricket approaching, "Tall Grass surely gave you the worst job." Shadow Fox laughed, and the other two laughed with him. Lonely Cricket did not reply.

"You must smell like a cow," Shadow Fox taunted; "we ought to throw you in the creek."

Twisted Rock laughed at the older boy's comment. Sparrow Yenri made no sound but looked at the ground.

Lonely Cricket said nothing.

Having teased and tried to humiliate, there was nothing more for Shadow Fox to do. "I guess I'll be heading home for supper. There's a nice stew waiting for me. You boys want to come back and eat." He used his finger to point at his brother and at Twisted Rock. It was clear that Lonely Cricket was not invited.

"Our fast is not over," Twisted Rock answered.

"Well, that's your choice," the teenager said. "I would rather eat a good stew. But in case you get too hungry, I figured I'd leave this for you."

Shadow Fox handed Sparrow Yenri some jerky and turned to walk away.

Turning back, he added, "You can share it with your friends." Fixing his eyes on Lonely Cricket, he added, "You, too, Ghost Boy. Real good jerky."

Shadow Fox walked away before Lonely Cricket could answer. In his heart, the younger boy knew that he would not break his fast.

The same could not be said for Twisted Rock who reached out to Sparrow Yenri. Even as Sparrow Yenri handed his friend a strip of the jerky, Lonely Cricket spoke, "My friends, did you take the bread which your mothers offered? You didn't. Neither did I. Now will you break your vow to fast because Shadow Fox offers us jerky?" He turned away and went to splash the cool water of the creek on his face. "I am hungry, too," he muttered; "but that is not the Ho-Chunk way."

Twisted Rock hesitated for a moment. Then he, too, went to splash his face with the fresh water. "You are right," he said. "I will keep this sacred fast."

Sparrow Yenri said nothing. He did not eat, but he did not join the other boys at the creek's bank. He tucked the jerky into the roll of his blanket. That night he would eat.

***

The boys had set a small fire to warm themselves. This night they were less eager, less excited. Still, they wanted to talk. The next morning, they were to visit Dreaming Woman. They wondered what story she would tell them and what tasks she would require in return.

"I don't like her," Twisted Rock said. "She smells of old woman and of dead things."

"She helped my mother when it was time for Many Fish to come," Lonely Cricket replied. "Besides, even the White people say that she knows great medicine. I heard Mr. Miller, the old man who keeps the White Man's saloon talking with Harry Cook one day. I had gone with Mr. Cook to help load some sacks of seed and tools from the general store, and they were talking."

"And what were you doing in that saloon? Indians aren't allowed," said Sparrow Yenri.

"They weren't in the saloon. They were in the store, and I was carrying packages out to the wagon and keeping an eye on Big Horse.

"Harry Cook asked Mr. Miller about doctoring for Leah Cook. He said she was 'feeling poorly in a woman's way,' and Harry Cook did not know what to do for her.

"Mr. Miller told him that the doctor in Fayette was not much use. He said that if it were his wife ailing, he'd take her to Dreaming Woman.

"Then Mr. Miller told about a terrible sickness that was killing people, White Man and Ho-Chunk. That was before the Cooks had come here. He said the White Man's doctor could not help. In fact, he came down with that same fever and was close to dying."

"Were they getting sick from the smell of Dreaming Woman?" Sparrow Yenri asked, and he laughed at his own words.

"Shss," Twisted Rock made the sound to quiet Sparrow Yenri. "I want to hear the rest of the story."

"Mr. Miller said he didn't know the herbs she used, not the ones she used for a tonic and not the ones she put on peoples' chests, but something worked because soon people were getting well. He said he was sick himself and he remembered her giving him that tea to drink and putting that poultice on his chest and then her singing. 'Some kind of Indian song,' he said. 'I got no idea what it meant. But something worked. Must have, because next week I was just like new.'

"I don't know what we will learn from her," Lonely Cricket continued, "but I know it will be worth knowing."

"Maybe one of us will learn her medicine," said Twisted Rock.

"Yes, you would make a fine midwife," said Sparrow Yenri. "Let's get some sleep." His stomach was complaining, and he wanted to eat some of the jerky his brother had given him.

When Lonely Cricket woke in the morning, he poked Twisted Rock to wake him. Then he went to poke Sparrow Yenri. But his blanket was empty. Sparrow Yenri was gone. He had had enough of fasting.

"What was your vision?" Talking Mountain would ask his son.

"In my sleep there were many trees, and I was lost among them. Then I saw a great fire in the sky, and I knew that I must follow it to find my way," the boy answered. He never told his father this, but Sparrow Yenri wondered if the vision of his dream was not caused by the fire in his belly, by too much jerky on an empty stomach.

***

Dreaming Woman perched on a log and lifted her arms so that her poncho took on the appearance of wings. Made from the White Man's cloth, the plain, light blue garb was yellowed and ripped with age. She seemed so old and fragile that Lonely Cricket wondered if the breeze might carry her away.

Twisted Rock made a face as if he had smelled something bad. Lonely Cricket did not respond but waited for the healing woman to speak.

ΩΩΩΩΩ

When the first people were in the world, they were happy. They hunted and fished and found berries and plants to eat. At night, they would gather around a fire and dance and sing of Ma-Ona the Creator.

Then the Trickster came among them as a man and he wanted to create discord and anger among them. So, he brought with him a woman of his creating. It was the first time the Ho-Chunk had seen a woman, and they were aroused by her. Each man vied for the woman's attention, for there were no other women in the world.

Instead of working together to hunt, each man hunted by himself in the hope that he would find the biggest deer or the best elk. Instead of fishing together, each man would look for the best place to fish and would try to catch the most fish—many more than anyone could eat. But they no longer hunted, or fished, or gathered plants for food but to impress the woman, for each man wanted her for his own.

When the night came, the people no longer built one great fire about which they might dance and sing. Each man built his own fire. Each man wanted his fire to be the biggest and the brightest, for they wanted to impress the woman, for each man wanted her for his own.

No longer did they share a large teepee, but each man built his own sleeping place in the hope that the woman would join him.

Our Grandmother in the Sky saw what was happening to the Ho-Chunk and she feared for them. She decided to give them women, not the Trickster's woman, but women of their same kind who could share their lives.

Since Our Grandmother could not create life, she used life that Ma-Ona had already created. Some of the women were made from thunder and some from eagles, hawks, and pigeons. These were people of the sky. Then she made other women from creatures of the earth: the wolf, the bear, the elk, the buffalo, the fish, the snake, the water as it moved, and the deer.

She made women from all twelve of these kinds, and Our Grandmother gave these women to the Ho-Chunk, who were very thankful. The people no longer felt they had to compete with one another for there were women enough for all.

They could go back to hunting, fishing, and gathering plants together. At night they could again gather around the fire to dance and sing. Only when it was time to sleep did they separate so that each man and his woman could be together.

Because the mothers of our people were from nature, they could understand the language of the world. They could hear the voices of animals and spirits to help guide the Ho-Chunk. The women reminded the Ho-Chunk how to work with one another and how to cooperate with the world around us.

ΩΩΩΩΩ

When her story was finished, the two boys thanked Dreaming Woman for what she had taught them. "What would you have me do in return?" each boy asked, for they knew it was their duty to repay the healing woman for her teaching.

Dreaming Woman took a plant from a pouch which lay nearby. She held it before Twisted Rock. "This is the food of the muskrat," she said. This cone, which is its flower, is to be ground into a powder. When people sneeze and are filled with the yellow liquid that is not good, they can use this powder in their noses.

"Now is the time to gather these flowers for the plants grow well in the rain of the spring. Go to the fields that have been flooded and filled with snow. There you will find this plant. Collect the flowers and grind them between two rocks. When you have filled this gourd, bring it back to me."

She also held up a small, deerskin pouch decorated with beads. "Fill this pouch as well and take it to your mother as a present, for every family has need of the food of the muskrat."

Then she showed Twisted Rock how to grind the flower, how to sprinkle tobacco over the rocks before he used them for the grinding, and the words that were to be recited so that the herb would work as it was meant.

Twisted Rock was happy with his assignment for he knew that the plant grew in great numbers where the stream had overflowed its banks with the melting snow. It would be an easy task.

When Twisted Rock had left them, Dreaming Woman took another plant from her bag. She handled it with care. "There are many sharp hairs that protect this herb, for it is sacred and its magic is great.

"It is the medicine of the heyoka. The clowns use it to heal their burns and scrapes and aches when they do their foolish things: when they fall from their horse and are dragged in the dirt; when they reach with their hands into pots to take food without thinking; when they dance until their legs can no longer hold them.

"The fruit must be gathered before the flowers grow. You will have to look hard for enough to fill this flask. When you have gathered the flowers, they must be prepared properly. You chew them into a paste even though they are bitter to the taste. When you do this, you must dance and sing as I show you and you must use tobacco to thank the spirits that have given us this herb."

She demonstrated the way of singing and of dancing. And she taught Lonely Cricket the way to thank the spirits.

When he had learned, she told him to search in the pastures where the deer most often fed but which cows did not favor. "Deer happily eat the medicine of the heyoka, but cattle and buffalo do not," she explained.

"Thank you, older sister," Lonely Cricket said. "I will return with the paste as you have taught me."

"It is not for me," the woman answered. "This is the medicine of the clown. Tomorrow, you will take it to Falling Cloud and learn what he will teach you."

Lonely Cricket was happy with his assignment for he knew that Dreaming Woman had faith in him. This was a sacred task, and the thought made him proud.

***

"I am so hungry," Twisted Rock complained to himself. "I wish that I had some of Shadow Fox's jerky." His mouth watered at the thought of the food he had refused the night before.

Nearby, a crippled meadowlark fluttered on the ground. "Careful, little bird," Twisted Rock said; "there are snakes here."

The bird dragged a wounded wing. Round and round she limped.

Thinking to help her, Twisted Rock pushed himself from the ground where he was lying in ravenous exhaustion. It was only then that the bird took flight. "Ha, you fooled me," the boy thought. "You must have eggs nearby."

It was then he saw the king snake winding towards the bird's thatched nest. Had it been warmer, the snake would have been quicker, and his supper secured before Twisted Rock could react. Instead, the boy grabbed a clod of dirt and threw it at the hunter.

As the creature slithered away, Twisted Rock was happy that he had saved whatever eggs there were inside the mound-shaped nest. He sat some distance from the nest and waited for the meadowlark to return. When she did and started to sing, he knew that this had been his vision.

In the years to come, Twisted Rock would revisit this moment and try to better understand the message he had been given. For now, the youngster was happy to know he could return to his parents' cabin. That evening he would eat his mother's cooking and he would tell himself that Ma-Ona had picked him to save the weak. Already the snake was growing longer in his memory.

***

Lonely Cricket's mouth hurt from preparing the nettles of the heyoka's medicine. His tongue was thick with the bitterness of the fruit that he had chewed. As he settled against a tree, he felt great sadness. Obviously, Twisted Rock, like Sparrow Yenri, had received a vision. His blanket was gone and, he must have returned to his parents' lodge.

Lonely Cricket imagined the other boys telling their fathers of the visions which they had been given. He wondered what was wrong with him that the Great Spirit had not given him a vision as well.

It was a fitful night for the boy. Animals yapped and bayed in the darkness. The sounds filled him with loneliness and fear. He threw more wood onto the fire and hoped the sun would soon appear.

Over and over he wrestled with the question: "What is wrong with me? Do I deserve a vision? When will Ma-Ona show me my way?"

No answer came. Instead, there was rain, which made the fire sputter and the boy even more miserable.

Lonely Cricket pulled the cloth turtle, which his sister had given him, from the waist of his grimy deerskin breechcloth. Holding it close to him, he spoke. "Perhaps tomorrow when Falling Cloud instructs me."

Lonely Cricket did not really believe this. After all, Falling Cloud never made sense. Still, it was comforting to hold the fetish that his sister had made.

***

Falling Cloud was stretched out in the mud. His head was cupped in his hands; his elbows on the ground.

Lonely Cricket did not want to lie in the mud; he was already uncomfortable. He would copy the older man—to do otherwise would have shown disrespect. He took the small container of heyoka's medicine and handed it to Falling Cloud who tucked it into his vest. Then he lay down to hear what he would be taught.

ΩΩΩΩΩ

When the First Man was placed on the earth, he did not know what to do or how to live. As he wandered, he came upon a medicine man, who was not a man but the Trickster in disguise.

"What am I to do; where am I to live?" the First Man asked.

"We shall see," the medicine man answered.

So, the Trickster told the First Man to take off his clothes except for the cloth that was wrapped around his loins and to jump into the river.

The First Man did as he was bid. He jumped into the water, which was very cold, so cold that soon he could barely feel his arms and legs.

"Stay there," the medicine man told him. "Stay until you can understand the fish who swim."

It was a cold day, so while the First Man sat in the river, that Trickster gathered grass and wood. He took rocks to make sparks and set a fine fire. Then he sat by the fire and warmed himself.

When the First Man was ready to pass into death from the cold, when he was ready to slip below the water and become food for the trout and the pickerel, then the Trickster

told him to come out of the water.

The man thought to sit by the fire, but the medicine man said, "Climb that tree and stay in its branches until you know the flow of the air and the flight of the birds."

It was a tall tree and difficult to climb. the First Man was scratched many times. Once he lost his hold and would have fallen to his death had he not grabbed a branch and pulled himself back.

Finally, he reached the top of the tree. There he sat as the medicine man had instructed him.

While the First Man sat in the tree and felt the wind trying to dislodge him, the Trickster was cutting branches and long grass and making himself a hut in which he could sit. Inside the hut there was no wind, and the Trickster fell asleep; for he wanted to take a nap.

By the time the Trickster had awakened from his nap, the First Man was barely able to hold on. The wind had become stronger and stronger until it was blowing the clouds this way and that, and the man was very tired.

"Come," the medicine man beckoned.

The First Man did and walked towards the hut, which the Trickster had built. He, too, was in need of rest.

"I did not build this hut for you," the Trickster said. "You must next learn the way of the mouse and the possum. Find a hole in the rocks and put yourself there to rest."

The First Man did as he was told even though he sorely wanted to rest in the hut. He found a small crack in the rocks, which formed a cliff nearby, and he lay down as best he could, curling his body into a ball. There were stones beneath him, and they poked and prodded him as he tried to sleep. Small animals ran by and he wondered and worried what they might be.

Meanwhile the medicine man had set a snare nearby and captured a hare, which he skinned and set in a pot.

The First Man was cold and sore, he could not sleep, and he was very hungry. All he could think about was that rabbit stew. He could stand it no more. He got up and strode towards the medicine man.

"Where do you think you're going?" the Trickster demanded. "Who do you think you are?"

"I know that I am not like the fish who must accept the cold river or die trying to find a better place. I know that I am not like the bird who cannot build shelter for himself but must allow the winds to blow. I know that I am not like the mouse and the possum who must live in fear that they will be killed and eaten.

"I am a man, I shall have fire, I shall live in a house, and I shall eat the rabbit stew that you have made."

ΩΩΩΩΩ

When the story was finished, Lonely Cricket thanked Falling Cloud for what he had taught. "What would you have me do in return?" the boy asked.

"I would have you become a man," Falling Cloud replied. He jumped to his feet and trotted to his pony. Mounting so he was facing the horse's rump, the heyoka yelled, "Whoa," and the horse moved away.

Lonely Cricket looked after them and wondered what he should do. "Perhaps I should find Tall Grass and ask," he thought, but he was embarrassed. He felt like crying, but he did not want to be seen.

Slowly, dejectedly, Lonely Cricket walked back to the campsite by the creek. There, at least, he could cry.

After the tears came sleep. It did not bring relief. Lonely Cricket woke still questioning. Surely, he was the least of the Ho-Chunk. Even the clown wanted nothing from him.

The boy sat on the bank of the stream. His thumb and finger stroked the cloth turtle and he thought of his sister. "Happy Turtle will be so disappointed." The thought made him cry once more.

It was then that he saw Barking Deer. The boy was young, only a toddler like Many Fish, certainly too young to be without supervision. Still, little boys like to wander. Lonely Cricket knew that soon his little brother would be wandering off as well.

Barking Deer saw something in the creek. Perhaps it was a fish leaping for a fly. Perhaps it was a polliwog testing his tail in the current. Perhaps it was a dragonfly darting to and fro. Whatever it was, the boy reached. Splash. Screaming with fear and wet, the child thrashed.

Forgetting himself and his misery, Lonely Cricket ran to help. He pulled the boy from the water, wrapped him in his own blanket even though it was still damp from the night's rain, and guided him as they went to look for Barking Deer's mother or sister. One of them was sure to be nearby.

Quiet Raven was gathering berries. She had not realized that her little brother had wandered off. Her eyes widened in terror as she saw Lonely Cricket bringing the miscreant back to her. Still, Barking Deer was all right. Disaster had been averted. Even as she scolded him for his heedlessness and thanked Lonely Cricket for his help, there was relief.

"Thank you," the young woman said to Lonely Cricket as he folded his sodden blanket. "Tell Happy Turtle that we must soon look for reeds to make baskets," she called to him as he headed towards his parents' home. The youngster's shoulders were hunched as he walked. He wished he could sit next to the stream forever, to never speak to another soul. But there was no point in putting it off; he would tell Lame Bear of his failure.

***

The boy looked down. He could not meet Lame Bear's eyes. Thought of the shame he had brought his father burned through him. "I am sorry that I have failed you." Tears welled as he added, "I am sorry that I have failed our people."

The sound that Lame Bear made was deep and guttural. Lonely Cricket had never heard it before. At first, he thought it the sound of rage. Then the youngster realized—his father was laughing, laughing at him. He could feel the blush of embarrassment flow through his body and into his face. He hung his head even lower.

Lame Bear wrapped his arms around his son's shoulders and held him close. When the boy's sobs had subsided, Lame Bear spoke. "The Great Spirit has many ways to send us his messages. To some he sends dreams. To some he sends animals. Only to the chosen few does he send his messages through other humans. What makes you think that the child was not sent to you by Ma-Ona?"

That night Lonely Cricket whispered of his experience to Happy Turtle. "You were with me," he said. "Without the turtle which you had made for me I would have given up. I do not know what the vision I have had means, but I know that I am lucky to have a big sister like you."

That night Lonely Cricket slept well. His stomach full, his mind at ease, his bed warm. It was good to be a young man of the Ho-Chunk. Pride again filled his heart.

Chapter ~ 5 Confusions

When Ezekiel Jones had learned of his assignment, Indian agent for the Ho-Chunk, it had sounded promising. Senator Arnold had assured him that Pierce was a town of promise and the job a plum. How could Ezekiel doubt his wife's cousin? After all, the Senator was a hero who had fought Indians with the Eighth Cavalry in the Arizona Territory.

Harmon Arnold had missed the War Between the States, but he had killed his share of Hualapai, been wounded twice fighting Apache, and come back to Nebraska ready for a career in politics. Getting spoils for his family had not been his goal but building a network of support throughout the state certainly was. If he played his cards right, the state senate was only the beginning; and unimportant relatives like Sarah Jones and her mangy husband were part of the deck.

For fourteen years, Ezekiel had suffered and resented his wife and her cousin for landing him in this backwater. The town of Pierce was no more than his agency, Old Man Miller's saloon, the general store that served White Men and Indians alike, the busted-down farrier, Angus Cooperman—not a real blacksmith at all—that pest of a preacher, Jeb Ludlow, and whatever foolish, old woman, the preacher could find to pretend she knew anything about teaching school.

The town of Pierce might be enough to the farmers hereabouts and was certainly more than those Red heathens deserved or could understand, but it was far less than Ezekiel Jones had promised himself when he had taken Cousin Harmon's offer. For that reason, he took every opportunity to enrich himself even if those opportunities meant Ho-Chunk doing without. Over the years, his account in the Fayette Bank had grown, as had his passion for the women at Miss Birdie's Rooming House and Sumptuous Parlor.

If his passion for those women of the evening had grown, whatever feelings there might have been between Ezekiel and his wife had dimmed. "Perhaps," he sometimes thought, "if we had a child, there might be something left of us. Instead, Sarah has dried within. Day after day she sits in the front room and stares out that damned window at this doubly-damned town."

Sarah Jones's weekly letters of complaint, which during those first years had jostled their way to Fayette and then to Lincoln, were no longer being written. Were her mother still alive and her cousin's father so disposed, perhaps then .... No, Sarah had resigned herself, and with that resignation had come an emptiness to match that of her womb.

When young McCabe banged on the door that afternoon, it had seemed more effort than she could muster to open it and inquire. Perhaps if she had for a moment thought someone might want her, it would have seemed less a chore. The truth was that she was never needed. Sometimes people came looking for the Indian Agent, but for his wife—never.

"Where's he at?" the young man demanded, not even bothering to take off his hat. "There's a fight at the saloon. Old Man Miller sent me to fetch him."

"Mr. Jones isn't a sheriff," Sarah said.

"No, he ain't, but he's responsible for them Injuns. This one's ready to kill a White Man. Get your husband over to the saloon before we got a scalpin', a hangin' or a lynchin' or somethin'."

The young man's fetid breath told its own story. The McCabes had failed as farmers and headed west looking for more of what they had never been able to find. This one youngster had stayed behind. Even in the rolling nothing of northeastern Nebraska, love could rear her ugly head, and John McCabe had been deeply in adolescent lust. Without family or prospects, the young man cleaned up the saloon and slept behind the bar. In exchange, he got more drink than was good and shared the old man's food whenever one of them thought to prepare some.

"Love is fierce dumb," Sarah thought as she reviewed the boy's life. Then she thought of her own and wanted to weep.

"He's not in town" she responded. "I don't know if he's out talking to his Indians or what, but I don't think you'll find him."

"Talking with his Indians?" Sarah almost laughed at the lie. She knew exactly where her husband could be found—in Fayette, at Miss Birdie's. It had been three days since he had been home. If the river ran true to its course, it would be at least two more before he would be back in Pierce demanding clean clothes, some food, and quiet. "Damn you, quiet. I need some sleep. Can't you see I've been working?"

"Well, somebody's got to do something, and quick," the boy demanded.

Sarah Jones tied her bonnet, pulled on a pair of gloves more appropriate for a dance in Omaha than the streets of Pierce, took parasol in hand, and stepped out into the summer heat and dust. What inspired her she didn't know. Was it boredom in need of relief? Or was it just too long spent knowing that there was nothing to be done?

The wearying heat of dead air stopped Sarah for a moment. She hesitated and then marched towards the saloon. Already she could hear the shouts. One man, an Indian whom she had seen from time to time, was standing his drunken ground. Surrounded by a knot of mangy

Whites, he whirled in all directions and yelled in the gibberish of the Indians with an occasional real word thrown in.

Old Man Miller did not allow Indians in the saloon, but he had no scruples when it came to selling firewater from the back door. Clearly this Indian had already poured any money he might have brought to town down his throat.

His White adversary, Nathan Wainright, who was kin to Harry Cook, had also been drinking heavily. Despite her penchant for seclusion and brooding, Sarah Jones knew Nathan's reputation: a sluggard and a drunk who liked to yell and to ride his dun hard and leave the poor beast—sweated and un-walked—while he indulged himself with as much whiskey as any man in town.

Sarah had no clue about why the two men were arguing. What she could see, however, was that the situation was getting dangerous. The derisive hoots of the onlookers were urging Wainright to violence. Already the Ho-Chunk had pulled out a knife and was stabbing futilely at the air.

Using her unopened parasol as a pry, she pushed her way between Jake Hobart and his brother Aaron. "Leave off," Sarah yelled as she marched towards to two combatants. Waving that parasol as if it were a battle-axe, she screamed again, "You men should know better. I declare I should set Mrs. Cole on the bunch of you. She'd tan your britches quick enough."

Some of the men looked down and pawed the ground like chastised children. A couple drifted away—certainly to go back to the saloon where they could savor the momentary excitement of the day.

"And you, Nathan Wainright, shouldn't you be helping your uncle? I warrant there's corn to be hoed and fences to be mended."

Nathan muttered in the direction of the Indian and marched towards Maggie who waited dispiritedly at the rail in front of the store. The horse sagged as he threw his weight into the saddle. The farrier took note of the dry sweat that marked the horse's withers and shook his head in contempt.

"And you!" Sarah Jones marched towards the Indian, her parasol still jabbing the air. "What do you have to say for yourself? When are you people going to learn you can't handle that firewater? Town is no place for Indians. Don't you have something better to do like chasing squaws and dancing around in circles?"

Her words went on, flowing in a torrent. Even sober, Morning Spring would not have understood a fifth of them. Well liquored, he understood nothing except his growing sense of anger. Morning Spring mumbled to himself as he backed away, "The White Man is a fool. Now he is gone, replaced by this crazy woman who jabs the air with her strange stick and fills my ears with buzzing words that mean nothing."

Morning Spring stalked away. That night he would tell the story. He would share the sound of the woman's voice—the raucous call of a magpie—and stab at the air as if battling ghosts. He would laugh at the White Woman. Morning Spring would not tell of his own knife flailing at nothing. He would not mention the whirling circles in which he had danced nor his afternoon's drunken sleep at the side of the road.

Later Morning Spring would tell of the White Man who had called him "Redskin" and "dumb." He would tell of the way the White Man had spat at him and gestured. He would tell what his heart had learned, that the White Man should be driven from the land of the Ho-Chunk.

***

"Well that was some ruckus we had us this morning." Old Man Miller spat; his spittle clanked into the bucket that served as a spittoon. "You know how she started?"

John McCabe settled into a chair. "Sure do. It was 'count of Mrs. Knox, you know Amos's wife. She come into town with him. Wanted to buy some of that cloth Jedidiah had 'em ship in from Omaha. Wanted to make herself a new dress, and…"

"Hrmph! Hrmph!" The older man snorted his impatience.

John continued, "she was walking cross the street when that Injun saw her, and him not thinking none because of the liquor, why he said, 'Howdy.' And she said, "Howdy," back. And Wainright he took 'ception count of him bein' an Injun and shouldn't be talkin' to no White woman."

The saloonkeeper stroked his whiskers and spat again. "Just, 'howdy?'"

"Yes, sir, 'howdy.'"

"That boy's got mean in his brain. He'd have taken exception if that Injun has passed wind." Old Man Miller hucked another wad of spit into the bucket.

"Yes, Sir. We gonna stop sellin' whiskey to them Injuns?"

The older man laughed—the sound of a goat bleating in surprise. "Hell no! You know what a good fight does?" He paused for emphasis. "Gets a man's thirst roaring. That's what it does. Sold more beer today than we do most weeks." He cackled again.

The door to the saloon had been locked, at least a stout of wood had been wedged against it. The saloonkeeper and his young helper were heating their dinner — the usual, beans with a few chunks of pork thrown in for flavor. John was always thankful to see his employer happy. When business was good, the old man was more likely to share those bits of fatty meat. Most days, the younger man had to settle for just the beans. Tonight's dinner was looking promising.

"You seen your share of fighting didn't you, Mr. Miller?" McCabe asked. He had asked the question many times. It was one of Old Man Miller's favorite topics — the years he had ridden with One-Armed Kearney, even helping the Captain off the field when his arm had been blown away at Churubusco.

Miller's story always ended the same way. "That was enough fighting for me. Enough of horses, too. Only thing I wanted after Army life was a good drink. That's why I went into this business. Good liquor and a good chaw. That's enough for any man."

When he would finish, the old man would always spit. Even if he didn't have a plug in his cheek, he would spit. Sometimes, if he were cooking their beans, he'd spit into the pot. "What the hell," McCabe would think, "it'll add flavor."

When he saw that Miller had actually given him a fistful of that pork, McCabe figured the saloonkeeper was in an especially good mood. "Mind if I ask ya a question?"

"Go ahead. Don't know as I'll answer but go on and ask."

"Your name?"

"What about it?"

"What is it?"

"Miller. Hell, you know that."

"Nah. I mean your Christian name."

"Folks call me *Old Man*."

"Well, I know that. I mean your real name—the one your folks gave you."

"They didn't."

"On your certificate or when you was baptized."

"None of that crap. My ma dropped me, and that was about all what she was ready to do."

"What did your pappy call you?"

"Before he rode out?" The old man lit the kerosene lamp. He ran his finger around the edge of his plate and sucked the last of the beans from his rough digit.

"Hell, all he said was, 'ain't no kith of mine.' Course I don't recall it being just a baby, but that's what my ma told me. Nope, only name I got's Miller. Course now folks call me Old Man, but I don't know as it matters. Miller's 'nough of a name for a barkeep." He took a plug and stuffed it into one cheek. The younger man could see the staining of Miller's teeth — the ones that had not yet rotted out.

***

Even as he swung his right leg over the saddle, Nathan Wainright yanked the horse's bit pulling the gelding's mouth to the left. He dug his heels into Maggie's flanks, yelled, "Come on, you worthless nag," and whacked at the dun shoulders with the reins.

Maggie's nostrils flared, and he galloped down the dusty street that was the town of Pierce.

Nathan was headed towards Fayette—summoned by its two saloons and possibly, if he could find the dollar, by that plump whore at Miss Birdie's. He might have made it had Maggie not stumbled. She might not have stumbled had Nathan been able to sit upright. When the rider lurched to the right just as the galloping horse planted her right front hoof, there was nothing Maggie could do to adjust for her drunken owner's weight. She stumbled, almost fell, and—gathering herself—raced on. Nathan tumbled to the ground where he lay on his back, for the moment damning his mount and all horse-kind and then passing into a well-liquored sleep—dead-to-the-world and to the sounds of his own snorts and snores.

It was about seventy yards before Maggie slowed. With a shake of his mane and a quick buck, the gelding turned around and cantered down the road—past her owner, through Pierce—where she was noticed only by Joshua Cooperman, who was pumping the bellows of his father's forge—and then across the fields towards Lame Bear's barn.

Lonely Cricket was hoeing beans when Maggie neighed. He turned, saw the dun's coat frothed with sweat, and he, un-ridden but still saddled and tacked, trotting into the barn. The boy dropped his hoe and ran towards the horse. Recognizing the flare of the horse's nostrils and the wideness of his eyes, Lonely Cricket slowed as he drew close and started singing a Ho-Chunk chant, one he often sang when he was feeding the animals. It was a song he remembered from years before. Had Yquili Sparrow sung it to him or perhaps Happy Turtle. It was a song that brought warmth to his heart and his singing often calmed the restive animals in their stalls. *Soon Huhawira will come to us. She will bring the stars. She will bring quiet and sleep. Soon all the world will hush. This moon brings dreams in which warriors rest and Hinugijá hold babies to their breasts.*

At the sound of Lonely Cricket's voice, the dun's muscles relaxed. The horse slowed to a walk and stopped at his stall.

"Easy, shkung, easy," The boy said over and over. The gelding's pinned back ears slowly relaxed. Even then, Lonely Cricket did not try to take Maggie out to the hitching post to remove his tack. He did not even try to tie the dun—although the horse was shifting in the aisle. He spoke calmly and rubbed the horse's flanks and shoulders gently with whichever hand was not otherwise occupied as he removed the saddle, blanket, and bridle, as he slipped the halter over her muzzle, and as he fastened the crown piece. He brought the gelding a handful of corn. While the horse ground the yellow kernels, the boy rubbed her with burlap. Once Maggie was calm there would be time to walk him. Once he was cooler, there would be time to give him water and feed.

When Maggie was relaxed enough to walk, Lonely Cricket led him out the door and to the field where Lame Bear and Harry Cook were working. The boy walked slowly, allowing the horse to stop from time to time to pull clumps of fresh grass, which he chewed as they moved along.

"What the devil?!" Harry Cook had many questions, but he quickly realized that the boy had no answers.

"I'd better go looking for him. That damn fool, you'd think he could do one day's worth of work. He's probably so busy drinking he doesn't even know his horse has run off."

"I go with you," Lame Bear offered.

"Nah, you take care of the wheat. We still got lots of work to do. I'll take the boy if you don't mind, just in case I need him to hold the mule. We'll take the buckboard so's I can throw my worthless nephew in the back."

"Go with Mr. Cook," Lame Bear said, but Lonely Cricket, leading Maggie at a trot, was already on his way to hitch Stubborn Mule to the buckboard.

"That boy of yours is a heap more help than Nathan, Bear. Good with the animals, too."

Lame Bear did not show the pride he felt at his friend's words. Instead, he nodded quickly and went back to his work. Bugs were threatening the crop, and the plants had to be carefully inspected.

***

By the time Harry Cook and Lonely Cricket found him, Nathan Wainright had awoken and managed to prop himself against a fencepost. With no greater purpose and no energy to do more, he watched an ant struggling to carry a leaf far bigger than herself.

When she had traveled almost beyond his reach, the young man held a small twig in front of her. Driven by the instincts of her kind, the ant climbed onto the stick. Nathan quickly lifted her into the air and deposited her at the spot where she had first entered his consciousness.

Over and over Nathan played this game until he heard his uncle call the mule to a halt. Using the twig as a spear, he impaled the hapless creature.

Chapter ~ 6 A Journey Begins

The great owl-scream of the white smoke whistle.

And then again. The sound pierced his ears.

The screak of wheels finding purchase on track.

A lurch.

Lonely Cricket was forced back in the wooden bench. His breath caught and then released.

Lonely Cricket watched through the dirty window as the train staggered from the station. He saw a man in a fancy checked suit and holding two cases talk through the grated window. He remembered the man who sat behind that grate—a small man perched on a high stool, a visor on his forehead even though there was no sun, his finger resting on the talking key, the one that tapped clicks and clacks along the singing wire.

A young couple stood on the platform—locked in an embrace, their lips touching, her head tilted back and his bent forward. They did not react, not even when the black-soot and cinder of the great locomotive drifted down.

Ezekiel Jones watched the train depart. As it gathered speed, he rubbed his hands together. Then he turned away, back to his buckboard and the gray nag that served him well enough. He thought to have a drink or two at The Wild Horse and then a different kind of ride with Rose-of-Sharon, his current favorite at Miss Birdie's Rooming House and Sumptuous Parlor.

Through the window, Lonely Cricket observed the town of Fayette going about its business. The blacksmith's assistant working the bellows. Two women, baskets over their arms, entering Grave's Mercantile. Lonely Cricket had never been inside that store; Indians were not allowed. Instead, if there was something to be bought, they went round to the back door and waited until gray-haired Tom Graves, who had fought the Sioux and hated "Injuns," would inquire what they'd be wanting and then decide how much extra price he'd ask. The boy's family did what little shopping as they might in Pierce, where Mr. Jacobs had a more cordial manner.

Lonely Cricket did not look for his father. Lame Bear had already left for home. It would take well past the high sun for him to make it back to their allotment, back to Lonely Cricket's mother, to his sister and his brother.

He imagined Lame Bear jiggling the reins and coaxing Great Horse on, the heavy load of fence wire bouncing and jangling as they went.

Two rolls of wire: that had been the payment given for Lonely Cricket's journey.

Far away there was a school for Indians—in a place called Pennsylvania. There he would learn from White Men. He would learn books and numbers.

"You will learn much and come back to help our people," Lame Bear had said when he had told his son of this school.

"But I don't want to leave you and my mother. I don't want to leave my sister and my brother. I don't want to leave my home and my people. I promise I will work harder," Lonely Cricket had tried to protest.

Lame Bear grunted and turned away. That evening, when the work was done and when they had eaten, he told his son a story.

ΩΩΩΩΩ

Standing Eagle and his friend were hunting. They saw a large deer and tracked him. The animal trotted away, keeping just out of range of their bows. He led the two young men deeper and deeper into the forest until they no longer recognized the place. Then, suddenly, the buck had disappeared, for it had been the Trickster and no deer at all.

A band of Arapahoe came upon Standing Eagle and his friend and took them captive. For many years the boys were kept prisoner. They were taught to dance in ways that were Arapahoe and not of the Ho-Chunk. They were told to speak in the language of the Arapahoe and to hunt as the Arapahoe. Their clothes were taken, and they were dressed as the Arapahoe.

For many years the boys lived this way. The other boy no longer thought of himself as Ho-Chunk. He fell in love with a young woman of the Arapahoe and asked to marry. Then he had no yearning to return to his own people.

But Standing Eagle never forgot his home. He never forgot his people. One night he snuck out of the camp and started walking. He was not sure where he would find his own people, but he knew that he must look for them.

Many days Standing Eagle walked. His feet grew sore from walking. His body ached from nights of sleeping on the hard ground without a blanket. His mind became confused with lack of food. Still, he walked. Still, he looked for a camp of the Ho-Chunk.

Finally, he found a hunting party. He did not recognize any of the hunters. They did not know him. They saw only his dress and thought him to be an enemy.

"Look," one of them called out, "it is an Arapahoe. We should kill him."

Standing Eagle wanted to tell them that he was a Ho-Chunk; but it had been years since he had spoken the language of our people. The words did not come easily to his tongue. He feared that he would sound as an Arapahoe. He feared the hunters would not listen, that the sound of his words would stir their anger.

Standing Eagle prepared in his heart to die at the hands of the Ho-Chunk. "At least," he thought, "I will die among my own people."

Standing Eagle did not try to run away. He held up his hands to Ma-Ona and waited for death.

One of the hunters said, "See this Arapahoe is a brave man. We should not kill him. We will take him prisoner and take him to the Medicine Man.

The hunters discussed this and decided that a brave warrior should not be killed like an animal. They took Standing Eagle to their camp.

"We have captured this Arapahoe," one of the hunters said. "What should be done with him?"

The Medicine Man, who knew things that men could not see, replied, "This man is no enemy. Within his heart he is one of us."

When Standing Eagle had found his tongue and told his story, the Medicine Man said to him, "No matter how far you have been from your people, no matter how long you have been separated from them, in your heart you have always been Ho-Chunk. Your heart brought you back to your people.

"Your heart will always know us, and we shall know you."

ΩΩΩΩΩ

When he had finished the story, Lame Bear shared a pipe of tobacco with his son.

***

Seven suns later they had hitched Great Horse to the wagon and ridden to Pierce. Talking Mountain had been there, too. With him was Shadow Fox; he would also be going to the White Man's school. His father, too, would receive fence wire. That had been the offer of the White Man's agent.

The two fathers had followed the agent's buckboard to Fayette and to the back of Grave's Mercantile. There the three men and Mr. Grave's son, Raymond, had loaded the heavy rolls of fencing onto the wagons.

"You boys might as well head home," Ezekiel Jones had said. His voice was high and tense, like the whistle of reeds. "I'll wait with the young-uns. I have to sign the papers."

He did not mention the government bounty he would receive for each youngster.

The agent had two pieces of paper, one for each father. Each man made his mark, and Jones, folded the papers and put them into his pocket.

That had been the required formalities—little enough for two young lives.

Chapter 7 ~ Towards the Rising Sun

Lonely Cricket spoke softly so the White Men could not hear. "I am Lonely Cricket, son of Lame Bear, child of the Sky and one with the Pigeon."

The boy sitting next to him didn't respond. Lonely Cricket lifted his hand to show his palm to the boy. He recited his name and lineage again. The boy's response was to pull back into the corner of the bench—to where it met the dirt-crusted window—and tightened his body in fear.

Lonely Cricket was about to try again, this time thinking to touch his own breast with his hands to make his intent of friendship clearer. Suddenly, the large, callused hand of the White Man named Frazier hit the side of his head. Lonely Cricket almost toppled with the force of the unexpected blow. He looked up in surprise. The man, a smile revealing his rotting teeth, hit him again, this time harder.

"Why…?"

The next blow was harder yet and set Lonely Cricket's left ear to ringing. "Keep yer mouth shut and yer eyes down, you fuckin' Injun." The words came too fast and slurred for Lonely Cricket to understand them, but the harshness of the man's voice made his intent clear. Lonely Cricket looked down and fought the trembling that plucked his body. With one more heavy-handed smack, the man seemed satisfied and started to move away. Then he turned back.

"You, too." He hissed the words as he gave the second boy a whack. "Keep them yammering mouths of yers shut till we tell ya otherwise."

The two boys dared to exchange a quick look and then went back to staring at the floor.

Slowly, Lonely Cricket reached into the waist of his pants and touched the worn nap of the cloth turtle he had secreted there.

He had not intended to take this talisman with him. When he rolled his few possessions and his clothing into his sleeping blanket, Lonely Cricket had decided to leave the turtle where he had placed it after his fast—tucked in the corner of a shelf near the spot where he usually slept. He thought that Many Fish would find it and would play with it. In this way he would remain with his brother to comfort him as the boy grew.

Only when Happy Turtle had come out to the wagon to say goodbye, only when she took his wrists in her hands and told him that he must remember her and her love for him, only when she told him that her spirit would travel with him to this strange place called Pennsylvania, only then did Lonely Cricket realize how precious the small cloth turtle had become to him. He ran back into the house even as Yquili Sparrow held Many Fish so the little boy would not dart under Great Horse's hooves or under the wheels of the wagon, even as Lame Bear climbed onto the wagon seat and lifted the reins. Lonely Cricket had grabbed the talisman, tucked it safely into his waist, and run back to the wagon.

"I won't forget you," Lonely Cricket said to Happy Turtle as he climbed aboard the wagon. "I won't forget, and I will return to bless your wedding as an older brother should."

Happy Turtle had smiled. Her face crimsoned. Her eyes glistened. She turned away and walked towards the barn. Lonely Cricket could hear the cows lowing. It was time for milking. It was time for life to continue.

As Lonely Cricket, fighting back tears of the heart and those from physical pain, recalled that morning's departure, Frazier—a mean smile on his lips—returned to his seat.

The other boy spoke softly, almost in a whisper. The clack of the train and the ringing in Lonely Cricket's ear drowned out the boy's words. Was his new friend's name Standing Oak? Lonely Cricket could not be sure. He would ask again, later, when the White Man was not listening.

***

Lonely Cricket slept. Both boys had slept—tilting towards one another until their heads rested together. Their bodies bounced and swayed, but neither boy's eyes had opened, not until the other White Man, whose name was Langdon, shook them lightly.

"Up, boys." He shook them again.

Lame Bear had already fed and hitched Great Horse to the wagon when he awakened Lonely Cricket that morning. It was still dark, only the faintest light came over the horizon. Lonely Cricket gathered his blanket and his clothes by the light of the kerosene lantern. They didn't use the lantern often; the fuel cost White Man money.

Lonely Cricket tried to collect his things quietly. He did not want to wake his mother and sister. He did not want to arouse Many Fish, who lay next to Happy Turtle. He had not meant to awaken them, but soon they were all stirring. By that time, he and Lame Bear had eaten some jerky and had drunk fresh water from the new pump, which Harry Cook had helped them to install.

The water was good and sweet. It came from deep beneath the ground and tasted of the earth and of life.

"We must go, or we will be late," Lame Bear said.

"But what of the animals?" the boy asked.

"Your sister and mother will take care of them today."

By that point, Happy Turtle had taken his wrists in her hands.

Lonely Cricket looked back as Great Horse plodded towards the road. Ahead lay Pierce, Fayette, and then that strange land far towards the rising sun.

***

The town of Pierce was just stirring. The storekeeper was putting on his apron and watching the sunrise. The farrier's son was working his bellows—soon the fire would be ready to soften iron.

At the Indian Agent's house, Ruth Ferguson was putting biscuits into the oven. Her employer had told her there would be four Ho-Chunk coming that morning. Sarah Jones hadn't explained the why of it, and Silas Ferguson's widow was of no mind to feed Indians. Her husband's death fighting Sioux was more than enough reason for her hating all Red Men. But she would do as told—if only to the minimum. There would be biscuits and bacon fat to dip them. "Let the heathens drink water from the pump and do without eggs. As for good churned butter, they'll get none from me," Ruth said to herself as she slammed the oven door closed.

Lame Bear pulled the horse to a halt. Before his father dismounted, Lonely Cricket had jumped down and was reaching for the reins. He ran to the back of the wagon and pulled an armful of hay, which he spread on the ground near the horse's head. He took an extra moment to rub the horse's broad, brown muzzle. Great Horse nickered in response before dropping his head to the hay.

Meanwhile, Lame Bear hastened to the shed with the moon and stars carved in its door that stood some paces behind the house. As he followed his father, Lonely Cricket could hear Lame Bear's grunts.

"Your father sounds like a bear in the woods." Lonely Cricket had not heard Shadow Fox walk up behind him. The older boy laughed and hit Lonely Cricket in the shoulder. "Does he make such sounds when he is with your mother?"

Lonely Cricket could feel the anger welling but said nothing.

When Lame Bear finished, Talking Mountain went into the outhouse. He, too, grunted as he relieved himself. Lonely Cricket thought of things he might say. *This mountain makes many noises, but they have no meaning. Do mountains make such sounds when they pursue clouds?*

He held his peace.

As Talking Mountain came out, Shadow Fox held out his arm to push in front of the younger boy. Still, Lonely Cricket held his voice.

When Lonely Cricket finally finished in the outhouse, the others were seated on a bench by the kitchen door. He walked over to the bucket in which Mrs. Ferguson had earlier poured hot water and by which there was a piece of gray-beige soap. The water had turned cold and was grimy. Still, he washed his hands in the manner of the White Man and dried them on the same shred of a towel that his father and the others had used.

As he washed his hands, Lonely Cricket could see the cook preparing eggs and bacon. He could smell the bacon frying and the great pot of coffee, which boiled on the stove.

Had this been the home of Harry Cook, it would have been Leah Cook preparing the breakfast, and Sapphira would have been helping. They would have sat together. Mrs. Cook would have offered a White Man's prayer of thanks for the food. They would have eaten together as friends.

This was not the home of Harry Cook. Mrs. Ferguson brought out four biscuits dunked in grease. "Get yourselves water from the pump," she ordered and bustled back into the house. It was a meager breakfast.

The agent's wife came out with two more biscuits—these well buttered. "The boys will have a long way to go before they can eat," she said and handed one biscuit to Shadow Fox and the other to Lonely Cricket.

Lonely Cricket offered the biscuit to his father.

Lame Bear refused it. "The White woman is right. You will be hungry today."

At the other end of the bench, Talking Mountain took the biscuit from his son's hand.

***

Lonely Cricket blinked his eyes into awareness. Langdon leaned over him and shook Standing Oak's shoulders. The man's eyes smiled, but his mouth was set with seriousness. "Reckon you boys could use the facilities."

The youngsters stared back uncomprehending.

"The toilet," he said, shaking his shaggy head. "The lavatory? The restroom? The privy?"

When they made no response, Langdon gestured for them to stand and follow him.

They followed the White Man through the swaying car. Lonely Cricket copied Langdon and grabbed the seat tops to keep his balance. The younger boy, who was behind him, was not so careful and four times fell against Lonely Cricket.

"Clumsy!" The first time, Lonely Cricket only thought the word. That was after the second lurch. By the fourth stumble, Lonely Cricket said it aloud as Standing Oak grabbed for his shoulders.

The younger boy mumbled something. Lonely Cricket could hear the beginnings of tears in the boy's voice.

"Be careful." This time Lonely Cricket used the voice he had often used to comfort Nathan Wainright's horse after the dun had been ridden too hard. He imagined Maggie's wide-eyed look. For a moment his mind wandered, and Lonely Cricket stumbled against the White Man. There was a moment of terror as the man turned towards him.

"Careful, boy." Langdon rested his hand on the youngster's shoulder. "This here train jostles about a mite."

They had traversed the car and were standing in a line in front of a brown curtain. The smell announced what was on the other side. In front of them in the line were Shadow Fox and the boy with whom he had been sitting. There was another boy in front of Shadow Fox. Lonely Cricket didn't recognize him. Vaguely, he remembered the train stopping while he had slept.

"Hurry it up." Frazier was by the curtain and spoke to whomever was behind it. "We ain't got all day, boy." His voice was the harsh wind that carried cold across the land.

There was a response in a language Lonely Cricket didn't recognize.

"Don't forget to wash them filthy Injun hands of yours."

There were other people in the wagon now—people whose skin was black and who had huddled together like they were scared when he had lurched by. Lonely Cricket had seen a few black people before. *Negras* Harry Cook had called them. Where they were going or why, nobody knew or cared. They bought provisions at Jacobs' store and waited patiently for Angus Cooperman to shoe their skinny horses. Then they passed on through.

"Don't know which is worse," Frazier said; "traveling with a bunch of Injuns or havin' to put up with *negras.* Guess the railroad lumps 'em together—baggage they don't want mixin' with real folks."

"Shut up, you fool," Langdon hissed.

"Injuns and *negras*—don't like either of 'em," Frazier responded making it clear that he wasn't going to listen to his companion.

The line moved forward towards the curtained corner that would be their outhouse. The smell had grown stronger. Lonely Cricket tried to block it from his mind.

The boy who was riding with Shadow Fox was next in line. Then it would be Lonely Cricket's turn. He hadn't thought about it before, but he needed to relieve himself. As bad as the smell might be, he wanted to get behind that brown curtain.

"I have to go bad," Standing Oak said.

Lonely Cricket could sense his companion shifting his weight from foot to foot. "You go ahead of me," he said and pushed Standing Oak in front of him.

"Hey, what do think yer doing?" Frazier demanded. "Get back in line like you was supposed to."

Lonely Cricket looked up to take the measure of the White Man. A scar ran down the man's left cheek standing out against the grizzled brown of his beard. The eye above the scar drooped. His left hand, the one with which he had hit the boys, was missing the little finger and half the finger next to it. The boy, his ear still ringing, wondered if the big White Man was going to hit him again.

"Hold on, Frazier." This time Langdon's voice was commanding. "The boy is just taking care of the younger one. Ain't that the kind of Christian thing this Injun school's supposed to be learnin' them?"

"First they got to learn to take orders. When I was in the army, it weren't about being no Christian. I can tell you that. No matter what Christ had to say, it was what the sergeant said that counted."

"Well, nobody told him nothin'. I just lined 'em up to use this shit pot, so leave the boy be."

Shadow Fox slipped out from behind the curtain.

"You wash your hands?" Frazier asked each of the boys the same question. Each time he accompanied the words with a pantomime.

The Shadow Fox grunted and pushed past the waiting boys.

"When my shit splashes up on you, I will laugh, Bird Head," Shadow Fox said to Lonely Cricket as he pushed past the younger boy.

"Hey you, keep your mouths shut," Frazier growled.

ΩΩΩΩΩ

One day, in the beginning times, before Ma-Ona had made humans, fox was very hungry. He went hunting for his favorite food, which was pigeon. He came upon a whole flock of birds who were eating maize and talking among themselves in the way pigeons do when there is nothing to scare them.

Fox said to himself, "Here are many pigeons, and every one looks delicious." He could not contain himself. With a bark of excitement fox chased into the middle of the flock.

There was a great whirr of wings as the pigeons took flight. Fox jumped at one and then at another, but they were already beyond his reach. All he had to show for his efforts were a few tail feathers and his frustration.

"I shall never eat," he moaned. "There was food everywhere, but now it is gone. If I see a meal again, I will take more care. I will not rush but sneak up on it until I am sure of my dinner.

The Creator took pity on the hungry animal and sent a mouse for fox to eat. Fox did not like mouse but something to eat was better than nothing.

While mouse was happy eating the roots of grass and looking for another mouse with whom he could nest, fox quietly crept through the tall grass. True to his word he did not rush forward until he was next to his prey.

Fox pounced. The mouse kicked and squirmed, but there was nothing he could do. Fox had his dinner—even if it was not the pigeon he had wanted. When he was finished eating, fox burped in satisfaction and he thanked Ma-Ona for the mouse.

As he went on his way, fox thought about what he had learned. Surely, he must hunt with stealth. But there had been a second lesson: eat with gratitude what the Great Spirit provides, for you cannot always have what you want.

ΩΩΩΩΩ

Yquili Sparrow had told him that story many times. Only days before she had told it again, this time to Many Fish who had turned his face away from the squash and beans she had made for their dinner.

When their mother had finished telling the story, Lonely Cricket and Happy Turtle had made a great show of eating so that Many Fish might follow them. The toddler had tried another bite, spit that out, and started to cry. Lame Bear had tskk, tskked at his son, but Yquili Sparrow had laughed at the little boy's reaction. She gave him a piece of cornbread, which was a food Many Fish loved.

"What of fox?" Lonely Cricket had thought, but he did not ask. Nor did he question the hard bread and syrupy drink that was their meal. He did his best to adjust to the sway and jolt of the train and to accept this new way of life that left his ear ringing, his throat dry with fear, and his stomach churning with food he did not want to eat.

Chapter 8 ~ Dreams That Come

Shadow Fox shuddered. Sleep had been long in coming and was filled with dreams. The White Man's iron horse was taking him far from his home. He was sure that he would never return, at least not in this life. In his dream, he saw the blue-coated soldiers riding towards him. He heard the bark of their guns, could feel the bite of their bullets, and knew that death was coming.

He woke with a start. His voice pierced the dimness of the railroad car. By the light of the one lantern hung in the center of the car, the white man called Frazier searched for the source of that yell. Uncomfortably, grabbing on the backs of benches for support and rolling as a man more used to riding a horse than walking on his own legs, the burly, heavily whiskered man made his way back towards Shadow Fox.

The smell of whiskey on Frazier's breath and the growl of his voice added to Shadow Fox's half-wakened terror. The man's hand lashed out and sent the youngster reeling. "Help," Shadow Fox screamed.

The young man with whom Shadow Fox shared the bench woke with a start. He looked at his seatmate and sneered. These Ho-Chunk were not worthy of his concern. Plenty Horses drooped his head against the window, pulled his blanket tight, and slipped back into sleep.

Frazier saw the fineness of the blanket and envied it. Properly aired of the smell of Injun, it would bring a good price. Before they arrived in Chicago, he would replace it with one of Army issue.

At the other end of the railroad car, Lonely Cricket heard the cry and started from his own sleep. In Lonely Cricket's dream, Happy Turtle was sitting by the river playing with Many Fish. The little boy was throwing sticks into the water and watching them float away. In his heart, Lonely Cricket wished he was with them, but he was happy that he could at least have the thought of his sister and of his little brother in his heart. Resting his head back against Standing Oak's shoulder, the boy fell back into sleep.

"Keep quiet," Frazier admonished Shadow Fox and slapped him again. The youngster cowered. "Now get back to sleep afore I get angry."

The man lurched back to his own seat, while Shadow Fox tried to remember where he was and why his father had sent him from their home. The young man whimpered quietly as he thought of death. For all his bluster around younger boys and especially towards Lonely Cricket, Shadow Fox was a coward. No matter how he might brag, he was not of the stuff of Many Deer.

ΩΩΩΩΩ

Three young men went hunting. It was the time of the colored leaves, and there were many deer and elk to be taken. Soon the village would feast, and the women would want them as husbands.

One of the men saw a small herd of deer nearby. So happy were they to see this prey ready for their arrows that they did not take care to watch for enemies. They did not see the hunting party of Crow, who were watching not only the deer but also the approaching people.

So intent were the young men on their hunt that they were totally surprised by the Crow, who raised a cry and came at them from all sides.

Even as the startled deer bounded into the forest, the three men realized that they had become the prey. Surely, they were going to die.

The first of the men filled his heart with terror and cried out for assistance. With that cry he ran back towards his village. His terror was so great that he did not see the enemy who had taken their place behind. Even as the terrified rabbit, who in his flight from the coyote does not see the hawk, this man was quickly killed.

The second man's heart filled with rage. With a cry of war, he ran forward, towards the main body of the Crow, his knife at-the-ready and his anger in his throat. Like the wolverine who charges towards the bait only to be captured by the hunter, that man, too, was cut down by the Crow who had taken their positions to the side.

Many Deer prayed to Ma-Ona and readied himself to die. He took into his hand the coup stick, which hung at his side, and waited for the Crow. Only when the Crow came forward to kill him with their lances did Many Deer raise his stick. He would, in the moment of his death, prove his courage by counting coup one last time.

Many Deer raised his coup stick and sang to Ma-Ona. "May my spirit join the hunt in the sky. May my enemies remember my name. May my people know I have come to you with honor."

Many Deer stood as a warrior stands, and the band of Crow muttered among themselves to see his courage.

The leader of the Crow, who had been intending to kill Many Deer, realized that this enemy was a man of courage, a man who faced death with the song of a warrior. He stopped walking towards the young man and pointed his lance to the ground. Seeing the action of their leader the other Crow also lowered their lances and stopped so they formed a circle around Many Deer.

The leader of the Crow took a string of beads from his own neck and offered it to Many Deer as a sign of friendship. Many Deer took the feather of a hawk, which adorned his own head, and gave it to the leader of the Crow that their friendship might be known in the world of spirits.

When Many Deer returned to his village, the people saw that he was alone and that he was wearing a string of beads of a style they did not know. The people asked him what had happened, and Many Deer told his story. The people honored him and called him by a new name, one which the Crow had given him.

Even to this day, we remember him by that name and tell the story of Strong Heart.

ΩΩΩΩΩ

Many times had Talking Mountain told his sons this story. Many times, Shadow Fox had told himself that he would face death bravely. Many times, the young man had lied to himself.

The train rounded a bend and the sleeping bodies swayed with the curve. Shadow Fox grabbed the top of the bench in front of him and held for dear life. Acknowledging for the first time that he could never be like Strong Heart, he felt the bile of hatred towards Lonely Cricket who was once again dreaming of the people he loved and whom he would miss. In this new dream, Sapphira Cook rode her horse across the fields towards his family's barn. Maggie snorted in anticipation of the rubbing and the food that he would give him. In his heart, Lonely Cricket knew that he would not be there, and in his slumber, the boy wept for the loss.

Chapter 9 ~ Wanderers

"Well, I'll be damned." The stranger stood swaying in the aisle of the train and stuck out his hand towards the two, seated white men. "Duke Frazier, what in blazes are you doing here? I thought you'd still be whoring away in New Orleans. Not that them Rebs would want you, but them Creole ladies surely did."

Ignoring the outstretched hand, Frazier stared into the tall, stooped-shouldered man's face, chawed his tobacco, and spit just missing the man's boot.

"Duke," Langdon questioned, "you know this fella?"

Saying nothing, Duke spit again.

"Ain't ya gonna say howdy to an old comrade-in-arms?" the stranger asked. "How many times do you run into an old buddy from the Indiana Twelfth?"

"You in The War together?" Langdon asked.

"Not exactly, not The War," the stranger replied. "More like we spent some time enjoying the beautiful ladies of New Orleans, though I s'pose we had battle scars of a different kind." He laughed a mule-bray hoot and again stuck his hand towards Duke.

This time Duke pushed the stranger's hand away. "Jones, I didn't want nothing to do with you in the army and I surely don't now. He turned to Langdon. "Nothing worse than stealing another man's woman."

"What woman?" The stranger, too, spoke to Langdon. "She was a whore, nothing more, and I paid her price. What Duke here thought was goin' on I can't control, but for me it was a good time, just another tawny-skinned good time."

"You may have paid her price, but you sure as hell didn't pay mine. She was my woman and you went behind my back."

"Just what do you mean your woman?" Langdon asked.

"I owned her. For Christ's sake, she was mine, my property. Everybody knew the money went to me, and Jones here cuts me out, like I'm no-account. Now he wants to glad-hand me like we're long lost buddies. He can go to hell, and you can go with him if you think otherwise." Duke was shouting, his face red, his muscles tensed, and his fists clenched.

"Maybe you'd best roost in another car," Langdon said to the stranger.

"I don't have no mind to be run off," the man replied. He had backed away from Duke, but his hands were balled into fists. He, too, was ready for a fight.

As tensions rose, one of the colored men muttered to his wife and children, and they moved towards the back of the car. Lonely Cricket turned to look at the white men. Standing Oak pulled on Lonely Cricket's arm. "The White Man will turn his anger on us. Do not look."

"I do not like this man Duke Frazier," Lonely Cricket whispered.

"No. He not a good man," Standing Oak agreed. The young Ho-Chunk strained to hear his neighbor's words through the ringing in his ear.

Langdon got to his feet. "Mister, perhaps you and I could step onto the vestibule and share." He pulled a flask from the inside breast pocket of his jacket—only far enough for Jones to see its silver, shot glass top.

Eyeing the flask, Jones nodded. "Don't mind if I do." He again held out his hand, this time to Langdon. "Jeremiah Jones and glad to make your acquaintance, sir."

"Robert Langdon and glad to make yours as well."

"Well, I'll be fucked," Duke muttered. "Well, I'll be fucked and damned."

As the other two men made their way to the front of the car, Duke looked around, deciding onto which of the young Indians he might vent his venom.

Langdon paused at the door. "Mr. Jones and I are going to share a snort and make the peace, Duke. You lay off these youngsters. I don't want to hear no screaming or yelling."

As soon as the door closed behind Langdon, Duke was up from his seat. Grabbing Lonely Cricket by the deerskin vest, Duke pulled him up and struck him across the mouth with the back of his left hand.

The boy made no sound, not even when the second blow came—splitting his lip and causing blood to drip down his chin and onto the front of his clothes.

"You know what makes an Injun good?" Duke asked the rest of the passengers, who watched in silence. "When he's good and dead." He raised his hand again and again.

In the back of the railroad car, Plenty Horses asked Shadow Fox, "Why do you not help your brother?"

Shadow Fox whispered his reply. "He is not my brother. If the White Man kills him, it will be a good thing."

"Coward." Plenty Horses spit the word into the night. His voice raised to be heard over the clacking of the train.

"What did you say, Injun?" Duke yelled towards Plenty Horses.

"Then I will stand up for the young Ho-Chunk," Plenty Horses continued to his seat companion but loudly enough for Duke to hear. Duke did not understand the words. That didn't matter. The man let go of Lonely Cricket's vest and started towards his new target.

Lonely Cricket slid down, landing first on the bench and then dropping to the floor. Plenty Horses slipped the blanket from his shoulders and stepped into the aisle. He was not sure what would happen, but he knew the white man was, like the Ho-Chunk next to him, a coward.

As Duke moved along the aisle, one of the colored men stuck out his foot—not too far, just enough to topple the bully to the ground. Before Duke could get to his feet, Plenty Horses was on him.

Had there been room for movement, had they started both standing, had the black man not added some surreptitious kicks, the fight would have gone badly for Plenty Horses. Duke, a full-grown man, was bigger and stronger, but the young Oglala fought bravely. They were grappling in the confined space of the aisle when Langdon returned. The other white man wasn't with him.

Seeing Lonely Cricket laying on the floor in front of his seat the blood running from his face and then seeing the struggle in the middle of the car, Langdon took the heavy Colt revolver he carried tucked in his belt and, waiting for the right moment, brought the butt of his gun down on Duke Frazier's skull.

When the man awoke and reached for his throbbing head, Langdon poked that same revolver into his ribs. Duke reached for his own weapon, but it was gone. "I put it in your bedroll with the rest of your belongings and some money for your services. You're going to be getting off at the next stop, and you won't want to be coming back.

"Course, if you've a mind to argue ..." Langdon cocked his Colt.

Duke said nothing. After a moment's wait, Langdon added, "I'll tell the Captain you decided to stop off and see your family; but if you show up in Pennsylvania, I'll tell a different story—one that'll make you out the trash you be."

When the train was just about to leave its next stop, Langdon threw Duke's bedroll off and pushed the man out after it. On the rough plank platform, Duke stumbled, went down to one knee, and hadn't regained his feet before the train pulled out.

It was only then that Langdon dealt with Plenty Horses. "I don't reckon the Captain has to hear about this." He held out his hand, and Plenty Horses took it with both of his.

"You were brave to take on that damned idiot."

Plenty Horses did not comprehend the White Man's words, but he understood and appreciated the tone of his voice.

Later, his lip puffy and a welt on his right cheek, Lonely Cricket made his way back to the toilet. He stopped at the bench where Plenty Horses and Shadow Fox were sitting. He touched his hand to his breast and then held it towards the Omaha.

Plenty Horses said nothing, only nodding his head.

Shadow Fox bit his lip and stared out the window at the passing trees.

Chapter 10 ~ Corn Dance

Lame Bear had awakened them early, before Wira had begun his journey across the sky. As Stubborn Mule slowly jerked them across the prairie, Happy Turtle could not sleep. Her back leaning against the buckboard's weathered wooden side, her sleeping brother's head cradled in her lap, she rocked with the sway of the wagon. The green smell of new grass and spring rain caressed her nose.

Happy Turtle ran the fingers of her right hand through her sleeping brother's hair. She rested her left on a mound of stiff fabric. It was the gown Leah Cook had made for her. Deep-red brocade with silver thread, Leah had brought the cloth from the East.

"I thought someday I'd have a grand house and a parlor room with windows that need such hanging, but it'll make a fine gown for your big dance."

To Happy Turtle's protestations, she replied, "Oh, I've enough for another for Sapphira when she has a need. Not too many dances to be had in Pierce, not likely we'll need more dresses nor drapes for fancy rooms."

"It is a White woman's dress, nothing fit for a corn dance. It should be deerskin and sinew. What will others think?" Yquili Sparrow said to her husband.

Lame Bear didn't argue with his wife. Neither did Happy Turtle.

Quiet Raven, Happy Turtle's best friend who lived near them and who would also be doing the corn dance, confessed, "I wish I had a dress made of the White Man's cloth. I know that the young men will look at you and see that you are beautiful. They will come to your parents' lodge and play the flute for you. You are lucky to have such good friends among the White Men."

Wira cast long shadows away from the left front of the wagon when they arrived at the dancing place. Quiet Raven and her family were already there. Her elder brother greeted Lame Bear and reached out to help the still sleepy Many Fish to the ground.

"Come, Many Fish, we must not see our sisters until we dance with them."

The boy hesitated and pulled toward his mother.

"We spoke of this, Many Fish. You are your sister's elder brother and must dance with her tomorrow. Until then you may not see her or the other girls who will dance."

Swallowing a tear, Many Fish allowed himself to be led away.

Tall Grass had already begun work on the shelter that would house the three girls who would be dancing the next day. Lame Bear and Quiet Raven's father went to help the medicine man. The girls must be safe inside the wigwam before Wira reached the top of the heavens and started his descent. After that, teepees must be erected for the others in their families and the dancing place prepared. There was much work to be done.

When the third girl arrived, her father, too, would help. It was known that she had no brother to dance with her, so her mother's brother would have the honor. Because he was a married man, he would not sleep with Many Fish and with Quiet Raven's brother but would build his own shelter near theirs.

Yquili Sparrow joined the women who were weaving tall grass into mats to form the sacred wigwam's walls. Happy Turtle started to follow her mother, but Yquili Sparrow held up her hand to stop her daughter. "Go with Dreaming Woman. She has much to teach you and the other girls. There is much that a grown woman should know."

The next morning, the breeze flurried the grass mat walls of the wigwam. The three girls, already half-awake, stirred and called to one another. Today they would do the corn dance. Today they would become women. All that they had learned from their mothers and from the other women of the tribe prepared them for this their day of maidenhood.

Happy Turtle knew she should be joyful. She knew she should be proud. Why then was she sad? Why did she cast her eyes to the ground and mumble her words? What was the bitter-sweetness that tore her heart? Elder brother would not dance with her; he was far away studying the white man's ways, learning their language and their books.

"Lonely Cricket, I miss you," her heart cried.

Her first older brother, the one of whom they did not speak, Gentle Hawk, lost in a great snow, before Lonely Cricket had come to them, before they had come to this place, this Nebraska, for him and for his memory her soul also wept.

The wigwam had been cold that winter Wisconsin day. The cattail mats did not keep out the Winnebago wind. "I'll get more wood," Gentle Hawk had said. Before their mother could say, "Wait," he was gone never to return from the white blown world.

Lame Bear, home that evening from an empty hunt, had looked for him, calling his name against the wind. "Gentle Hawk, your mother weeps. Happy Turtle needs your helping hands. She cries your name."

Yquili Sparrow's tears for their son had not ceased. The river of her discontent carried them to a new home in this new place far from the sacred lake, far from their ancestors' mounds.

"Today I will do the corn dance, but elder brother will not dance with me," Happy Turtle said to herself. "Many Fish is young and does not know the steps. People will smile at him, but in my heart, I will mourn my brothers who are not here."

When Tall Grass beat the drum, and Dreaming Woman shook the sacred, bean-filled gourd, the three girls led their partners into the circle where they would dance. Each girl's head tassel and flower wreathed. Each carried a basket in her arms, baskets into which their partners would gather magic from the air and ground. From the direction of the rising sun, they entered the dancing space and followed Wira's path: East, South, West, and then to darkness North.

Quick. Quick. Dance. Quick, step, step, step. Dance.

Turn and turn.

Yellow sacred pollen from deer skin pouches sprinkled on maiden heads.

Quick. Quick. Dance. Step, step, step.

The drum's steady beat. Rain beating on a wigwam roof. Life's river rapid in its course.

Goddess Atina taught this dance that corn might grow, and people live.

Bend, Elder Brother. Bend, make your sister's basket full. May she have many children. May Ma-Ona watch and keep the Trickster's wiles at bay. May Atina remember us when winter comes to take Father Sun away.

After the dance, they shared a feast. Talking Mountain had killed a deer. One Tree's wife brought hearth-baked bread. Yquili Sparrow offered a dish of rabbit and a squash stew, and she had brought Leah Cook's White woman's beans sweetened with molasses and made with pieces of pork.

Small Deer had brought his gifts for the three young women, pairs of moccasins with beads traded from the white man store.

The girls sat in the honored place.

"Whom will you marry?" Quiet Raven asked.

"A chief," Rippling Water, who was the third girl, replied.

"A man who is like my brother." Happy Turtle hid her face.

The others laughed.

"Many Fish will make a fine husband." Rippling Water's laughter brought tears to her black-lashed eyes.

"I think Small Deer would have you," Quiet Raven spoke softly. "Do you not see the moccasins he made for you have golden thread—"

"And many beads and bells," Rippling Water added.

"A man who is like my brother," Happy Turtle repeated. She knew of Small Deer's desires, but her thoughts were far away in Pennsylvania.

"Did I do it right?" Many Fish sat next to his mother.

She reached down and patted his head. "You did very well, my biggest boy."

Lame Bear leaned against an elm and turned his mind to the three acres that Harry Cook would be plowing that day. "We'll plant 'em to wheat, Bear. Make us some cash money. Won't have to trade for things. Know what that means? We can buy stuff, not just take what Jedidiah Jacobs wants to give."

Lame Bear grunted acquiescence.

"Consider it a gift to your girl, Bear. Nathan and I 'll plow and plant 'em whilst you're celebrating."

Lame Bear grunted again. "I do not believe Nathan will help," he thought, but kept the words to himself. He wished he was there to help guide the great dappled grey horse back and forth across the field, the metal plow digging deep furrows in the rich prairie turning over the secret-rooted grass, the happy yellow Susans, the orange Impatiens, the purple-belled stalks of Lead Plant.

"Harry Cook is a good friend, but the White Man's farming is not kind to Mother Earth," he said to himself.

Chapter 11 ~ Happy Turtle Goes to Town

The great gray horse strained against the traces. The wagon, loaded high with fresh harvested corn, moved slowly along the rutted way. Harry Cook clucked and urged as the horse picked his way along the not-yet-sunlit road. Beside him, his wife held fast to the plank-wood seat. Behind, their daughter chattered away about the new dress she wanted, the one her mother would make from material purchased that very day.

Herodotus Mercier's agent Abner Banner — bulbous drinker's nose, hanging belly, long fingernails, and cash in hand — would be waiting for the stream of local farmers. By nightfall Mercier's wagons would be loaded and on their way to the railhead in Fayette.

"Best to arrive first to get the top price of the day," Harry had explained to his partner, and, not adding, "before that damned idiot is too drunk for reason."

Everybody knew that Mercier only tolerated Banner for his agent's wife, and buxom, wonton Mrs. Banner was happy to satisfy Mercier's whims and suggest many of her own devising.

Herodotus Mercier's peccadilloes were known to all, except perhaps to Mrs. Mercier. That fine lady, preoccupied as she was with the latest fashions from New York and London, cared not a fig for what her husband might do as long as it was not in her bedchamber. For all his desires, Herodotus would not stray far. It was her father's money that had bought the fleet of wagons, the warehouses, and the barns that bore the Mercier name. And, it was her uncle's bank in Lawrence that lent the money Abner Banner dispersed to the farmers in her husband's name.

Harry Cook had seen no purpose in sharing any of that gossip with his partner. It was sufficient for Lame Bear to know he would drive a fair bargain for them both. It had been a good year, corn, wheat, hay, even soy had filled the fields for miles around. Soon coins would jingle in farmers' pockets and wives would be searching Jedidiah Jacobs's shelves for cloth, patterns, notions and buying those staples and treats needed for the coming winter.

"Hup! Hup!" The farmer cracked his whip. Their pace did not change. The horse was plodding his best speed given the load. The urging and cracking were for effect, putting on a show for his wife and daughter.

Her feet hanging from the back of the wagon, Happy Turtle was wrapped in her own thoughts. Only the day before, Lame Bear had told his daughter that she would go to town with their neighbors. "Collect money, buy things mother tell. Mrs. Cook will tell what buy to make White Man clothes for you and Many Fish."

Harry Cook nodded his head while Lame Bear spoke. "Don't you worry, girl; my wife will make sure you don't get fleeced."

Happy Turtle had not understood the broad-shouldered white man's meaning. She nodded anyway and knew that her father trusted his friend. She was less trusting of herself. Would she remember the list her mother had given her? Over and over she worried it in her head. How would she tell the storekeeper so much salt, so much coffee, so much rope, and which kind? Leah Cook would help with the words.

And the cloth. So many kinds. White Women wore clothes of many colors; how could she decide? How did Sapphira tell her mother what colors she wanted? And the way the clothing would look? Mrs. Cook had called the pieces of paper patterns. But how was she to know?

At least she didn't have to worry about the money. That the Cooks would take care of for her—collecting her father's share for the corn and paying the storekeeper for her purchases. It was good to have the Cooks as friends, as neighbors.

And always in the back of Happy Turtle's mind, in the midst of all those other questions which tumbled in her head as her body jounced on the high-piled corn, was the thought of a letter. Would there be one? Would there be word from Lonely Cricket? First, before the store, while Mr. Cook was selling the corn, she would go to the agent's house and ask. She missed her brother so. Was he well? Did he like the White Man's school? Did he wear White Man clothes? Did he think of her and of their family?

"There must be a letter. There has to be," she begged the spirit world.

From a hillock, Small Deer watched the wagon pass. He raised his hand in greeting to Happy Turtle. She did not respond. It was only when Sapphira Cook yelled to Small Deer that Happy Turtle looked up and raised her hand. Immediately, her thoughts returned to her faraway brother.

Small Deer watched the wagon bounce down the road, the dust of the dry autumn days billowing behind. He trotted after it, down the slope of the hillock, waving as he ran. Happy Turtle did not look up again.

The young man dropped to the ground. Taking a knife from his waist, he worked at the arrows from his quiver. He would kill many rabbits and bring them to Lame Bear's home. Yquili Sparrow would make a fine stew for her family, and the skins would become moccasins for their feet.

Sapphira had written a letter to Lonely Cricket and had asked Happy Turtle if she, also, wished to write some words. "I hope he count many victories," the girl had said.

Sapphira gave her a pencil so she might draw a picture for her brother. She drew a cricket hopping away from a teepee. In the opening to the teepee was a turtle watching the insect depart.

That letter was now in the purse which Leah Cook clutched in her left hand. Happy Turtle knew they would give the letter to the Agent Jones. Mrs. Cook had written on the outside telling the White Men how to find Lonely Cricket. Happy Turtle wished she, too, knew how to find him.

The young woman remembered the story Dreaming Woman had told her. The Medicine Woman had been stirring soup on her cooking fire. Happy Turtle sat quietly as the woman tasted, added herbs, stirred one more, added more herbs, and —finally satisfied—sat on the floor and told the tale.

ΩΩΩΩΩ

When Spotted Horse was hunting buffalo, the Trickster decided to fool the people and come in his place. He disguised himself so the men of the tribe would think he was their chief. The Trickster planned to lead the people to their enemy, The Crooked Feet, so the Crooked Feet might kill them and make them slaves.

When the Trickster came appearing as Spotted Horse, he told the men of the tribe that he had found a place with many buffalo and with deer and rabbit. He told them he had found a lake where there were a lot of fish and otter and ducks. He told them they should pack the camp and come with him to this new place. The hunting had been bad for some time. The fishing had been bad for many moons. The men of the tribe were happy to hear this news.

"Quickly, quickly," they told the women and children and the old people, "we must get ready to follow Spotted Horse to this wonderful place."

Everyone set to work except Spotted Horse's sister Dark Raven. She sat by her fire and ignored the entreaties of the other women. She stirred her soup and ignored the yells of the men. She left her teepee standing and ignored the cries of the children and of the old people.

"What is wrong with you?" one of the women asked.

"It is not with me but all of you that something is wrong," Dark Raven answered; "For you are following the Trickster and do not know him."

With her words it was as if a veil were lifted from their eyes, and the people saw that Dark Raven was right. They picked up stones and threw them at the Trickster who changed into a coyote and ran away.

"How did you know it was not Spotted Horse?" somebody asked.

"When my brother left, he told me that when he returned, he would teach me a new song. But when the Trickster came in imitation of my brother, he did not have a new song to sing."

ΩΩΩΩΩ

Jouncing on the back of the corn-filled wagon, Happy Turtle remembered the story Dreaming Woman had told. Would Lonely Cricket be changed by his journey? Yes, that was most likely. but he would remember her. He would still be oldest brother and she would still be oldest sister.

She hoped that none of the Cooks would see her tears.

***

"Hey you, squaw!"

Tobacco juice spittled from the drooping corner of the bald, heavyset, white man's mouth and stained his greasy beard. In drunken disorientation, he lurched towards the great wagons on which were heaped corn, wheat, and butchered hogs. Happy Turtle recognized Mercier's agent and, remembering Harry Cook's warning, walked towards the general store without turning.

Abner Banner would tolerate no such insolence, but especially not from an Indian. He changed course, lurching after her.

"I'm talking at you, Injun," he bellowed, arms waving in disorderly emphasis.

Happy Turtle froze. Torn between the desire to flee and the knowledge that this drunk was somehow important.

"He's a bad man, Turtle, a real bad one. You stay clear. Mean as a jaybird when he's drunk, and nobody ever seen him sober. Can't cross him though. Mercier's man. God knows why, but Mercier's man and used to having his way."

Now the white man with his big nose and waving hands was next to her, his whiskey-stinking breath, his tobacco spit spotting her face.

Happy Turtle was too terrified by the hulking presence to hear the footsteps as John Macabe crossed the street towards them.

"There you are." The young man took her arm and whirled Happy Turtle around.

"Where did he come from?" she wondered.

She did not recognize this young White Man: slim, with brown hair and green eyes. He spoke softly. "Mr. Jacobs found some of that cloth you were wanting, sent me to find you."

"This White Man must be crazy. What is he talking about?" she said to herself.

The young man tipped his hat to Banner. "Sorry, sir, but the storekeep says I should fetch her right back.

He pulled Happy Turtle along towards the general store. "Just keep walking, miss, till we're clear of that fella. He ain't nobody you want to be doing with."

John Macabe turned towards her as he spoke. He smiled ever so slightly, just enough. It reassured her the way she had been reassured as a child when Yquili Sparrow would grind corn and sing of a faraway place which had once been her people's home. Happy Turtle could only vaguely remember that place. They had moved to Nebraska when she was very young, not even as old as Many Fish.

"Everything will be all right," Happy Turtle realized. "This White Man will not hurt me."

***

Sapphira Cook sat on one of the rockers outside of Jacob's store sucking a candy and watching little pockets of dust swirl in the breeze.

"Momma got one for you, too." She held another candy towards Happy Turtle.

"You know this young lady?" John Macabe asked.

"Yep. That's Happy Turtle. Her daddy and mine are partners."

"And where's your daddy at?"

"He brought corn to sell. I guess he's still down to the wagons doing business with Mr. Banner."

John snorted. "That drunk. I sure wouldn't want to do no business with him."

"My daddy says there ain't no one else."

"True enough. Anyway, Banner's been in the saloon getting himself right drunk, so Old Man Miller told me to keep an eye on him make sure he didn't fall down or go getting lost. People need that money he hands out, and Mr. Miller needs them to have it so's they can pay him. Guess that's the way of things.

"I just figured when he went after this young Injun lady it wouldn't end no good." His smile was broad and full.

Sapphira grinned in response.

Happy Turtle stared at the young man. She knew that his smile was meant for her. In an almost inaudible voice she said, "Thank you." At the same moment, she took the candy from Sapphira's hand. That way, this kind stranger could not know if she was thanking him or her young friend.

Happy Turtle licked the candy and beamed. Was it from the taste or in response to him? That was something John Macabe would wonder over for the rest of the day.

That night John asked his boss's advice. What he didn't know about women. What he didn't understand about the Indians. Hell, he couldn't even talk with her. Still, John hoped that smile had been meant for him.

Old Man Miller harrumphed, spat, and cogitated a spell before responding. "A squaw?" He asked and waited for the word to sink in.

"Yes, sir." John's voice trembled as much with arousal as fear.

"Folks won't like that."

"No, sir."

"Nope, I reckon not." The saloonkeeper scratched himself and thought on it some more. "Not the white folk nor the Injun."

"I reckon not," John echoed.

"Still, boy, if it's meant to be."

John waited, his heart sounding tympani in the silence. "Yep, if it's meant to be," Old Man Miller repeated.

The older man laughed. "Course you ain't tolt her yet."

"No, sir."

"Fact, you don't know what she thinks or no."

"No, sir."

"Well, if it's meant to be." The saloonkeeper blew out the kerosene lamp.

"Yes, sir," The younger man said as the silence closed upon them. How would he tell this young Injun maiden that he was smitten?

Chapter 12 ~ Rape

Happy Turtle leaned against a poplar and sorted through the reeds she had collected. Selecting a length of light green canary grass, she clenched it between her teeth and pulled; Dreaming Woman had taught Happy Turtle well. As the fibrous reed slid between those clenched teeth, it would flatten and soften, right for weaving the basket that the girl planned to make. In another moon's time, her mother's brother's daughter, Swift Steam, would make her first sun dance. Happy Turtle was making a special present for the occasion.

Woven into the straw and mint colored container would be the sign of a bear in brown and red, for Swift Steam was of the Bear Clan. There would be a black geometric design circling the top of the basket, but Happy Turtle would be careful to leave a small gap in that design so no spirits might be caught unawares and be unable to escape.

The thought of trapped spirits took her back to Gentle Hawk, the brother who had died. That had been many years ago. Trapped in a sudden snow, he had perished. Happy Turtle had been very young, slightly older than Many Fish, a toddler. Still she remembered the day her mother had told her, "Oldest Brother has left us to join the spirit world."

They had buried Gentle Hawk with his toy bow and lance, wrapped in his deerskin robe. They had buried his bowl as well, but first Lame Bear had knocked a hole in the bottom. "A portion of Older Brother's spirit is in this bowl, and we must set it free," he had explained to the little girl.

Some moons later, after their long journey, after they were settled in their new home in the place of the flat river, which is called Nebraska, Lonely Cricket had joined them. "This is Oldest Brother," her father had explained. Yaquilli Sparrow had said nothing, but her daughter could see the tears in her eyes.

Happy Turtle still remembered Gentle Hawk; she remembered his combing her hair and holding her when she was scared. Of course, she remembered Lonely Cricket more clearly. Now, he, too, was gone. They had not buried his bowl. Instead Yaquilli Sparrow had given it to Many Fish. "Now you are old enough to feed yourself," she had said and given him the bowl.

"You must now call him Oldest Brother," Yaquilli Sparrow had told Happy Turtle. Lame Bear had nodded his agreement.

Happy Turtle wanted to ask what this meant. She wanted to know if Lonely Cricket was never to return. However, the way her mother spoke and the solemn way in which her father nodded made it clear—there would be no discussion.

Happy Turtle worked on preparing the reeds and reflected on her missing brothers. It was sad thinking of them, but it was right to do so. The sun dance was a big event. The Great Spirit would be watching the young women as they performed the ritual. It was a time for serious meditation.

The girl was so engrossed in her work and her thoughts that she didn't hear the footsteps. He grabbed her shoulders, and she was helpless in his rough grasp even before she knew that Nathan Wainwich was there.

His unwanted kisses cascaded on her face.

"Please, do not." Happy Turtle's protests didn't deter him. Nathan was too intoxicated to care. Was it whiskey or desire that held him in his inebriation? He smelled of both.

Happy Turtle writhed and pulled. The man held her fast. He ripped at her blanket and then at the blouse she wore beneath. The blouse had been a gift from Leah Cook, a simple thing, but the checkered blue, cotton fabric had felt good against Happy Turtle's maturing breasts. Now those breasts were exposed, and the white man was kissing and biting at them in the frenzy of his arousal.

She begged again and again.

"Be quiet," he growled. One rough hand squeezed her left nipple; the other covered her mouth.

Squirming her face from his hand, Happy Turtle continued to plead. He snarled in response, "You know you've been wanting this."

Happy Turtle moaned in terror. She felt the knife-cut-pain as Wainright forced himself through her virginity and passed the clenched resistance of her womanhood.

"Noooo!" Her voice a shriek.

"Shut up." Nathan's right hand cracked her face. Three frenzied times he stuck. Her lip cracked, and blood trickled from the corner of her mouth. Her left eye swelled.

Happy Turtle cried in terror and in pain.

Her tears did not deter him.

When Nathan had finished, when he had violated her, when he had rolled off her and in the satiation of his wanting had loosed his hold on her, Happy Turtle fled. She didn't think to gather her blanket against the chill of the spring afternoon. She didn't try to stop the flow of tears down her dirt-streaked cheeks. In naked pain and terror, she fled. As she ran, her voice reached out to the heavens with her suffering and outrage.

Lame Bear and Harry Cook were churning the dirt in a section that was soon to be planted in wheat. Great Horse had already dragged the plow through the ground. Now, the two men were breaking up clods and turning over the rich soil with spades. Dirt-blackened sweat ran down Lame Bear's neck. His muscles strained with the effort. He didn't hear his daughter's voice.

Yaquilli Sparrow did not hear Happy Turtle, either. She too was busy; dinner had to be prepared.

It was Many Fish who heard his sister's screams. He ran across the field towards her adding his own voice to her terror.

"C'iyé!" Happy Turtle called out to the little boy. "Oldest brother."

***

"Oldest Sister are you not well?" Many Fish pulled at his sister's robe. Huddled in nausea, the girl could hardly respond.

It had been over a moon since Happy Turtle had been raped. During that time, she had not spoken of that day. Neither had she spoken to the Cook family. Often Sapphira had waved to her from the garden where she was helping her mother weed. Happy Turtle had looked away and quickly ducked inside the barn.

Once Sapphira had mentioned that Happy Turtle was avoiding her. Leah Cook replied, "Sometimes we women have problems with our bodies that make us unsociable."

Sapphira, whose own—only recently begun—menstruation was easy and predictable, nodded her head in understanding and hoped that her friend was not suffering the pain and discomfort of which some of the other girls from school complained so bitterly. "Perhaps I could bring her some broth? Would that help, Mother?"

"I'm sure Yquili Sparrow knows what to do. You just wait. Soon enough Happy Turtle will be fine."

But the young Ho-Chunk woman was not fine.

When the nausea did not abate, Yquili Sparrow asked her daughter hard questions. "Have you lain with Small Deer? Have you been a foolish girl and done things without thinking?"

"What do you mean? Small Deer? Why would I do things with Small Deer?"

"Have you lain with Small Deer?" Yquili Sparrow asked again. "Are you with his child? Should you move into his teepee?"

The girl began to cry. Her mother went to the door and called out, "Lame Bear. Lame Bear."

"Please, do not ..." Sobs consumed Happy Turtle.

Lame Bear, followed closely by Many Fish, came through the cabin door. "What is the matter?" he asked.

"Your daughter has been with Small Deer and now she is with child."

"That is not a reason for tears and shouting," Lame Bear responded. "Daughter, have you become a grown woman? I did not realize."

Lame Bear's words brought an even great cascade of tears from the Happy Turtle. She crouched next to the cooking fire and hid her face in her arms.

"Older Sister!" Many Fish ran to his sister and wrapped his arms around her. "Did Nathan Wainright do this to you? I will kill the White Man if he has hurt my sister."

"What are you saying, child?" Lame Bear demanded.

"Many days ago, the White Man hurt Happy Turtle. She came to me in tears, but when I said that I would tell you, she begged my silence.

"Is this true, daughter?" Yquili Sparrow asked.

Later that day, Nathan, swaying in the saddle, whipped Maggie into the Cook's yard, where the exhausted horse almost stepped on a chicken before sliding to a stop. Nathan teetered for a moment and then toppled to the ground. Grabbing the reins, he tied them to the flimsy wire fencing that protected Leah's flowers from the feeding birds. "Damn you," he shouted at the horse as he brushed brown dust from his clothes.

"And damn you," Harry Cook shouted from the outbuilding where he had been sharpening scythes and sickles. A fine gray dust covered his face, which made his black eyes stand out.

Even drunk, Nathan started at the ferocity of his uncle's voice.

"My best friend's daughter. And an Injun! You may be the dumbest man to ever walk this earth. I should kill you myself. No doubt Lame Bear will kill you if he gets the chance, and that would be a waste of a good man. Him being in prison, not you rotting in hell."

The muscular farmer grabbed his nephew by the shirtfront. "Half an hour and no more."

"What?" Nathan's voice wavered.

"You've half an hour to clear out. Take your belongings and be on the road in thirty minutes, or I swear, kin or no, I'll kill you myself."

"What about Aunt Leah?"

He had not seen his aunt come out of the cabin door. She held a large cooking knife and waved it in his direction. "Aunt Leah would cut your testicles from your body and feed them to the pigs. You'd best listen to your uncle. Thirty minutes and not one more."

Leah Cook slammed into the kitchen in a trail of muttered oaths.

***

The next day, Small Deer left his parents' home. "Where will you go, my son?" his mother asked.

"I cannot stay here. I cannot see Happy Turtle without tears in my heart. I cannot speak of her without rage in my stomach. I cannot speak her name without pain in my tongue. I will go to our brothers in the place the White Man calls Wisconsin."

Small Deer's father heard his son's words but did not believe them. "He will go after the White Man," he said to his woman. "He will seek vengeance for Happy Turtle."

"The White Man will kill him," Small Deer's mother replied.

"That White Man is a coward, but if Small Deer succeeds in this purpose, other Whites will surely kill him."

"Even if he does not succeed but tries, they will hang him from a tree and leave his eyes open for the crows."

Still, the couple did not argue with their son as he gathered his blanket and his bow. They did not argue with him as he took food for the trail. They did not argue with him as he walked towards the setting sun. They did not argue, but they believed he would follow Nathan Wainright until one or both were dead.

When Happy Turtle heard that Small Deer had left his parents' home, she, too, supposed he would seek revenge for her. "It would have been better," she thought, "if he had offered to take me with him." Despite those thoughts, she knew she would not have gone. "Perhaps, someday, when I was older, I would have lived in his teepee, but I would not bring the White Man's child. I would not ask Small Deer to care for such a child as his own."

When Happy Turtle thought of the baby in her womb, her tears would flow as the rapids in a river. Seeing his sister so distraught, Many Fish would try to comfort her. He would bring her water to drink and food to eat. He would hold her hand and put his arm around her. Once he had offered her the cloth rattle which Sapphira Cook had made for his naming present. Although he no longer played with the toy, Many Fish still treasured it.

The proffered gift brought a smile through the storm of Happy Turtle's tears. "I wonder what toys my child will play with?"

"He can have my rattle if he wants." Happy Turtle could hear the catch in her brother's voice as he made the offer.

As she held the rattle, shaking it without rhythm, Happy Turtle wondered about the Cooks. They had not visited her—not once since Nathan Wainright had left. "No, I would not welcome them," she thought, but still she wondered why they had not come.

Twice, Sapphira had bought bread her mother had baked, but she had left it on the doorstep, not entering, not even yelling a greeting. Furtive visits as if atonement for the now disappeared man's sins.

Lame Bear and Harry Cook still worked the fields together, but Lame Bear no longer called the White Man friend.

Since they were seldom visited by other Ho-Chunk, it took some time for Lame Bear and his family to realize that many others of their tribe had also stopped coming to their home.

Dreaming Woman did not come—not even when Lame Bear went to her cabin and asked for her to help his daughter.

"I do not know the way of the White Man's baby. You must ask the White medicine man. Tell Yquili Sparrow that I have pain in my heart for her." The birthing woman turned back to the berries that were simmering on her stove. In her heart she cursed the cowardly White Man, but she could not bring herself to curse his unborn child.

Neither did Tall Grass come—not even after Lame Bear visited his teepee.

"It is unwise to trust the White Man," the shaman said. "He may appear to be your friend, but he wants only for himself. You and Yquili Sparrow have lost a great treasure to this White Man's greed." The old man chanted as he heel-toe walked away from his teepee and towards the stream where he would wash away the evil of Lame Bear's misfortune.

"What of my daughter's treasure?" Lame Bear thought as he trudged back to his cabin and to his sorrowing family.

Even Falling Cloud did not come—not even when he heard that no Ho-Chunk would visit the home of Lame Bear.

Lame Bear did not visit the clown's campsite. He had stopped asking himself painful questions. Instead, he grew quiet and bitter within himself. He did not tell Many Fish the stories of their people. He did not show his young son the ways of a man. He no longer lay with Yquili Spirit in the night, nor did he embrace her during the day.

As for his daughter, Lame Bear had no words to offer Happy Turtle, who seemed to grow fuller with each passing day. "Soon her child will be born," Lame Bear thought with sadness, "who will want this child or his mother?"

Only once did a member of the tribe visit the cabin of Lame Bear and Yquili Spirit. Talking Mountain came with war markings on his face and his quiver filled with arrows. "This is what happens to the Ho-Chunk who welcomes the White Man into his teepee." Talking Mountain muttered words, stomped his feet on the ground, and turned three times against the circle of the sun. Lame Bear knew that Talking Mountain was calling a curse on their home and on his daughter, but he did nothing, he said nothing. What was there to say or to do that could undo what Nathan Wainwright had done.

Still, Lame Bear worked beside Harry Cook. They seldom spoke, only working together that they may not lose everything they had made together.

One morning, when Lame Bear had hitched Great Horse to the plow and the two men were working hard ground that was soon to be planted with rye, Harry Cook spoke of the situation. "Lame Bear, we're leaving. Going out to meet up with my kin near a place called Butte. They say it's a growing place, good money to be earned if a man ain't 'fraid of work. Leah and me we cain't stay here, not with you folks. Not with what Nathan done to your girl.

"You keep it all." He swept his hand in a great arc to indicate his homestead. "God knows it's little enough. When that boy of yours comes back from that school in Pennsylvania, you give him this place so's together you can care for Happy Turtle and the child.

"I wish there was more ..."

The rest of that day the two men worked without speaking.

Lame Bear did not want his neighbor to leave, but it was torment to have the Cooks remain.

The next day, the Cook family loaded their wagon with all the mule could haul. Lame Bear watched as Harry hitched the mule to the wagon. "You take the horse. He's better for the heavy work. And all the rest of the animals, too. I reckon they wouldn't survive the journey."

Harry Cook offered his hand in the white Man's way and Lame Bear took it in his. Yquili Sparrow watched from the doorway of their cabin. Many Fish would have run to say goodbye, but his sister, who sat on her sleeping robe, held him in her arms.

Leah Cook climbed onto the wagon seat and said nothing. She wanted to cry but willed herself to not. She dared not feel sorry for herself and the fact that she was leaving her home. "How can God ever forgive us?" she had asked herself every day since the truth had been known.

Sapphira Cook did cry. Before she climbed onto the wagon, she handed a letter to Lame Bear. "This is for Lonely Cricket," she said. "Tell him that I will miss him very much."

Lame Bear took the letter and grunted. Perhaps someday Lonely Cricket would return. Perhaps the boy would have learned to read the White Man's paper. For now, the man only wished the pain in his soul would stop—the pain for his daughter and the pain for his friend.

Chapter 13 ~ Small Deer

"Where does he go?" Small Deer would ask after every story his father told him as a child.

"Of whom do you speak, Small Deer?" the father would ask.

"The Trickster, Father, where does he go. He disappears from each story you tell me, but where does he go?"

"No one knows," the father would reply.

"Don't be difficult, Small Deer," his mother would say. "Stories take place in the land of tales, and the Trickster goes from story to story with no need to be in this world."

Small Deer had stopped asking that question aloud but never in his own thoughts. Then Nathan Wainwright had come into his life and into the life of Happy Turtle. From the first, the Ho-Chunk youth had not liked Wainwright. While he had no quarrel with the White Men, Small Deer knew little of their ways and few of their words. He had drunk their strong drink and found it made him braver. He had eaten their bread of wheat and learned it made his bowls loose. Some of the women bought his moccasins for their children's feet. The wife of the agent Jones had arranged the selling and given him the White Man's money which his family could spend at the backdoor of Jedidiah Jacob's store.

No, Small Deer had no quarrel with the White Man, but with Nathan Wainwright, that was another story. The young Ho-Chunk had no question; this White Man was the Trickster, and he was trying to lead Happy Turtle into a bad place. Small Deer had known this from the day of Many Fish's naming. He had watched the Cook family arrive bringing this new White Man, and Small Deer had not liked the way Nathan Wainwright looked at Happy Turtle. He had not liked the way Nathan Wainwright did not look straight into the eyes of Lame Bear. He had not liked the way that Nathan Wainwright had looked through the food and drink and then taken nothing to his lips—not even that which Leah Cook had made.

Later, he had seen Nathan Wainwright drunk on his horse, a horse the White Man rode without care or thought. Wainwright was often in fights with other men in the town. Especially, he was quick to start a fight with any Ho-Chunk man who walked down the street.

Small Deer was convinced that Nathan Wainwright was a bad man even before he knew of the rape of Happy Turtle. "He is the Trickster and I must follow him to the place he hides. I must kill him before he can hurt another. Then I shall come back to marry Happy Turtle. I will bring back the White Trickster's scalp and put it at her feet and ask her to marry me for revenging her." With that thought in his mind, Small Deer set out to follow Wainwright.

The first place to look was easy. Everyone knew that Wainwright was always to be found at Old Man Miller's saloon. Small Deer went to the back door and asked "Wainwright, White Man?" The Indian was shaking with anger and with fear that he must kill a White Man.

"He's not here. Been and gone," John McCabe, who had come to the back door, answered. "You look upset. Perhaps you need to set a spell." He indicated a bench by the door. "I'll fetch you something to drink. You have money?" He took a coin from his own pocket to indicate what he meant.

Small Deer took the coins from his deerskin pouch, a pouch made with the same care as the moccasins that were his great skill.

"You sit right there. I'll be back with the best in the house."

Small Deer didn't understand much of what McCabe said, but he knew the White Man had told him to sit, so he waited.

The young man returned with a bottle of whiskey. "Best in the house," he said as he opened the bottle and handed it to Small Deer.

Of course, it was not the best in the house, but McCabe knew that Small Deer wouldn't know and that Old Man Miller would be pleased with him for selling a bottle of cheap for dear.

"You drink up. It'll make you feel better," the white Man said and mimed the act of drinking from the bottle.

Small Deer slept beside the back door of the saloon that night. And the next. And the next day after that he begged for coins that he might have more of the White Man's drink.

When his parents heard of Small Deer's behavior, they wept for him. "He is a victim of the Trickster," Falling Cloud told the Ho-Chunk, but who would listen to a heyoka?

Happy Turtle did not hear of Small Deer; nobody was cruel enough to add that tragedy to her sadness.

***

As enthralled as he was, it was not easy for John McCabe to do anything about his feelings for the Indian girl he had rescued from Abner Banner. A painfully shy man with a romantic soul, McCabe couldn't imagine going to Happy Turtle's family's home, which he imagined to be not a cabin, but a teepee made of buffalo hides, to ask after her. Once or twice since that day, he had seen the blonde–haired White girl whose daddy was Happy Turtle's father's friend, but even saying something to the young woman was beyond him.

"You takin' that Injun under your wing?" Old Man Miller asked one night after closing.

"Nah, but like you said, nothing wrong selling liquor to them Indians if they can pay. Besides ..."

"Perhaps," McCabe thought, he knows Happy Turtle. Perhaps he can tell me how I might let her know how I feel."

When Ezekiel Jones heard that yet another of his wards was night after night lying drunk in the alley behind Miller's saloon, he went to have a talk with the barkeep.

"The poor lad doesn't seem to know what he's doing," Miller said. "I figure he's a lost soul trying to drown his pain in drink as many a White Man would."

"Lost soul or no, it's 'gainst the law and good judgment to sell hard drink to that Injun. Send him packin' or I'll have a federal marshal close you down."

"You speak their lingo, Mr. Jones. Maybe you can talk with him. Find out what his problem is," John McCabe interjected.

"You think that'll help?" Jones's laughed. "He's an Injun and a drunk Injun at that. Best thing to do is run him off."

"The boy has a soft spot for one of them young squaws," Miller explained. "I guess that makes him soft on 'em all."

"You're hankering after a squaw, boy? Why didn't you say so? Most of 'em will go with you for a new blanket."

"Ay, you don't think much of them folks, do ya, Ezekiel?"

"Nope, Old Man. I've worked this post too long to have illusions. There ain't half a dozen of them worth a lick."

"So, who's this girl your wanting?" the Indian agent asked McCabe.

"Her name's Happy Turtle. You know her?"

"I've heard the name. Her father Lame Bear, he's one of the few good ones. Worked his place in tandem with Harry Cook till Cook up and left. I heard he went to Montana. Funny thing that, the way he lit out. They were doing right well—him and that Injun."

The Indian agent scratched his head. "You know, I did hear something about that fella Cook's nephew. Now there was a no 'count. You must have known him, Old Man. I reckon he spent more time in your saloon than helping on that farm. Wainright's his name."

"That piece of turd." Miller spat the words along with a glob of tobacco-stained saliva. "Weren't a man in town don't despise him. I remember the last day he were in here. Three drinks, one after the other, then he says, "I'd best be out of here," and out he goes. Jumps on that poor horse and lights out of town. Ain't been back since, and I don't mind saying he ain't missed even if he did buy enough cheap liquor to pay this boy's salary."

"What about her? What about Happy Turtle?" McCabe asked.

"Hell, boy, if it's that important to ya, I'll see what I can get from this drunk Injun. We'll palaver, and I'll give him some of your cheap stuff. See if a drink or two will loosen his tongue."

Taking a bottle from Old Man Miller, Ezekiel Jones headed for the back door of the saloon. "Nope." Suddenly he wheeled around. "If I'm going to drink it, give me a bottle of your best."

Old Man Miller held out his hand.

"Let the boy pay for it." The agent thrust the bottle of cheap liquor towards the barkeep who exchanged it for a bottle from under the bar. "This better be the good stuff," Jones said as he went out the door.

Chapter 14 ~ What Sapphira Doesn't Know

"Please," she begged. "It will only take a minute. Just stop and ask." Ever since Lonely Cricket had left for that boarding school faraway in Pennsylvania, Sapphira had hoped for a letter. She missed him terribly. After Nathan Wainright's rape of Happy Turtle, the gulf between the young woman and her friend had seemed to grow ever wider in her mind. "If only he would write, then I could write back. I could tell him how much I miss him. I could tell him about Happy Turtle and how awful Nathan was to ..." She was never able to find words—not even in her private thoughts—to describe the horror of the attack. "I'd tell him why we're moving and how we're leaving our allotment for him. I'd tell him ..."

At such times of reverie, the teenager would begin to weep. She would do her best to hide her tears from her parents, but they knew how she felt. That was just one more reason they decided to leave Nebraska. Of course, they would never tell Sapphira that part of their thinking. "She has enough to bear," Leah Cook told her husband. "There is no need for her to feel guilt for our leaving our home."

"It's surely none of her fault," Harry Cook would agree. "If I could wring that bastard's neck, I'd do it in a moment." At such times, the farmer would storm about their holding banging and hammering so that the drumbeat of his rage could be heard for leagues. All that pounding did not relieve his rage. "Please," she had often begged. Harry Cook had many reasons to go into the town of Pierce. Sometimes he would see Small Deer huddled in the alley next to the saloon. Each time was a reminder of the trouble his nephew—*that piece of shit Wainright* as the farmer called him—had made for everyone. On each such trip, Harry stopped at the agent's office to enquire. "Any letters from the boys who went back East to school?" he would ask. "If there are, I'll take 'em to the families." Of course, he hoped that there would be one for his daughter, one from Lonely Cricket. None had come. "Please," the girl begged over and over. "We're going through town anyway; it won't hurt to stop."

Leah nudged her husband. "The girl's right. At least she'll know that we care."

"Whoa." The farmer pulled the reins. The wagon filled to brim with the Cooks' worldly possessions jounced to a stop in front of the Indian agent's house. "Oh, all right, child. I know there'll never be an end of it if we don't ask one more time. Go on then, knock on the door. But, mind, be right quick. No time for dallying. The day is half gone and there's many mile 'tween here and Montana."

***

Dare Sapphira, the letter began. It was a strain to make sense of the letters. Still, it was a letter, the one for which she had been praying. As the Cook's cart bounced along the ruts and hillocks of the dirt road towards Fayette, she read the words over and over.

Plese read this lether to my perenets. I wood rite lether to them but they not reed. Plese tell my mother and fater that I am well. Not all the boys hare are well but i am. There is many sikness becose we live in a big room. It to hot and some time to coled and we sleep in beds in line with blankets like army not comfortable robe of bufalo. When we come, Major Pratt say we cut hair like whit man and wear whit man cloths. Many boy never wear cloth befor. I show how to put on pant. Have to wear cloth like army men. Not comfortable. Major Pratt say we have pictur takin first in cloth we wear then in army cloth. I think new cloth not good as old. Other boy say same. We not alow talk our words. Use English or get punished. Some hit us. Some yell. I not yell at much because good with animal. Good with horse. I help lot. Major Pratt say I hard work.

Learn englis reed and rite. Hard to learn. Learn numbras and add take away. Some time they teach about whit man knows. Tell us about electricy. Take us see lightning macheen. Maks noise then lightning come when science man tuch. Many boy scare. I not scare becose I trust whit man. He look like Harry Cook. When Major ask me new whit man name, I say Harry. I think your fater good whit man. Tell him and mother I say hello. Soon I come home to Brasker and see you. Tell mother and fater I miss them. Tell Hapy Turtel I miss her. Tell Meny Fish I thoht of him lot. Plese pat Mage on nost tell him he gud horse. I come give apple.

Miss you much and hope you well, your frend,
Harry who is also.

Next to the last word he had drawn a picture. "What is this?" Sapphira wondered. Then she laughed aloud. "Oh, it is a cricket. How lonely he must feel."

***

It had taken months for Lonely Cricket to write a letter. He asked the White Man Langdon what to do. Langdon squinted at the young man and asked, "You got somebody can read?"

"Sapphira Cook read."

"Then you send it to her. The school'll pay the post long as it goes to the agent what signed you. Just put his name and hers on the outside and give it to the Major's secretary. Of course, that secretary read the letter before posting it. All the students' mail was checked. "This boy seems to be all right," she thought as she added Lonely Cricket's envelope, now sealed with mucilage, to the outgoing pile. "No complaining. Not like some."

The youngster had not written many things that he thought. How could he tell his friend and his family of the nights spent crying in bitter loneliness? Of the strange foods that made his stomach hurt and left him with painful diarrhea? How could he speak of the beatings? How could he write of the ringing that had not left his ear? Nor would he speak of the other boys, those who had grown sick and those who had died. Those who could find no place to feel safe. At least he had the stables. And the White Man Langdon, who was in charge of the animals, was never cruel. "He treats me as good as he treats the horses," the boy thought.

***

"We should go back," Sapphira said. "I should read Cricket's letter to his parents."

Harry Cook hunched his back and urged the mule on. "I don't think they would welcome us," Leah said. "Not even with a letter from the boy."

"But they will think that he has forgotten them." Sapphira rubbed the tears away from her eyes. "Or worse, that he has died."

"Hush, child," her father replied. "Leave bad enough alone." He flicked the reins on the mule's flanks. The animal didn't respond. "Get on," the man yelled and flicked again. "Don't take it out on the animal," Leah commented. "God damn," Harry Cook yelled. "God damn and damn again."

"I'll write him a letter from our new home," Sapphira thought. She wondered what she would say. She wondered how she could tell him about Happy Turtle. How she could explain …

Chapter 15 ~ A Proposal

Many times that summer John McCabe had hitched a livery nag to Old Man Miller's buckboard and driven the rutted way to Lame Bear's cabin. Each time he brought a simple gift from Jacob's store: cloth, notions, candy for Many Fish.

"Howdy," he would say and wait for Lame Bear to call Happy Turtle to come outside.

Each time her belly more prominent. Each time her smile a little quicker. She would take the presents he brought and call to her mother and little brother to take them inside. Then the two young people would walk—never beyond Lame Bear's watchful eyes.

They spoke little but groped towards learning a language they could share.

The first time, John had not come alone. Ezekiel Jones had agreed to come—more to make sure that there would be no complaint made to Washington than to facilitate romance. "This boy loves your daughter even though they have only met once. He knows that she is with child and what happened. He would ask your permission to visit her. He hopes that over time you will think of him not as a White Man and not as a stranger but as a son. He hopes that someday Happy Turtle will wish to make a home with him. He hopes that someday her child will call him father. These are the things he says, and I believe his words are true."

"I will talk with my woman and Happy Turtle." Lame Bear took the blanket which McCabe had brought as a present and draped it over his shoulders. The Indian called his wife and Happy Turtle to him.

John McCabe and the Indian agent stood at a distance while Lame Bear talked with Yquili Sparrow. Happy Turtle said nothing, but from time to time looked at McCabe and once smiled in his direction.

When the talking ended, Lame Bear announced, "He may come."

Once, McCabe brought cold chicken and biscuits. "Food." he said as he held them out.

"Eat," Happy Turtle responded in her own language, gesturing to define the word.

"Chicken."

"Biscuit."

"Corn."

The words came slowly. Some Happy Turtle remembered from the Cooks, but with those words came memories—happy and sad.

"Kiss."

"Love."

"Hand."

"Hand in hand."

Their shared vocabulary grew.

"Baby."

"Boy."

"Girl."

"Man and woman."

"Family." Of all words that was the hardest—not to say or to learn but to make come true.

One-night John found Small Deer crouched behind the saloon. "Give drink," the Indian begged.

"I got news, Small Deer, great news. Me and Happy Turtle are getting' hitched."

At first Small Deer did not understand the White Man words, but with the few Ho-Chunk words he had learned and with gestures, John got the news across.

Small Deer stared at the White Man. He could not comprehend. Happy Turtle and this White Man would share a life. It was more than Small Deer could consider.

"Give drink," he begged again.

John went inside the saloon and brought a bottle from under the bar, a bottle of the cheapest.

Chapter 16 ~ Shadow Fox Returns

"Major, I'd rather drive a team of a jackass and a thoroughbred than chaperoon them two." Langdon hitched his lanky form to attention. "Them boys ain't no good with nobody, but with each other; well, sir, I couldn't picked two worst."

"And why is that, Mr. Langdon?" Major Richard Henry Pratt nested his steel-nibbed pen in its holder and rested his hands on the travel documents he had been preparing to sign.

"Well, sir, that Sioux boy thinks he's a dang chief. Better'n anyone 'cept maybe yourself. The other youngsters don't cotton to that. And the other one, that Aaron boy, he don't have a friend in the world. Always makin' trouble and worse, the boy's a coward. Always whining and 'plaining. If it ain't the work, it's the food or the clothes. And, when somebody goes to discipline him, well, sir, all hell breaks loose with tears and cryin' and runnin'. Even Matron Fox cain't stand his caterwaulin'. Says he gives her the jeebies, if the Major knows what I mean."

"Which, Mr. Langdon, is why I need you to take the boys. I can't rightly send them back alone, especially not William. He may be full of himself, but his father is a chief. It's bad enough the boy is leaving school. We'll never have another Sioux in Carlisle if his father is angered. As for the other, I'd soon as put him in a sack and ship him back to Nebraska in a baggage car, but that wouldn't look good when the Congressmen come around to inspect the school, and they'll be coming next month."

"Yes, Sir, I understand, but couldn't some—"

"No, sir, somebody else could not. You're one of my best men. I can't spare a teacher from the classroom, and it would be a disaster to send one of the Apaches. I can imagine what the newspapers would be saying about that. Nope, Langdon, it's you.

"Tomorrow afternoon's train. Make sure the boys have their all belongings. Matron Fox will give you two carpetbags."

He took the pen from its holder, dipped it carefully in the inkwell, and signed the papers laid on his mahogany desk. "These give you authority in case you're asked and these others you give to the railroads for passage."

Pratt opened the top drawer of his desk and took out a leather wallet. He counted notes and held them out to the other man. "Here's cash for expenses. Keep a record but take ten dollars for yourself. The least I can do is make this less a chore and more a leave. When William is safe in his father's teepee, you take a couple days 'fore you come back. Lord knows you deserve something." He mumbled his next words, "We all do; this is no easy job."

"Yes, sir." Langdon resisted the impulse to salute, did an about-face, and started for the door. Just before opening it, he turned back. "Funny thing, sir."

"What's that?"

"The other boy, the other Ho-Chunk."

"Harry?"

"Yes, Sir."

"He's doing right well. I was worried for a bit after his young friend died."

"Terrible how sick these Injuns get. Tell me, Major, do you think it's in their blood or their diet and such they can't stand up to mumps and measles the way a White Man does?"

"The doctor says it's them bein' not quite human … lacking the faculties as he puts it. He says he can feel the difference in their lumps." Pratt ran his fingers through his medium long hair as if straightening the graying strands. "Danged if I can tell the difference from one head to the next."

"Well, sir, I know the doc's right smart and educated, but he was sure wrong about Harry. Never saw a boy took more natural to horses nor one so willin' to learn. Doc said he had the head of a farmer. How'd he put it? 'The brains of a plow mule.' Well, I guess he missed a bump that day." Langdon laughed.

"Mr. Langdon, phrenology is no laughing matter."

The subordinate immediately straightened himself to full attention. "Yes, sir. No disrespect for the doctor intended, sir."

"But you are right, Harry is going to make our school proud. Mark me, Langdon, he is going to be a credit to us and to his people."

"Yes, sir, that's what I mean. Two boys from that same tribe. One is, well, no better way to say than plain—that boy ain't worth spit. The other good a boy as ever we got." Langdon turned again towards the door.

As he walked through the orderly's office and onto the porch of the house, which served as Pratt's home and the school administration, Robert Langdon was still wishing that somebody else would escort Shadow Fox and the Sioux chief's son to their homes.

***

For all the torment and teasing he had received from Shadow Fox, Lonely Cricket was not glad to hear that the older boy was leaving. Although the other boys considered Shadow Fox a coward and a liar, Lonely Cricket always remembered that they were both Ho-Chunk. Lonely Cricket remembered a story of their people.

ΩΩΩΩΩ

When the Ma-Ona gave the people the knowledge of words, he sent a great white buffalo to teach them the way of saying the sacred words, the way in which to call on the spirit world and the way to ask Isanaklesh, our mother earth, to bring forth the three sisters, the ways in which to speak to the wind and the rain, the prayers to offer in the times of snow and in the times of dryness.

So sacred were these words, that the white buffalo spirit warned Many Voices, who was then chief among the people, that they should only be said on top of the great mounds on which the people lived. "That way," the buffalo spirit told Many Voices, "your enemies will not be able to steal these prayers and take their power from your people."

The Trickster was envious that Ma-Ona had given the people such sacred and secret words. He desired to learn them for himself. So, the Trickster stood outside the circle of the people dressed as one of them and said, "I am also of the people of the word, but I am from a different and distant village. May I rest with you for a time?"

The people brought him to the council fire and Many Voices welcomed him as a brother who has been lost but who has now been found. "Welcome stranger who is one of our people," Many Voices spoke. "Eat venison with us, for today we have killed two deer and have much meat. Eat corn with us, for today Isanaklesh has been good to us and given us the sisters from her body, the corn, and beans, and squash that we might have much food. Drink with us, for today the spirits of the rivers have given us clean water that we might quench our thirst. Sleep with us tonight, for today father sky has given us good weather that we might watch the stars and watch the great bear chase his prey across the heavens. All these things we have asked, and the spirits have answered our prayers.

And the Trickster, dressed not as a spirit or an animal but as a man from the people, responded, "Thank you, Many Voices, for your kindness. Truly the spirits have listened to your prayers. They must be good words of great power that Ma-Ona has talked to you.

When the Trickster spoke. Many Voices knew him for who he was. "All Ho-Chunk know the words the great white buffalo has taught the people. You are not one of us but the Trickster in disguise. Leave this place, for the magic which is of the people belongs to the people and to every member of the people—even to the lowest—but those who are not Ho-Chunk shall have no part, even the chiefs and great warriors who are not Ho-Chunk shall not have it."

And the people recognized the wisdom of Many Voices and made oath they would share with one another the wisdom of the people—even to the lowest. From those who are not of the people these words shall be kept secret.

ΩΩΩΩΩ

The night before Shadow Fox, whom the white men called Aaron, was to leave the school and return to his family, Lonely Cricket went to him and said, "As we are Ho-Chunk and share the secret words of the people, I ask that you tell Lame Bear and Yquili Sparrow that I am well. I ask you to remind Many Fish that his brother will come back to teach him the things he is learning of the White Man's ways. I ask you to tell Happy Turtle that her big brother will soon return to give her in marriage. I ask you all these things.

"And I ask that you give this letter to my family that they might ask their white friends to read it for them." He handed the older boy an envelope that contained two lined sheets of paper on which he had carefully written the words of the White Man, which Matron Fox had helped him to do.

"Of course, Little Brother, I will tell your family as you have asked and I will give them your letter in the White Man's language," Shadow Fox replied. He made a great show of placing the envelope into the carpetbag that Langdon had given him for his belongings. "I will go to see them as soon as my father permits."

When Lonely Cricket returned to his own dormitory, Shadow Fox removed the letter from his bag and tore it into pieces. "Fool," he thought, "why would I help an enemy? You stay here with your white friends; I will go home to be a true Ho-Chunk."

***

As they pulled into the station at Fayette, Shadow Fox did not notice the new wooden platform. Nor did he observe the new stockyard filled with cattle or the sign above it, "MERCIER CATTLE AND SHIPPING." The boy did hear Nathan Wainright worrying with slurred words at a new batch of steers, which he prodded with a long pole.

“I heard tell you took that Injun girl without her say?” Abner Banner, scratching his bulbous nose, had asked when Wainright applied for a job.

“Sure did.” Nathan had puffed himself up with the thought of conquest.

“Then I guess you’re right enough fer me.” Banner spit tobacco juice towards Maggie’s front leg.

The horse pulled back against the reins. Wainright yanked against the gelding’s mouth and asked, “Does the job come with a decent mount?”

“I guess we can fix you up. What’ll ya do with this one?”

“Find some dumb farmer take it off my hands.”

They sealed their contract with a drink from Banner’s silver flask.

Neither Shadow Fox or Robert Langdon knew of these things as they stepped from the train onto the wooden planking that fronted the ticket office. “I’ll be leaving you here.” The White Man spoke slowly. The adolescent Ho-Chunk grunted a meaningless response.

Shadow Fox ignored Langdon’s outstretched hand and the lanky man’s once more repeated admonition. “You wait on that agent Jones. Sent him a telegram from Chicago and another in Des Moines. He’ll fetch ya back home, boy.”

None of that mattered to Shadow Fox. Soon he would be back among his people. Already he was fashioning tales to tell them. Stories of the White Man’s evil and of how he, Shadow Fox, had survived the worst they could do.

He would save the story of the science man with his lightening machine to tell the other boys, but he would tell the elders of cutting of his hair and the prediction of the darkness of the sun. He would tell them of the Jesus religion and how it caused Red Men to die with faces swollen and breath hot. He would tell them that fools trusted the White Devil and how the Ho-Chunk must not trust these tricksters who came to promise them knowledge.

Shadow Fox sat on the bench, which stood against the station wall, his carpetbag with his real clothes and other possessions at his feet.

The day was dusty-hot, and the water bucket and ladle set against the station wall beckoned both passengers and townsfolk. Nathan Wainright, wishing he had a whiskey or beer but settling for less, pushed his way past two ladies making their gingerly way to the dry goods emporium, and climbed the steps to the platform. Reaching for the ladle, he saw Shadow Fox watching him.

“What you lookin’ at, Injun?” Wainwright demanded. He moved closer to the boy. “Fact, what you doin’ up on this platform? Don’t you know your place? No Niggers and no damned Injuns allowed up here.”

He reached out a foot and nudged Shadow Fox's leg. "Move off a here or I'll feed you to them steers of mine." He added a harder nudge aimed at the young man's left shin.

The station agent, hearing Wainright's raised voice, came onto the platform. "Do as you're told, boy," he said. "This bench ain't for Injuns."

After that, the boy sat in the dirt leaning his back against the west wall of the clapboard station. He nursed his anger and waited; waiting until the sun passed overhead and started to drift downwards in the sky.

The shadows were long when Ezekiel Jones finally arrived. He showed up smelling of whores and whiskey. "You the boy from that Injun School," Jones asked, not caring to remember that he had delivered this and another youngster to the train many months earlier.

Shadow Fox nodded.

"Well, get on board and I'll take you back to Pierce. From there you can hoof it back to your folks. They know you're coming?"

"I think Maj—"

"No mind. Get on up here and let's go. We got a distance to go, boy. A distance to go."

As they trotted out of town, Shadow Fox did not notice Nathan Wainright as the man drifted down the main street and into Sapphire's Saloon.

"Hey, Wainright," a voice called from within the establishment, "you want we should deal ya in?"

"Let the man have a drink first 'fore you take his money."

Laughter engulfed Wainright as he entered. "Let me have a drink 'fore I take yours," he answered.

***

Ezekiel Jones pulled his rig to a stop in front of the stone building that served both as the agency office and his home. "You can make it home on your own, boy."

Shadow Fox stepped to the ground, pulled his bag from the rear of the buggy, and turned towards the road.

"Hold on, boy. You hungry? Don't want your folks complaining 'bout my not feeding their little heathen."

Shadow Fox said, "Yes, sir." It was the way he had been taught to respond to the White Men at school and came out without thinking. Later, walking down the road chewing the jerky the agent had given him, the teen played the moment over and over again. He hated the White Man for the feelings of stupidity and guilt that welled within him. He hated himself for taking the jerky even as he enjoyed its taste. "I wish

I could have fought with Sitting Bull and Crazy Horse," he thought. "I wish I could kill all the White Men. I would start with this Indian Agent."

Those were his thoughts even though he knew that they were lies. He would never be a warrior. His heart filled with hate.

"That you, Shadow Fox?"

Shadow Fox was passing Old Man Miller's saloon. Small Deer sat in the dirt and manure, his back against a hitching post, a bottle in his hand. "That really you, Shadow Fox?" he repeated.

Shadow Fox turned towards the young man.

"Back from White Man school?" Small Deer held the bottle up. "Come. Share White Man drink. Welcome home."

Shadow Fox turned away and took a step down the road.

"Wait!" Shakily rising to his feet, needing the post for support in the effort, Small Deer nearly dropped the bottle. But, holding on to it with both hands, he wobbled forward towards Shadow Fox. "Have drink with me. Celebrate home."

Shadow Fox hesitated. It was said the White Man drink would make one feel better, would take away worries and doubts. Thinking of his family and the other Ho-Chunk and of the questions they would ask, the youngster felt many doubts and many worries. "Perhaps ..."

"Yes, Small Deer, I will drink the White Man drink with you." He reached for the bottle.

***

The splash of soapy water woke Shadow Fox. The Chinese washerman stood over him, an empty pail in hand. "Injun drink too much." Turning abruptly, the man walked away leaving Shadow Fox choking on the smell of vomit; his head churning with nausea and confusion, and his throat rasping and dry. "Ahhh." It hurt to lie there. "Arrr." It hurt to rise. "Where is Small Deer?" Shadow Fox asked himself. He tried to remember. The last thing was the White Man money. He reached into his pocket. It was gone. Three dollars and six bits, the money Major Pratt had given him.

"Wages for the work you did on the farm," the Major had explained. "You tell your people we don't cheat you boys here."

The money would have pleased Talking Mountain. Perhaps he would have bought a White Man gun. Shadow Fox would say there was no dollars; he would say that the White Man did not pay for his work. He would tell a story of hard work with no reward. What would such stories matter? His father would not know, would not see him lying against a tree while other boys worked. Would not see him sharing bottles of White Man liquor with Small Deer.

Talking Mountain—the thought of his father forced Shadow Fox up from the ground. He went to the pump, which stood behind the saloon, and worked its arm until a stream of water flowed. Soaking his head first and then trying to wash himself clean. He took off the school uniform and took his own clothes from his carpetbag. Shadow Fox had grown during the months in Pennsylvania; his old clothes bound him tightly. He thought that Matron Fox might help adjust them and then realized that she and the school were many days journey away. He would have to make do. Stuffing the school clothes into the carpetbag, he headed out of town.

The sun, dust, and, most of all, his hangover took their toll. The young man shuffled down the road cursing the White Man's drink even as he wished that he and Small Deer might have another bottle to share.

Chapter 17 ~ Wisconsin

The young Ho-Chunk woman lay on the metal frame bed, the straw ticking of the thin mattress prickling her back. The baby at her breast suckled noisily. Wandering Woman, as she was now called, did not understand this new life. She was terrified of the great noise and busyness of Milwaukee. Even with her husband, she was afraid to venture into the streets. By necessity, she would climb the three flights of stairs and back to the pump and the privy. By necessity, she would use the tubs set for washing; the baby's swaddling and John's overalls and shirts, smelling of Valentin Blatz's brewery demanded laundering.

If John McCabe could learn to work in the lauter tun, to drain the liquid from the grain so as to waste none. If he could wash the tun over and again with a heavy mop and have it ready for the next batch of mash, she owed him decent food and clean clothes and—if he asked—her body.

She did not desire him. She desired no man. She thought of no man except Nathan Wainright, and for him she felt loathing. He had raped her and left her reviled in her home. He had raped her and left her shamed. Once she had been Happy Turtle, a lover of the peaceful life which had surrounded her, a lover of her family and of her Nebraska home. That was no more. Now she would have no family, no home. She must wander in the White Man's world.

Talking Mountain had said the words of accusation. "Happy Turtle, you have lain with the White Man. You carry the White Man's child. Your child does not belong with the Ho-Chunk. Now you accept another White Man to lie on your pallet. You no longer belong with the Ho-Chunk. You belong with the White Man. You bring shame to our people."

No one had spoken for her. Lame Bear did not speak; his voice was blocked with tears. Small Deer did not speak; his words would have been filled with the White Man's fire drink. Lonely Cricket did not speak; he was too far away in the White Man's world. John McCabe might have spoken, would have spoken, but his words would not have been heard.

Tall Grass said his heart was filled with sadness. "Happy Turtle is no more. This woman must become a wanderer in the world of the White Man. Wandering Woman your White Man will take you far from this place. That is a good thing."

With those words, the leader of her people had turned away, and she was alone. Happy Turtle was no more. The life inside her womb stirred as she climbed onto the cart the saloonkeeper had given McCabe. McCabe urged the half-blind stubborn mule, a gift of farewell from her father Lame Bear, "Hey yuh! Hey yuh!" He slapped the reins on the animal's tough hide. The cart jolted forward, towards the northeast and Wisconsin.

The young woman's plan had been to join her people by the great lake where the evil smelling monster dwells. The Ho-Chunk had lived in that place since the beginning of time.

"The Ho-Chunk people are there," Yquili Sparrow told her daughter, "but they will not know you. Those who remember us will no longer wish to remember you. They will remember your brother Gentle Hawk, but they will say that you are the one who has died."

ΩΩΩΩΩ

The Trickster had gathered the enemies of the people. So many were there that the people could not fight them. Instead, they fled toward the sun of the afternoon. They ran as fast as they could, but they reached the bank of great lake and could run no further.

Wise Owl, who was the chief of the people, sent scouts—some in the direction of the morning sun and some in the direction of the evening sun— to find a place where the people could cross the water. "If we must fight with our back to this great water, we shall surely be fed to the fish who live here," Wise Owl told the leaders of the two scouting parties.

Strong Fish led the scouting party that went towards the evening sun. Strong Fish was a great warrior. He did not wish to run from the enemies of the people, not even from the large number of enemies whom the Trickster had assembled.

When the scouting party that Strong Fish led camped that evening by the great water, Strong Fish did not mean to sleep. He made a fire by the water's edge and spent the night in vigil praying to Ma-Ona to help the people and to show him what he must do.

During the night, Ma-Ona sent a spirit dream to Strong Fish and cast sleep into the warrior's eyes. In his sleep a giant fish appeared to Strong Fish. "Cast yourself into the lake, and where you drown the water will grow narrow," the sprit instructed.

In the morning, when they awoke, the rest of the scouting party could not find Strong Fish, but they found his bow and quiver and the stick with which he counted coup. Nearby was a channel where the lake grew narrow. "We can cross the lake here," one of the warriors said.

"But this place smells of evil and death," another of the warriors said.

"All the better, for our enemies will not want to cross the lake in such a place," replied the first warrior.

While that warrior stood guard over the place where the lake narrowed to make sure no enemy made ready to attack the people there, the others ran back to Wise Owl and told him that Strong Fish had disappeared, but that they had found a place where they could safely cross the great lake.

The people quickly headed in the direction of the evening sun and made their way towards the narrow place.

When they arrived at that place, Wise Owl knew at once that Strong Fish had worked magic to make this place of crossing. "This is not the odor of evil and death" Wise Owl said, "but the smell of Strong Fish's bravery. Do not hold your noses at this odor but breathe it deeply that you might be as brave a warrior as Strong Fish and that you, too, might someday rescue our people.

The people followed Wise Owl across the channel in the lake. Some of them listened to the words of Wise Owl and did not hold their noses against the stench. Some of them did not listen and held their nostrils tight to not smell it.

When the enemies of the people, who were following them in order to kill them, came to that place, many turned back because of the odor. Some were brave enough to climb down the bank and into the lake.

When the enemy were all in the water, a giant fish appeared and ate them all. It was Strong Fish, who had saved his people by sacrificing his life as a man.

Later, when the people knew they were safe, there was a great council. Wise Owl spoke. "Those who did not hold their noses at the smell of Strong Fish are great warriors and shall make the people feared by our enemies. Those who held their noses and did not fill them with the odor of Strong Fish shall become farmers and raise the three sisters for us all.

ΩΩΩΩΩ

Word had traveled before them. "You have lain with the White Man. You carry the White Man's child. Your child does not belong with the Ho-Chunk. Now you accept another White Man to lie on your pallet. You no longer belong with the Ho-Chunk. You belong with the White Man. You bring shame to our people." The words of Talking Mountain had condemned her not only in Nebraska but also in Wisconsin. The people had rejected her.

John McCabe had said, "Don't fret, gal. This place don't smell right anyways. We'll make our home in the White Man city."

With no better reason or direction, John McCabe had brought them to this place of many people—many of whom spoke a White Man language from a place known as Germany. Here people were stacked one above the other so they did not rest on Mother Earth. Here people lived next to one another so she could hear the words of strangers through the walls and hear them cry out to one another in the night. Here they lived without a place to grow crops or keep animals, without a place to seek quiet or shade by a stream. Here they lived—not with Ho-Chunk but with people of many nations. Here they lived without customs or legends, and Wandering Woman wondered if Ma-Ona knew them in this place.

"This is not a home. It isn't even a place to live. There is no one here who can give my child a name." Wandering Woman said these things to herself, but never to John McCabe.

The young Indian woman sat on the floor, her back against one of the thin walls of their barely furnished room. She held her little boy to her breast until he had suckled his fill and then laid him on a blanket beside her. She gave him a metal spoon for a toy. He banged it against the metal bedstead. Wandering Woman did not notice the clanging. She did not notice the tears coursing her own face and dripping from her chin. She was oblivious to all except the loneliness and misery that engulfed her.

Coming home at dusk, his body coated with the salt of his sweat and stinking of the lauter tun, John McCabe hoped—as he did every day—that his Happy Turtle would be returned to him, that she would once more smile, that she and the child would truly be his family. When he found her, once again sitting on the floor, once again lost in tears, his heart broke as it had so many days since she had agreed to be with him.

"If only I knew what she wanted," he questioned himself for another time. "If only I knew how to make her happy." It was difficult to fight his own despair, but he wanted so desperately to make her happy. "And the child? What about him? She cares for the poor tyke, but ..."

He bent down and gently stroked Wandering Woman's face. "Has it been any better today?"

"How many times have I asked that question?" he thought. "And the answer always the same, a grunt. A weak un-meant 'yes.' I wish ..." It seemed there were so many thoughts that went uncompleted.

Over their meager supper, McCabe tried again. "The boss says I'm due a raise, that I'm hired good now. Says I'm a good worker."

There was no response.

"Means we can have a bit more to eat, maybe buy the boy some'n to wear 'sides my old shirt, maybe even get you a new dress." He babbled on and hoped for some response.

"Who give my son name?"

McCabe almost leapt with joy. She had spoken. She had given him a problem, something about which he could do ...what? "Well, Hap ... Wandering Woman, he sure can have my name. Yep, I'd be right proud to have him called McCabe."

"But that not name. Not name friend call. Not name family call. You John. Who give son name?"

"Well, my Ma and Pa named me; didn't your folks name you? Didn't they call you Happy Turtle, I mean till yer people changed it?"

"Lame Bear and Yquili Sparrow not name me. Name given Dreaming Woman. Boy name given Tall Grass. Who give name here in White Man city?"

"Well, since we's living in this here White Man city and all, maybe the boy should have a White Man name. Someday if'n he goes to live with your people he can take a name there like you took Wandering Woman stead of Happy Turtle. Maybe, he—"

"How White Man get name?"

"Like I said, my folks gave me my—"

"How they know? Tall Grass have story. Dreaming Woman have story. They tell name story. How John McCabe parents know name."

"Is that what's been fretting you so bad? Well, in the White Man world, folks pick someone they want to remember, someone they love a lot, and they use that name. Like I was named for ... heck I forget who it was, but it were somebody.

"We can pick somebody you like, maybe some White Man you thought was good. How about that friend of Lame Bear, that Cook fella?"

Wandering Woman shrank back at the words. "No. I think him and I think his family. I think ..." Tears sprung to her eyes.

"Oh, yeah, that fella. Course. Weren't there no other White Man."

"You. You good White Man."

"Well, if you want, I s'pose we can call the boy John Jr. Course folks will call him Junior, but that ain't so bad." He spoke slowly, not sure of his own hesitancy. Then, to his surprise, he said, "If he were my son, I'd name him fer Old Man Miller. He was more of a pappy to me than my own father. I barely knew my daddy. Went off to fight fer Jeff Davis and died somewheres—never did know where. Can you believe that, he were from Illinois same as Old Abe and he joined the Rebs? Left my mother with six mouths to feed and nothin' to do with.

"When Old Man Miller took me in, that were all the difference. Reckon I'd have ended up decoratin' a tree somewheres if he hadn't taken me under his wing. Gave me a job and taught me how to read and do numbers, how to be honest and to care 'bout people. Yep, I'd want my son carryin' his name."

"Old Man good name," Wandering Woman observed.

"Well, we can't call him that. White folks wouldn't understand that kind of name, and I don't right know his Christian name. Never used it; just went by Old Man Miller. I guess we could call him Miller. How 'bout that—Miller McCabe—that got a nice ring."

"Miller McCabe," Wandering Woman echoed. A small smile flickered at the edge of her mouth. The sight of it filled McCabe's heart with joy.

***

After they had eaten their supper of cornbread, beans, and bacon fat, Wandering Woman again held the baby to her breast. As he suckled, she whispered to him, "Do not worry, Miller McCabe, your mother is here to care for you. Do not worry, Miller McCabe, your father is here to protect you."

The baby cooed in satisfaction. She held him over her shoulder and gently tapped his back until he burped. For a moment, the small room smelled of the child's satisfaction.

"He's a good boy," John McCabe said. The man pulled off his outer clothing and lay down on the bed in his rough-cloth union suit. He lay as he had every night, far to one side to make room for Wandering Woman and her child. He lay as he had every night with his back turned to them so that Wandering Woman could sleep in peace.

The young woman climbed into bed next to McCabe and laid her son next to herself, not between them but to her side. This was not what she had done every night before. She reached out to the man who lay so still and stroked the back of his head and then his shoulder.

"John McCabe," she said quietly into the darkness, "you good father. You good man."

Almost asleep, McCabe smiled at the words and wondered that good things might yet lie ahead.

Chapter 18 ~ The Sorrow of Many Fish

Lame Bear no longer told stories. No longer did he show Many Fish how to care for Great Horse and the other animals. The father did not take time to explain how to plant or weed, and his son was filled with the bitter tears of remorse.

"What did I do that my father is so angry with me?" he asked Yquili Sparrow.

His mother hid her face so he could not see her tears. "You have done nothing. It is what the White Man Wainwright did to your sister. Now, she has gone and the White Man Cook, who was your father's friend, has gone. There is pain in Lame Bear's heart, but you are not the reason for it."

That night, when his parents slept, Many Fish thought about his father's pain and his mother's explanation. He knew that his mother's words were true. Still, he was sad that his father did not spend time with him, and it hurt his heart that Lame Bear was so unhappy.

"There must be something I can do that will ease my father's pain," he said to himself. "I will ask Falling Cloud what to do, for he knows how to make people remember their laughter." With the quiet of night, Many Fish crept from his sleeping mat and put on his clothes.

Many Fish dressed back to front as Falling Cloud would do so that the man would know that he came seeking knowledge. By the half-moon's light the boy followed the path to the jester's lodge.

"Why are you here, Son of Lame Bear?" the heyoka asked the next morning when he found the boy asleep. Slouched against the side of Falling Cloud's cabin, Many Fish had dreamed of his sister. Clutched tight in his left hand was the remains of the rattle he had been given on the day of his naming.

"I need to know what I have done wrong that my father no longer smiles at me. I want to know how I can make him laugh again and how I can dry the tears in my mother's eyes."

Falling Cloud went back inside his cabin and came out with two pieces of rabbit and a jug of water. Handing the meat to the boy, he said, "Let us eat and I will tell you a story."

ΩΩΩΩΩ

Angry Antelope and Morning Star had a daughter who was very beautiful, filled with fun, and able to do many things. Her name was Red Chili and all the young men of the tribe wanted her hand. Every night there would be the sound of courting flutes playing outside the lodge of Angry Antelope. Every day the young men would bring hides and furs and haunches of venison to the cook fire of Morning Star.

"Red Chili is too young to leave her mother's fire," Angry Antelope would tell the young men.

"Red Chili is too young to leave her father's lodge," Morning Star would tell them as well.

Her parents' words did not deter Red Chili's suitors. "She is beautiful."

"She is filled with joy."

"She has many talents."

The young men of the tribe would not take no for an answer.

No matter what Angry Antelope and Morning Star would say, still the nights were filled with the sound of flutes and still the gifts were brought to the cook fire.

Red Chili enjoyed the admiration of the young men. She dressed in cloth of bright colors and put beautiful shells around her neck. In her hair she wore flowers. The more beautiful she looked, the more the young men wanted her.

She relished the songs of the young men. She would call to them in the night and share the laughter of her voice. The more she laughed, the more the young men wanted her.

Red Chili delighted in the gifts of the young men. She would make fine clothes of the hides and furs and delicious food of the meat that they brought her. The more she did, the more the young men wanted her.

Then a stranger came to the village of the tribe. He was not of The People but was a White Man. He did not wear moccasins but the boots of the White Man. He did not wear a deerskin vest or the leggings of a man but the clothing of the White Man.

This man came to the village and he begged them to let him eat with them and to spend the night in their lodges. "I am without food and have no place to sleep," he said. "Will you make me welcome?"

"We will have a feast in your honor," Angry Antelope said, for he knew that the gods and spirits often came as strangers.

The village ate well that evening. Venison and rabbit, buffalo and elk, elk and trout—all were served. Corn, beans, and squash were also provided. Berries had been gathered from the fields and sweet plums and tart cherries from the trees of the forest.

After they had eaten and had smoked tobacco, the people went to sleep. So tired were they from the great feasting, that the young men did not play their flutes that night. All was quiet and nobody stirred in the darkness.

When Morning Star woke, she called to her daughter, "Red Chili, it is time to light the cook fire. It is time to make the porridge of corn and squash."

The young woman did not answer. Her mother went to look for her. Red Chili was not at her sleeping pace, nor was she at the stream fetching water, nor was she gathering berries in the fields.

Neither was the stranger in the village. He was not at the stream washing himself, nor was he in the fields gathering berries or looking for a rabbit to bring to the stew pot. His bedroll and rifle were nowhere to be found.

Morning Star awakened Angry Antelope, calling him back from the world that can be seen but not touched. "Husband, our daughter has disappeared, and the stranger is nowhere to be found. I fear that he has taken her. Quickly, take your bow and follow him. Bring Red Chili back to our people."

Angry Antelope gathered the young men who desired Red Chili's hand and said to them, "This stranger has stolen my daughter, whom I know you love. Help me to find him, to slay him, and to bring Red Chili back to her mother's cooking fire. The man who slays this stranger shall have my daughter to live in his lodge and to sleep by his fire.

Quickly they took up their bows and their tomahawks and set off after the stranger and Red Chili.

At first, the trail was easy to follow. Branches had been broken and grass had been bent. The mark of the White Man's boot was clearly visible in the dirt. For two days, the men followed the trail. But, on the third day, when the sun came from his lodge and woke the world, they realized that they had been travelling in a great circle, that they were near their own village.

"How is this possible?" one of the young men demanded.

"This is magic," another replied.

"This was no White Man but the Trickster who has stolen Red Chili," said a third.

Discouraged, the men returned to their lodges. Even Angry Antelope returned to the village to tell Morning Star what had happened.

"I cannot live without my daughter," Morning Star insisted. "You must look some more. You must bring her home to me."

That afternoon, Angry Antelope again went to search for Red Chili. This time, none of the young men went with him. He went alone and searched in a great circle around the village and then another and another. When he completed three great circles around the village, he sat on the ground, closed his eyes and prayed to the Great Spirit that his daughter would be safe.

"Her mother pleads for Red Chili's return," he said. "She says that without our daughter to help with the cook fire the food will have lost its flavor."

When Angry Antelope opened his eyes, he saw a new plant, one that he had never seen before. From the same stems as the green leaves hung bright orange-red cocoon-shaped berries. He picked one of these fruits and broke it open to taste the flesh. The taste was like fire but pleasant to his tongue.

He held his hands to his face to smell the odor of the fruit. His fingers came close to his eyes, and they burned and burned, and tears came.

Picking many of the fruits, he brought them back to Morning Star and said, "The Great Spirit has given us these berries to remind us of our daughter. They will bring taste to our cooking pots and tears to our eyes."

ΩΩΩΩΩ

When the story was done and the rabbit eaten, Falling Cloud said, "It will be hard for Lame Bear and Yquili Sparrow to accept what the White Man trickster has done. Happy Turtle will be missed by all of the people.

The jester mounted his horse and rode away leaving Many Fish seated against the lodge. Because Falling Cloud rode with his face towards the tail of his horse, he could see the tears streaming down the boy's face and he could also see the cloud of anger that filled the youngster's eyes.

***

"Your mother will cry for you," Lame Bear said when, on the next morning, he found his groggy son—still seated next to the jester's cabin—stretching and yawning. "She will not light the cook fire for her lodge is empty. What is a sparrow to do when her nest is barren? I cannot make you do so, but you should come home to her."

"And what of you, father?! Do you also cry for me?"

Lame Bear nodded his assent and tenderly touched the boy's forehead. Folding his son in his arms, the father remounted Great Horse and turned the beast back towards their cabin.

"The White Man can be a good friend or a great enemy," Many Fish said.

"That is true," his father replied.

"But, the drink of the White Man is always an enemy."

"That, too, is true," answered Lame Bear.

From that day, Many Fish's young heart was turned against the White Man and he vowed to punish any Ho-Chunk who took up the White Man's way of drink.

Chapter 19 ~ The Hearts of Girls

Sapphira Cook rested her head on her folded arms and tried to stifle the sound of her sobs.

Leah busied herself with fry pan and pot while ineffectually waving her hand at the smoke that escaped the cracks in the metal stovepipe. It was no more than a shack, this new home of theirs. At least Harry had found employment in the mine, and the company provided this one room cabin—just like the scores of other cabins clustered near the company store.

"What is it, child?" Leah asked, no longer able to maintain the fiction that her daughter's tears were unnoticed.

"I want to go home." Sapphira did not lift her head, but she tried to keep her voice from going shrill. "I'm homesick, Ma."

"You are home. This is our home now, and The Good Lord knows your pa works hard enough to make it so." Leah banged the fry pan onto the stove.

"I know he does. I know that." Sapphira lifted her head. Her eyes brimmed with red and tears. "But ... but, I still want to go home, to Nebraska. We shouldn't have left. We should have ..."

Leah Cook had no answer for her daughter, not this time, not again. How many times had this topic been broached? How many times could she speak of Harry's cursed nephew? How many times could she speak of her own sense of shame and loss? How many times could she cry in her husband's arms while he tried so hard to be brave?

"There's work to be done, Sapphira. The floor needs brooming and I'll be wanting coal for the stove." She wiped the sweat of her brow with her sleeve and surreptitiously shook her head.

"Yes, Ma, I know pa works hard. I hate that he has to work in that mine. I know he'd want to be back home and you know it, too." The girl grabbed the broom and set to work before her mother could remonstrate.

That night, when Harry—caked with dust and sweat and tired beyond enduring—had eaten another meal of beans and corn and lard, Leah held herself tight to the man she loved and again whispered in his ear of their daughter's unhappiness.

"What would you have me do? She can't go back to Nebraska. We can't go back. There's nothing there for us but the shame and the hurt we left behind. Could you face them folks? I fear this is home now. Just gotta be. It may not be much, but if we save some pennies perhaps there'll more."

"No, not Nebraska, but I was thinking."

Quickly, before Harry could object or think about the cost of a railway ticket and travel, she laid out her plan. "My cousin Elisabetta has a drapery in New Albany, Indiana. She's a spinster and I'm sure would love the companionship and what better employment for a girl who loves to sew?"

When Harry made no reply, she added, "I'm sure they have an athenaeum where the girl could study some in the evenings, maybe become the teacher she always wanted."

Leah paused for a moment and then, with a deep breath and not daring to look at her husband, continued, "I think we owe her that—a chance to have the life we'd have given her if that monster hadn't come to—"

"I'm so sorry," Harry moaned as he did each time Nathan Wainwright was mentioned.

"As am I, Harry, which is why I think we must."

"Have we the means?" The man rolled to his back and stared at the ceiling. "And will your cousin take her?"

"I'll write to Elisabetta and ask. As for the funds, I have my necklace."

Harry groaned. "I cannot allow that. It was your mothers and hers before."

"And it would be Sapphira's someday as well, which is all the more reason it should be used for her now."

"B ... but, but ..." Harry sputtered and grew still.

"Perhaps we can use," Leah fought to keep her voice steady, "the pawn."

"You mean borrow against it?! How do we pay it back?"

"I'll get work. With the girl gone, I can find a job ... perhaps as a cook at the hotel or cleaner."

"My wife working for a wage?! I'll not hear of it. Such things are beneath—"

"Nonsense. Work is dignity itself. And once the pawn is paid, we can save my earnings and soon be gone from this place and back to our own farm."

***

"I'll miss you terrible." Sapphira wiped her eyes with the already soggy bit of muslin that served as her handkerchief.

Her parents fought to hold back their own tears.

"Here's a few dollars for the trip." Harry Cook slipped a collection of coins into his daughter's hand.

"Pa, you mustn't. I don't need all this. You and Ma will go hungry till your paycheck." She tried to push the money back into his hand, but he held fast.

"You be a good girl and mind your Cousin Elisabetta. Work hard and she'll give you a decent home and a wage as well. Make a good life for yourself. Study. Become a teacher. The things of which you've dreamed. Remember, girl, your pa and I love you and want the best." Leah's voice broke.

"Don't waste your life and talent on some no-account. If you marry, make sure he's worthy." Harry gathered his daughter in his arms and whispered, "And if you someday have a child, I hope she will be as dear as you to me."

Putting his callused hands on Sapphira's shoulder, Harry propelled her towards the steps that led onto the train and on to her future.

As the train pulled away from the station, Harry and Leah waved. Long after the caboose had reduced to a dot against the horizon, they stood on the platform and watched.

"What will become of her?"

"She'll be all right, Leah. She'll be just fine. God knows we'll miss her, but He'll keep her in His care, of that I'm sure."

In the second of the three passenger cars, Sapphira sat stiff, eyes closed, her case and hatbox held close.

"Where you headed, Miss?"

Startled by the conductor's voice, Sapphira dropped her hatbox to the floor. "Nebraska," she answered without thought.

"That's quite a ways, young lady." He held out his hand for her ticket.

"I mean Indiana. New Albany, Indiana."

"Either way, I'll need your ticket. This train will take you to Chicago. From there, well, Miss, it's up to you."

"Yes, thank you. Indeed, it is up to me."

***

Lonely Cricket had been a toddler then, not much older than Many Fish. "Go to sleep," Yquili Sparrow had told him, and Lonely Cricket had obediently lain on his sleeping mat and pulled the buffalo robe over himself.

But he had not slept. Instead, he listened to the story their mother told Happy Turtle. In two days, his sister would attend the sunrise dance. Even though she was still a girl and would not dance with the girls who were coming of age, Happy Turtle felt like she was becoming a woman. She was excited, and Lonely Cricket was excited for her.

ΩΩΩΩΩ

When the first people reached the third level of the world, they were afraid to continue their journey upwards. They camped by the silver river and thought to stay in that place forever. However, Red Horn knew the people would grow sick and perish without the sun's warmth. As it was his pledge to help the people and to keep them safe, he sent Cha'tima, The Caller, saying, "Convince the people to continue their journey to the surface of the great tortoise."

So Cha'tima came to the camp of the people and told them of the bright world that awaited. "Build canoes and follow the silver river until you reach it," he instructed.

But the people did not believe his words, and Ogima, which is the name that was given to the chief of the people, said, "We will not follow you. This is a good place, and we are safe here. You may be The Trickster in disguise come to lead us to danger."

Cha'tima went to Red Horn and said, "The people would not listen to me. They are afraid."

Then Red Horn sent Eagle to the people bearing a giant fish in his talons. Eagle set the fish before Ogima and said, "Red Horn has sent you this proof of the good things that await at the next level of your journey."

The people cooked the giant fish and it was good to eat. Some of the people said, "Perhaps we should do as Cha'tima instructed;" and they set about building canoes.

Some of the people did not agree. They spoke to Ogima saying, "Great Chief, here we have much food and good water. Why should we take this great journey because of one fish? Are there not already fish in the river?"

When he heard these words, the chief was moved, and he ordered the men to stop building canoes. "We will stay here in this good camp," he said, and the council of warriors agreed.

Eagle flew back to Red Horn and told of Ogima's decision, Red Horn was angry that the people did not continue their journey. He was determined that they would come to the surface of the great tortoise which is the world. So, he called White Otter Woman to him and told her to visit the people.

When Ogima saw White Otter Woman his heart was moved. Instantly he fell in love with her and asked her to share his tipi.

Knowing that Ogima loved her so strongly that he would follow her, White Otter Woman slipped into the silver river and swam away.

Ogima ordered the people to make canoes, and jumping into the first canoe, he paddled furiously after White Otter Woman. He followed her all the way to the surface of the world, where he saw the sun and realized that Red Horn had sent his messengers so the people could live in a place of bounty.

Because it was White Otter Woman who brought the first people to the world of the sun, we women do the sun dance and honor Red Horn and the help he has given us.

ΩΩΩΩΩ

"Remember, my daughter," Yquili Sparrow continued, "men may carry the bows and throw the lances. They may even shoot the guns of the White Man, but it is women who truly lead because we know the ways of the heart, the ways of love and desire, and they are more powerful than any weapons."

Many years later, Happy Turtle and Sapphira Cook had talked of love. "Small Deer loves you, doesn't he?" Sapphira had asked.

"I imagine he does, but I do not know if I love him. Whom do you love, Sapphira?"

The young girl had thought for a moment, smiled, and answered, "I do not know. Perhaps I shall someday find another world in which I shall truly love."

When she heard Sapphira's words, Happy Turtle had understood her mother's story.

The train jerked away from the station. Sapphira looked back, waved to her parents, then turned her head to the east. "Once I dreamed of finding a new world in which there would be someone for me to love, she thought. "Perhaps I will find a new home in Indiana. Perhaps I will find a man whom I will want."

The young woman drifted off to the rhythm of the wheels and the thoughts of perhaps.

Part Two ~ The World Awaits

Chapter 20 ~ Home

"Dinah." At her mother's voice, the girl stiffened, tightening her hold on the shallow basket which she held against the curve of her hip. She turned her almond-brown face towards the great red barn and wished herself inside currying one of the horses. Dinah loved horses; she was less fond of her mother. Rachel Tideswell may have loved her only child, but Dinah couldn't quite suppress the resentments she felt in return.

Slowly, Dinah took another handful of feed and held it out, allowing the seeds and kernels to drop undistributed to the dusky, bare ground where the family chickens competed for their food. It seemed too much effort to move her arm in an arc and spread the feed. If only she were a boy, then she'd be working in the barn. Perhaps she'd even be helping to build the new structure, not as grand as the barn but even more enthralling. That was where they would be kept, the new animals, brought by railroad from the far West. Real Injun horses. "The best riding horse on the continent," Broadmore Tideswell had declared, and as the breeder of the finest animals in Pennsylvania, perhaps the entire United States, he was surely the one to know.

Dinah took another handful of feed and again dribbled it through her fingers. Her mind was on the drawings her father had shown them one night at table. Those horses, with their spotted coats—some dark with white spots and the others just the opposite—were said to be stunning. Their faces looked so calm yet intelligent. At least that was what the magazine article said. Reading that article, Dinah had fallen in love with Appaloosa ponies and with the wild tribe of Indians who were so determined to evade the cavalry. She imagined herself astride one of those ponies riding away from the tiny Pennsylvania town of Newville, to where she had no idea, but away to freedom from her mother's insistent voice.

"Dinah, I need thee." Straightening her back for a moment to ease the strain of ironing, Rachel shook her head sadly. Broadmore did not stint in hiring help for care of the horses and fields, but she had only their twelve-year-old daughter, and she more interested in the animals Broadmore raised and sold than in cooking, laundry, and cleaning. "No help at all," Rachel had often said, "not even with the garden or the chickens."

Of course, there was Molly Stillwell. "Thank God for The Widow Stillwell," Broadmore had laughed more than once as he tucked into a loaf of bread or a fresh apple pie. For all her domestic skills, Rachel had never mastered the art of baking. Molly came three days a week with new loaves, cakes, pies, and the like. In return, she received five dollars every week and the care of her horse and buggy. Three times a week—Tuesday, Thursday, and Saturday—her buggy, loaded with food, Molly would come no matter the weather. The two women would sip a cup of dandelion tea and share what news there was. Newville offered little excitement and the labors of womenfolk offered even less time for sharing. Even though Molly was a Mennonite, she was company, and Rachel was duly thankful for those three hours of conversation each week, as thankful as Broadmore was for the good baking.

"Where is that child?" Rachel used the back of her hand to push sweaty hair back from her eyes.

"Dinah!"

Her mother's tone left no room for dallying. "I'm coming, Mother." Dinah took one last handful of feed and threw it to the ground.

"I was feeding the chickens," Dinah said as she strolled through the kitchen door.

"As slowly as thou couldst, I'm sure." Rachel saw but did not comment on her daughter's smirk. That evening she'd have another talk with Broadmore, and he would, no doubt, take his belt to their daughter's backside. A tactic that had never helped. Even as a baby, Dinah had been difficult, but now with womanhood approaching she had become intolerable. These last months she had menstruated, and her breasts had ripened.

"I'd like to give her back." How many times had Rachel sad that only to have her husband respond with a clucking or a "There, there," as if she did not mean her words.

"You might take in one of those Indian girls," Molly had suggested weeks before. "Major Pratt trains them up right well, and you only need pay them one dollar a week as long as you give them good Christian teaching."

"A lazy Indian to help Dinah find ways to not do her chores? I think not." Despite her comment, the idea had not left Rachel's mind. Now Miriam, a Sioux from the Dakotas, was helping Molly bake Broadmore's favorite shoofly pies and the yeasty rolls she so loved, and Rachel was going to present the idea at dinner that evening. Just today, Molly had brought a fluffy honey cake which would provide the perfect timing to introduce the notion.

"Why she'll be saving us, not costing. No need to have Mrs. Stillwell do our baking when we have a girl to do that and more for a dollar a week and found." Surely that would do the trick. Broadmore could never resist a savings, except where his precious horses were concerned. Those animals were the food on their table and the roof over their heads, and for that, Rachel Tideswell was grateful. But, her husband's preoccupation with them, the love and care he lavished on them, that was another matter.

Dipping her hand in the starch-water, Rachel sprinkled Broadmore's white shirt, the one he would wear to meeting on the morrow. Brushing back her hair once again, she took a hot iron from the stove. Wetting her finger with spittle, she tested the plate.

"Take these clothes upstairs," Rachel instructed, accompanying the words with a gesture of her head, "and mind thou puts them away properly."

"Yes, Mother." Dinah did not move.

Rachel glanced up—only for a moment lest her husband's best shirt be scorched. "Why dost thou linger, daughter?"

"I was wondering ...?"

The silence hung.

"If thou hast a question, then ask it."

"I ..." Dinah watched the rhythmic movement of her mother's iron, watched her mother's mouth purse with concentration, and knew that she had to ask.

"Yes?"

"Why can I not help with the horses?" she blurted out.

There it was, her great desire. It would surely be an answer to her frustrations.

"Again? How many times have we had this discussion? It is not seemly. Thy father has said this, I have said this, even Elder Brandon has said this. Thou are a woman, not a stable boy. Now, do as I have said."

Rachel could hear the basket of clean, ironed clothes banging against the walls as Dinah stomped up the stairs.

***

The three Tideswells ate their noon meal in the dining room. Sometimes they were joined by a visitor, perhaps Elder Jonathan Brandon. He led the worship at meeting and was the finest harness-maker and lorimer in the county—some said in the entire commonwealth. Or, Jeremiah Cooper, the farrier, and from time to time a customer wanting a fine carriage horse, a brood mare, or even the services of Free Mason or one of the other fine stallions, whose seed was prized by farmers, carriage owners, and draymen alike. It would have been easier to eat in the kitchen, but Rachel demanded that their one "family meal" of the day be more formal, more genteel. "How else will Dinah learn proper etiquette?"

Broadmore, having no adequate response and not really caring, had agreed. So, whilst the hired help ate their lunches in the barn or fields, Broadmore would join his wife and daughter—all the while wishing he were back at work with his horses. For all her efforts and wishes, Rachel could not make those lunches more than silent, quick repasts. Some days, the only time her husband would speak at table were a few words of thanks to the Almighty. "Thank Thee for these victuals and for Thy blessings on this house." And oft as not, he would add, "And may Sunrise's new foal be healthy," or if there were a visitor, "May Free Mason stand well to stud."

Breakfast and dinner were, however, very different. Those were eaten family style around the great oak table in the kitchen. All seven of them would be there, even Mose, the negra who had manumitted himself from the rice plantations of the Carolinas during the late war and who seemed to Broadmore to know more about horses than any man should.

Rachel would, with grudging assistance from her daughter, bring great platters of food to the table. Then one of them, more often than not Burton Miles, whose father had apprenticed him to Broadmore in exchange for two fine draft horses, called a blessing down on them all. It was not that Burton was particularly religious, but he was a growing boy and always hungry. There was no way he was going to allow the chicken or roast to go cold waiting for somebody else's words. "Bless this house and all within. May the horses thrive, and the hay be sweet. In Jesus name we say—"

And the others would chorus "Amen."

The conversation would turn and twist. Matthew and Luke, the Frazier boys, whose father— the Elder Brandon had told Broadmore— had gone off to save the Union when they were toddlers and never returned, telling tales and jokes while stuffing their faces and pushing at one another like they had never grown. When their momma died, some say at her own hand, the two boys had found their way from one home to another until Elder Brandon intervened. "Broadmore, you take these boys in and work them hard, and I'll see to their moral teaching."

Seeing only cheap labor, Broadmore had agreed. Three years later, he often rued the day. Two lazier young men had never lived, nor more careless, nor hungrier. At least the members of the meeting respected him for his charity, and the Frazier boys, if separated from one another and properly supervised, could shovel the stalls and lay fresh hay.

"Molly Stillwell says she is most excellent trained. Thou canst taste the proof." Rachel licked the last of the honey from her fingers.

"I will think on it," Broadmore replied, "and we will talk."

"If she can bake like this," Matthew commented, "she would make somebody a fine wife." He nudged his brother under the table.

"And why would she marry you when she could have me?" Luke demanded, nudging back.

"As long as you invite me to dinner, I don't mind which of you she marries," Burton said.

Mose, ignoring the discussion, asked, "Might there be another portion of that fine cake?" And before the others realized, he was well tucked into the last piece.

Dinah said nothing. Another pair of hands would certainly help with the chores she so detested, but they would not get her a step closer to the horse barns, and they would certainly not solve the biggest problem of her life. She saw no solution for that, and the helplessness burned as rage within.

"Wife, thou must tell Molly Stillwell to add honey cake to my list of favorites." Broadmore took a long draught of buttermilk. "Well, boys, bed the horses well and then off to your prayers. Tomorrow comes soon, and we have work to do. Those Injun ponies will be arriving in but three days, four at most, and we must have the new barn and paddocks ready."

Chapter 21 ~ Sin

The air was cold and there was a hard pack of morning frost still on the ground. Dinah Tideswell was on her way that morning to receive instruction in the Quaker faith. She pulled her shawl tight with her left hand, wishing that her blue sweater, the one Grandmother Foster had knitted just for her and only a year earlier, still fit. But Dinah's breast had budded; even when she bound them as her mother had taught her, the sweater was too tight. Soon it would be passed along to a younger girl, one from the meeting who was not yet maturing. That would be soon, but Dinah was loath to give up such a dear possession.

In her right hand, Dinah carried her Holy Bible, The Rules of Discipline, and her slate. She hurried along, aware that Elder Brandon would be waiting.

"Thou dost not want to grow up a heathen." How often had her mother enjoined her thus? How often had her father added, "Thou must find God before thou findest a husband"? Finding God was not easy. Sitting in meeting waiting for God to find her was even more difficult. Every First Day meeting, Dinah's thoughts were not of the Almighty but of the great barn in which Matthew and Luke were no doubt sleeping off their breakfasts.

"We'd surely go with thee were there not so much work, Mr. Tideswell," they would say, "but there's tack to clean and currying to be done."

Broadmore always relented. In the tug-o-war of his heart, his horses always won, even if he knew right well that the boys would give a lick at this and a promise at that before taking advantage.

Burton might have preferred staying with the Frazier brothers, but his parents attended the same meeting and it was understood that sharing worship with them was part of his apprenticeship. And, while he would have died of embarrassment to admit it, the young apprentice was more than glad to see Ann Lancaster and perhaps even receive a smile in return for his adoring gazes.

Mose, a man of deep faith and Baptist conviction, rode the grey mare to the colored church near Osterman's Crossroads. Most Sundays he didn't return until after dinner. Rachel would leave him a covered plate even though he often told her, "Never you mind, Mistress Tideswell, I get fed real well by Widow Jones." Each time he said, "I get fed real well …" Mose would chuckle like it was a great joke, and Rachel would answer, "God understands your need."

God may well have understood, but Dinah hadn't an inkling.

On this day, as they did once every month, Dinah and two other girls would meet with Elder Brandon. "For thy religious education that thou might better follow the Lord," her mother had explained. Dinah disliked the hour spent in talk of scripture, but it was better than the interminable hours spent in First Day silence waiting for somebody, anybody, to speak.

And when they did speak, what did such comments matter? Why should she care if they sent money to help bring the Word of God to heathens in places like Idaho, the Dakotas, and that mountainous place filled with Blackfooted savages? Once, Frederick Clwyd had spoken of making a joyous noise and had said he wanted to sing praise. Within the month, he had left the meeting. "Joined the Methodists," Broadmore had said, as if Mr. Clwyd had condemned himself to death.

No matter, when the Clwyds needed a new draught horse, Dinah's father had been more than willing to do business, even giving them the same ten-dollar discount he gave all the members of the meeting.

At least on Sabbath days for meeting, the Tideswells used the Rockaway pulled by the handsome gelding Prince. Her father would sit in the front tipping his hat and nodding to the drivers of passing coaches and traps. Broadmore also kept a wary eye on Burton, who was learning the art of driving and whose hands and mind often drifted away from the task.

Dinah would sit with her mother in the rear seat. It would have been an ideal opportunity for a mother-daughter conversation, but Rachel wouldn't talk before meeting. "Hush, girl, I must set my thought on Him." It was as if the meeting had already begun even on the way. And on the ride home, Rachel was always on about the chores that lay ahead. If the hours spent at Meeting and then mingling had lightened the burdens on her spirit, for Rachel it was clear that those hours had increased the burdens on her time.

Dinah wished her father would allow her to ride to these meetings with the Elder. Her parents may not have approved of her interest in the horses or her un-ladylike skill astride, but they certainly knew that she could safely trot the two miles on one of the ponies.

"It would save an hour and leave me less tired for my duties," Dinah had tried.

Broadmore might have given in, but Rachel held firm. "Better thou shouldest think on thy lessons, Daughter. The time thou spendest walking home can be put to better use for thy spirit than for any of thy earthly chores."

A dog barked from the adjacent field, squeezed under the rail fencing, and ran to greet her. Dinah stopped for a moment to pat her, allowing her shawl to drape open on her shoulders. "Art thou a Friendly dog or a Methodist?" Dinah asked. "I'll wager thy voice is better for howling than for hymns."

Shivering, Dinah pulled her shawl tighter and walked on, the stray hard by her heels. The girl looked down at her new companion, "Why, thou art pregnant. Who might the father be? Was it that hound of the Peterman's? I hear him baying often enough. My father says he is always after one or another female. Indeed, Father says he might just go after the mares or the cows if he dost not find a willing bitch."

With a companion by her side and occasionally jumping up to snatch at her shawl's fringe, Dinah was reminded of the better side of this monthly religious discussion, the two other girls who would be there. Polly Smyth was a good enough friend, someone with whom Dinah would share an apple while walking by Big Spring Creek on a late summer day, even someone with whom she might talk of her dreams, dreams of someday visiting Philadelphia or even New York City.

But it was Ann Lancaster who really mattered. A second cousin on her mother's side, Ann was only a year younger than Dinah. They were, to use her mother's phrase, "thick as thieves." After meeting, if Broadmore and Rachel were not in a mood to rush home, the two girls would sit under a hickory or climb the old Beech and talk away as if they had a lifetime of absences to share.

They would chatter away until Burton would come looking for Dinah. "Thy father told me to find thee," he would say. The girls would giggle knowing full well that he had volunteered. It was no secret that Burton was in love with Ann. He had told Mathew and Luke, had even asked advice from Mose, who had assured him that Lady Love came in time and there was no way to rush her.

Thinking of her friends, Dinah found the walking easier. "It is chilly," she said to the dog, "but it is a lovely day."

***

Elder Brandon's black mare was hitched by the meetinghouse door. She whinnied once hoping for a treat. Dinah bent down and patted the dog one last time. "Go home," she commanded. The dog backed off a few paces and lay down in a patch of sun.

Dinah pulled a handful of grass and walked over to the mare. "Here you go," she whispered in the horse's ear as the animal chomped on the grass.

"I have been expecting thee," Elder Brandon called from the meetinghouse door. "We have much to discuss this day."

It was only after she had passed through the entrance hall with its scrapers for snowy and muddy boots and its hooks for coats and capes and had entered the dimly lit great room of the meetinghouse that Dinah became uncomfortable. "Where are the others?"

Usually, Dinah was the last of the girls to arrive. This day neither Polly nor Ann was there.

Elder Brandon busied himself with the Franklin stove. "'Tis chilly out today," he said as he clunked pieces of split log into the firebox; "we shall be wanting some warmth."

"But where is Ann?" Dinah asked. "And Polly?"

The man slowly straightened. "I wanted to speak with thee alone, Miss Tideswell. Polly and Ann are younger, and there are things which thou shouldst know but of which they are too young." He rubbed his hands together and then gestured towards one of the benches. "Sit thee down, and we shall discourse." The stocky man's breath, heavy with garlic and tobacco, drove the girl back. Almost faint with the smell of it, she sat on the bench nearest the stove. Despite the heat, she kept her shawl tight around herself. Being alone with Elder Brandon made her uncomfortable. While the meeting had agreed John Brandon would supervise the education of their young, the adults had not asked the children their opinion. If they had, the great preference would have been for Elijah Crenshaw, who was the elder responsible for the building maintenance. Indeed, it was Elder Crenshaw who had piled the wood with which Brandon had so wastefully overfilled the stove. For all its size and the leakiness of its simple shake walls, the great room was soon overheated.

Elder Brandon had been talking about prison reform, a topic given great attention in the current Rules_of_Discipline. Since the end of The War Between the States, two topics had taken on great weight within the various meetings: prison reform and the Indian wars. In John Brandon's eyes the solution to both problems was clear and singular. "If people, be they fallen or savage, come to know Christ, then they, like George Fox, will come to know that *'here is one, even, Christ Jesus, who can speak to thy condition.'*"

Pacing back and forth in front of Dinah, speaking with great energy, and gesturing with each word, Elder Brandon repeated that oft quoted line so central to the teachings of the *valiant sixty*, "*'here is one, even, Christ Jesus, who can speak to thy condition.'* Dost thou understand, Miss Tideswell, what this means?"

Dinah, not knowing what the correct answer might be, nodded her head.

"It means that thou must submit to the will of God, that thou must trust Christ Jesus to know what is best, that thou must accept thy condition no matter what it may be as part of His plan for thy betterment. Dost thou know what it says in the scripture?" The Elder continued without waiting for her answer, "'Humble thyself therefore under the mighty hand of God, that he may exalt thee in due time.' And how dost thou properly humble thyself?"

John Brandon stopped his pacing. He was standing directly in front of Dinah, looking down at her, his eyes filled with an intensity that confused and scared the young girl. He took off his coat and unbuttoned and removed his vest revealing the perspiration that had soaked though the linen of his collarless shirt. Putting the coat and vest next to Dinah, he stared at her for a moment which seemed in her mind to stretch on forever.

His hands fumbled with his wide, black galluses, slipping them from his slightly stooped shoulders. When the suspenders hung by his sides, he reached down and pulled at the shawl, which Dinah now held with tightfisted terror. Brandon pulled harder until Dinah's grip gave way.

"Today, thy test is a simple one; canst thou return the love of one who truly lovest thee? Can thou understand that the love of a good man is like unto the love of God and that thy submission is a show of thy reverence for Christ Jesus?"

As he spoke, Brandon was fumbling with the buttons of Dinah's dress, pulling at the cloth with which she had bound her breasts, touching her in ways that made her feel confused, angry, and unclean. She pulled away and pleaded with the older man to stop, but he did not. He kissed her on the mouth and on the breasts. His fingers found her maidenhood even as she screamed in terror.

Brandon slipped the button of his trousers. As they fell to his ankles, he pulled down his long, cotton underwear revealing his genitals.

It was only in that moment that Dinah understood the full nature of what the man intended. Even as he mauled at her, even as her heart filled with horror, Dinah thought of Peterman's hound and of Free Mason's excited neighs and stomps when a ready mare had been brought to his service. In that moment, Dinah laughed. She was not sure why. Assuredly, it was part in fear. But there was more. For all the times she had seen a tumescent cock in the barn and the fields, she had never before seen a man's. And this man, so old, so indifferent of frame or face, and so filled with himself; how small he looked. Why the Billy goat that shared a stall with Prince was better endowed. There was no question that even Burton, the youngest of her father's workers, would be a better stud, and he only a boy.

Dinah looked at Elder Brandon standing revealed and tumescent with desire and expectation, and she laughed harder than she had ever laughed before.

Embarrassed, the man mumbled incomprehensibly, pulled his underwear and pants up, slipped his arms through his galluses, grabbed his coat and vest, and—without finishing his dressing or saying another word—fled the meetinghouse. She heard the whinny of Brandon's horse, then the man's angry shout. Dinah knew the poor horse would pay the price of her own laughter.

Dinah straightened her appearance, but she didn't stand. Suddenly, the laughter ended, she felt a sadness so profound as to seem that the darkest of nights settled upon her. Even when Mose came to find her, riding the sway-backed, grey mare and leading Lightening, the gentlest of her father's stock, she sat statue-still, making no sound.

On the ride home, Mose asked, "Miss Dinah, why is you so late? There be something the matter you stay so long when the other girls and the elder done gone?"

Dinah made no response. She knew that she would never speak of that day, not to Mose, not to her parents, not even to Ann.

As she and Mose rode home that afternoon, a shell of hardness formed around Dinah's heart. Only God would understand its cause. "*Here is one, even, Christ Jesus, who can speak to thy condition.*" Dinah thought, and she cursed God for what had happened.

It was only when they arrived at her parents' farm that Dinah realized she had left her books and slate at the meetinghouse. It didn't matter. She hoped she would never see them again, but she knew John Brandon would make sure that she did. He was not a man who would let this day's embarrassment or his desire pass.

Thus had begun the anger and sadness which burned inside Dinah Tideswell. Her mother's scolding and her father's strap did nothing to relieve the pain; they only hardened her heart against them and against that Christ Jesus who did not speak, not one word to her condition.

The Elder Brandon had not touched her again, not with his hands, but with his eyes and with his words, that was another matter. How often had he visited the farm since that day, sitting at table and staring at her until Dinah, unable to bear another moment, would avert her own eyes? How many times had he said the grace and thanks be to God for the "beauty" of this world? What was it about the way he pronounced that word? Perhaps it was the way he would look up, look at her, and lick his lips and all the while his hands, those evil hands, folded in the mockery of piety. Dinah had wanted to scream, but she knew there was nothing she could say, nothing that her parents would believe, nothing that would not hold her up to ridicule and perhaps ostracism. She held her tongue but certainly not her inner peace.

Chapter 22 ~ Arrival

The apple trees were turning from white flowers to tiny green fruit. The farm was awash with sweet odors. From the barns and paddocks newborn voices were trying their new whinnies. Spring was a wonderful time unless one suffered, as did Luke Frazier, with fits of sneezing and running eyes. So constantly did the young man rub at his nostrils with the rough calico handkerchief that his nose had turned raw and red.

Matthew took no pity on his younger brother. "Stop that honking," he would enjoin with every painful sneeze. This comment always set Burton to laughter. Part of Burton's humor was based on truth. Luke's sneezing did sound more goose than human and without the distraction of his brother's allergic discomfort, Matthew would often turn his skills at torment towards the younger boy.

Dinah sat at the parlor window watching the empty road. It would only be a matter of minutes before her mother would call to remind her of the work that needed doing. Today they were beating rugs. Too heavy for clothesline, the rugs were dragged, one at a time and set on a pole which Broadmore and the Frazier boys had specially erected for the purpose.

Her father had groused and grumbled about the enterprise as he had done every spring Dinah could remember. There were better things to be done he said, what with the stock to be cared for and especially with the new Appaloosas, which had been delivered weeks before. Broadmore was enraptured with these new horses. Dinah was as well, but she was not allowed into the new, small barn where they were housed. Whenever possible, she watched them cavort about their paddocks. Her heart had been stolen by the week-old foal who followed his mother, poking at her teats and then, suddenly flicking his tail, would buck and gambol off almost tripping in his enthusiasm.

"Get back to thy mother. She needs thy help," Broadmore had said to her more than once. Dinah didn't care if her father disapproved or not, she loved horses far more than housework.

"What's taking thee so long, Dinah?" Rachel called. "That small rug needs a good beating." Even as she spoke, Rachel shook her head at her daughter's dallying. "Perhaps it would be more use to beat that child than the rug," she thought.

Dinah picked up one end of the throw rug that lay by the parlor door and dragged it down the hall toward the kitchen.

"Pick it up! Child, thou becomes more exasperating with each day."

Had the doors not been open to the beauty of the day, Dinah wouldn't have heard the buggy arrive. "They're here," she yelled as she dropped the edge of the rug and ran out the front door.

Rachel followed her daughter down the hall. She had been expecting this arrival, expecting and reluctantly accepting, but anger still welled within.

"Thou hast the girl," her husband had said, "she should be help enough." Rachel, disappointed, thought that had been an end of the matter. Molly Stillwell's suggestion had been dismissed as easily as Broadmore might slip off his boots at the end of the day — an act which all too often left crumbled mud and a crust of manure piled next to their bed for Rachel to clean come morning.

But it had not been an end. The horse farmer had contacted Major Pratt and his Indian school in Carlisle. His purpose had been not help for her, but another hand in the barns, an Injun boy to work with his new Injun horses. "He'll know their ways better 'n a white man or even Mose, 'count of them being his kin," Broadmore had explained his decision and taken his pipe to the porch where he smoked and rocked until Rachel, having given up in frustration, had stomped to bed.

Broadmore knew his wife was unhappy but help with the Appaloosas was important. It was after all business, that which kept the food on their table and the clothing on their backs. "Besides," he told himself, "Dinah will come 'round. She's a mite difficult, but John Brandon won't give up on her. Surely in time she'll find her way to Christ. We've given her a proper home and upbringing, and she shall come around." Of that Dinah's father was sure, as sure as he knew the new horses would prove profitable and that the first Appaloosa foal would be just fine for all the colt's tendency to trip over his own feet. "Just let him grow into himself," he had told Burton. "Just like thee, it's a question of growing into himself."

Broadmore hoped his new helper would grow into himself faster than Burton or the Frazier boys seemed to be progressing. "They say this Major has them lads well trained up," he had told Elijah Crenshaw after meeting two weeks before.

The elder had nodded his agreement as the two men shook hands. It was only that First Day evening, after he had talked with Elijah Crenshaw and a few of the other men, after they had finished their supper, that Broadmore Tideswell announced his plans to his wife. Once again, he had sat on the porch smoking whilst Rachel sat on the edge of their bed and cried for his bitter insensitivity.

The new Injun boy was due this very morning. As glad as she was for the interruption to spring housecleaning, Dinah was ready to hate the new farmhand. After all, he would be where she dreamed of being, working with the horses, while for her, his presence would mean one more plate to wash and one more meal to prepare.

The girl stood at the bottom of the porch steps and watched the buggy bounce up the rutted drive. She didn't turn around as her mother came to a stop beside her.

"Go tell thy father that the Major and his Injun are here," Rachel instructed.

Dinah did not respond.

"Didst thou not hear me, child?"

Dinah muttered and walked slowly towards the barn. Rachel wanted to call her back to ask what she had muttered, but the mother decided another fight—especially in front of this well-known stranger, would be a fool's pursuit.

Instead the woman stepped forward. "Major Pratt? Welcome to our farm."

There were three of them in the buggy. The major, an older, taller man wearing an army uniform sat in the back. The two on the front bench also wore uniforms, but not of official army issue. One was older, a full-grown man. The second was a boy, presumably the new hand. It was the boy who was driving the two-horse team. Rachel noticed how the boy's body seemed to rise and fall with the horses' gait. "Just what Broadmore wanted," she thought.

The full-grown man jumped off the front seat and offered his hand to the officer. Pratt stepped down, ignoring the proffered assistance. "Mrs. Tideswell?" he boomed as he moved forward.

Although the reins fell loose in his hands, the boy easily held the team in check.

"Major Pratt, won't thou come in? Our daughter has just gone for Mr. Tideswell."

"Get down, Harry, get down," Pratt said to the boy. "This is your new home. You listen well to what Mr. and Mrs. Tideswell tell you and do as they say, and this will be a happy place for you, of that I'm sure."

As Pratt spoke, the boy cocked his head to one side.

"You might notice he holds his head a trifle queer. Don't pay that no mind, Ma'am. Boy's a bit deaf in one ear; nothing that gets in the way of his work."

Broadmore reached them and said, "Major Pratt, delighted to meet thee, sir. Is this our new worker?" he added looking at the older of the two men by the buggy.

"No, no." Pratt chuckled. "That's Samuel. He drives for me. The boy here, Harry, he's your hand, and a good one I might add, real good with horses."

Broadmore looked the teenager over. "Not much older than Dinah," he thought. "Sinewy, but doesn't look any stronger than Burton. Most likely dumber than Luke and Matthew combined. Don't know what I'm getting into."

"What about religion?" Pratt asked suddenly, interrupting Broadmore's thoughts. "I understand you folks are Quakers, and we have a firm policy that the children must receive good Christian education. You folks have a Christian can teach him right from wrong?"

Broadmore knew there was no point in arguing questions of faith. Besides, he wasn't sure how the rest of the meeting would react to an Indian boy worshiping with them. That wasn't the same as charity, not the same as sending money and old clothes to naked savages far to the West.

However, Broadmore had already been told of the possible problem, and it had been easily solved. "One of my hands, Mose, he's a Baptist, goes to the colored church over to Osterman's Crossroads. He'll take the boy on Sundays. I don't imagine there'll be any problems. Course, he'll have to come back on his own. Mose spends Sundays with his own kind, and he made it right clear that church was one thing, but—"

"That'll be just fine," Pratt responded. The two men shook hands.

"You get your roll from the back of the buggy, and Mr. Tideswell'll show you where you'll be sleeping." As he spoke, Pratt ran his hand through the boy's brown hair. "You do right by these folks, Harry, and I'm sure they'll do right by you. Work hard and do as you're told."

While the officer spoke, the boy, his head still cocked to the side, looked up at the man's face and nodded. "Yes, sir." He stood almost at military attention.

"Your roll, boy," Pratt reminded.

Harry moved towards the back of the buggy, stopping twice to look back at the Major, who gestured him onward.

"Burton," Broadmore yelled. The boy appeared from the corner of the house. Broadmore was sure that the other hands were hiding there as well, hiding and watching this new addition.

"Take Harry here to the barn and show him where you all sleep. Then have your lunch, and make sure Harry is fed as well."

"Major, wouldst thou break bread with us?" Broadmore asked. "Thy driver and the boy can join the men while thou joins Mrs. Tideswell and myself."

As her father spoke, Dinah moved forward as if to remind him of her presence. My daughter, Dinah." She bobbed a curtsey, and the major doffed his cap.

"A pleasure to meet you, Miss Tideswell."

"And, of course thou hast met my wife."

"A pleasure to meet you, Ma'am." Pratt's deep bow was accompanied by the martial click of his heels.

"Thou best hurry, Burton, all the victuals will be gone before thou and this Injun lad get to them."

"Yes, sir." Burton trotted off.

With quick glances over his shoulder, the boy followed Burton around the edge of the house and towards his new life. It had been almost three years since the Indian Agent had put him on the railroad heading to Pennsylvania. Lonely Cricket had learned much during that time, but there were still nights when he thought of his parents and of his sister. On those lonely nights, he would hold the cloth turtle his sister had given him, and he would tell the turtle's spirit that someday he would return to his home.

It had been almost three years, and now he was in a new place with new people who would call him Harry.

Chapter 23 ~ If We But Listen

"Is that thy god?"

Lonely Cricket had not heard her coming. He turned towards the girl, his mouth slightly open in surprise, and did not answer.

She asked again, "Is that thy god?" She pointed at the cloth turtle he held in his left hand.

Lonely Cricket laughed. "God? Like your Jesus?" He held his arms out at shoulder height.

Dinah started to laugh stopped herself. "Thou must not mock the Lord."

"It is toy. My sister give when come Pennsylvania. I talk to turtle and think sister hear."

They stood silent for a moment—he looking at the stars and the half-moon above, she searching out the boy's features in the dim light. His arms where sinewy yet muscled—his nose jutting from between raven-black eyes and his dusky skin—not so like Molly Stillwell's girl but ruddier more than red. And, the way he held his head cocked to one side as she spoke.

"Why art thou out here?" she asked. "Thou should be in bed. There is work to do in the morning, there will be—"

"Talk to sister. Talk to turtle. Talk to stars, moon. Lonely Cricket need talk."

"Lonely Cricket?" she repeated the words.

The boy put his hand on his chest. "Lonely Cricket my name."

There was another moment of silence. "Oh, I thought thy name is Harry?"

"When Pennsylvania, Major Pratt say must have White Man name. Harry Cook my friend. I take name. Major Pratt want my name Absalom from Jesus book, but I say, 'Harry' and Major say all right."

"But thy name is Lonely Cricket?"

"Yes. Lonely Cricket."

"What does it mean?"

He imitated the sound of a cricket. Dinah laughed. Lonely Cricket looked down.

"I'm sorry. I did not mean to laugh at thee."

He shrugged his shoulders, which Dinah noted were broad for his frame, and looked towards the sky. "It cricket sound. I am cricket all by self."

After another pause, Lonely Cricket asked, "What you do here?"

"It's my home. My parents' home."

"No, what you do here?" This time he pointed to the ground at their feet.

"Oh, I came out here to pray. Do you know pray?"

"Our Father, who art in Heaven …" He stopped.

"No, not that kind of pray. Yes, that kind, but not those words. My words, talk with God." Dinah could feel her tongue stumbling to find the right words.

"You talk God? What God say?"

"I don't know. Some of the grownups in meeting say they hear God's voice, but I cannot."

"It hard to hear words of silence."

Her mother had warned Dinah to be careful of this strange boy. "He may have come to Carlisle to learn, but he is still a savage."

To Dinah the young Indian didn't seem a savage at all; he seemed the gentlest of all the boys she knew.

"Do you like the horses?" she asked.

"Yes, the Appoosas," he said, mispronouncing the breed.

Dinah laughed. Even though he knew that this time she was laughing at him, the boy was not embarrassed. The sound of her laughter reminded him of Sapphira Cook. It carried the warmth of the summer yet to come and of secrets to be shared. Tears came to Lonely Cricket's eyes. He wiped them away with the back of his hand.

"I'm sorry. Don't cry. I did not mean to laugh at thee."

"I not cry because of laugh. I cry for friend. Does she think of Lonely Cricket? Do sister … parents think of Lonely Cricket?" He buried his eyes in the back of the cloth turtle.

"I love them," Dinah volunteered, "especially the foal. Isn't he cute the way he stumbles over his own feet?"

Lonely Cricket didn't answer. He was thinking of Maggie and wondering if Sapphira still rode the gelding to school. He hoped Nathan Wainright was taking care of his horse, but Lonely Cricket feared for her. He stood looking into the dark and said nothing.

"I suppose I should go back inside. It's getting a bit chilly." Dinah shivered slightly. She knew it was not the temperature.

"Yes, he good animal. He grow be good horse."

It took Dinah a moment to realize that Lonely Cricket was answering her question.

"That's what my father says."

There was silence except for a slight rustling of new-sprung leaves.

***

"He's a good boy," Mose reported to Broadmore Tideswell. "Cares something fierce about them horses."

Perhaps that was the problem, that Harry cared too much about the horses. Perhaps it was that the Frazier boys wanted no part of an Injun. Perhaps it was just their way, especially Matthew's, just plain meanness to others. Whatever the reason, the Fraziers tried to torment him. What they could not understand was Harry's patient acceptance of their taunts and pranks. He would not rise to their bait, preferring to think while the Trickster might test him—try to lead him astray—a man must trust in himself and in the ways he knew to be right.

Burton Miles didn't follow the two older boys. He was afraid of them, so he didn't oppose their tricks and taunts; neither did he join in. Sometimes, like this morning, he even tried to help.

The Fraziers had dropped manure and dirt in the two troughs from which the Appaloosas normally drank. Taking care of the five horses and the foal was Harry's primary responsibility. He had taken the horses to the paddock that morning and watched them approach and then crow-hop back from the two large containers. Now the troughs needed to be emptied, cleaned and refilled.

The cleaning finished, Burton was helping Harry carry pail after pail of clean water from the pump. "What are you going to do?" Burton asked.

"Do?"

"To get even. To teach them."

"I do nothing. If they not learn, they never be men."

Burton weighed Harry's words. While his new friend's words were much like the words he would hear each week at Meeting, Burton couldn't suppress his own anger at the two bullies.

"He's a hard worker all around," Broadmore observed. "Even when I put him to something new, he learns quick and works hard."

"He's right good with all the stock; gets milk from the cows just as easy as he drives a horse or gathers eggs. Never scares them. Never rough," Mose added.

"Burton seems to have taken a shine."

"Yes, Massa Broadmore, he sure has. Works harder around the Injun than around those other two."

"They just seem more worthless than ever they were."

Mose laughed. "Worthless ain't the half of it. They downright mean; make the rest of us work extra." Mose, having often heard their whispered slurs directed at himself and seen their mischief, had for some time hoped his employer would let the Fraziers go. Mose knew that Broadmore could find better help. If nowhere else, Mose could find him two good men at the Baptist church. There were many more

Negroes who had drifted north since the war, men who would be happy to have a job for good grub, a place to sleep, and a dollar a week.

"I know. I know." Broadmore scratched his head. "They ain't worth much, Mose, and I've surely been tolerant of them. I'd let them go were it not for John Brandon. I know not his reason, but he has taken interest in those two and asks my Christian forbearance.

"As an elder in the meeting he has asked and as my friend he has asked. It is hard to know how—"

"If they was to leaves on their own, what would Mister John say then?"

"Thou hast a plan, Mose?"

"Not a plan, sir, but a thinking. If we had Harry and Burton take care of all the horses and had them two clean stalls and haul manure and do more of the heavy work, maybe they'll decide farming ain't for them."

"Maybe. But how wouldst thou tell them so's they wouldn't go complaining to John Brandon? I don't want him saying I was unfair to them two."

"Well, they's bigger and stronger. I reckon I can tells 'em so's they think it's me payin' them a compliment. And if they complain to Mister Brandon, you can tell him it was me lookin' to get stronger backs for the work."

The last of the water had been hauled. Harry and Burton were sitting against a hickory drinking from one final bucket. "Sure is hot, today," Burton said.

They watched the foal, now growing into his body, buck and cavort about the paddock.

"Horse no mind hot," Harry answered. He stood up. "Time clean stalls."

"I'd help thee, but I have to take the cows out to pasture."

As Harry walked towards the Appaloosa barn, Mose yelled across the garden. "Where you goin', boy?" Both of the boys turned to him and answered.

"Taking the cows out to pasture," yelled the one.

"Clean stalls," said the other.

"Harry, Mister Broadmore wants to go into town. Harness Prince to the buckboard. Boss wants you to go with him. I'll have Luke do your stalls. Seems to me you've done your share of cleaning up after him and his brother this morning."

Harry saw the brief smile flick across Mose's mouth before the colored man turned away.

"Thou wilst drive," Mr. Tidewell told him. Harry was all too happy to follow that order. As Prince walked smartly down the driveway, he could hear Luke's voice raised in protest.

"Clean them stalls like I said, or you don't get no supper tonight and no pay come the Sabbath." Mose's voice was not so loud but firm.

"It ain't fair," was Luke's response.

Harry looked straight ahead and tried to not react to the voices. Broadmore chuckled once and settled his corncob into the corner of his mouth. A cloud of pipe smoke wreathed around their heads as they wagon turned left at the road.

"How didst thou learn to drive so well?" Broadmore asked as Prince settled into a comfortable trot.

"Samuel teach."

"That the fellow who came with thee and the Major?"

"Yes. Samuel say Lonely Cricket good with horse. Major has White Man friend come school, touch student head. Feel bumps. Tell what they do. What head good for. He say, 'No good horse. Lonely Cricket only good work in field.' But Major Pratt listen Samuel. Samuel good friend."

"Thou have many friends at the school, Harry?"

"Samuel. Plenty Horses good friend. They call Abner" Harry flicked the reins. There was a moment's hesitation. "Standing Oak was friend," Harry continued. "But he die."

"Oh."

"Many Indian die. White Man sickness. Maybe when cut hair. White Man say Indian hair too long, cut. Many sick. Many die."

Broadmore sucked on his pipe. The dry summer dust kicked up by Prince's hooves gave both a good reason to say no more.

***

The White Men were not all brutal, not like the man they called Duke Frazier, but they were quick with their hands and even quicker with a leather strap. If a boy spoke his own language, there would be the sharp snap of leather against arm or leg. If a boy didn't show respect, the punishment was quick and painful. If a boy used his name or the name of another boy instead of the Bible book names they were given, the "young heathen" would rue his tongue.

If some of the boys believed that they had been sent to this place to die, most were determined to show no fear, not of death, and certainly not of the White Man's punishments. "Do not cry out," they would enjoin each other. "Do not shed tears before White Man. Do not beg mercy."

One day, Lonely Cricket saw Plenty Horses carrying wood into the kitchen. Without thought the younger boy called out, "Plenty Horses do you need help?" Before he could understand his offense, Lonely Cricket's legs stung.

Mr. O'Brian, who managed the stores in addition to teaching history, was one of the cruelest of the staff. The blows didn't stop. Lonely Cricket's arms and buttocks, his legs and back. Over and over. And the man kept shouting, "No damned heathen names allowed. No damned heathen names allowed."

Lonely Cricket did not cry out. He did not ask for mercy. He took blow after snapping, stinging blow until the old man tired.

"Get away from me, you Injun fool. I got no more time for you. Just you remember this beatin' and no more heathen names. You understand me, boy?"

"Yes, sir."

Lonely Cricket walked away hoping to find a quiet spot where he could rub his bruises with a bit of gunny as he would have rubbed a horse who had been hurt. It was late that night, after the lights had been extinguished, after everyone but the watchman was supposed to be asleep, that Lonely Cricket had felt a hand on his arm. He woke to find Samuel and two of the other Apache standing by his bed. These were not schoolboys, they were grown men who had been taken under arrest from the Chiricahua Mountains where their people lived, brought to Florida by Major Pratt, and then brought by him to this Pennsylvania place.

Indicating that he was not to speak but to follow them, Samuel led the way.

They walked some distance without words and came to an abandoned farm. The farmhouse had burned to the ground. Under the debris, a root cellar remained. Within, other of the Apache men and some of the other students stood in a circle. Plenty Horses was among them.

Lonely Cricket was shown to stand in the middle of the circle facing in a certain direction. Samuel and Plenty Horses stood in front of him. Plenty Horses held a small deerskin bag.

Samuel began to speak. In a soft voice, he told this story.

ΩΩΩΩΩ

When Great Spirit created the earth and set the first man on her back, Trickster laughed. "This is the puniest of the animals you have created. They have not hair nor hide to protect them from the weather. They have not claw or fang with which to fight their enemies. They have not the eyesight of the hawk, the strength of the bear, the stealth of the owl, or ability to smell of the coyote, or the hearing of the rabbit. They cannot hide as the toad or strike as the snake. They cannot even run as the deer or the elk. Why do you place them above all the world?"

"All that you say is true, "Ma-Ona replied, "but these humans have one trait that all other creatures lack. They have courage—not just the ability to fight, to win or to lose, but the courage to stand in the face of danger without fleeing and without lashing out."

Trickster did not believe Ma-Ona's words. He did not believe that humans had true courage. He resolved to show Great Spirit that humans were not brave but were the weakest of all the animals who rode the back of the great tortoise.

Trickster came down from the sky in the form of an old man, a shaman who knew the secrets of the stars and the riches of the earth. He went to a village of the people and asked, "Who among you is most worthy of my knowledge. I am old and will soon die; to whom should I tell the secrets that are worth knowing? Who will keep these secrets safe for your children and from your enemies? For these are the secrets that will allow your people to survive and prosper; without them you will surely die."

The elders of the village met around the sacred fire and talked for three nights and two days. Each warrior of the tribe was called before them and asked if he was ready to receive this great knowledge. Some said they were not worthy. Some said they were not brave. Some said they were not wise. Some said they would prefer to seek the company of women. Only one man accepted the challenge. His name was Fresh Spring, and he came from the clan of the bear.

The elders laughed at Fresh Spring. He was the smallest of the men. In games he was not fast and at the hunt he often came back to the village without. The young women did not blush at him, for none wanted to live in his teepee. Even the children did not respect him but made fun of him when he passed.

The elders told Fresh Spring that they would have to talk to all the men of the village, but they would tell him their decision. They did not mean to do this, but that left them free to continue their search.

Again, they went through the list of warriors. For another three days and two nights they talked. Not one man had changed his mind. Not one man had accepted the challenge. All of them knew that with such knowledge they would be envied by other villages. All of them knew that with such knowledge other villages would hunt them and take them prisoner. All of them knew that with such knowledge they would be tortured to reveal those secrets.

Only Fresh Spring was willing. Again, he came to the council fire. Again, he accepted the challenge.

There was nothing the elders could do. Somebody had to learn the secrets that would allow their village to survive and prosper.

They draped Fresh Spring in a new robe and put a garland of honeysuckle around his head. They led him to the edge of the village where the old man waited.

"Here is Fresh Spring," one of the elders proclaimed. "He will receive the great wisdom which you offer. He will keep it safe from our enemies and for our children."

"Trickster, in the form of the old man, laughed to himself. "If this is the most courageous from among these people, surely Ma-Ona will see the error of his decision.

Taking Fresh Spring from the village into the forest, Trickster told him stories that meant nothing and promised him that soon he would understand these magic words. So, into the forest they journeyed until they found a dark place. There Trickster took a small bag made of deerskin and into it he placed some small stones. With the stones he placed tobacco so Fresh Spring would believe they were sacred. Carefully, he tied the bag with a thong and attached an eagle feather to the bag.

"These are the secrets I promised you," Trickster said as he dug a hole in which to bury the bag. "You must come back in three days' time and recover this bag. When you do, all the words I have told you will be revealed. When you do, all the knowledge you need to protect your village from its enemies and allow it to survive and prosper. But you must be careful to keep this bag a secret. If your enemies learn of it, they will have the power to destroy your people.

With those words he led Fresh Spring to a large rock even deeper in the forest. "Wait here for the five days to pass and then return for the bag."

With those words Trickster disappeared.

Fresh Spring sat by the large rock and waited. He did not know that Trickster had changed his guise to an old woman and gone to another village. "I heard one of your enemies brag of hiding a bag of magic deep in the forest." The old woman's bones cracked as she moved. She looked so old as to have come again from the grave. The warriors of the village strained to hear her words. From the way he talked and from the way he did not remain where he had buried it but went instead to rest near the big rock that sits among the birch trees, I know the bag must contain great magic. You should capture him and make him reveal its whereabouts. Make him give that sack to you, and the magic will be yours.

The warriors thought this a good plan, so they sent a party into the forest. When Fresh Spring saw them, he tried to hide behind the big rock, but the warriors dragged him from hiding and demanded he tell them where the bag was hidden.

Fresh Spring did not answer the enemy warriors. Not even when they lashed his hands and hung him from the limb of an oak. Not even when they beat him with thongs of leather. Not even when they piled kindling beneath his feet and set it on fire. He had sworn that he would protect the secret of the bag for his people, and that oath gave him strength.

By the end of the allotted three days, Fresh Spring was almost dead. As a last act of torment, the enemy dragged him through the forest. They did not know that Ma-Ona guided their path. When Fresh Spring's spirit left his body, the enemy abandoned his body for the coyotes and vultures to consume. They did not know he lay in the very spot where Trickster had buried the deerskin bag.

When the people of his village went to look for Fresh Spring, they could not find him. His body had disappeared. But in the place where he the enemy had left him, his people found a new spring that gave sweet water. Two of the women dug into the loose dirt to increase the flow of water that they might fill their water pots. One of the old women, who was Fresh Spring's mother, found the sack.

The elders opened the bag and looked inside. Ma-Ona, having sorrow that Fresh Spring suffered so for his village, had changed the stones into the yellow seed from which grows corn, the first of the three sisters. Truly it has been a gift that has allowed our people to survive and prosper.

ΩΩΩΩΩ

When he had finished, the other young men came up to Lonely Cricket, grasped his left forearm in their left hand, and placed a small present in the sack which Plenty Horses held. Some gave a bit of corn pollen. Some gave him a bit of tobacco. Each gift was placed in that sack. With each offering the giver said, "I welcome you, Lonely Cricket, into the company of warriors."

Finally, Samuel came up to Lonely Cricket with an eagle feather and a small thong of deerskin. He bound the sack closed and then tied the feather to it. Giving the bag to Lonely Cricket he said, "We are proud that you are one of us. We are proud that you are strong. We are proud that you are good. We welcome you into the company of warriors."

On the way back to the school, Plenty Horses accompanied his young friend. "Only those who have shown courage in the face of the White Man have been given this honor. Only those who have not cried when the White Man has punished them have been invited into this brotherhood."

When he returned to the barracks that night, Lonely Cricket hid the sacred bundle that he had been given. It would protect him and connect him to other Indians just as his cloth turtle would always keep him close to Happy Turtle and his home. That night Lonely Cricket slept well in the knowledge that he had been accepted by the company of men.

***

When the last corn was in the barn and the moon of the horses' coats growing thick was nearing its end, a celebration was held at the school. It was a day without classes and without most chores. Instead, the White Men talked many words and hours about thanks and how it was good that The War was over and how it was good that the Indians were learning the ways of the White Man. The Major talked, the chaplain, Matron Fox, and the teachers; even two of the Apache who had come with Major Pratt from Florida talked. Lonely Cricket tried to listen to all the words, but his mind was elsewhere.

His friend Standing Oak was ill. Lonely Cricket didn't know the sickness which made his friend's cheeks puff like a squirrel's filled with nuts. He did not why his friend burned with fever and tossed and turned and did not know where he was. The matron called it mumps, but that was just another White Man word that made no meaning. Lonely Cricket didn't know the illness, but he was sure of its cause. His friend was too far from his people, too far from life.

Three other students were sick. The matron had put the four in a room, which sometimes she called an infirmary and sometimes quarantine. Whatever the name of the place, Lonely Cricket was not allowed into the room. Twice, when the window of the room was propped open, Lonely Cricket had stood outside and called to Standing Oak. First, he called by his name and then by the name the White Man had given him, "Joshua, Joshua."

Standing on his toes Lonely Cricket was able to see into the room, to see the beds with their dull white sheets, grey ticked pillows, and army blankets left from the White Man's great war. He could see Matron Fox and the other White Woman with their starched aprons and their hair bunched in the back carrying glasses of water and bowls of soft porridge. He could see the boys turn their heads away from the food, and he could see the tears that rolled one by one down the boys' cheeks.

Once Standing Oak had answered Lonely Cricket's call. The sick boy had talked of hunting with his father and how much he missed his mother. He spoke of the cool water that flowed in the stream near his village. It was good to remember such things, but it was also sad. Lonely Cricket knew that Standing Oak's words were not meant for his ears, that his friend spoke from the fever of his sickness.

That evening, Lonely Cricket talked to the cloth turtle his sister had made for him. He spoke of the loneliness he, too, felt at school and of his fear that his friend would die.

The next time Lonely Cricket had stood outside the open window and called his friend's name, Standing Oak did not answer. One of the other boys, whom the White Man called Thomas, told Lonely Cricket that Standing Oak was sleeping. "He is very sick," Thomas said. "I do not think he will awaken."

That had been two days before the day the White Man called Thanksgiving. In three days, Thomas's words came true. One of the other boys also died. The two boys were buried in their uniforms, and the Major said kind words over them.

"Among the Israelites there was a man named Saul who persecuted and punished and beat many Christians. He sent them to prison and did not speak out when they were killed. Great was the fear of Saul among the Christians.

"And Saul, yet breathing out threatenings and slaughter against the disciples of the Lord, went unto the high priest, and desired of him letters to Damascus to the synagogues, that if he found any of this way, whether they were men or woman, he would bring them bound unto Jerusalem.

"And as he journeyed, he came near Damascus and suddenly there shined round about him a light from heaven. And he fell to the earth, and he heard a voice saying unto him, 'Saul, Saul, why persecutest thou me?'

"I am sure that Saul was terrified at that moment just as I know that our young friends Joshua and Benjamin were terrified by the sickness which struck them. It is a fearful thing to be struck down in a strange place, but what happened to that terrified man? He became a believer and an apostle of our faith. His name changed to Paul, he brought many to our Lord and because of him those many have been admitted into heaven.

"Indeed, today our young friends are with Jesus and with Paul in heaven, for they, like Paul, have traveled the great journey of faith. It started many miles from this place and now it has ended in a better place, a place where someday we shall join them.

"That is the promise of our Lord and Savior. Let us pray in Jesus's name."

Lonely Cricket did not cry when the Major spoke, nor did he cry when the preacher said his God words over the two boxes that held Standing Oak and the other boy. He did not cry as the boxes were placed in the ground and dirt was shoveled on them. That night, when he thought the other boys in the dormitory could not hear, he wept, burying his face in his pillow.

They had heard, but the other boys said nothing. They, too, were sad that their friends had died. Perhaps they, too, wondered if the White Man's sickness would kill them as well.

In the morning, Follow Rivers, who was a Lakota, put his arm around Lonely Cricket's shoulders. "The White Man will kill us all. We must be brave in the face of death."

Lonely Cricket knew that many of the other Indians believed the White Man was their enemy, but he did not think so. He thought about Harry and Leah Cook and especially of Sapphira. No, all White Man were not his enemy, nor were all Indians his friends.

That next morning he had gone to where Standing Oak had been buried and had spoken his own words to Ma-Ona.

"You saying words for your friends?" The Major had surprised Lonely Cricket.

Lonely Cricket nodded and did not look the Major in the eye.

"That's a good thing to do. Thought I might just do the same."

The Major knelt next to the graves. He didn't speak aloud, but Lonely Cricket knew that the White Man's heart was full.

Shadow Fox had seen Lonely Cricket standing by the grave of Standing Oak, and he had seen Major Pratt kneeling there as well. "Lonely Cricket is trying to become a White Man," he told some of the other students.

Later that day two of the older students were taunting Lonely Cricket. "So, you want to be White Man," one said.

"If you become White Man, do you think to boss us?" the other asked.

Lonely Cricket said nothing, which only made the two older boys angry.

"See, Harry already thinks he better than Indian."

One of the two boys pushed him.

Lonely Cricket still said nothing. He was pushed again and again. Words of cowardice and fear were jabbed at him. He tried to walk away, but the two bigger boys would not allow it. They circled him and pulled at his clothes.

"Even the Ho-Chunk do not want you."

"Shadow Fox told us this."

Lonely Cricket was sure this was true. He knew that Shadow Fox would say mean things, but it saddened him to know others believed Shadow Fox's words.

Three girls were watching, which made Lonely Cricket feel red with shame. One of the girls, whom the White Men called Sarah, was laughing.

The sound of Sarah's laughter encouraged the two bullies. They pushed harder. So intent were they on tormenting Lonely Cricket that they didn't notice Follow Rivers and Plenty Horses coming from around one of the school buildings. Even if they had, the two bullies would not have cared; what difference would it make to have another witness to their cruelty?

"Coyotes," Plenty Horses shouted as he trotted towards the scene.

Plenty Horses grabbed one of the boys and threw him to the ground.

The other backed away. "What matter to you? We teach him be Indian."

Plenty Horses took a step forward, and the second bully ran.

"I know Harry from train ride," Plenty Horses yelled. "He plenty brave. He plenty good. Him man. You coyotes want hunt? You hunt mouse not man."

The second of the bullies scurried to his feet and ran.

Now, all three of the girls were laughing, but their laughter did not sting Lonely Cricket's ears.

Chapter 24 ~ Mose

Mose often groaned in his sleep. This night the old man tossed on his straw pallet and kicked against the rough felt blanket that covered him. He had found the Army-issue blanket on his long trek from South Carolina. Perhaps the soldier who lost it had also lost his life. Perhaps he had simply dropped it by the road and run. At the end of The War, many soldiers had deserted—not from fear but from a longing for their homes. Mose and other Black Men had run the other way.

The old man's groans woke Lonely Cricket. They shared a small room off the new barn. Broadmore Tideswell planned a larger room for tack.

"Massa Tideswell," Mose had begged, "I'd sure like a space for myself. I'se too old to be with those boys. "Sides, them horses 'll do better if theys smells a body in the barn with 'em."

Broadmore had agreed and a flimsy wall had been erected to divide a small room off from the greater. The entrance into Mose's sleeping area would be through an open doorway in that insubstantial wall—nothing elaborate but sufficient, even with a small stove for the winter and a castoff chest of drawers for clothes.

It had been Mose's idea that Lonely Cricket share that room. "Them horses knows his smell better 'en mine," he explained to Broadmore, which was true enough. The real reason was the sadness the old man felt night after solitary night. Lonely Cricket was clearly his favorite among the young men, the hardest worker, and the boy with whom he rode each Sunday to church. Not like the other three, not worth spit.

"Harry, you might set your pallet in my room so's you can be near them Appaloosas," the Black Man suggested.

Lonely Cricket didn't hesitate in accepting. The Frazier brothers did all they could to torment him. It was only their fear of Broadmore's rage that kept them in check. As it was, they called him names and made rude sounds when he was near.

Often, Lonely Cricket was reminded of Shadow Fox. Even at the end, just before he told Major Pratt that he could no longer stay in Carlisle, Shadow Fox was still tormenting Lonely Cricket. "You may fit in here, Harry, but you will never be a true Ho-Chunk. Our people are as glad to be rid of you as the White Man will be glad when I have left this place."

Lonely Cricket responded with a hunch of his shoulders. He knew that Major Pratt and the other Whites were not happy to have any Indian leave, not even one who seemed as incapable of learning as

Shadow Fox. He knew that the Major had tried to convince Shadow Fox to stay at the Carlisle School. "Abner, you still have much to learn. Your teachers say you may yet become a cordwainer, perhaps good enough to work in a White Man's shop."

Shadow Fox had not cared about Pratt's words. He was tired of being scolded and hit. He was even more tired of being looked down on by the other students. Among them he was not seen as a man.

The other students were not sad when the Major told Solomon to drive Robert Langdon, Shadow Fox, and the uppity young Lakota William to the rail station. Nor had the two Indian boys looked up as the buggy in which they rode passed the remaining students assembled on the parade ground and then through the school's gate. With a flick of the reins, Solomon urged the horse to a trot. Behind them, the school returned to its normal life.

"William is nice enough," one of the students said. "I suppose we'll miss him."

"Not worth missing. Put on too many airs," another replied.

Nobody spoke of Shadow Fox. He certainly would not be missed.

***

"You hurt much in sleep, Mr. Mose."

"What you mean, Boy?"

"Is it from slave days? Beatings make bad hurt."

"What you goin' on 'bout, Harry?" Mose was hurriedly dressing. "I want to shave before breakfast. No time for talkin'; got these whiskers to tend to." He pulled his shirt over his head. It was one of the two the old man wore for work. There was another—white—that served for Sundays. Even though Broadmore paid him a decent wage, the old man spent little on himself.

"What doest thou save for?" Broadmore asked more than once when Mose had asked his employer to keep most of his pay in the bank. "Art thou planning to buy a farm of thy own?"

Mose always gave the same answer, "No, suh. Mose just savin' case he find some'in he want."

"What might that be?" Broadmore had inquired a few times.

"I don't know, just some'in."

The way Mose shifted his feet and looked away from his eyes, told Broadmore that his foreman was not being honest. Still, it wasn't his business. If the Colored Man was saving for something, that was his business and his alone. As long as Mose was honest in his dealings and hard-working, as long as he taught the younger men and made sure their work was done correctly, what reason did Broadmore have to complain?

"He is a Christian," Broadmore's wife had said more than once. "He goes to church regular and gives his tithe. That is surety enough."

Rachel's words didn't reassure her husband. Secrets perplexed him, and the fact that his hired hand held them back worried at him. "What if he takes that money and leaves when I need him? When it comes foaling season or if the horses get sick? What can I do without him?"

"Well, thou hast the Indian boy. If he's as good as Mose says, thou dost not have a worry 't-all."

"That's if the boy stays. Who knows when that Major will want him back at his school or maybe he'll just decide he wants to go home. I suppose he misses his people."

"Thou worriest too much, husband." Rachel turned her attention back to darning her husband's socks. Often, she thought, "I wish Broadmore would worry as much about me as he does this farm." But those words would never be added.

Lonely Cricket would not be put off. He had come to love Mose. The older man had taught him so much, not just about horses but about the White Man's ways. Every Sunday they rode to the Baptist church. As they rode, the two would talk. Mose asked questions about Lonely Cricket's family, and the boy would talk of his home, of the crops and animals, of his sister and brother, and of the Cook family who were White but who were his friends.

Sometimes, Lonely Cricket asked Mose about his life. Those questions went mostly unanswered.

"A slave ain't got no life," Mose said one Sunday morning as their horses ambled away from the farm. "'less you call's bein' beat a life."

"Do scars hurt?" Lonely Cricket asked.

"Not the scars, but the memories. Yes suh, Harry, them memories never stop hurtin'."

"You hurt much in sleep, Mr. Mose. Is it beatings make bad hurt or memories?" Lonely Cricket asked.

"If I tells you the story tonight when I gets back, you gotta swear you'll not tell no one, not Massa Tideswell, not them other boys, not even the preacher."

"I swear, Mr. Mose. I keep your secrets as I would father's."

***

Mose propped himself on his elbow so he could look at Lonely Cricket. The young Indian lay flat on his back, his arms across his chest, his head cocked towards the older man.

"I was solt by my mammy's owner when I was a boy, younger than you. His name were Essex, and they called me Mose, so I was Mose who b'longs to Essex. Then he sells me to Mr. Marshall, so's I was Mose who b'longs to Marshall. Now, I calls myself Mose Lincoln. Course I never knowed nobody name of Lincoln, but every nigger in this country feel like we knows Father Abraham.

"Well, I goes to live on Massa Marshall's plantation. First, they puts me to work in the house. Tell me to fetch this and bring that. Sometimes I help the cook. Sometimes I help the maids. Sometimes I sweep and sometimes I beat them rugs. I works in the house 'till I grow big, and Massa Marshall say I'se earn my keep more pickin' and hoein' then sashayin' round that kitchen. So's he set me in the fields workin' rice. That was what Massa Marshall call his 'money crop', and we grows a lot of rice.

"I weren't much good as no field hand, and they beat me a few times. Didn't do no good 'cept to make me want to run away, run far as I could. But I saw what they does to Niggers what run, so I stay there and get beat.

"One day, Massa ride out to see how that there rice o' his is growin', and his horse shies. Massa he thrown off and that horse run off.

"Luck have it I grab that bridle and horse stop. I didn't have no idea how to talk to a horse, how to calm him down. I just talked to him the way I'd talk to another slave, the way I talk to you boys here. I talked quiet and kept sayin' 'It'll be all right. Just you calm down and it'll be all right.' I rubbed horse's nose and kept talkin' till Massa come. He say, 'Boy, you got a way with that horse,' and he tells the foreman I should work in the horse barn instead of them fields."

"I know that story, Mr. Mose," Lonely Cricket interrupted. Everybody's heard about you and that horse.

"Quiet, Boy. It's my story, and I'm gonna tell it the way I want or not at all. Now, you wanna hear it or not?"

Lonely Cricket nodded.

"Good." Mose wiped his lips with a frayed piece of checked flannel and looked upwards before continuing.

"Life was better workin' in the barn. I loves horses, and the White Man who run the barn saw I was a hard worker. Trouble was I had me time to think, time to talk with other niggers, time to meet Susanne.

"She was one beautiful girl. Not just her body. Not just her face. But inside, she was beautiful as well.

"Massa Marshall done bought her for his wife, to help Miss Sarah dress and take care of her clothes. Get her bath ready. All them women things."

The old man stopped for a moment to dab at his eyes before continuing. "I cain't say for them other darkies, but I loved that girl more 'en life. I wanted her to be my wife, and I reckon she wanted that, too 'cause when I asked, she said, 'yes' and kissed me right off."

Mose stopped talking. By the dim kerosene light, Lonely Cricket watched the tears silently run the course of the old man's face. He wanted to say something. He wanted to urge his friend to go on. But, with the same sensitivity he brought to a skittish horse, the boy waited without a word or movement.

"I asked the massa and he said, 'No.' Just like that. He says, 'That girl ain't got no business getting' herself pregnant. She here to take care of my missus and not go worrying with any of you darkies.' That's what he said and my heart broke.

"When I told Susanne, her heart broke, too. That girl cried and I cried. But there ain't nothin' a slave can do. 'Cept we didn't listen. Not like we was supposed to. Whenever me and her had a chance we was kissin' and lovin' and talkin' bout followin' the dipper."

"What mean followin' dipper?" Lonely Cricket asked.

"Means you run off. You head north and keep runnin'. That old dipper in the sky'll show you the way." Mose paused and then added, "You's just keep runnin' till you's free.

"See, Harry, that's when I decided I weren't gonna stay no slave. 'Sides I couldn't live not havin' her bein' mine. Havin' to look every which way 'fore I could touch the woman I loved. I 'cided to run off.

"Susanne begged me to not. 'They'll beat you dead,' she said. I figured if they caught me, that's 'actly what they'd do. I didn't care. I loved that girl so much I wanted to be dead if I couldn't have her.

"I'd heard stories of run'ways goin' up North. One night I took off. Didn't tell no one, not even Susanne. Just followed that dipper and I run and run till I could't move one leg or t'other. Next mornin' I run some more.

"I run, but they caught me. Damn them slavers. Drug me back in chains and the Massa he said, 'Beat me till I was dead."

"The White Man run the barn told Massa Marshall, "Don't kill him, 'cause Mose best boy with horses he'd ever seen.' So they's beat me, but not to killin' me."

Mose shuddered with the memory of the beating he endured.

"Next day, I hear they's gonna sell Susanne. Sells her far away where I'll never see her never again." That was worse'n the beatings. That the memory hurt most. They sell her to Mis'sippi to be a field hand. "'Fore she go, he rape her. Makes sure I's know he done it. And her carryin' my baby." Mose's voice broke into sobs,

Forcing himself to continue, the Black man said, "'Fore she go I get her a message. I tell her if I ever get free, I'll run to the North and she should do the same. I said we'd find us, and we'd be married here, up here in the North. Tolt her someday we'd be together. Her, me, and our baby. Someday, on the great gettin' up day.

"That's why I'm savin' up. Someday she'll get here. Someday ..." His voice trailed off.

Lonely Cricket's voice was hoarse with the tears he held back. "Lonely Cricket hope this come true, Mose. I pray next Sunday. Jesus God hear prayer and bring her."

"You know the cruelest thing, Cricket? I never go to see my child. Never go to ..." Once more, sobs took the man's words.

"That White Man deserve die." Lonely Cricket's voice cracked with emotion.

"Nope, he deseved worse 'en that, and he got it. He came back from that war o' his and he couldn't walk. A Yankee bullet done hit him right in the spine. So there he is with no slave 'cause we all left. Just him and his wife and their boy, who weren't no better'n his daddy. Yes sir, they probably starved to death or maybe worse."

The Black man once more dabbed at his eyes with his piece of flannel. "I knows I should forgive 'em. That's what Jesus would tell me. But, Boy, I cain't stop hatin' him long 'nough to forgive."

Mose stood to blow out the lamp. A moment of kerosene smell and smoke, then darkness and quiet.

Once again that night Mose's cries woke Lonely Cricket. In a quiet voice, the boy said, "It'll be all right. Just you calm down and it'll be all right."

Chapter 25 ~ Moments

The moon, ahead of the clock, was full in the eastern sky. The dry air of the early autumn evening felt cool against his skin. Lonely Cricket was happy.

Sky nickered, whirled to the right, and took off around the paddock. The yearling galloped twice around before he skittered to a stop. Lonely Cricket held out his hand, and the horse arched his head forward, keeping his muzzle just out of the young man's reach. Lonely Cricket stretched forward from his perch on the split rail fence. Sky took a small step away. The boy sat back and dropped his hand; immediately the horse inched closer.

Lonely Cricket squirmed an apple from his pocket. Using a small knife, he cut a piece of the fruit. Immediately, the horse was there, ready to take his treat.

"That horse really loves thee, Harry"

Lonely Cricket turned at the sound of Dinah's voice. "Horse love apple not Lonely Cricket."

She moved forward until her hand rested on the top rail near him. "And, I think thou lovest her as well."

"Horse not Lonely Cricket's, belong your father. He sell Mr. Crenshaw.

"No! How dost thou know that?"

"Lonely Cricket hear talk. Other day Mr. Crenshaw say he pay whatever Mr. Tideswell want for young horse."

"But I want Sky. I have asked him over and over." Tears sprang to her eyes.

Almost unconsciously the young man touched her hand with his. "There be other horses. New stallion good. We have foals next spring."

"Oh, you don't understand."

Sky reached for the remaining apple. Lonely Cricket pulled it away from the horse's nose and cut two slices. He handed the pieces to Dinah. "You give horse apple, he love you."

"There is much I do not understand, especially about this girl. But horse and apple, that I know," the young man thought.

The girl took one slice of fruit and held it on the palm of her hand. As Sky took his treat, Lonely Cricket swung down from the fence.

"There work. New horses not use here." That was true, three more Appaloosas, arrived only three days earlier, needed to learn the routine of the farm. Especially, Peaceful Warrior, the new stallion. Mr.

Tideswell had named the stallion. "Harry boy," he had said just that morning, "I am calling this one after thee."

Later, after Broadmore had gone about other business, Mose had whispered into Lonely Cricket's ear. "That man think the world of you, boy."

"What does Mr. Crenshaw want with Sky?" Dinah asked.

"Sky good horse. Two years make a fine horse for Mr. Crenshaw son."

"You think Elder Crenshaw is going …" She could not bring herself to say the word.

"To what?"

"To … to change him?" The girl glanced towards the horse's genitals. As if on cue, Sky extended his shaft and loosed a stream of urine.

Embarrassed and confused, the adolescent boy said, "Lonely Cricket not know White Man plan." He ducked his head and walked quickly towards the barn. "Sky good horse." It was more comfortable to think about horses than about this young woman who so often appeared at the barn and in his dreams. He looked back just as the colt took the second piece of apple from Dinah's palm, snorted, and pirouetted away.

Maggie, too, had loved apples. Sapphira Cook would share pieces of the fruit with her cousin's horse. Maggie would follow the girl, nudging her back, whinnying, and Sapphira—acting as if she were reluctantly giving in to the horse's importuning—would hold the bits in the palm of her hand and giggle with delight at the touch of the horse's lips.

It pained Lonely Cricket to remember Sapphira. Still, he couldn't bring himself to forget. There had been no letters during the many moons since he had left his home. He yearned for word from her, of her, and of his family. Even after Shadow Fox had taken his letter back to Nebraska, there had been no word.

The Indians at school spoke often of their homes, but seldom to the White Men. It was a subject for nights, when their words would not be overheard. The Apache who had been in Florida spoke often of the mountains of their faraway land. They did not speak so much of the people who remained there. But the younger boys and girls thought often of their friends and families. The memories burned their hearts. Many did not believe they would ever return to those homes, that they would die in this strange place. For many, like Standing Oak, that would be their fate. Lonely Cricket did not want to die far from his home.

Since coming to the Tideswell's farm, Lonely Cricket had often thought of his family. Even though he could now write well enough to write a letter without assistance, he did not ask Broadmore or Mose for pen and paper. He did not want to tell Sapphira Cook about Dinah. He did not want to mention the feelings that came in the night and left his blanket wet with dreaming.

Lonely Cricket leaned on a pitchfork. The stalls needed cleaning, but the youngster could not break away from his thoughts. He was unaware that the girl had followed him into the barn.

"That fork isn't meant for a leaning post, and those stalls won't clean themselves." She tried to sound stern and demanding like her mother, but Dinah could not hide the warmth of her feelings. "Wouldst thou like my help?"

She put her hand on Lonely Cricket's arm. Even through the long sleeves of his shirt, he could feel the trembling of her fingertips. "Your father—" His words were interrupted by the touch of her lips on his.

At school the students were not allowed to kiss. If they were caught, a boy would be strapped, and the girl would be forced to wash floors on her knees until her back groaned with pain. Not even the Apache, who were much older, were allowed to kiss or fondle. Of course, they did so in hidden places. Sometimes students would hide in a cellar or take to the woods. Lonely Cricket had never done so. In his mind, he was pledged to Sapphira Cook. In his mind, she was waiting for him in Nebraska.

The touch of Dinah's lips on his, the feel of her hands on his body, the thought of their togetherness in that moment: such things excited Lonely Cricket, but they also confused him. He wondered if he could ask Mose about the feelings that coursed through him. He wondered if those feelings were similar to the feelings Mose had experienced with his beloved Susanne.

Even as he thought such things, he pictured Sapphira Cook. He knew that she must have changed in the long time he had been away, but he could not imagine that difference. In his mind, he saw her as she had been—a girl. Here before him was a young woman. As their bodies came together, he could feel her breasts against his chest. He was aware of something, not really a smell but still some difference of odor. Most of all, he was aware of the excitement in his own loins.

For the first time in his life, Lonely Cricket knew the power of sexual desire. He pulled Dinah to himself and showered her face with his kisses. At first, she responded and then suddenly grew quiet. Removing her arms from his neck, Dinah placed her hands on Lonely Cricket's chest and pushed him away.

"Have I done wrong?" the boy asked.

"Not you," Dinah managed between the sudden sobs which wracked her body.

"What then?" he called after her as she ran from the barn.

"I not understand women," Lonely Cricket said to Mose that evening.

"That, Boy, is the beginning of understandin' 'em."

That night both man and boy writhed in the discomfort of their sleep.

***

Broadmore and Rachel sat in the parlor; he, reading the latest horse journal and she the good book. It was, Broadmore thought, a great frivolity to take this time for reading when there was much work to do. Still, he had to agree that Rachel's idea had made their lives more pleasant. "Only one hour," she had begged. "Surely we can spare sixty minutes for quiet and contemplation before we take to our bed."

In truth, there was little to be done in the twilight. Perhaps some evenings the accounts, but those could be done in the parlor as easily as they could in the small side room where his desk stood. And Rachel assuredly was happier, which meant less conflict with their daughter.

The idea had started one evening at dinner. "What doest thou think is the best time of day?" Burton had asked.

"Morning, when I first get up. Least this time of year. Before I'm tired," Luke Frazier replied.

"'Bout mid-morning," Mose opined, "'when my body's still happy to be workin' and my stomach ain't complainin' for no food."

That had made everyone laugh.

"What about thee, Harry?" Dinah had asked. The youngster cocked his head to better hear her. "What's thy favorite time of day"

"When sun not yet gone. Animals know night come. Work done. Stomach happy with Miss Tideswell dinner. Before clean stalls for night, Lonely Cricket like talk moon as she come see what trouble sun has done. It good time for quiet. When Nebraska, Lame Bear and Harry Cook smoke tobacco and plan next day. Happy Turtle tell little brother story. Best time. After father and Lonely Cricket care horse and cows. Mother and Happy Turtle put chicken in pen and make sure garden fence keep safe from rabbit. That when world seem peace."

Rachel Tideswell noted the Indian boy's comment. It was the most words Lonely Cricket had said in her hearing. That night when they lay in bed, she commented to Broadmore that she understood why the Indian boy so impressed him. "That boy's got a brain," she said.

Broadwell had snorted and said, "Well, I'll warrant the boy is good at his work." The next day, he agreed to the hour of quiet each evening. For almost four weeks they had enjoyed these hours sitting in their parlor, sometimes with Dinah sometimes not but always the two of them.

The slam of the front door broke Broadmore from his reverie. Dinah thudded up the stairs. Her footfall echoed overhead. Then another slam, this of her bedroom door.

"Now what?" Rachel demanded of the air.

Broadmore stomped up the stairs after his daughter. Without knocking, be pushed open her bedroom door and found her collapsed on her bed and sobbing.

"Who has done this to thee?" he thundered. Suddenly his rage at Dinah had transformed to solicitation. "Who wert thou with?"

"We kissed," she whispered. "It was nice, the way I had dreamed. Suddenly, I couldn't—"

"Kissing, who kissed thee? Which of those scoundrels— "

"No, Papa, I kissed him. He didn't do anything wrong."

"Who?" Broadmore thundered. "Who?"

"Harry." Her whisper even fainter.

"That heathen. I knew no good would come of his coming here. I tried to warn thy mother, but would she heed my advice? I swear I should kill him with my bare hands, but I'll leave that to that sanctimonious Pratt. Thinking he can calm the wild Injuns by teaching them to read and write. Sooner teach them the fastest way to heaven or more likely hell."

While Broadmore ranted, his daughter tugged at his sleeve. Finally, as he turned to leave, she shouted, "Father. Lonely Cricket did nothing wrong. It was I who kissed him. It was I who wanted— It was I who ran away, not because of anything Harry had done but because of what it reminded … Elder Brandon; it was Elder Brandon."

"What are thou talking of, child." Rachel had followed her husband up the stairs and into Dinah's bedroom. "Did Elder Brandon not warn thee of your impulses? Did he not teach thee of chastity?"

The words tumbled from Dinah's mouth. How months before the Elder had touched her. How she had wanted to say something but feared their anger. How she was sure she was not the first and would surely not be the last.

Rachel listened with rage, delighted to lay every problem with her daughter on Johnathan Brandon's doorstep, even those which had existed for years.

For Broadmore, processing his daughter's words was difficult. Jon Brandon was his friend, had been for years. They had not only worshipped together but also done business. "How better to know the morality of another than to do business with him?" Broadmore asked himself. "This makes no sense."

With difficulty, Dinah convinced her father to not speak with Harry. "He's the sweetest boy," she said; "and the hardest worker. The Appaloosas would never forgive you if you ran him off. I think Sky would run away to follow him." She did not add her thought that she might run off as well.

Finally, he agreed to wait until morning. "If he is honest about what happened, if he doesn't try to lie about kissing thee, I shall tell him never again and let that be," were his final words on the subject.

That night, while Lonely Cricket and Mose's sleep was roiled, Broadmore's mind was also troubled. It was well past midnight before he slept and well before the rooster that he woke in sudden distress. It was all the sturdy horseman could do to keep from shouting out. He was sure that were he to do so the anguish of his cry would bring banshees and hobgoblins to their knees. Instead, he shuddered, gasped for air, and damning the truth that could never be again spoken resolved that business came first and that meant silencing the outrage that tore within.

Chapter 26 ~ The Pain of Emotions

Dinah Tideswell's sleep was no less troubled than her father's. The memory of Jonathan Brandon's hands and the smell of his breath had driven her from Lonely Cricket's embrace. Even though the evening was warm she pulled the comforter close and buried her face in its cotton softness. "Will I ever trust a man to hold me?" she wondered. Still, never before had she wanted to kiss in that way. Never before had she wanted her lips to touch a man's, her tongue to find his in sweet communion, her breasts to harden against his, her loins to desire him.

Never before had Dinah understood the words of books, the whisperings of other women, or even the Song of Solomon, that book of worship that made so little sense to her and of which her mother had said, "When thou art ready to understand, Elder Brandon shall instruct thee. The meeting and your parents trust him to teach thee in godly ways, for he is well learned in scripture and has—since his dear wife's departure from this world —devoted his life to its study."

"Let him kiss me with the kisses of his mouth: for thy love is better than wine. Because of the savor of thy good ointments thy name is as ointment poured forth, therefore do the virgins love thee. Draw me, we will run after thee: the king hath brought me into his chambers." The passage ran through her mind.

"Yes, I want to run to his room in the barn, to be with him." The thought of Lonely Cricket moistened her maidenhood. Hugging her pillow and smothering it with kisses, Dinah fell asleep only to start again into doubt. "Will I ever trust a man? If he puts his arms around me, if he touches my breasts will I flee from his caresses?"

With the turmoil of her heart two competing images came to her mind: One Lonely Cricket, his body lithe, young and strong, his eyes deep with feeling, his mouth moist and full, his head cocked to the side as he strove to hear her words. The other the old man, his great hands dirty and gnarled touching her, probing her, behind them small eyes gleaming with sin, his tongue a serpent's—forked and flicking. With the one image Dinah moaned with pleasure and with the other choked with horror.

Yet, even in her pleasure there was fear that she might sin for was it not a sin to be with a man? And, even in her horror, there was a fear of wrongfulness, for was it not wrong to reject the commandments of her parents and her elders?

The gasps, moans and tears of her daughter's sleep woke Rachel, whose own slumber was shallow and fitful. She padded into the girl's bedroom and pulled a high-backed chair next to Dinah's bed.

Patting the girl's head, the mother whispered—hoping at once that she would not waken the girl and at the same time that her words would bring comfort and calm. "I wanted to protect thee from those boys, and I delivered thee to that man. I wanted thou to grow to a woman, and I have taught thee to fear being a maid. What am I to do, my daughter? In protecting thee from sin I have sinned against thee."

Rachel's tears dropped on her daughter's cheek.

"I do love thee," Dinah moaned through her sleep. Rachel was reassured by the words, she did not know they were meant for Lonely Cricket. "I would be with thee forever."

***

"What will Lame Bear say if I bring White Woman as my wife? Will he accept her into his home or reject us both? Will Yquili Sparrow teach her the Ho-Chunk ways or turn her back. Will Happy Turtle be glad for me or will she mourn the loss of her brother?" The thoughts tormented Lonely Cricket.

And, worst of all, "What of Sapphira Cook?" The greater his feelings for Dinah Tideswell, the more Lonely Cricket thought of his childhood friend.

ΩΩΩΩΩ

Walker of the World could not sleep. The sound of drumming kept him awake. But when he looked out of his teepee, the sacred fire was not lit, no one was drumming, the rest of the village were sleeping soundly. Only Walker of the World could hear the beating of the ceremonial drums. It was a new song, one he had never heard, a song that made his feet ache to dance. The drumming called to him from beyond the village, and he could not resist it.

Taking his buffalo robe and his bow, Walker of the World left his village resolved to find the drums he heard and to learn the song they played that he might return with it to teach its beauty to his tribe.

Through the night he followed the sound. No matter how far he walked, the drumming seemed always at the same distance. "Perhaps it is The Trickster who summons me," Walker of the World said to himself, "but I will follow those drums until I find them.

By morning, Walker of the World had traveled far. As the sun greeted the earth, Walker of the World, too tired to travel on, wrapped himself in his buffalo robe and fell to the ground in a deep sleep. All that day, he did not wake, not even when crows came to inspect his body, not even when coyotes came to see if he was food for them. All day Walker of the World slept, but he was in no danger for Ma-Ona had sent the spirit of the owl to watch over him.

When the sun left the sky to sleep and his sister the moon had come to light the night, the drumming sounded again, and this time woke Walker of the World. He gathered his robe and his bow and once more walked through the darkness. Still the drums did not seem any closer. Walker of the World was sure that it was the Trickster beating those drums, but he could not stop. The song called to him with the power of great spirits; his feet demanded that he go on.

Once more the day came. Walker of the World did not know the place to which he had come. He had no idea of where he was or in which direction lay his home. Afraid that the Trickster was planning to kill him, Walker of the World huddled in the warmth of his robe and waited for death. But death did not come. Instead, he fell into a deep sleep, a sleep which lasted until the stars appeared in the sky.

Once more, the drumming woke Walker of the World.

"I am weary, Trickster, what do you want of me?" he shouted into the night.

There was no reply, only the drumming—still at a distance, still calling to him.

Weary as he was, tired as he was from the great distance he had traveled, Walker of the World again picked up his robe and bow and followed the sound. He knew that he would follow that sound until he reached the edge of the Great Tortoise on which we all dance.

When the sun rose into the sky the next day, Walker of the World saw a strange village before him. These people did not live in the teepees of the Ho-Chunk but in lodges built of logs and mud and set atop a large mound so that the rain would run down from them and so that they could rain their arrows down on enemies who might attack them.

A drum was beating to announce Walker of the World's arrival. It had been the rhythm of that drum which Walker of the World had been following all that time and distance.

Walker of the World climbed the mound and stood outside the circle of the lodges. "I am Walker of the World," he called out, "and I have come to learn the song of your drum."

A beautiful maiden came from the circle of lodges to greet him. She wore a robe of great beauty and many colors. Her hair was adorned with plumage of birds Walker of the World did not recognize. Her moccasins were decorated with shells that shone with the brightness of stars. "You are welcome, Walker of the World," the maiden announced. "I am Love Woman and I have called you here to dance with me."

For many weeks Walker of the World stayed with Love Woman. Many times, they danced, and Walker of the World learned the songs by which Love Woman had called him forth.

When it was time for Walker of the World to depart and to return to his people, he asked Love Woman to come with him. At first, she refused, but every day he would plead with her until Love Woman could resist no longer.

Together they walked the great distance until they came to the place of Walker of the World's village. Walker of the World called out to his friends and neighbors. "I have returned to you and I have brought my bride to live among us."

When the other men of the village saw Love Woman, they coveted her for their own teepees. When the women of the village saw the desire in men's eyes, they grew jealous of Love Woman and hated her.

When Love Woman beat the ceremonial drum and Walker of the World danced to the song, the men of the village were driven to madness by desire and the women raged against Love Woman with words of hatred. The longer Love Woman played, and Walker of the World danced, the greater was the upset of the village. Arguments broke out. Friends yelled at friends. Brothers struck brothers. Women screamed at their husbands. Sisters turned away from sisters. There was great anger among the people.

Finally, the elders called Walker of the World to the ceremonial fire. "Love Woman must leave the village," they decreed. "You may stay here, but you must not play this song you have learned or dance this dance."

The next morning, "Love Woman could not be found. Nobody knew where she had gone or when. Walker of the World stayed in the village for three moons, but in the end, he could not live without Love Woman, so he set off to find her.

It is said by the people that he never did find Love Woman again. That he still looks for her unless, perhaps, he has fallen off the edge of the Great Tortoise.

ΩΩΩΩΩ

Lonely Cricket remembered the story of Walker of the World and Love Woman, which Lame Bear had told him many moons before.

"Did my father Lame Bear speak of Dinah Tideswell?" Lonely Cricket asked himself. He knew that the tales of his people could not be ignored.

Chapter 27 ~ The Straying Elder

"Help thyself."

"Thank you, Rachel. I don't mind if I do." Molly Stillwell deftly took the slice of ham she'd been eyeing from the plate, held it between her right thumb and forefinger, and took elegant bites, which she chewed carefully, each followed by a mouthful of tea. Then taking a slice of the fresh baked pumpernickel which she had brought that morning, the smiling lady took the lid from Rachel Tideswell's blue French butter keeper, dipped a knife into soft, pale yellow creaminess, and slathered the bread before taking far less delicate bites which she chewed with gusto. "What a fine collation you have set for me." Molly took a moment to smooth the skirt of her floral-patterned dress. "I am glad for the company of another woman," Rachel replied, also smoothing her plain calico skirt.

"And, I thank you for allowing my girl Miriam to visit with your heathen. The poor Indian girl is missing her home something fierce. I suppose that is normal enough, although, when I think of the dreary lives they must lead compared to ours ..." The sturdy woman paused to sample of the cookies which she had also brought. "I can't imagine how she would abide it having sampled civilization."

"Dost thou think they know one another?" Rachel asked. "Are they of the same tribe?"

"I doubt that matters. They all speak the same lingo and have the same heathen ways. If nothing else, they must have knowed each other at that school. I just hope talking with the boy will ease her a mite. If that girl leaves why I have no idea how I'll keep up with the baking. To think I didn't think she'd be a help and now." Molly took a small, chintz handkerchief—not at all a match for her clothing—from her sleeve and blew her nose.

"Perhaps they'll be attracted." Rachel's voice sounded strangely anxious to the other woman.

"What do you mean, Rachel Tideswell? Are you worried about that boy of Broadmore's?"

"No, not about Harry. He's fine." Rachel busied herself pouring her visitor another cup of tea. They were using her best china—unpatterned but ghost white and delicate—the cups far daintier and smaller than her every day.

"It's my daughter Dinah," Rachel finally continued. "She has become ... about the boy... I fear what they, what she—"

"Lord have mercy, are you saying that heathen and your daughter?"

Rachel shook her head. "That and more. She told us ...she claims that Jonathan Brandon." The usually self-assured woman buried her eyes in her own, plain white handkerchief.

"Has that devil been at your daughter? That man is worse than any heathen."

"Devil? How can you say that of him? Jonathan Brandon is an elder of our meet—"

"He's a womanizer and worse. Do you and Broadmore not know the stories 'bout the Fraziers?"

"What stories? What gossip art thou telling?"

"And, you giving those two boys shelter and Broadmore learning them the horse trade," the baker continued; "I'd have thought you'd have known."

"Molly Stillwell, I've no notion of what thou art saying. Voice thy stories if they be worth thy telling." Rising suddenly from the ladder-back chair, Molly moved quickly about the room. "You know, Rachel, for all the times I've been in your home, this is the first I've set in this front parlor."

"I thought not the kitchen today, that we might be proper for a change."

Molly went to the fireplace and inspected the scrimshaw flute in the place of honor on the mantle. "Why, wherever did you—"

"Oh, Molly Stillwell, if thou hast stories worth telling, then tell them. Don't keep me in the web of thy distraction or I shall burst with apprehensions."

Molly Stillwell did not turn around to answer. "You know, of course that Mr. Brandon comes from quite the distance."

"Of course, we all know he moved to Newville a few years back after his wife died."

"Yes, yes, all the way from Shippensburg, but not ... no, it wasn't his wife, it was his mistress who died birthing their child."

"Are you sure, Molly? That's—"

"Quite sure." The woman walked back to her chair. Took a moment to examine the remains of their tea and select another cookie before retaking her seat. "Quite sure, for my cousin lives in Shippensburg, has lived there all her life. I even know the unfortunate lady's name, Sarah Frazier."

"You mean the mother of those boys, the two he asked Broadmore to take on, are his—"

"No, not Jonathan Brandon's sons, more's the sin. Sarah Frazier was married to someone else, to Robert Frazier; and Robert Frazier was as ne'er-do-well as ever lived and sad to say a drunk as well. Quite the figure of ridicule in the parish was what my cousin wrote. When well sozzled, the man would claim royal blood, fancied himself a duke she said.

"Her words exactly as she wrote me them, 'For the price of a draught he'd grant a royal patent till the tavern would be filled with lords and earls and all as laughing at him for the sport.' Seems that soon enough the town took to calling him a Duke. Men would be taking off their hats and ladies curtseying when e'er he passed and all the while laughing at the sport of him. 'Duke Frazier,' they would call and bow and bob and laugh."

Dabbing the corner of her mouth with one of Rachel's red gingham napkins, Molly examined the cloth for crumbs, picked two off, popped them in her mouth, and continued her story. "Not a scrap of dignity to the man, not a scrap. Let others laugh what care Duke Frazier as long as his jug were filled. Let his boys go without shoes and his wife without a bonnet as long as he had a pint to drink. A wastrel. A scoundrel. A drunkard. And mean they say, mean as any, especially the morning next. Mean to her and mean to his boys. And mean to anyone who had less than he. Bullied the weak and cursed the fearful.

"No wonder, the missus took up with another. And, he, your Elder Brandon, your Jonathan Brandon, he without a wife no more, well who might blame him for the loneliness. Not that with the war bein' fought there weren't men enough away he'd have his pick of women. Why he chose Sarah Frazier, that no man can tell. I warrant she was a comely lass; you only need look at her boys to see." Molly paused.

It took a moment for Rachel to realize that some response was called for by the bread and pastry maker's last comment. "Yes," she finally agreed, "they are both handsome enough." Pursing her lips, she took a moment to add, "Except for their eyes. Mean eyes they have."

"Eyes like their pa's," Molly agreed. "Most likely turn to drink as well if given half the chance."

"Not on this farm they won't. Broadmore won't tolerate—"

"I'm sure he wouldn't. I'm sure not. But the acorn doesn't fall too far from the tree."

Both women nodded their heads in agreement with the aphorism.

"But what happened to the father?" Rachel inquired. "Where is he?"

"Duke Frazier run off. Not a scrap of pride 'cept when it came to her and that not enough to stand and fight. When every man in Shippensburg had taken to calling his missus Mrs. Brandon and laughing at the joke of it, Duke Frazier could abide no more. Off he went leaving her with naught but debt and dreary more.

"'Twere Jonathan Brandon took her in. Refused to knuckle to the rumors or the laughs. Said he'd duel any man had ought to say again' her. Beat one man, don't recall his name, severe enough the sheriff came. Brandon paid a fine and recompense. After that, things quieted down; not one else wanted the same at his hands.

"Soon after with the babe due, he took her and the two boys to live, not with him but in an outbuilding fit enough. He dressed those boys and paid tuition for their school—fine waste that was the two having not the brains of chipmunks.

"And, when she died giving birth, why he sold off his farm not from shame but loss. Brought the boys with him and asked your husband to take them in." Molly Stillwell stopped to scratch her nose before continuing. "And, you never knew? My goodness, did you or Broadmore never ask or did Brandon tell you some story more cunning than true?"

Swallowing hard, Rachel replied, "I don't think we ever asked. Elder Brandon asked and Broadmore, needing help and having little to pay, was glad to take them. Not that they've shown much effort for their feed, but it takes little wit to shovel manure or bed a stall and we've Mose to harry them."

"I hope you'll not hold against them. I'd feel awful guilt, Rachel, were you and Broadmore to drive those boys off for the story I've told or what their parents done."

"Drive them off? No, least not for that. But they have their daddy's meanness streak and that might yet be enough to drive my husband to wrath. Our younger boy, Burton, and the Injun, they're hard workers and those brothers, well ..."

***

"I miss my home." Miriam spoke softly. "Miss Molly not bad. I like cook. Learn from her. But, miss home."

"I miss home, too." Lonely Cricket held out his hand to take Miriam's.

The two young Indians leaned against the corral fence and watched Sky bucking and prancing with the pleasure of the autumn day.

"Why not come back with me?"

"I miss home, but happy here." Lonely Cricket furtively glanced at Dinah, who was propped against an oak tree trying to look nonchalant as she watched them.

It had been her mother's request. "Keep thy watch on Harry and this girl. They have permission to talk but I want no touching, nothing unseemly," Rachel had instructed. Rachel had been surprised that

Dinah had immediately agreed to the assignment. For her part, Dinah feared what might happen between Molly Stillwell's girl and her Lonely Cricket. "Did they know each other in school?" she had asked Molly Stillwell when a few days earlier, the baker had stopped by with some unasked-for rolls and her request that Miriam be allowed to talk with Harry. The two older women had been sitting at the kitchen table when Rachel had called her daughter to join them.

"I suppose they must. They were both students. She's not mentioned him, but who can say." Molly had scratched her nose and thought for a moment before adding, "Who can say anything with these savages. It's not like we talk the same language. Most of the time, it's me showing her how to bake this or that and her doing. Who's to say what words she understands and how much is just her copying of my actions."

Dinah nodded as if agreeing. She certainly had no interest in sharing the depth of her conversations with Lonely Cricket—not with her mother and certainly not with Molly Stillwell.

Now, taking the moment to gently scratch her back against the oak, Dinah wished she were closer so she could hear the softly spoken words. "Of course, they're probably speaking Injun," she thought; "so's I wouldn't understand anyway."

It was difficult enough to understand Lonely Cricket when he spoke with her.

"Molly says she wants to go home," Dinah thought. "I wonder if I'd miss this place if I were to go off. I surely don't think so, except Lonely Cricket. I'd miss him."

The teenager savored the smell of horse that wafted from the barn. "I'd miss the horses, too. More than that if Pa would allow I could work with them."

The sound of Mose's voice caught Dinah's ear bringing another thought, "I'd miss Mose—not a lot, but some—more than my parents."

Bitter tears sprung to the young woman's eyes. She was glad to be alone where no one else could see them. She wiped her face with her hands and realized that they were dirty. "Now, I've smudged my face right funny," she thought. At least that thought brought the corners of a smile to her mouth.

"I not tell Miss Stillwell, but Dancing Crow reason I go home;" Miriam hoarsely whispered.

Lonely Cricket nodded, cocked his head, and waited for Miriam to continue.

"When I home, we marry. I know he love me. I love him. We make home. Have babies. Now, I cook good bread. White Man buy. We live in town."

"Not with your people?"

"No, people not let Dancing Crow and Short Poplar marry."

"Why not?"

"He for Bear Clan. I, too, Bear Clan. Not allow marry."

The young man squinted as he thought about what Miriam had said. "It hard you love when parents and tribe not accept. It hard when you break rule. Clan important."

The young woman nodded, and Lonely Cricket could see the tears at the edge of her eyes. He sighed and said, "Rules important, but love important, too. Is that why parents send Short Poplar to school?"

"Yes." The woman shuddered slightly. "They say I forget Dancing Crow. They say I comeback and marry another brave. I not want another brave; I want Dancing Crow."

Lonely Cricket squeezed the young woman's hand, which he still held in his. "Love hard, not make life easy."

Unconsciously, Dinah dug the nails of her left hand into her palm. "Ouch," she said, not loudly enough for the two Indians to hear. Looking at the bruise marks she had inflicted on herself, the girl thought, "Feelings can make a fool of thee, Dinah Tideswell."

***

Lonely Cricket and Miriam, whose name was Short Poplar, talked more. They wearied of standing by the corral and sat on the half-log bench Broadmore Tideswell had made years before when he had felled a great beech.

"Some day when Dinah is interested in a young man, she can sit on this bench and talk with him and you will be able to watch over her," Broadmore had told Rachel.

At the time, it had seemed a foolish thought. After all, their daughter was only a young girl. Seeing the two young Indians seated there, Rachel thought, "At least that silly bench is some use."

Lonely Cricket thought long about what he should say to his friend. He remembered a story Tall Grass had once told him. "Not know why he told story. It hot day. We sit by stream near parents' home."

ΩΩΩΩΩ

It was in the time of the White Men who wore long dresses and spoke a different tongue. They came among the people and traded for furs. They sought the fur of the beaver and of the muskrat, of the mink, and the otter. They told stories of a god who created the heavens and the earth and who would save us from death.

Some of these men stayed among the people and lived among them, but they had brought no women with them, so they lusted after the women of the people. One of the White Men, the one whom the others called Brother and who led their songs, fell in love with Singing Small Bird.

"I must not love you," he told her; "for I have promised to never love a woman."

Singing Small Bird laughed at his words, and her laughter sounded like the bird of the broken wing, the bird that calls the hunter to lure him away from her babies. Her laughter sounded like the music of bells and chimes to the White Man who loved her even more.

Each day, the White Man saw Singing Small Bird going about her chores in the village, helping her mother and the other married women with the preparation of hides, with the making of food, and with the tending of the three sisters. He heard the men of the village say, "Soon Singing Small Bird will make one of us an excellent wife." All these things made the White Man love Singing Small Bird even more.

When he could no longer withstand his desire, the White Man went to Singing Small Bird's uncle and asked if he could take her as his wife. "I will stay with your people and make them as my own," the White Man said. "If the people will allow it, I will fight in your battles. I will kill in your hunts, and I will worship your gods, for I love Singing Small Bird more than I love the ways of my own people, more even than I love my god."

For many moons, the White Man stayed among the people. Each day he would go to the uncle of Singing Small Bird and repeat his pledge. And, each day he would follow Singing Small Bird about the village helping her and saying sweet words to her until she came to notice him and to smile when he came near her.

The White Man whom the other White Men called Brother asked the young men of the tribe what he should do to win the favor of Singing Small Bird and they taught him how to shape a flute and to play music outside of her family's lodge. They taught him how to trap the small animals and to give the skins to Singing Small Bird that she might make moccasins and gloves. They taught him to hunt so that he could bring meat to the fire of Singing Small Bird and her family.

The more the White Man did, the more Singing Small Bird felt of him within her heart. She spoke of him to her uncle and said, "Uncle, I would marry this White Man, for he loves me, and I love him."

Singing Small Bird's uncle called the White Man to his fire and told him that he could marry Singing Small Bird. The White Man's heart was filled with joy. He worked hard to be worthy of her hand. He hunted so there might be a feast to celebrate their marriage. He gathered wood and skins to make a lodge in which they might live.

When it was time for the ceremony of marriage, the medicine man asked the White Man, "What will your name be now that you are one of the people?"

The White Man had not thought of this. He said, "Could you give me a name as you give the names to the young children?"

The medicine man said that he would ask Ma-Ona to tell him the White Man's new name. "Come back tomorrow, and I will give you your name."

The next day, the White Man came to the lodge of the medicine man and asked, "What is my name to be known among the people?"

"You shall be known as Man Who Is Not Who He Was," replied the medicine man.

So it was that Man Who Is Not Who He Was came to live among the people.

He tried to be a good member of the village. Every day he would get up and go about doing the things that people did. Every day he would talk to other men. Every day he would hunt and fish trap and prepare for battle. And every night he would sleep with Singing Small Bird as had been his hope. But never did he know who he was. Never did he know what arrow of fate Ma-Ona had placed in his heart. Always, Man Who Is Not Who He Was could only think of the past he had given up, the past he had left behind.

ΩΩΩΩΩ

When Lonely Cricket finished his story, he said, "I ask Tall Grass why he tell me story. He say, 'Remember, Lonely Cricket, life is to be lived. Do not dwell in the house of your regrets.'

"Short Poplar, you not want be 'Not What I Was'. Go back to Dakota, marry Dancing Crow."

The young woman ran her right hand over the rough-hewn seat of the bench. "Life like bench. Look smooth but many splinter." She pulled small bits of wood from her palm.

***

"Matthew, hast thou had enough on thy plate?" Rachel asked the older of the Frazier boys at supper that evening.

"Thank you, Ma'am," the boy responded. Taken by surprise, it was only later that he regretted not asking for more of the excellent chicken.

"I'm surprised she knows your name," his brother commented later when they were reading for bed. "Even more she knows I might have an appetite. At least if Broadmore is gonna favor that Injun, it'd be nice if his missus were to take an interest in our plates."

Whatever Matthew's hopes might have been, at breakfast the next morning Rachel had forgotten any solicitations. "Hurry on boys, thou hast much to do," had been her only proclamation to them all.

Chapter 28 ~ Coupling

Shirtless, the straps of his overalls flapping to his sides, Lonely Cricket leaned on the rail fencing and enjoyed the play of the evening breeze on his body. It had been changing of late, and Harry enjoyed the changes—the toughening and firming of muscle, the increase in height, even the growth of hair around his parts, under his arms, and now patch by patch on his chest.

Only the downy hair on his face was a bother, requiring as it did being scratched away with the razor that Broadmore Tideswell had presented him one morning just after breakfast.

"Mose will show thee how." He handed the blade to the young man. "Like as not there will be some blood shed afore thou hast the hang of it. Not like the women folk whose blood is ordained by The Almighty, but thou'll get the hang. Won't he boys?"

The others had laughed. Matthew Frazier muttered—his voice just loud enough for his brother Luke to hear, "I hope the dumb Injun slits his throat."

When they left the table, Mose had shown him the way of shaving: the sharpening, the heating of water, the soaping, the scraping clean, the washing, and finally the bits of paper to staunch the flow of red. "Don't worry, boy, as the Mister says, you'll get the hang."

And get it, he had, for which he was thankful every third day when he took his turn with the basin and soap. Only an occasional nick—better than the Frazier boys, far better than Burton, whose face often appeared pocked with bits of corn silk used to staunch the flow of blood. Almost as good as Mose, who had become his mentor and best friend.

The breeze tickled ever so lightly against his torso. Harry looked down and without thought counted the hairs on his chest. It seemed there were more—more today than yesterday—more yesterday than a week before.

Dinah tiptoed close and touched her fingertips to Harry's left shoulder. His first reaction was a quivering of muscles much like a young horse reacting to a fly. It was all the girl could do to hold back the giggle in her throat.

She touched again. This time he reached across with his right hand to scratch, Dinah pulling back just in time to escape detection.

With the third touch, a little longer and stronger, he turned. "What?"

"Beautiful evening is it not?" she asked, trying for innocence in her voice.

"Best time; no work, peaceful."

She leaned against the fence next to him—her right side at his left—close enough that arms touched, that hips osculated. Ever so slightly Dinah leaned against Harry. It aroused him in ways he didn't understand. His parts grew as they did some mornings when he awoke. There was a stirring he did not understand.

One night, when Lonely Cricket was still a boy, just before the birth of Many Fish, Lame Bear had spoken of such feelings. Harry had not understood his father's words, but he knew they were the words of adults.

At the Tideswell farm Harry had watched stallions mount their mares and had listened to Mose talk about the needs of a man and how on a Sunday afternoon, after church, he would relieve himself with his Leah. Still, Harry was amazed to have that need erupt within his own body.

"Dost thou like me?"

He nodded.

"I like thee," she said.

The boy said nothing.

"I like thee a great deal."

"That good." Harry knew that the girl wanted him to say something, to do something, but he had no fathom of what.

She reached in front of him and took his right wrist in her left hand. Harry did not resist, allowing her to reposition them so they were face to face, her breasts touching his chest, her mouth slightly below and just inches from his. "Wouldst thou wish to kiss me once more?" Her voice hushed and deep.

Without waiting for his response, Dinah pushed onto her toes, thrust her lips against his, and pushing her tongue ever so slightly into his mouth, kissed him in a way that aroused him even more.

"Aren't thou going to kiss me in return?" she demanded.

And he did. And again. And again. Their mouths met, their tongues caressed, and their hands—having taken on an energy and immediacy of their own—roamed and touched and stroked.

***

The Major called him Samuel, but to the other Indians the Apache was known as Arrow Who Speaks Truth. It was he who convened the group of young men who had received the medicine bundle of a warrior. In their cellar meeting place, they would dance, sing the songs of their people, and tell the stories they had learned in their tribes. There they would share a pipe of friendship and talk of the White Man's knowledge and of the Red Man's wisdom.

Once, when a Cree boy and a Lakota girl had been caught by Matron Fox kissing and fondling among the blooming apple trees, the Major called an assembly and the White man chaplain told of the first man and the first woman, of how the Trickster had come in the shape of a snake and how the woman listened to that snake and brought evil into the world. Later that same night when the White men slept, Arrow Who Speaks Truth called the young warriors together to talk of men and women.

ΩΩΩΩΩ

When the people were first created the men and women lived in separate wikiups. They did not know of touching and of pleasure. Sparrow With Empty Nest was lonely. She prayed to Spider Woman to have pity on her that she might have someone to share her cooking fire. Spider Woman took pity on Sparrow With Empty Nest and sent her a child, a fine baby who would grow to manhood.

That should have made Sparrow With Empty Nest happy, for she was no longer alone; but it did not. Now she had to find food for her child as well as herself. So, Sparrow With Empty Nest again prayed to Spider Woman to have pity on her that she might have someone to help gather food and take care of the child. Spider Woman took pity on Sparrow With Empty Nest and told her to search among the men for one who would share her wikiup and be father to her child.

That should have made Sparrow With Empty Nest content, for Spider Woman had told her what she must do; but it did not. She did not know how to search among the men and how to find one who would want to share her wikiup and be a father to her child. So once more Sparrow With Empty Nest prayed to Spider Woman to have pity on her that she might learn how to find a man. Spider Woman took pity on Sparrow With Empty Nest and told her to adorn herself with colors and shells, with robes and feathers. Spider Woman taught Sparrow With Empty Nest how to spin a web that would capture the heart of a man.

When Sparrow With Empty Nest walked among the wikiups of the men, many men came forward and followed her. "How should I choose the right man to share my cooking fire and be a father to my son?" Sparrow With Empty Nest prayed to Spider Woman.

Spider Woman was wary of taking pity on Sparrow With Empty Nest, so she answered only, "Trust what your heart tells you."

So it is to this day that we men may follow the women of the people, but it is the woman who must choose among us knowing only the wisdom of her heart.

The man whom Sparrow With Empty Nest chose was a good choice, for he loved her and took care of her child. Together they had many more children, and she became known as Sparrow Whose Nest Overflows.

ΩΩΩΩΩ

When Arrow Who Speaks Truth finished his story, the men laughed and agreed that they were powerless before the tricks of Spider Woman. As Plenty Horses said, "On the hunt, we may see a handsome antelope and pursue it, but it is the spirit of the animal that allows us to kill. So, too, with women; they attract us, and we follow, but they must allow us to enter their wikiup and lie by their cooking fire."

"It is the will of the spirits that we do so," said one of the others. "The Great Spirit would be angry if we did not."

***

The night of their second kiss, Lonely Cricket found it difficult to sleep. He stared up into the shadowy darkness lit by a low-flickering candle and thought of Dinah.

And then he thought of Sapphira Cook. It had been many months since he had last heard from her. Thoughts of Nebraska and of his childhood filled his head.

Kneeling next to his straw-mattressed cot, Lonely Cricket dug into his carpetbag and pulled out the small cloth turtle his sister had given him. Tattered and dirty though it had become, he held the toy to his eyes and spoke to the spirit within it.

"What are these feelings that come when I am with Dinah? Why do I think so often of home? What should I do? Am I a man or a boy? What would a true warrior do?"

He dug again into the carpetbag and pulled out his medicine bundle. To keep it from prying eyes, Lonely Cricket kept it wrapped in a union suit. Holding the turtle in one hand and the small bag in the other, he lay back onto his cot. He stared into the darkness and thought of the meanings of these things, of childhood and of being a man.

He didn't know when he passed from consciousness to sleep. In the morning, the medicine bag was still clutched in his left hand. The cloth turtle had slipped from his right and lay next to the cot.

***

Fireflies darted about. In the paddock, three mares stomped and whinnied. The muffled sound of their foals echoed from the barn where the weanlings were penned far from their mothers' teats. Overhead, with only a wisp of moon to outshine them, stars and planets sparkled in the cloudless night.

She waited, as planned, under the great beech that had been a sapling when the first Tideswell had taken deed to the land and sailed from Plymouth in search of peace, tranquility, and service to God. Although it was never spoken of, Dinah knew that she was the only child, that her husband, whoever he might be, would someday with her inherit the two hundred thirty acres, the house, the barns, the crops, and of course, the animals. It was a rich birthright, but not one she coveted. At the moment, the girl only wanted to run as far and as fast as she could from this place and her parents—from her mother's never-ending list of boring chores, from her father's refusal to accept her love and understanding of horses, and from the Quaker meeting and its hypocritical elder, Jonathan Brandon.

Dinah waited.

In the barn, Harry finished bedding the horses.

Waiting, Dinah imagined the life ahead. Perhaps they would run away to Nebraska and live with his people. Perhaps they would marry, and her parents would have to swallow their pride and accept their half-breed grandchildren. Perhaps she would never be Mrs. Lonely Cricket; that would be a waste of the needlepoint she kept hidden under her mattress. "Dinah Tideswell," her name, on one line. A curlicue divider in the middle. "Harry Lonely Cricket" on the second. The entire surrounded with flowers and sundry decorations. She had been working on it for weeks. Her mother would disapprove of such a frivolous project.

"Ppsst." Harry's voice interrupted the young woman's reverie.

The smells of hay, horse, and leather preceded him.

Dinah patted the ground, and he sat next to her. "I thought thou would not come."

"Why not come?"

"I know thou preferest other girls."

He stared at her and mumbled, "No understand."

"Other girls. Thou thinks they are prettier than I."

"Dinah pretty like sunset."

She smiled. "Dost thou really think so?"

"Dinah handsome woman." He blushed with his declaration and reached his hand toward hers.

She pulled back. "Dost thou love me, Lonely Cricket? Dost thou truly love me?"

"Stallion make love mare; make foal. Dinah want foal with Lonely Cricket?"

Dinah laughed. Her laughter grew strident, raised in pitch until the sound pierced the night.

Harry stared without comprehension.

Her laughter turned to tears, to great rending sobs.

"What matter?" Harry reached for her. This time, Dinah didn't pull away but allowed him to envelop her in his arms. They rocked back and forth; she locked in his arms, her own hands held to her face, the tears flowing and her breath in gasps.

"What matter?" Harry repeated as the girl's sobs subsided.

"No, I don't want to make a foal with thee." The deluge resumed.

"Then no make love." Harry reassured her at the next diminution of her sobs.

"I want thee to love me, not rut with me," the girl explained even while realizing that the words would only confuse Harry.

"Love not rut?" Harry didn't understand, but at least she was again laughing. "Laugh good."

"Yes, laugh good," Dinah agreed. "Love is good, too, in heart. Making love like a horse is not good."

"Make foal good. Make baby good, too."

"Make foal very good. Making babies? I'm not ready for that, Harry. I don't trust men. Not since ..."

They sat in silence. Harry's right hand entwined with Dinah's left.

"God-man at school say make baby first must make marry."

"Is that what they taught thee?"

"Say no marry and go Hell. Bad place Hell."

"Is that what they say at the colored church?"

"Pastor Morgan not talk make babies, not talk marry, talk do right, talk not hate White Man, talk help, talk go Heaven. Say Hell for White folk, God love color people; not send Hell."

"Not even if they make babies without marrying?"

"Man, woman at church make baby. Get married after. Pastor Morgan say love good. Baby named Michael. Pastor Morgan say Michael child of love, baby good,"

"Well, what dost thou believe, Lonely Cricket?"

"Lonely Cricket believe Great Spirit love people, give world to people, not punish people love. Not punish people make baby. Send Mother Moon watch over man, woman love each other. Lonely Cricket know White god-man fooled by trickster. Pastor Morgan know Ma-Ona thinking because Pastor not White."

He leaned forward and kissed her again.

"Lonely Cricket believe Dinah right. Love in heart good. Make baby another time." He bent forward once more and kissed her gently.

Soon the young couple was a knot of arms and legs entwined.

The dew had started to form. A glow framed the eastern sky. In the nearby copse a whippoorwill sang and another answered. The teens kissed one last time.

Harry rushed to the barn. When Mose awoke, he would be brushing the foals. After that would come feeding the anxious mares who pawed the ground and perked their ears in the direction of the barn. Harry would not tell the colored man how he had spent the night.

Dinah slipped into the kitchen door. Carefully avoiding a squeaky tread, she climbed the stairs, changed to her nightdress, and climbed into bed. She would wait for her mother's call—not the first or even the second—before she would sleepily announce that she was awake.

The coming day would be difficult for them both, but a reasonable price for the night's pleasure.

Chapter 29 ~ A Theft at the Church

The day promised more snow. The air felt of chill, but resting, as she did, in one of the sunbeams that sneaked through the western windows of the Ebenezer Black Baptist Church, Louisa Murrow could dream of the coming spring. She didn't mind waiting for Pastor Morgan. Her church cushion was soft enough that the steep-backed pew was tolerable. The boys playing at snowball war made a pleasant tableau outside the window, albeit not so agreeable as the birds that sang in Louisa's dreams. In spring, such songs were God's call to waken her to each morning's possibilities and to each day's joys.

This morning, when not dozing off, the old woman's thoughts were of her sister and of the letter she had received that week. Once the minister was done teaching that Injun boy his letters, why then, it would be her turn.

Pastor Morgan would read Amelia's letter to her and then help pen a response. She would mark it at the end and wish once more aloud that she had learned to read and write. "The Holy Word," she would say, "if only I could read the Holy Word." The preacher would pat her shoulder and reassure that it was more important to live by scripture than to read it.

When Cedric Harvey peeked in the window, Louisa had slumped over. "The old woman's asleep," the mahogany-skinned youngster thought. "Hell, maybe she's gone and dead."

For all his quick mind and good looks, Cedric Harvey was not a good boy, no, not even a scamp. He was a bad seed in the parish. Had there been a way, Pastor Morgan might have excluded the boy from the church, but O'Day Harvey was one of the church elders and Elvira was a pillar of the women's guild. So, their only son, the notorious Cedric, continued his role as rascal bane.

The other boys tolerated him only so far. True, Cedric, at thirteen, could hit a ball farther than most of the older boys. True, he could run faster than many. And snowball in hand he could terrorize any girl in the parish, even those older and bigger than he. Surely, he could tell a story quicker than most, and one that could almost have them believing. But Cedric was a cheat. "He never touched me … I never missed it." Smile at the ready, he denied everything, even what the others had clearly seen.

"You was too killed," the boys had chorused. Cedric, throwing his cap to the ground in outrage, had stalked off the battlefield. Nobody was watching. Nobody knew the old biddy was there. "What might be in her bag?" The question rose immediately in the young thief's mind.

He slipped around the building to the graveyard and then through the side door, which was usually reserved for after burials. After the corpse had been returned to the earth, the pastor and the next of kin would return through that side door for a moment of silent prayer while the congregation would, with respect and deference, remain outside talking of the departed and—for the men at least—passing a small jug of comfort.

"Perhaps she's dead. Serves her right." Cedric lost no love on anyone, but he had a particular dislike for the old woman whose body slumped precariously close to falling off the pew and to the roughhewn floor of the church. Louisa Murrow was one who clucked often at him and the other youngsters of the church. Had she not only that morning, before the service began, told him his face needed washing as the Lord would see it? "As if God would notice a boy's dirt-smudged face with all the sins of his elders to count." Cedric had had his comeback framed, even on the tip of his tongue, but his mother approached, asked the old woman what was the matter, and then directed him to the wash basin set outside the front door.

"Don't argue, boy," his father had added for emphasis. How was it that the old man always knew when he was about to give his mother a difficulty?

Cedric stepped as quietly as he could. Louisa's slumped body had pushed her bag to the floor. Cedric picked it up and quickly rummaged. Three coins, no four! Now that was a treasure worth a boy's stealing.

Something else caught his eye. He had seen Louisa wear it once or twice, a brooch of shining stone and metal. Surely not gold or silver, but lovely in a woman's way. A large pink stone and filigreed metal work. Something a boyfriend might give. Something he might hide away at least until the old woman was surely gone and forgotten. Then perhaps he'd find a girl who'd do for him the way a woman should. Yep, that would be her payment for getting him in trouble. That brooch could buy him nights of pleasure from the right girl. "Maybe even a white girl, one of them stuck up rich white girls, he told himself and licked his lips in anticipation.

"Or perhaps, I'll sell it," was his next thought. There were plenty of young men who'd pay good money for such a trinket to give a girlfriend. The Warwick boys always had money in their pockets and their eyes on one or another pretty girl. Hadn't he seen Johnny Warwick ice-skating with Ann Lancaster just the other day.

"That's perfect, them Lancasters bein' Quakers, she'll never wear it where her folks might see. And Johnny'll get his money worth and more." Cedric wished he could give the brooch to Ann himself. She was one of the long list of White girls whose secret places he longed to explore. Of course, he never said such things aloud, that could get a Negra whipped, but he did have a hankering. "Maybe someday." For now, he would take Johnny Warwick's money.

Pocketing the coins and the brooch, Cedric replaced the bag, careful to set it upright so nobody would think to check its contents until ... well, possibly never. After all, she was probably dead.

A sound disrupted him. The pastor's door was opening. Quick but silently, crouching low, Cedric slipped through the church and—fearing being seen by whoever was coming out of the study—hid behind the pulpit. In the confusion of finding the old lady, he would slip out and then come in, the innocent bystander drawn by the excitement.

From the pulpit he saw Harry, the Indian boy who came each Sunday with Mose who worked at the Tideswell farm. Of course, the minister's pet, the boy who wanted to learn reading and writing and sums. The boy who was getting a name for helping folks, especially with their horses. If there were anyone Cedric hated more than the Old Biddy Murrow, it would surely be that Injun.

Lonely Cricket saw the older woman slumped in the pew near the center of the three western windows. He ran to her, calling for help as he took a score of long strides to reach her. As the youngster reached Louisa, Pastor Morgan came out of his office already yelling, "Why are you shouting in ..." The minister took in the situation and rushed towards his fallen parishioner, the tail of his jacket flapping with each portly step.

"Quick, Harry, get water and call some of the women." The preacher knelt by Louisa, feeling for the pulse in her neck. "Thank God, she's alive," he muttered.

Lonely Cricket was already at the front door yelling to some of the women to come quickly.

Cedric, seeing his moment, slipped into the pastor's study. He listened to the hubbub crescendo in the church and clambered out the window. Carefully tucking himself together, he nonchalantly moved around the church and joined the throng of heavily wrapped congregants who now peered inward and stomped their feet against the cold.

Meanwhile, Lonely Cricket, almost colliding with Mose's friend Sally Goodnuff and with Mr. Zachariah, who was one of the elders, had brought a pail of water from the well. Mrs. Morgan was already crouched next to her husband and the stricken woman. Louisa had been laid out on the floor, her head resting on two pew cushions. Dipping her husband's handkerchief in the pail of water, Mrs. Morgan gently sponged the older woman's face and wrists.

"Ohhh." Louisa groaned once and then again. She blinked. "Where...?"

A murmur of satisfaction swept through the throng. Louisa was going to be all right. Louisa was going to be just fine.

Cedric fingered the coins in his left pocket. The brooch he had carefully stuck into his waistband. He could not help smiling at the thought of even more money in his pockets.

***

Mose rode to the Meeting house and asked Broadmore if he might borrow the Tideswell's sleigh to take the old woman home.

With Sally Goodnuff's help, he tucked the old woman under a thick wool robe and clucked the horse to start him on his way. Sally climbed up beside the stricken woman, held her hand, and made soothing small talk as if everything were normal as normal could be.

"Cricket," Mose called out, you bring the horses home. I'll be back soon's I see Miss Louisa safe and take Sally home as well."

With a snap of the whip, the horse pulled forward. The sleigh runners crunched against the snow, hesitated, and then moved ahead.

"Get up!" Mose called and snapped the whip again. Lonely Cricket knew that was unnecessary. No matter how he might be mourning for his lost Susanne, Mose was showing off for Sally.

***

Yquili Sparrow seldom told stories, but she had told this to Happy Turtle and Lonely Cricket, sitting far from the cooking fire they had heard what their mother said.

ΩΩΩΩΩ

The woman of Strong Bull had died. Sorrow fell on him and he could not play his flute or sing songs of joy.

He sang only of his sorrow and of the woman he had lost. His people gathered in council without him. They built a great fire and gathered around it. In the front row were the old men who had much wisdom. In the middle row were the warriors and hunters who had much strength and energy. In the last row, farthest from the fire, were the women—old and young, who had much emotion.

"What shall we do about Strong Bull?" the people asked. "His sorrow over his woman's death has stopped the songs of his flute and has blocked the gladness of his heart. It is not right that a man grieves so."

"He must be told to find another woman," one of the young men suggested.

It was agreed by many that Strong Bull should find a new woman to fill his teepee and to share his sleeping robe. But whom? The council listed all the women of the village, even those who were with men.

"If Strong Bull had wanted one of these women, he would have pursued her before," one of the warriors suggested, "but always he pursued his woman who has died, only her. Why would Strong Bull now want one of the women of our village."

"That is true," agreed one of the older men, whose own woman had died moons before. "In time Strong Bull will forget his pain. After a time, he will sing songs of joy and play his flute."

Other of the older men agreed. One who no longer had teeth and could no longer chew the meat of the buffalo spoke of growing old. "With age comes acceptance. A young man longs for the hunt and for battle. A young man looks forward to sharing the night with a woman. But an old man learns to forget those things and take pleasure in the gruel that remains"

Many agreed that time would heal Strong Bull's loneliness. But, it did not. Moons passed and Strong Bull still did not play his flute or sing songs of happiness. Once more the village met in council.

"What shall we do about Strong Bull?" they asked again. "His sorrow over his woman's death has stopped the songs of his flute and has blocked the gladness of his heart. It is not right that a man grieves so."

"He must be told to find another woman." The same young man who had said this at the first council repeated his suggestion. This time even more people agreed with him.

From the back circle of the council a woman spoke. There was a gasp of surprise that any woman would speak at a council fire, but this was no ordinary council for even the women who were with child had been invited.

"Strong Bull must not be told to do this. You cannot tell a person to love or to stop loving. Strong Bull still loves his woman and he cannot be told to stop loving her. If you tell him to find another woman and he does as he is told, his woman will come back and haunt his heart."

The other women murmured agreement.

"Then what are we to do about Strong Bull?" one of the chiefs asked. "His sorrow over his woman's death has stopped the songs of his flute and has blocked the gladness of his heart. It is not right that a man grieves so."

The woman who had spoken replied, "The journey of life is far and winding. Each man must find his own path. Trust that Strong Bull will find his path again and when he does, he will again sing of gladness and he will again play the flute."

The women all agreed with her. Many of the men were discontented, but they had no better solution to offer, so the village waited while Strong Bull sang songs of sadness and did not play his flute.

After many more moons, the tribe attacked another village. One of the young women of that village found Strong Bull's manly desire. She was not as beautiful as his woman who had died. She was not as skillful in the making of clothes or the cooking of food. But she caught his eye and he took her to share his sleeping robe.

Once more Strong Bull played his flute and once more, he sang happier songs. Though he never sang songs of gladness as he once had, the village knew that Strong Bull had once again found his path.

ΩΩΩΩΩ

Lonely Cricket was glad for his friend Mose that he again had a woman, that there was someone for whom he would crack the whip over the horse's head.

***

Louisa Murrow did not miss her brooch for days. When the pastor looked in on her she again thought to write to her sister Amelia. "It were our momma's," she explained as she searched her bag for the jewelry, "a gift from her mistress. Old Ms. Murrow done man'mitted us all when her husband gone. Gave our momma that paper and this fancy brooch, called it payment for her sins.

"Momma passed it on to me, but Amelia's the one with chil'en. Her older girl ought be old 'nough to 'preciate it. I don't wear it but Easter and Christmas to church."

"That's a lovely thought Miss Louisa."

"She's a good wife," the pastor thought as he helped himself to another of the sugar cookies his wife had sent along to the recovering parishioner.

Louisa's search became frantic. "Where is it? Where did I put my brooch?" She dumped the contents of her bag onto the small table at which she did her sewing, ate her meals, and today entertained the pastor.

"It isn't here. Oh my! How?" The woman flustered and fussed. The preacher feared she might faint.

"Now, now, Louisa, we'll find it." He licked the sugar from his lips. "Where do you usually keep it? Perhaps you put it away and don't recall."

She shuffled to the chest of drawers that stood in the corner of her one room cabin.

Meanwhile, the pastor took a log from the pile and placed it carefully into the fire.

The old woman searched the drawer and then again. "No, Pastor Michael, it ain't here. What my goin' to do? What my goin' to do?"

"Perhaps you dropped it at church, when you fainted. I'll ask Horace if he found it when he was cleaning on Monday." Horace Zachariah was an elder and the sextant as well as Michael Morgan's best friend and fiercest critic.

"I'll stop by his farm and ask," Morgan offered. The preacher dreaded the extra riding on such a bitter cold day and knew that his friend would have at least an hour's commentary on his Sunday sermon. Worse, Horace, a bachelor, always offered him a piece of stale jonny cake "made in my own oven by my own hands."

"No amount of water can wash this abomination from my throat," the preacher often thought as he forced himself to swallow yet another bite of that coarse bread.

"Please!" The old woman's voice was filled with tears. "It's all we have of Momma. Please Pastor Michael, find my brooch."

***

"Our reading today is short. It is found in Exodus, 20:15, and it is simple, clear and sure."

There was a chorus of "amen," and Sally Goodnuff added, "Praise the Lord!"

The preacher continued. "'Thou shalt not steal;' that's it, the entire lesson. God don't say, well it's okay to take it if you means to put it back. He don't say it's okay to take it if you needs or think you needs it more'n the man what owns it."

"No, suh," one of the congregants said. That too was greeted with calls of "Amen."

"No, and God don't say it's all right to take some'n that ain't yours cause you find it on the floor, not when you knows who it b'longs to. If you know some'n b'longs to another and you finds it on the floor, thing ta do is give it back. You pick it up." Michael Morgan stepped away from the lectern and mimed lifting a great weight and iterated, "You pick it up, and you give it back to the person whose it is."

"Yes, you do," somebody yelled from the back of the congregation.

"Some may say I cain't be bothered. I'll leave her where she lay, and the Good Lord will lead the owner back. Now, is that stealing?"

One man mumbled, "No, it ain't."

"Perhaps it is and perhaps it isn't," the pastor continued. "But there's another word from God that tells us pretty clear what we should do. We find that in Matthew 7:12. 'Therefore all things whatsoever ye would that men should do to you, do ye even so to them: for this is the law and the prophets.'

"Now, I can't speak for Jacob back there or anyone else, but I know if I lose somethin' I prize, like say a piece of my dear wife's jewelry, maybe her brooch or somethin' I was carryin' 'round for her, I'd sure want the person who sees that brooch lyin' on the ground to pick her up." Again, the heavyset minister bent and picked up an invisible object. "And bring it to me."

"Sure enough" one of the women in the congregation shouted, which was followed by another chorus of "Amen."

"So, there it be; short and simple. You find somethin' b'longs to somebody else and you knows it does, you pick it on up and gives it back. That's what the Good Book tells us. We don't put her in our pocket. We don't leaves her lyin' on the ground. We gives her back."

Everybody in the congregation had already heard about Louisa's brooch, but the pastor didn't leave it there. He announced it right out. "Somebody in this congregation must have found Sister Louisa's brooch. We figure she lost it when she fainted couple weeks ago. Remember that?"

A nodding of heads and murmured comments followed the question.

"You probably remember her wearin' it Christmas or Easter, special occasions. A big pink stone and fancy silver holdin' it. Real nice piece of jewelry."

Sally Goodnuff yelled out, "Louisa, I always did 'mire that brooch of yours."

"Maybe you picked it up meaning to return it; but she ain't got it, and that's what counts. Maybe you just tucked it in a pocket and forgot all 'bout havin' it; but she ain't got it, and that's what counts.

"Amen." The pastor abruptly sat down, and his wife began singing "Lead me, Lord, Lead me in Your righteousness …"

Chapter 30 ~ If Lies Be Told

"I hate to say it, Pastor Morgan; but I saw him clear as day." Cedric Harvey practiced his lie quietly and planned his strategy. "I'll look down so's he doesn't see my smile if I can't hold it in. All I gots to do is tell hows I saw Harry stealing that brooch and nobody'll doubt it. Them Indians is thieves. Everybody knows it's in their blood."

"I hate to be the one carrying the tale." He started his recitation again. "I knows the other boys won't like me telling, but it ain't right, Pastor. It was just afore he started yellin' about needing help. That Indian boy of Mr. Mose's was bending over and taking things from Miss Louisa's bag. At first, bein' I didn't know nothing was missing, I thought he was just picking up what she might have dropped. But there he was. I was right over there by that window." Cedric motioned with his head towards one of the windows that looked onto the church burial plot. "I hate to say it, Pastor Morgan; but I saw him clear as day."

"Yas sir, that'll do the job," the boy thought.

Cedric's hatred for Harry was fueled by the Indian boy's efforts to learn reading and writing. "Even arithmetic," O'Day Harvey had pointed out to his son. "How come that heathen's learning his sums and you don't try to learn as much as your ABCs?"

"I can too read," Cedric had rebutted. That was true he could read some and scratch his name and add numbers up to some twenty or more, but it was also true that had Cedric Harvey applied himself with half an effort he'd be Pastor Morgan's star pupil.

"I try to teach him," the reverend had told O'Day; "but he doesn't make an effort."

"I know what you mean," O'Day Harvey replied. "The other day I asked him to cart in the wood for his mother's cooking. He brought in three sticks and set himself on a stump. I said, 'Boy what you doin' sitting there when there's all that wood to carry.' And he says to me, Daddy, I'se worked so hard I'se plumb down to the pit.' And him grinnin' that smile o' his that says, 'I'm lyin' and gettin' away with it, too."

"Well, you think so much of that Indian, how do you feel now everyone knows he's a thief?" Cedric was now rehearsing the conversation he would have with his father once the pastor had believed his story.

***

"Yes, sir, right through that window. Just as clear as day. It was that Indian boy comes with Mr. Mose. I seen him right good. Him bending over Miss Louisa's bag and her lyin' there still as dead. I was gonna run and get you or my pappy, but then he starts hollerin', so I just watched and saw you come out of your study. So, I didn't make no more of it till you preached us about stealin' on Sunday. I was gonna tell my pappy, but then I figured just as easy to come over and tell you direct. No need I shouldn't talk up, not when somebody done wrong."

"You're sure it was Harry?" The minister asked for the second time. Perhaps if another boy had told him the tale, but Cedric Harvey's word was as good as fool's gold or one of those salesmen who periodically came through Newville selling medicines to cure everything from a common cold to old age, from brain fever to tumors. Still, the boy's words couldn't be dismissed—not out of hand.

Cedric nodded his head as he repeated, "Yes, Sir, Pastor Morgan, it was Harry and no other. I seed him right from there."

"And what were you doing in the cemetery, Cedric?" The sternness in the Pastor's voice might have caught a lesser perjurer than Cedric Harvey, but the boy was ready with his answer.

"I guess I have to fess up," he said trying to make his voice quaver and carefully studying the ground in front of his toes. "I had me some tobacca and corn silk and was looking for a place where nobody … you know how it is, Sir. My pappy would tan my hide fierce if he knew I was smoking tobacca. You won't tell him, will you?"

For Cedric, taking blame for something—even if he hadn't done it—was a good strategy for getting adults to believe his lies.

The minister gave an indeterminate grunt. Cedric knew his father would hear it all. Small worry a hiding if it gave his story the ring of truth. It wasn't like he hadn't been hided often enough for smoking and for more. "Your son is a heathen," O'Day Harvey regularly said to Elvira. "It's a father's job to raise a son," she always replied.

***

Rachel Tideswell was putting away the clean wash carefully folding Broadmore's union suits and hoping it would be soon be spring with warmer temperatures and less wash. She took a moment to look out the bedroom window and catch a glimpse of the first crocuses poking from the mud of the front yard. "Tarnation, now what do they want?" she asked herself.

The delegation of negroes was coming up the drive. In the front was a one-seat buggy with a man dressed in black and a woman equally somber. She recollected meeting them once. "I do believe he's the minister over to that Black church Mose attends. That must be his wife. Who them others might be …"

The old gray pulling the buggy looked thin and near collapse. "I suppose they've come looking to buy a new one." She started towards the door and down the stairs. "Best call Broadmore. I hope they don't expect a discount 'cause of the cloth."

At the front door, Rachel—now clutching a wrap to herself—called in the direction of the older barn. "Broadmore, thou hast company."

Her husband was already exiting the barn door, buttoning his coat as he came. Taking a quick look at the delegation coming up the drive, Broadmore helloed and strode towards the front of the house. As he walked, the horseman took in the small group, the two people in the buggy and three mounted men.

He, too, recognized Pastor Morgan and figured the woman to be his wife. Quickly, he reached the same conclusion as his wife, "They're needing a new beast. I wonder what they can afford."

One of the other men was mounted on a plow horse that looked old but cared for. "Not much of a seat," he thought. With a quick look at the horse's legs Broadmore added, "Not many furrows left in him either."

The second man was on a mule that looked in fair health if too small for his rider's legs. The man's worn boots, hanging free of stirrups, almost raked the ground. The third rider was on a good-looking dun that had obviously been curried that morning. His saddle and tack were newly polished as well. "I know that fellow. O'Day something. Proud fellow. I recollect selling him a horse, but not that one."

Cedric Harvey was supposed to be mounted behind his father on that dun, but he had begged to be excused. "If them boys tell I was there, all the other boys will think I told. Nobody likes an Injun, but they hate tattlers more."

O'Day Harvey had bargained with the boy. "You shine Emperor up nice and pretty and you can stay home."

"At least he can do a lick of work when he's proper moved," the man had reflected as the delegation had left the church and headed towards the Tideswell farm.

"Hello," Broadmore called again. "Can I help thee?" Then, turning back to the barns he hollered, "Luke, Matthew, these gentlemen need thy help with their animals."

Slowly as they dared the Frazier brothers pulled on their coats and walked across the yard.

Meanwhile, Broadmore had reached the buggy. Touching the brim of his hat, he nodded to Mrs. Morgan. "Ma'am." Then he turned to the men, nodded again and asked, "How can I help ye?"

Before the men could reply, the Frazier brothers had come closer. Taking a look at the four animals and their owners, Matthew said, "You want us to help?"

"I do. Make sure they are cooled properly, watered, and given a bit of hay. It's a chilly morning and hard hauling through the mud. They'll take ill if they're not attended proper."

"But—"

"No buts, boy, do as thou art told." Broadmore turned again to the five Negroes. "And what would ye have of me, gentlemen?" Again, he turned to the minister's wife and nodded.

"It's not you we're seeking, Mr. Tideswell," Horace Zachariah said as he dropped to the ground from his mule. "We've come to speak to Mose—"

"That is if it's all right with you, Sir," Michael Morgan added.

"Of course, Pastor, and Mrs. Tideswell will be honored to receive thy Missus whilst you talk with him."

He gestured with his head in the direction of the front porch, where Rachel responded, "Wouldst thou care for some tea whilst the men do their business?"

"Thank you, Ma'am," the woman answered from deep inside her heavy cloak and cover, "but I think I must be part of this discussion."

"My goodness, what hast Mose done that requires thy concern?" Broadmore inquired.

"It ain't so much Mose as that Indian boy he brings 'round to the church," O'Day Harvey answered. He still sat atop Emperor and tried to look every bit the proper owner of such a splendid mount.

"Harry?" Broadmore took a moment to rub his hands together. "Now, ye know it ain't rightly Mose who's responsible for the boy. So, if ye needs be talking about him, I'd best be part of the conversation as well." He added a bit more loudly, "Whatever it is, I'm sure some tea and a bit of cake won't be remiss after. Rachel wilt thou and Dinah prepare refreshments for our friends?"

"Of course, Broadmore." She didn't bother to add her reflection that Dinah was probably someplace in the barns or even in the back corral where Harry usually schooled the young Appaloosas each morning. "I don't know if it's the horses or the boy who draws her most," Rachel had confided to Molly Stillwell one morning over tea.

"Give the girl her head and she'll get over both," Molly had opined.

Heading back to the door, the lady of the house mumbled to herself, "God Almighty, now he has me feeding Niggers. There's no end of that man's foolishness."

Turning to the five visitors, Broadmore said, "Here I thought ye folks came wanting some animals. I must say, friend, thy horse has seen better days." This last remark directed to the man atop the aged plow horse.

"I reckon he do," said the man as he pulled his stumbling steed towards one of the Frazier boys. "If I had me the money, I sure would admire something a bit younger."

"And you, Parson," Broadmore added. "I fear that horse of thine has seen better days as well."

"Perhaps another day, Sir," O'Day Harvey said. "We all know you have fine horseflesh to sell, but today's is another matter."

"So it is. So it is." Broadmore gestured towards the barns. "I suppose we'd best find Mose and then the boy." He moved forward and bellowed, "Mose. Mose. Where thou at Mose?"

They all heard Mose's answering shout. "I'se in the new barn, Massa Broadmore."

Turning slightly, Broadmore led the way towards the new structure. "Well, looking to buy a new animal or not ye will see my Appaloosas. Fine horses they would be for thee as well."

***

Harry, muffled against the morning cold, smoke flaring from his mouth and nostrils, had been shoveling space in the snow-laden paddock. Soon the snow would be melted, and the ground turned to mud. Both surfaces too slippery for young animals. He spread a coat of hay on the ground to give purchase to hooves.

"The little ones need to gambol," Mose had instructed that morning. It had been days of snow and freeze. As he spoke, they could hear the animals' nickered impatience.

Once the enclosure was ready, Harry brought them out: first the fillies for their romp and then the colts. Warmed by the work and the first sun in days, the young man—standing at the rail and watching the foals—wished that he, like the Appaloosas in his charge, could spend the morning at play.

Dinah had the same thought as she slipped up behind him and wrapped her arms around his chest. "Canst we not slip off whilst they frolic?" She asked.

"Much work. Clean stalls while horse outside."

"Thou work too much, Lonely Cricket." She kissed him on the neck.

"You help?" He turned and smiled at her. "You want clean stall?"

"That's not fair. Thou know I would, but my father forbids. He says, 'Women should not work with horses. That's a man's job.'"

"Broadmore Tideswell good man. Know much about horse but not know daughter."

"That's true enough." Dinah picked up a handful of snow, shaped it carefully and threw the snowball at Sky's rump. The young horse bucked and broke into a gallop, startling the other foals who joined in his run. Harry had bent down for another handful of snow when he and Dinah heard Mose's call, "Harry, you'd best come here." Behind the foreman's voice they heard a tussle and then came the shouts of the Frazier boys: "You're in it now."

"This'll teach that Injun." And, the yell of Burton Miles, "Hey, that ain't right. You leave his stuff be."

"That be enough," Broadmore boomed. His command was followed by quiet. Then Mose called again.

Harry and Dinah looked at one another. Dinah started for the barn, but Harry grabbed her arm. "You go back house. Father angry you here."

"I don't care. If he's going to be angry at thee, then he can be angry at me as well. What's wrong in my watching the animals play?"

"That not what he angry at."

"Well, there's nothing wrong in the way I feel about you either." She pulled free and walked with long strides towards the door of the barn, which was closed against the lingering cold breezes of the day.

Harry rushed to get to the door first. In his hurry, he almost slipped in a pile of not-quite-dry manure. Reaching out to right himself, he caught Dinah's shoulder and almost pulled them both to the ground. Looking at the pile of horse dung into which they might have tumbled, Dinah laughed. Harry couldn't resist joining her merriment.

They were still laughing when they entered the barn and saw everybody standing in a circle outside the cubicle that Harry shared with Mose. On the ground at the feet of the two Fraziers was the contents of his shelves. Everything was spread out on the floor. The remains of the cloth turtle that his sister had made for him was lying there. Even the sacred deerskin bag he had been given by Samuel, Plenty Horses, and the other young men at Major Pratt's school was on the ground; its contents dumped.

Before Harry could speak the outrage that clawed in his throat, Broadmore demanded, "What kind of heathen paraphernalia is this? Do you not know this is a Christian home?"

Chapter 31 ~ Confusions and Corrections

The voices cascaded over Lonely Cricket. He cocked his head to one side and tried to sort the noise of them.

Broadmore Tideswell shouting about being a Christian.

The brothers Frazier shouting gleefully, they'd told him so. "He ain't worth shit," one of the young men yelled as he stirred Lonely Cricket's possessions with his feet. The other repeated over and over, "You cain't trust no Injun heathen!" He did his own little war dance.

Dinah, clutching Lonely Cricket's arm, said, "Stop it. Stop it," so quietly that no one but he could hear her.

Mose, too, was trying to stop the madness. "You boys oughtn't have done that. Ought they, Massa Broadmore?" The Black man spoke with quiet authority. In ordinary times, it was a voice that would have stopped the Fraziers in their tracks, but not now, not in the heat of their triumphant rage against Harry. Even as he spoke, Mose observed Matthew Frazier jab his brother in the ribs and grin. Behind Mose, Pastor Morgan was saying, "It isn't here. If he took it, where did he hide it?"

"Don't you worry, Reverend," O'Day Harvey replied. "We'll find it. Sure as rain, we will." The two other Black men murmured their assent, while the pastor's wife nodded her head.

"Quiet down, all of ye!" Rachel Tidewsell's command took them all by surprise. Having come to tell Broadmore that tea and cakes were ready in the dining room, the lady of the farm had been taken aback by the chaotic scene. "What on earth is going on here?" she now demanded.

Before anyone could respond to Rachel, Burton called out his question. "What does it look like?" It was a question he had asked twice before. First, he had asked the Negro lady, the pastor's wife, earlier, while her husband was asking Mose if he knew where "Miss Louisa's brooch might be," and Burton had received no response.

Then he had asked it more loudly of everyone, when the one of the Frazier boys yelled, "Don't you worry, Mr. Broadmore, we'll find it," and the two of them charged into the room where Harry and Mose slept and started ransacking Harry's possessions. Again, there had been no response to Burton's question.

This time, Burton yelled at the top of his voice, "What does it look like?"

"What does what look like, Burton?" Dinah demanded.

"The brooch," Burton replied. "What brooch? What art thee going on about?" Rachel asked.

Quickly, Broadmore filled his wife in.

"Did you take that lady's brooch, Harry?" Rachel stared into Lonely Cricket's eyes.

"Not thief," was the teen's answer. "Not take."

"And who says the boy did?" Rachel demanded of her husband.

Before Broadmore could answer, Burton asked again, "What does it look like?"

"What in tarnation difference does that make?" Broadmore asked.

The apprentice looked at Dinah and answered, "'Cause I might know where it's at. Dinah and me might know."

Catching Burton's glance at her daughter, Rachel asked, "Did Harry give thee that purloined bauble?"

Ignoring her mother's question, Dinah nodded to Burton. "Go ahead, tell them," she mouthed.

"At meeting, on Sunday," the youngster said. "One of the girls had a pin looked like this." He sketched with his finger in the hard-pack floor."

"The stone was pink," Dinah added. "I think the pin was just tin, but it was shiny and pretty."

"To whom did he give it?" Broadmore thundered. "Which girl."

"Ann," Burton mumbled the name.

"Who?"

"My friend Ann, Ann Lancaster," Dinah said.

"How does Harry know her?" Broadmore questioned. "Did you intro—"

"Don't … oh, Father, what are you going on about? It wasn't Harry gave her anything!"

"Then who?"

"Her boyfriend," Burton answered. "Johnny Warwick's his name. He ain't a member of the Friends. They met up at school."

"I knew that school weren't nothing but trouble," O'Day Harvey opined. "Children should be at home learning things that need knowing."

Before anyone could take up that topic, Rachel Tideswell asked, "Harry did thou sell that brooch to this Warwick boy?"

Lonely Cricket repeated his earlier words, "Not thief. Not take."

The youngster knelt on the ground and gathered the remains of the multi-colored cloth turtle and the contents of his deerskin bag. Looking up, he spoke again—this time looking directly at each of the men who surrounded him. He spoke slowly. "Not thief. Not take from Miss

Louisa. You thief. You take from Lonely Cricket. You throw on ground. What you do wrong."

Rising to his feet, the few things he had gathered clutched in his hand, Lonely Cricket walked out of the barn. Nobody spoke. Nobody tried to stop him.

Dinah started to follow the young Indian. "Where art thou going, young lady?" her father demanded.

"With Harry. He needs me. He needs somebody." She whirled to look directly into her father's face. "Thou should be ashamed of thyself. Thou say thou art a Christian. Lonely Cricket is far more a Christian than thou can ever be."

As she walked away, Broadmore reached to stop her. His wife's hand stopped his. She shook her head.

"If Harry didn't steal that brooch, who did?" Pastor Morgan demanded. "Somebody gave it to that boy who done give it to that girl at your meeting?"

Mose stared at the minister for a moment and then asked, "Well, who 'xactly said it was Harry?"

Mrs. Morgan turned to O'Day Harvey. "It was your boy, weren't it?"

"We's sorry we done bothered your day, Mr. Tideswell," Pastor Morgan said as he led the others from the barn. His wife was five paces ahead. "Please, tell your missus we 'preciate her trouble, but I don't rightly think we'd be enjoying tea."

Broadmore gave no answer, only calling to his help, "Bring their horses." When nobody appeared, he called again. "Mose, these folks need their mounts."

Mose came out of the new barn and answered, "Yes, suh, soon as those two finish picking up Harry's possessions they done dumped on the floor, why they'll bring out them horses." The Black man turned back to the barn door. Just before he entered, he called out so everyone could hear. "We done a bad thing here. We done real bad."

"Mr. Tideswell, sir." Michael Morgan had returned to Broadmore's side.

"What?" Broadmore's voice was filled with outrage.

"Might you go with us?"

"Go with ye where?"

"I don't 'spect the Lancasters gonna want to talk with us Negras 'bout that brooch."

"What the devil?"

"We wants ta get it back, suh. That old lady. It may not be worth a lot of money, but she sure does set a store by it."

"And if I do?"

"Yes, suh?"

"If I do, you still got to deal with my Injun boy. When he comes back to thy church, what are ye folks going to say to him? How are ye going to make this right?"

"Yes, suh. We do. We got to be thinkin' some on that and hope he can forgive us." The pastor gulped. "And, suh, so does you."

Chapter 32 ~ Grace

They waited in silence. Broadmore Tideswell, seated at the head of the table, stared at the kitchen door. To his right, Mose looked down at his plate. Rachel and Dinah Tideswell stood near the stove stirring pots and hoping that dinner wouldn't burn for the waiting. The Frazier brothers poked at each other and exchanged glances and smirks. Burton, seated next to Luke, squirmed uncomfortably on the wooden bench. The place next to Burton was empty; Lonely Cricket had not come to supper. Not when Mose had rung the bell by the back door. Not when the Black foreman had returned to ring it again and shout, "Hallo."

"I don't know as he'll come, suh." Mose finally spoke. "You wants I should fetch him?"

"Burton, say the grace," Broadmore said. "I don't suppose it would do much good to force the boy to eat."

"No, suh, Massa Broadmore," Mose replied. "I don't s'pose it would." After serving the others and without asking permission, Dinah fixed a plate and took it to the new barn. "Lonely Cricket," she called as she entered the dusk-darkened building. There was no answer. She went to the small side room that Lonely Cricket shared with Mose. It was empty. The blanket had been removed from Lonely Cricket's cot. "Now, where's he gone?" she asked herself.

Setting the plate and a mug of milk on the bed, she returned to the house.

"Did thee find him?" Broadmore asked his daughter. "No. I left the plate on his cot." She didn't mention the blanket.

"Who knows what that Injun'll do," Matthew Frazier commented. Broadmore and Mose fixed their eyes on the young man and he dropped his eyes back to the hunk of beef and mound of beans set before him. Under the table, Luke nudged his brother's foot. Then he whispered, "Hopefully, he'll starve his-self." "Thou hast something to say?" Broadmore demanded.

"No, sir. I was just remarking that Harry's missing a right fine supper."

***

The young Indian wasn't at breakfast either. "Never slept in his bed," Mose told their employer. "Took his blanket, so I guessed he found someplace else to hold fer the night." The Black man put the untouched plate of food Dinah had brought to the barn on the counter. "Didn't eat nothin' neither."

"You see if thou canst find him, Mose. Talk with the boy."

"Yes, suh."

"Meanwhile," Broadmore turned to the two Fraziers, "ye two will do his work and your own." Matthew grunted his opposition. "If thou hast objection, do not speak it. Harry has cause enough to burden ye both." He coughed once before adding. "And be sure ye doest that work rightfully."

Luke Frazier managed a weak, "Yes, sir," as he nudged his brother. The Fraziers need not have worried. By the time they got to the new barn to help Burton clean those stalls, Lonely Cricket had already cleaned them all, not even waiting for the apprentice to help. Having curried some of the animals already, the young man had taken two of the pregnant mares to the back paddock where he was urging them move about.

Clicking his tongue against the roof of his mouth he walked next to one of the animals, his hand stroking her withers. As she moved forward, the other mare followed. "Guess we should tell the boss that Harry's working," Luke said.

"Why? Let him think we did it all."

"Yeah, and then when Burton says something."

"I'll knock his teeth in," Matthew replied.

"Maybe we should mind our Ps and Qs afore Broadmore fires us."

"Afore Broadmore fires us and leave himself with only dumb-assed Burton and slow-Black-assed Mose to do the work? Not likely." Matthew spit on the ground to emphasize his point.

Just then Mose came around the corner of the barn. "I come to check up on you two," he called. Then seeing Lonely Cricket with the two mares, the foreman added, "You boys get back to the other barn. Make sure the cows are proper milked and fed. Then you can clean the chicken coop. Lots of work needs doin', and Massa Broadmore 'spects you to be doin' it."

***

"Thou must eat." Dinah handed Lonely Cricket his lunch plate. "I put honey on the bread," she added. "My mother did not see." She smiled. "And, I brought thee milk instead of water."

"Thank you," the young man muttered. He was sitting on the beech stump watching Sky frolic in the paddock. He looked at the double-heaped portion in his left hand, took one piece of the thick white bread in his right, took a large bite, chewed for a moment, and his mouth still partially full, said, "Give colt piece of bread. He like honey, too." Dinah took a piece of bread, broke off a section of crumb and held it over the fence. Sky trotted over, sniffed, shied, and then took his prize.

"Good eat. I hungry." The young woman held out the mug. Lonely Cricket took it and took a large draught before setting it on the ground. The milk left a white rim on his newly growing moustache. He licked away the froth. "Thirsty, too."

"Thou art welcome." Dinah stepped over and kissed him lightly on the mouth. "My father does not know what to do about thee. He says thou are not a Christian and that troubles him. Yet, he knows that thou didst not steal the brooch and that the Frazier boys were plumb wrong in taking thy belongings."

"Mmmm."

She waited for him to say more. When he didn't, Dinah continued, "And Mose says he don't know what to do either. He says that colored lady has her jewelry back and the boy who lied about you has been punished. But he doesn't know what'll happen at the church. Only thing he knows for sure is that thou got a right to be angry.

"My father says thou got the right to be angry, but thou should forgive. Says that's the Christian thing to do. Says it's the right thing."

"Forgive good," Lonely Cricket answered. "Not steal, not lie. Respect others. They good, too." She inched her way next to him on the stump. He edged over slightly to make room, took a spoonful of succotash, and chewed thoughtfully.

Sky's neighs filled the quiet of the chilly, brightness of the early spring afternoon.

***

Nobody asked the question out loud, but seven sets of eyes were fixed on the kitchen door. The five men sat at the table ready for their dinner and the two women stood near the stove ready to serve it. The door handle moved. In the silence of the moment they heard the latch scrape. Lonely Cricket opened the door and walked in.

Nobody spoke. The young man walked across the room, took one of the extra chairs that stood against the far wall and moved it into the space between Mose and the chair place that was set for Dinah. He reached across the table and took the place setting that was meant for him and moved it in front of the chair. Sitting down, he waited for some reaction. Other than Matthew Frazier's slight jostling of his brother's arm, there was none. At the head of the table, Broadmore Tideswell harrumphed once, cleared his throat, and said, "Burton, wilt thou say grace?" The youngster rose. Before he could speak, Lonely Cricket got up. "I say grace."

There was a moment's silence. Burton looked to Broadmore. It took a moment for the head of the household to speak. "Well, Harry, I guess thou may if it is thy wish." Burton sank back to his place on the plank bench. There was another silence. Everyone looked at Lonely Cricket. Even Rachel—ignoring the pots of food bubbling on the stove—fixed her eyes on the young Indian.

Reaching into one of his pockets, Lonely Cricket pulled out the remains of the cloth turtle that his sister had given him years earlier. "This not god. It toy. Sister give to remember her. I keep. Think of sister." He left the remnant on the table and reached again into his pocket. This time he pulled out the deerskin pouch he had been given at school. "This not god thing, either," he said as he put the pouch on the table in front of himself. "It gift at school. Give Lonely Cricket say I am brave, say I am man. Gift from other men. Older."

Waiting for a moment for his words to sink in, the youngster looked around the table. Then he continued, "Man not lie. Man not steal. Man not afraid." He held out his hands in front of himself, his elbows touching his ribs. "Jesus teach man treat others as self. Man give others love. Man give others respect. I pray all in this house have love. I pray all in this house have respect. Amen."

Nobody made a sound as he slipped into his chair. All eyes, except Lonely Cricket's turned back to Broadmore. He gulped twice, stirred in his chair, and finally said, "Amen."

"Amen, amen," chorused Mose.

Dinah and Burton echoed the interjection, Dinah with a smile and Burton nodding across the table. Rachel mumbled her response.

The Frazier brothers stared down at their plates and remained mute. "I said, 'Amen,' Broadmore repeated.

"Yes, sir, Amen," Luke replied. Then his brother echoed the word.

Chapter 33 ~ Bad Cake and Good Truth

"You go on in and talk with her," Horace Zachariah pointed to the front door of Louisa Murrow's rickety cabin. Lonely Cricket gave one more bewildered shake of his head—he had shaken it often on this ride from the Tideswell farm—and slipped from the sway-backed, grey mare Mose usually rode. Tying the horse's reins to a post, he asked once more. "Why lady want speak to me?"

"If I knowed that, I'd tell you. All I knows is after church she asked the pastor and he asked me. So here you is. I done rode over to Mr. Tideswell's and asked him if I could fetch you, and he said, 'Sure 'nuff', so's I did."

The lanky church sextant watched his mule's ears flick, watched for a moment, and shooed the fly that was buzzing the animal's head. "I knows Mose weren't happy you takin' his mare. He said somethin' 'bout visiting Sally Goodnuff today."

"He not want stay back from church. Mr. Broadmore say I not stay if Mose not there. Say Matthew and Luke make trouble." "I reckon they would. And, I reckon no way you wants to be at church."

"No, sir." Lonely Cricket patted the mare's flank. "Folks at church not want me. Think me thief."

"They don't ... least not all o' them." The church elder stopped himself. The day before he and the pastor had argued over this very thing. "We should send somebody to talk to the boy," Pastor Morgan had told his friend. "Too much feelin's for that," Horace had replied. "I hope he stays home. Best let things simmer down 'fore the boy comes back."

Neither man had imagined that Louisa Murrow would bring Harry up, but she did, right after services. "Where was that boy?" the old woman had demanded. "I want to talk with him."

"You stay, wait for me?"

"No, boy. You think you needs me to protect you from an old lady?" Horace clucked to his mule. The animal took a reluctant step. The man clucked again, this time adding a quick nudge with his heels. The mule walked away as Lonely Cricket mounted the stoop and knocked on the cabin door. It took a few moments for Louisa to open the door. When she did it, the hinges squeaked and the door—once free of its frame—hung askew. "You want see?" Lonely Cricket asked.

"I sure do, Harry. You come in and sit. I've got some cakes in the oven and some good tea brewin'. You set down and we'll have a feast."

She gestured to a seat and bustled as quickly as her arthritic legs allowed to the stove.

"Why you ask come?"

"Why?" The woman turned briefly and then returned to her cooking. "Why to thank you for finding my brooch."

"I not find. I not take. I not—"

"Course you didn't take it. That little thief Cedric Harvey took it. O'Day brought him 'round the other day to apologize. Said, "Miss Louisa, I'se sorry as can be.'

"I don't know if he were sorry 'bout my brooch, but he sure was sorry 'bout the hidin' O'Day done give him. Boy couldn't even set down." Louisa chuckled.

Taking a Johnny cake from one pan and something resembling a crazy cake from another, the old woman cut them into pieces which she put on plates. She poured tea from a chipped, white pot into two chipped, unmatched mugs and added teaspoons of sugar to both. Slowly making her way back and forth between the table, where Lonely Cricket sat, and the stove, she set their repast in place.

Finally, she spoke again, "You help yourself, Harry. Least I can do, you findin' my brooch and all."

Without moving towards the food or tea, Harry repeated, "I not find."

"No not 'actly, but if Cedric hadn't lied 'bout you nobody would of known where it were. His lie 'bout you must have been part of God's plan 'cause otherwise I'd never get it back." She pointed to the brooch which she wore pinned to her faded, blue dress. "So, I figure them folks goin' 'round to Mr. Tideswell and accusin' you save this here for me so as I can send it to my sister in Indiana."

"Glad you get pin back," the young man responded. "Not need thank."

"Need or not, I surely do. Now, you eat up." Lonely Cricket took a piece of the crazy cake and bit into it. Swallowing with difficulty, he reached for one of the mugs. "You enjoy that cake, boy," Louisa Murrow said. "Lord knows it's least thing I can do for you."

"Thank you." The words struggled out of his mouth. Swallowing another mouthful of tea, he asked, "Cedric apologize?"

"Yep, sure did. Right here in this room. I told him I forgave him. Not that it meant much to him, but I figure O'Day got 'nough troubles with that boy. Don't need no more. "Then I says to him, 'Cedric, you got to apologize to somebody else.' He say he already done ask God to forgive him. I says, 'That weren't who I meant.' He asks who and I say, 'What 'bout that boy you lied on? You gots to talk with him.'"

The old woman took a bite of Johnny cake and chewed it methodically. "You help yourself," she said once more to Lonely Cricket.

Forcing himself, the young man took another bite of cake and quickly followed it with a gulp of hot, sweet liquid. "What Cedric say when you tell him he talk to me?" "What he say?"

The old woman laughed. "He say what 'pected he'd say. He say you're an injun and no one care 'cause injuns all thieves. That what he say and his daddy just noddin' like that boy is talkin' sense.

"So, I tell 'em I'se tired and needs to lie down. They go on home and this morning there they was bold as brass in church and actin' like that boy is just fine. Worse part, some of the folk they actin' like he ain't done nothin' wrong. They talkin' to O'Day and his missus and that boy just standin' 'round and sayin', 'Howdy.' That's when I told the preacher I wanted to talk with you. Said, 'Somebody ought to tell you thanks and sorry.'"

"I talk to Cedric tell him? Talk to Pastor, tell him?"

"No sense in that, Harry. One thing I reckon every negra knows is a man who's done you wrong and cain't ask you to forgive him, he ain't ever gonna get over bein' angry at you. It'll fester and rile till he cain't stand it nor you no more. And, you forgivin' him ain't gonna make it better. He'll hate you all the more. So, you forgivin' that Cedric Harvey or no, it don't make no difference. You got an enemy there, boy, and you'll have him hatin' at you no matter what till he decides it's done. And there's gonna be some who's gonna hate you with him, just 'cause of him. They gonna sides with him and some's gonna sides with you."

"What should I do?" Harry asked.

"No should here, Harry. You gots to find your way. Just you don't forget what you is about."

"What about Pastor?"

"Oh, Michael Morgan, he's a good man. Lots of them are good folks some as 'll take your side and some as 'll say you ain't one of us, not like Cedric Harvey is. Don't matter which is which. You figure who you is." The elderly woman pushed on the arms of her straight-backed chair and struggled to her feet. "Now you head on home, Harry. I know it ain't right what that boy said 'bout you. I know it ain't right what them folks done, neither. Only thing I know is right is that I should thank you for my mother's brooch and me gettin' it back." Tears welled in her eyes as she shuffled forward and hugged him to her frail frame.

"I hope you find way give brooch to sister." Lonely Cricket spoke softly.

"Me, too, boy. Now I got it, I have to find a way before I dies."

Chapter 34 ~ Memory

Although he had set out from Louisa Murrow's house with the energy of youth, calling back to the woman, "Thank you for your words," Lonely Cricket got only half a mile before his thoughts became more urgent than the chores waiting at the Tideswell barns. Perhaps it was the cakes the old woman had served him and the sweet tea, but his mind focused on Cedric Harvey and a saddening question, "Why didn't Pastor Morgan believe in me? Why didn't he tell them all that I ..."

Immersed in his thoughts, the young man didn't urge his horse on, allowing the swaybacked mare to sample the shoots of new grass along the trail and to admire the budding trees. Sitting motionless on his mount, Lonely Cricket saw a young boy and his father walking towards him.

"Lame Bear," he said. "Many Fish." He spoke without realizing that he was seeing not what lay before him but a memory, not of his brother but of himself as a child.

In the moment, the vision was so real that he could hear his own squeaky voice of protest. "But the fish was too small, so I threw him back! You told me that we should not take the life of that which we cannot eat."

Lame Bear patted his son's shoulder and said, "You may have done the right thing, but in doing so you caused an argument with Twisted Rock and Sparrow Yenri. It is wrong for brothers to fight with one another."

The young boy nodded his head and tried to understand. He knew that his father was not pleased with him, but he also knew that yes, he had done the right thing. The fish Twisted Rock had caught had been much too small to eat. If he hadn't thrown it back into the creek, it would have died and that would displease the Maymaygwayshi who lived by the stream. Surely, it would also displease Ma-Ona, who had created this world and the next. That was why he had thrown the trout into the water despite his friends' protests.

"I will tell you a story of our people," Lame Bear said. "Come sit next to me and we will talk." He sank to his knees and then sat with his back against the hickory from which they had been gathering nuts.

It was a good year. The tree was thick with nuts. Each time Lame Bear pushed and shook the giant tree, more of the brown treasures would drop to the ground. Their sacks of the White Man's burlap were almost full.

Dropping his sack next to his father's, the boy sat cross-legged in front of him and tried to hold back the tears of outrage from his eyes. "Why isn't he praising me?" was Lonely Cricket's thought. Nevertheless, he tried to listen to his father's story.

ΩΩΩΩΩ

It was, as now, in the moon of the birds flying south, when a young man of the people had gone hunting for nuts. In those days, it was not as it is now. It was women who gathered nuts and roots to add to the cooking pot. However, this young man, who was named Many Calls, was in love with a girl named Wandering Flower. Wherever she went, Many Calls would also go. So, when Wandering Flower's mother sent her to gather nuts in the forest, Many Calls followed behind her bringing his sister's basket.

Some of the other young men laughed at Many Calls and called him of two-spirits saying that he did the work of a woman, but Many Calls would not be deterred, for his love was very strong.

As was the custom, Many Calls did not speak to Wandering Flower. He only followed her through the woods and picked up nuts that she had left on the ground.

Because she had feelings for Many Calls, Wandering Flower left many nuts on the ground so that his sister's basket would be filled. Sometimes, she stopped to watch him pick up the nuts she had left on the ground. When he would look up, she would smile at him and he would smile back. He hoped that someday he would earn the respect of the other men and could go to the father of Wandering Flower to ask that he might play the flute for her and that she might come to his wickiup and join him at his cooking fire and under his sleeping robe.

The two young people wandered far from the village of the people looking for different kinds of nuts. Perhaps they wandered too far, for Many Calls heard the sounds of talking and the words were not of the language of the people. Motioning to Wandering Flower that she should wait for him, he crept forward until he could see who was talking. It was a band of Ojibwe. The Ojibwe wore the paint of war on their faces and brought no women with them, so Many Calls did not speak to them but withdrew and, taking Wandering Flower with him, hurried back to the village.

When they returned to the village, a council was called and Many Calls, even though he was young, was summonsed to tell the elders what he had seen. Everyone said good things about Many Calls for his bravery and his wisdom in returning so quickly to the village. But Tree That Grows From Rock was not impressed with Many Calls's actions.

Tree That Grows From Rock also loved Wandering Flower and he was angry that Many Calls had been with her. Tree That Grows From Rock was determined to take vengeance on Many Calls. He hoped to make Many Calls look bad so that the father of Wandering Flower would not allow his daughter to go to the wickiup of Many Calls.

At the council, a plan was developed for how to deal with the threat.

"First," one of the chiefs said, "we must determine if these Ojibwe mean us harm or if they are going to another place to make war."

Many of the elders agreed that this was a good point.

"But still we must appoint war chiefs," another of the chiefs said. And, that, too, was agreed.

"But how shall we see their plan and at the same time protect the village?" one of the women of the tribe asked.

It was decided that the warriors of the tribe would be split into two groups. One group, dressed for the hunting of deer, would go towards the setting sun in the direction of the Ojibwe band. They would stay just to the south of that band and make enough noise and show enough activity that the Ojibwe would know of them.

The second group, who would be painted and dressed for war, would skirt to the north and move quietly so the Ojibwe would not know they were there.

A few of the fastest runners who were also skilled in the calls of the birds were sent to hide between the two groups of the people so they could communicate between them. "If the Ojibwe are enemies," the war chief, who had thought of this strategy, explained, "then the hunting party will fight until the second group can attack this enemy from the rear. Then, we shall surely have a great victory. If, however, the Ojibwe do not attack the hunting party, we shall let them pass in peace."

Everyone agreed this would be a good plan. Even though they were young and had not yet added feathers to their coup sticks, both Many Calls and Tree That Grows From Rock asked to be part of the war party. Since it had been his discovery that had warned the people, the war chiefs could not say no to Many Calls. And, since everyone knew that both Many Calls and Tree That Grows From Rock were rivals for the hand of Wandering Flower, it would be unfair to not allow Tree That Grows From Rock a chance to prove himself in battle.

When, in the evening, the Ojibwe heard the hunting party making noise and readying themselves to hunt deer, they decided to raid the hunters' camp. One of the people who had been sent to watch what the Ojibwe would do, made the sound of a loon. And that call became the whoop, whoop of the Prairie Chicken, and then the warble of the Redstart. And so, the news was passed man to man until the war party of the people had been alerted.

What was going to happen was soon clear. In the first light of morning, the Ojibwe would attack the hunting party. Clearly, even if the hunters realized the danger, the Ojibwe were sure they could defeat that small band.

To the north, the warrior group from the people were moving closer. Come dawn, as the first cries of battle were called, those warriors would throw themselves at the Ojibwe. Clearly, before the Ojibwe would realize what was happening, the people would have destroyed their war party.

Just before dawn, somebody from the war group of the people shouted. What they said was not something that anybody understood. But that did not matter. The Ojibwe warriors heard the call and, realizing that there was a second band to their north, quickly ran away.

In vain, both groups of the people chased after the Ojibwe. Finally, returning to the village, they asked one another, "Who was it that yelled and warned the enemy?"

There was much confusion and discussion. Nobody came forward to admit calling out. Nobody came forward to point their finger at another. Only later, after people had dispersed to their wickiups and lit their cooking fires, after they had lain down beneath their sleeping robes, only then did Tree That Grows From Rock slip into the lodge of the chief who had been in charge of the war party. "I know who cried out," the young man said; "it was Many Calls. He grew afraid as the moment of battle approached and cried out in fear."

"Why did you not say this before?" asked the chief. Rising from his sleeping place, he went outside of the wickiup and stood looking into the distance.

Tree That Grows From Rock followed him outside and answered, "I did not want to cast shame on him. He is young and I know that in a moment fear can overtake even the strongest warrior's heart."

"Then why do you tell me now?"

"Because there will be other times of battle and he must not endanger our people."

The next day, the war chief called the sachems together to discuss what Tree That Grows From Rock had told him. In the manner of rumor and gossip, word passed from lip to lip and story from ear to ear. Soon, the entire village had heard that Many Calls had grown afraid at the moment of battle. Everyone believed this except for one warrior who had not spoken of what he had seen. Now he came forward and spoke to one of the women who led the tribe. "I stood next to Many Calls as we waited for battle," that warrior said. "He did not call out. He stood ready for battle with his coup stick in one hand and his lance in the other. This story cannot be true."

When the warrior's words were shared in council, it was decided that Many Calls should be called before the sachems.

"Did you call out and warn our enemies?" one of the leaders asked.

"No, I did not call out and give our enemies warning," Many Calls responded.

"Were you afraid to face battle?" a second sachem asked.

"No, I was not afraid of battle. I was only fearful that I would not count coup before I was killed," Many Calls answered.

"Why have others said that you called out?" a third leader asked.

"I cannot speak of the hearts of others," Many Calls replied. He knew that it was Tree That Grows From Rock who had started the rumor and that Tree That Grows From Rock was his rival for Wandering Flower, but he would not speak of such things in order that no one should gossip about his love. "I do not know who called out," he continued even though he had his suspicion.

"We are sorry that we doubted your bravery," the chief of the war party said. "Whoever started this rumor that you cried out must have been in error, for we know from another warrior that you did not." He did not speak of Tree That Grows From Rock or how the rumor had spread. After the council met, there was much discussion in the tribe. People spoke one to another and argued among themselves. "Did Many Calls become frightened?"

"No, it could not have been him."

"If it wasn't Many Calls, then who cried out?"

"I know that it was not Many Calls because another warrior was with him."

"What will the council of elders do about Many Calls?"

"They will do nothing for he has done nothing wrong."

The arguing and discussing went on and on, everyone wanted to know the truth. Many Calls was very sad that some of the people believed he had called out, but he was even sadder that there was dissension in the village. He went once more to speak to the council of elders and said, "Even though I have not yelled to warn the enemy, still the story of that raid is being told. It is dividing the people. That is the worst thing that can happen. I will leave our village so that there can be an end to this argument."

The next morning, Many Calls left the village. Tree That Grows From Rock was happy to see his rival's heels. He thought of Wandering Flower coming to his wickiup.

That evening, Tree That Grows From Rock went to the lodge of Wander Flower's father. "May I play the courting flute for your daughter?" he asked.

"You have come too late, Tree That Grows From Rock," Wandering Flower's father answered. "My daughter left the village this afternoon. She has gone to follow her love for Many Calls."

ΩΩΩΩΩ

Having finished the story, Lame Bear stood and gestured towards the hickory against which he had rested. "The greatest strength is sometimes in standing firm, but sometimes it is in bending before the wind." With long strides Lame Bear headed towards the last of the corn that needed harvesting. Lonely Cricket had to trot to keep up with his father.

***

After recalling this memory, Lonely Cricket, pulling gently on the reins and squeezing with his legs, turned the horse back to Miss Louisa's.

The old woman sat on the porch of her small house. She hummed a spiritual and watched a hawk glide through the sky. The hawk screaled. "Mr. hawk you sayin' there's a visitor coming?" Louisa asked aloud. The bird screamed again and dove towards a field. "No, I ain't makin' him no dinner. I already fed the boy all them cakes.

"Bird speak; you hear?" Lonely Cricket said as he walked to the side of the porch.

"Oh, I hears' 'em all the time. Don't mean I got to listen to what theys sayin'." She stood slowly and creakily made her way to the cabin door. Lonely Cricket stood at the step to the porch. "You comin' in or no, Boy?"

"I not come for dinner."

"No, I reckoned not."

"I decide what do."

"That's what I figured."

Lonely Cricket stood on the ground by the porch step and made no move to mount it. Louisa stood, her back against the doorframe, and stared at the young Indian. The silence continued for a few minutes. Finally, the old lady asked, "So what did you decide yourself to do?"

"This not good place for me. Make people angry. Make people at church angry. Make people at Tideswell farm angry. I go home. Go back to my people. Go back Nebraska"

"When you gonna leave, Harry?"

"Not Harry. My name Lonely Cricket. That my Ho-Chunk name, not White Man name."

"Lonely Cricket," she repeated. "That's got a nice sound to it. What's it mean?"

After Lonely Cricket had explained his name, she asked again, "So, when you gonna leave, Lonely Cricket?"

"Leave when all foals born this spring. Not leave without help Mr. Broadmore."

She nodded her head. "I knew you's was one of the good uns." He turned and walked towards his horse. "Lonely Cricket, you want something to eat?"

"No," he laughed. "You already tell hawk you fed all them cakes."

"That I did." The old woman joined his laughter. "Afore you go ...," Louisa Morrow called as loudly as she could. The frailty of her voice like that of a bird trying to distract a snake in search of eggs.

He turned around. "Something you need Lonely Cricket do before go?"

"Not now, not right this ... no, when you go. When you go to Nebraska. Would you bring that brooch to my sister?"

"You trust me with jewelry?"

"Course I do. I know you ain't no thief."

Chapter 35 ~ A Decision

"Youch!" Stems of hay poked through the burlap sacking and stuck into Dinah's back and buttocks.

"I hurt?" Lonely Cricket shifted his weight, putting more on his knees and elbows.

"Yes, but that's different. The hay is poking me."

"Indian learn not cry out when pain. Not alert enemy."

"Well, that's fine, but I'm not an Indian, and this hayloft sounded a lot more romantic than it is."

"Not romantic? You want stop?" He shifted slightly to the right. "We not need make sex."

Dinah wrapped her legs around his hips. "Yes, we do. When we finish, we need to talk as well." Despite the scrape and poke of the stems of grass, her body shuddered with arousal and relief as Lonely Cricket's manhood entered her.

"Talk about?" He pulled backward—the movement a combination of choice and nature.

Using her legs Dinah pulled him closer. "Yes," she screamed. "Yes. Oh, dost thou love me?"

"I love," Lonely Cricket replied. "I play flute for you."

"Well, that's another dumb idea." Suddenly, Dinah released her legs and pushed him away and to the side.

Lonely Cricket's still erect member trailed sticky wetness across her left thigh as he rolled to his right. "What wrong?"

"Play flute. My parents will think thou art mad."

"Not angry. Play flute to show—"

"To show thou loves me. I know. But, dost thou love me?"

"Already answer question. Yes, I love Dinah."

"Then why didn't thou tell me?"

"I did tell. I tell many times. I make sex-love with you."

"I don't mean that way. I mean, why didn't thou tell me thy plan? My father says thou art leaving when the last foal is standing."

The young woman sobbed. Lonely Cricket touched her shoulder. "Go Nebraska."

"That's what he said, but ... but what about me?"

"Not understand."

Raising her voice in exasperation, Dinah again asked, "What about me?"

"Shsh. Others hear."

"I don't care who hears! What about me?"

"What want, Dinah?"

"I don't want thee leaving me."

"I not leave you. I leave Pennsylvania. Go home."

"Dost thou expect me to beg?"

"Not beg. I not want beg."

"But, thou dost not ask." Her voice once again rose.

"Ask what?"

"Ask if I will go with thee. If I will leave my parents' house and go with thee to Nebraska."

"You want come to Nebraska, you come."

Dinah sighed. "I guess that's the best I'll get from you, Harry."

"I make angry?"

"No, but thou will surely drive me mad."

"Harry, you up in the loft?" Burton's voice rose from the barn floor. "Mose says one of them Appaloosa mares is foaling. Told me to find you. Says he needs you in the new barn."

"How did he know we were up here?" Dinah hissed. Lonely Cricket nodded.

"Burton friend. Not tell what we do." He gathered his clothes.

"Did thou tell him we were—?"

"Not tell. Burton see more than he tell."

"Well, now I got to go with thee. He may not tell here, but at meeting." Her face reddened. "Oh, Harry, how could you?"

"What do wrong now?" He stopped pulling on his clothes, took Dinah by the shoulders, pulled her forward, and kissed her. "Must go help Mose."

"Fine. Go ahead. I'll wait here before I—"

"You come Nebraska?"

"Oh, Cricket, dost thou want me to?"

"You want, you come. Make Lonely Cricket happy."

Throwing her arms around his neck and kissing him, Dinah replied, "Yes, I want to go with thee."

Part Three ~ Almost Like Home

Chapter 36 ~ Returning the Brooch

"New Albany, New Albany, Indiana," the heavyset conductor sweated as he shoved his way through the packed passenger car. The humidity of humanity clung to the air. Wondering if there might be some beer in the caboose's ice chest and against the railroad's regulations, he loosened the top button of his starched, white shirt.

"New Albany, New Albany, Indiana."

The conductor stopped long enough to tap Lonely Cricket on the shoulder. When the young man looked up, the conductor carefully enunciated, "New Albany, Indiana. The stop you asked fer, young fella. Don't know why you're stopping. Your ticket takes you clear out to Nebraska."

The conductor had taken an interest in the young Indian and his girlfriend back in Pittsburg when he noticed how the youngster cocked his head to one side and stared when the conductor spoke.

"Reminds me of my brother," the older man said to himself. "Lost his hearin' in the Peninsula; that boy's tryin' to read ma lips."

"Have to return Miss Louisa's brooch," Lonely Cricket replied. "Promised to return. Promised Miss Louisa, promised Pastor Morgan, and Mose. We find Miss Louisa's sister and then we go to Nebraska." Unconsciously, he reached through the placket of his dark blue, school uniform tunic and touched the deerskin pouch Plenty Horses had given him. Inside were the talismans from the older students at school, the brooch, and the remaining shreds of the cloth turtle his sister had sewn for him over four years earlier. Next to it was another small pouch, this of cloth and containing his accumulated wages plus a gift from Broadmore Tideswell, another from the congregation of the Baptist Church, and yet a third from Mose.

"Thou art a fine young man, Harry," Broadmore had said handing him the pile of silver coins. "Better than many a grown worker I've known. Here's thy wage and more." He shook Lonely Cricket's hand and abruptly turned away. That had been two days before the youngsters had taken the train and headed for their new life.

Lonely Cricket had added the coins to the small bag and thought, "I will give money to my father and mother. It make them proud. They will know I have done well among the White Men."

"Well, you two young'uns be careful; lot of sharp horse traders in this town." the sweaty conductor pulled at his collar with his left hand and patted Lonely Cricket's shoulder once with his right.

"No trade for horses, just return brooch."

"Yeah. I meant … oh, the heck with it. You just take care."

The conductor pushed forward. Dinah stirred, raising her head which she had nested in the young man's armpit.

Lonely Cricket carried their two bags, his a scarcely filled cardboard case provided by the Carlisle Indian School and hers a carpetbag made of stiff, flowered material and nearly bursting with all she could take from home.

"Aren't you going to take all your clothes and stuff?" Mose had asked him the morning of their departure.

"No take. Burton have. When I get back to Nebraska, maybe I wear Ho-Chunk clothes. Mother make. Sister make. White Man clothes good for work on farm, good for school. But Lonely Cricket not take."

Burton had thanked him profusely, started to walk away, came back, and threw his arms around Lonely Cricket. "I'm gonna miss you something fierce, Harry." The boy's voice broke. He pulled away and shuffled towards one of the Appaloosa's stalls. "Don't worry none 'bout these horses. I'll take care like you taught me."

Lonely Cricket might have responded, but he was enfolded in Mose's bear-hug. "Boy, you're good as they come. Me not knowing my own child, seems like youse more a son to me than any man could wish. I sure want you ta stay. I knows Mr. Tideswell wants it, too. Course, he don't want nothin' going on between you and Miss Dinah. But, he sure ain't got no 'plaint about your work."

"Time to go back to my people, and Dinah want to go with me. She says we in love. We build cabin and farm with father and Harry Cook."

"Yeah, I knows. Just … Mr. Tideswell he say, 'Mose, thou drivest them to the train station and see them off. I cannot do it. Mrs. Tideswell and I …. He couldn't speak after that, so I just said, 'Yes, sa.' He went off with the Mrs. I don't knows they want to be here when …."

The big Negro blew his nose on his sleeve. There was nothing more to say, not then and not at the station while he waited for the train from Philadelphia.

"You got your tickets?" Mose asked as the train chugged in and shrieked to a stop. "Your money?"

"We're fine, Mose," said Dinah. She gave him a peck on the cheek. "Now, don't you forget Miss Louisa's brooch," Mose called after them as Dinah climbed the steps of the train.

"Harry not forget," Lonely Cricket replied, but not so loudly that the black man could hear.

***

As they stepped off the platform and onto the sweltering street that fronted the depot, the noise and confusion of the big city overwhelmed the two youngsters. Hawkers and buskers everywhere. People hurried this way and that. "Where are they all going?" Dinah asked.

As Lonely Cricket stepped into the street, two people perched precariously atop large wheels–their legs working furiously—rushed by.

"White Man always in big hurry," Lonely Cricket observed as he jumped back onto the wooden sidewalk.

"Can I help you with those bags, young fellow?" A tall, thin man wearing a long coat and top hat and carrying a buggy whip asked. The man came too close to Lonely Cricket for the youngster's liking. He stepped back as the man held out his hands. "I got a buggy outside. We can get you where you're going quick as a wink."

"Lonely Cricket carry bags," he replied. "You know Miss Amelia?"

The cabby removed his hat, bowed, took Dinah's hand, and kissed it. "Miss Amelia I'm honored to make your acquaintance."

In addition to the cabby's odor of horse, whiskey and tobacco, Dinah noted his bell-like laugh, twinkling blue eyes, and fine-chiseled features.

"Thou are—"

"That not Miss Amelia, that Dinah."

"Ah. Then I am honored to make your acquaintance, Miss Dinah." Again, he took her hand and bent to kiss it.

"Miss Amelia live Crandle Street at Pirrip house. You know where that is?"

"This is a big town, son. I don't know everyone. But Crandle Street? I sure do. It's a long way. You'll be needing that ride and that's a fact. Can't say I know the Pirrip house but if it's on Crandle, it won't be difficult to find. Who lives there, that I got no way of knowing. Like I said, New Albany's a big city. Even Jim Wickham can't know everybody.

"Come on, this way." He edged away from the depot. "Twister'll get us there in no time."

"How much you charge?" Lonely Cricket put the two bags down.

"Thirty-five cents. You won't get a better deal from anybody." The cabby walked along the platform towards the waiting street.

"Too much. Hard work make money."

"Tell you what, my friend. Since you're new in town, I'll give you a deal and that's a fact. Usually, it would be thirty-five, but for you let's say two bits. How's that, eh?"

The cabby again moved towards the street, but Lonely Cricket hesitated.

"Oh, don't fret so about money, Harry. Thou sounds as miserly as my father. I'll pay for a ride." Dinah smiled at the cabby, who grinned in response.

Under her breath and thinking that only Lonely Cricket could hear, Dinah added, "Besides what I've saved over the years, my mother gave me some as well. Said, 'If thou must go off with that heathen, then I'll give thee something so thou canst come home when thou hast a mind.'" She laughed bitterly. "I have a mind and I'll pay Mr. Wickham. I won't have thee carrying my bag all that way."

Stung by the brittleness of her words, Lonely Cricket still hesitated even as the cabby again turned and walked down the sidewalk. Dinah followed right behind. "Humph," the youngster snorted and picked up the two cases. "We need be careful with money," he thought as he followed the other two. "Easy to spend and hard to make."

They walked another block and a half before they came to Wickham's two-bench buckboard. The cabby helped Dinah up to the front bench. "You sit besides me. Less bounce up front."

Lonely Cricket had put down the bags and walked over to the horse. "This Twister?"

"Yeah, that's him. Steady as they come."

The youngster looked the horse over, noting the gray animal's splayed front feet. "Horse not good. Need care." He ran his hands down one foreleg and then the other. "Not good make horse work."

Dinah got down and walked to where Lonely Cricket was standing. She, too, touched the horse's legs and then felt his shoulders and withers. She turned to look at the cabby, "Lonely Cricket's right. This horse should be in the barn. He needs care not work." She rubbed the animal's chest and when the gelding lowered his head, she patted his muzzle.

"Come on, Lonely Cricket. We'll find our way." Dinah picked up Harry's case and started walking back towards the depot. "We'll find somebody else to take us."

After waiting in line at the ticket window, they asked directions.

"Crandle Street? Go two blocks that ways—long Market." The clerk pointed in the direction from which they had just come and where the cabby probably was still standing—probably cursing his poor horse. "And then a right on Main." He gestured to the right to emphasize his instruction. "Next corner's Crandle. It ain't long. One block runnin' to the west and one to the east. More than likely, you'll be wanting the block that runs east. Pretty block. Kind of a park in the middle, benches and trees; real nice. Couple nice homes on that block. Anyway, you ask. Somebody'll know the house if it's there."

"Lot of sharp horse traders in this town," Lonely Cricket muttered as they walked away from the station.

***

The hinges squeaked as Lonely Cricket opened the white picket gate. "It very big. Did not think Miss Louisa's sister would live in such fine a house."

"What a grand tree." Dinah stopped to admire each tree, bush, and flowerbed in the large front yard.

"No reason be afraid. We bring brooch not steal it."

"I know, but the way I look." The girl brushed at her soot covered clothes and tugged them straight. "I wish I had a mirror."

"You fine look. We give brooch and go back to train station."

Dinah looked at Lonely Cricket and brushed at his tunic.

Laughing, he moved towards the three front steps and she followed. The young couple climbed onto the porch and set down their suitcases. Lonely Cricket lifted the heavy bronze ring held in a lion's mouth and let it drop against the wooden door.

The door groaned open.

"What you be wanting?" a dark-skinned woman asked, her voice skimming irritation. She was not much older than Lonely Cricket but there was a look of age, anger, and haunting in her coal black eyes.

"Return Miss Louisa's brooch," Lonely Cricket replied.

"Miss Louisa? Who in tarnation's that? This here's Miss Abagail Pirrip's home and we ain't wantin' whatever you be sellin'. What you after anyway?"

"Miss Louisa ask bring brooch to sister."

"Miss Louisa? Miss Louisa? You keep goin' on 'bout her. Miss Pirrip ain't got no sisters. Had a brother, but he dead and buried at Sharpsburg. Same as Massa Raymond. God be praised that one's gone."

"We're from Pennsylvania," Dinah tried to explain. "A Colored lady there asked Lonely Cricket to bring this brooch to her sister. Since we were travelling to Nebraska, she wanted to make sure her sister received it."

"Colored lady. Well, the only coloreds we got here are me and Amelia. She da cook."

"Yes, Miss Louisa say sister name. A-me-ia." The young man tried his best to sound the name. Give cook lady brooch and we leave."

"Well, if youse come to give som'en to Amelia, youse go 'round back. Youse got no business knockin' on no front doors."

"Esther," a thin voice called from inside the house; "To whom are you talking?"

"Nobody, Miss Abagail. Just young folks looking for Amelia. Says they gots som'en of hers."

"Are they from Pennsylvania?"

"I don't know where they's from, but that's what they says, ma'am."

"Well, bring them through. Amelia's been waiting for them. I dare say they've brought something from her sister."

"Yes, Ma-am." The maid held the door open and gestured for Dinah and Lonely Cricket to come into the foyer.

"So, you have brought Amelia's brooch? How very kind of you."

Lonely Cricket turned toward Miss Abigail. She stood in a doorway to his left. Short, slightly bent with age, gray-haired, her voice thin but firm, the woman wore a shiny blue dress made of a fabric he did not recognize. The young man stared at the woman, taking in the pearls that circled her neck and the way that her hair was done, piled on her head and held in place with combs made of shells that reflected the light from the window in the room behind her. He wondered how the room was filled with the aroma of sweet flowers when there were no plants to be seen and realized that the scent came not from blossoms but from this woman whom he had never met yet who knew so much about him.

"I know sister Miss Louisa in Pennsylvania."

"Oh, yes, you must be the Indian boy. Harry, isn't it?"

Lonely Cricket couldn't think of words but ducked his head in agreement.

"Yes, ma'am," Dinah spoke for him. "This is Harry, but his real name's Lonely Cricket, and I'm Dinah Tideswell. We're on our way to Nebraska and, well, we ... Harry, wants to give your cook her sister's brooch."

Abagail Pirrip nodded her head in understanding. "Miss Murrow wrote that you would be coming, Harry. She did not mention you, Miss Tideswell, but you are both welcome." Seeing the look of confusion on Lonely Cricket's face, she continued, "Since Amelia can't read, I serve as her secretary when it comes to that. And as mistress of the house I know you are most welcome."

"Esther," the lady of the house now turned her attention back to her maid, "take these folks to the kitchen and make up the second guest room for the young lady. Now you know why I had you ready the front room the other day. I did tell you we would be having company."

"We've prepared a room for you, young man but now I see you'll be needing two." She paused a moment, "Or perhaps you'd prefer to share the one?"

"Oh, no, ma'am," Dinah rushed to explain. "We won't be staying. We didn't mean for thee .... We'll just leave the brooch and be on our way."

"Nonsense. You must be tired from your travels and hungry, too, I'd dare say. Amelia roasts the best chicken I've ever eaten. Says it was her mother's recipe, so perhaps you've already enjoyed it."

Unable to croak out a word, Lonely Cricket shook his head in response.

"You must have some and some of her apple pie as well. If she doesn't feed you after you came all this way to bring her that family treasure, Amelia will be mortified. And, I'm sure she'll want you to meet Dorothea. That's her eldest, the one your Louisa meant to wear their mother's finest piece of jewelry. A lovely girl. Teaches in the local Colored school. 'I never gots to learn,' Amelia always said to Dorothea when she was growing up. 'I never learned me to read, but, girl, you gonna read and write just like the White folks.'"

Miss Pirrip took a small white lace handkerchief that was tucked into the cuff of her left sleeve, dabbed at her eyes, and cleared her throat. "And after that, I'm sure a bath and a comfortable bed would do you right.

Lonely Cricket stared open-mouthed at the older woman who had so suddenly taken charge. Stammering a bit, he got out the words, "But, we not want take advantage—"

"More nonsense." Her words rushed out faster than Lonely Cricket could comprehend. "You young people aren't taking advantage. In fact, it is I who will be taking advantage of you. In two days there will be races and a horse sale at the fairgrounds. My coachman Danforth tells me that we simply must replace Bathsheba, who has been drawing my buggy for years. He says the mare's legs are breaking down. I suppose that is true, but if you are as good with animals as Louisa has told her sister, why perhaps you might see what can be done for her. And, if she must indeed be retired, possibly you could go the sale and advise me on her replacement.

"I will, of course, pay you for your time. And, it will be a pleasure to have you stay with us. I look forward to hearing about your life in Pennsylvania and your plans for Nebraska." The tempo of her words slowed. "I understand Omaha is quite the city and the new capital named for our late president is growing quickly." `

"Oh, no, Miss Pirrip." Lonely Cricket, glad to have the rush of the woman's words slow, broke in. "Not go city. Go home family. They live Pierce. Small town, but good place. I happy get back."

Miss Pirrip blanched and reached for the nearby doorjamb to steady herself.

"Miss Abagail, you look like you done seen a ghost," the maid exclaimed. "You need I get the smellin' salts?"

"No! What? No. No. Oh dear. Pierce you say? I have …." Settling awkwardly on a nearby cherry wood, Queen Anne chair, the woman added. "We must talk more. I have questions about …. First, go deliver this brooch." She wrung her hands. "I fear I have been taken by the vapors. Perhaps some salts would help." Pushing her hands down on the chair's arms, Abagail Pirrip tried to rise and heavily sat back. "Best I lie down. Yes, I think that would be a good … but at dinner, then …. Esther, please take these young people to the kitchen and tell Amelia to …. No, no. I'm sure Amelia doesn't need my instructions. Just take them to the kitchen and then perhaps you would be so kind to help me upstairs."

"Can help?" Lonely Cricket moved towards the woman.

"No, child. You go with Esther and deliver your treasure."

Yes, ma'am. I'se be right back."

The maid turned to the two young guests, "Youse comes this way."

Chapter 37 ~ Of Daughters

"Thank you, Lord! Thank you, Lord!" The dark-skinned, heavyset woman's mezzo voice filled the kitchen.

Lonely Cricket was just able to register the multiplicity of smells that packed the room before he was enveloped in Amelia Robert's embrace and pressed against her bosom.

"I swear I never thought I'd see it again. Our Momma's brooch, Dorothea's gonna be so proud wearing this." Amelia took the brooch, which Lonely Cricket had first held out and then, just before being clenched in the cook's arms, had slipped onto a nearby counter. She held it out for Esther to see. "Ain't this the most beautiful?"

Not waiting for an answer, she pinned it on the bodice of her teal dress and pranced arthritically around the large kitchen humming a song Lonely Cricket had often heard when he and Mose had gone to the Baptist Church.

"Yes, it surely is," Esther answered even though she knew the cook was no longer listening. "I'd best see to Miss Abagail. She said you was to feed these young folk and I'se goin' to make sure they's bags up in their rooms. They's stayin' a while and Harry here's gonna help find Miss Abagail a horse to replace Bathsheba."

With that, the maid bustled off to tend to her mistress leaving Dinah and Lonely Cricket to deal with the sashaying, singing, ecstatic cook.

"You sit right down here," Amelia ordered. "I'll be making us some tea and nice little cakes; the kinds Miss Abagail likes. Then we'll sit and talk, and you can tell me all about Louisa and Pennsylvania.

"Never had tea to drink," Lonely Cricket said.

"Would you—?"

"No. Only mean new ... try."

"How about you, young lady? I don't even know your names. I'm so excited I—"

"Tea is fine," Dinah replied. I'm Dinah Tideswell. He's Lonely Cricket and he worked for my father."

"Lonely Cricket? My sister said—in her letters—that you was Harry."

Already, she was again bustling about the kitchen getting their tea.

***

"Pork good." Lonely Cricket pushed another hunk of pan-fried pork chop dripping with white gravy into his mouth and followed it with a forkful of mashed potatoes. "Potatoes good, too."

Nervously, the youngster looked down to make sure he hadn't dropped any food on his new white shirt. Louisa Morrow had given him the shirt when she had entrusted him with the rose and silver brooch for her sister. "I made it big, Harry, on count you still growin'." With those words, she had kissed him on the cheek and patted his hand.

For her part, Dinah was happily spooning the golden, lumpy sauce of apples and alternating it with chunks of the white bread covered with butter. "Hmm. This is delicious, Amelia."

"Miss Abagail, she didn't know when you was comin' so I didn't kill no chickens. Tomorrow night I'll show you just how our momma used to make a hen. Won't I, Dorothea, won't I just?"

"Yes, Momma, you will." The handsome, young woman in a scoop-cut, mauve dress that showed off her almond brown skin and wearing her grandmother's brooch centered over her cleavage, nodded her head.

"That's a handsome piece of jewelry you're wearing," Jerome Danforth, the one-legged coachman and gardener observed. Knowing that there was to be company at the kitchen table that evening, he had worn his best, the remnants of his cavalry uniform complete with his medal. "I won that 'gainst the Apaches," he had explained in response to Lonely Cricket's inquiry.

"Thou fought Indians?" Dinah had questioned.

"Sure did and rebs, but mostly Injuns. I joined 'cause I wanted to help free them slaves, but once you is a soldier, why you go where they tell you. Course, when I lost this," he slapped down on what remained of his left leg, "weren't no place to send me but back home. Lucky, Miss Pirrip needed a man 'round the place even if he didn't have enough legs."

"And lucky for me," Esther added.

"Mm hmm," the cook punctuated the conversation. Getting up from the table, she quickly returned with another skillet of sizzling chops—forking one onto Lonely Cricket's plate and another onto the coachman's. She was about to add one to Dinah's plate, but the young woman held up her hand.

"Oh, no, Amelia, I couldn't eat another bit."

"Well, you'd best get that appetite back 'cause I got me two pies that surely needs eating." The woman laughed to herself as—ignoring her daughter's gesture to not—put the last chop in the skillet onto Dorothea's plate.

"It is a shame Miss Pirrip isn't feeling well enough to join us." The young teacher enunciated her words carefully.

"She took sick a sudden this afternoon," Esther explained. 'Said she's feelin' better when I took her supper up. Just a bit of bread and an egg. Sometimes that woman worries me. Hardly eats worth a bird. I declare, Amelia, and your cookin' bein' so good.

"Course, long as Jerome and me's around it won't go to no waste."

"Amen to that," Danforth added as he took knife to chop.

"That is a shame. Has she seen the brooch?" Dorothea pointed to the middle of her chest.

"No, not yet," Amelia replied to her daughter.

"Miss Dorothea doesn't talk like most people. Not like her mother or Esther. Not even like Miss Pirrip." Lonely Cricket thought when they were first introduced. "She sound like a teacher." He had smiled to himself. "No, not a teacher. She sound like Sapphira Cook when we play school."

Remembering his friend, the young man wanted to laugh aloud and to cry for missing her.

Esther brought another round of plates and set them in a pile before Amelia's seat and then she fetched the coffee pot and some blue porcelain mugs. Filling the mugs, she set them before each place.

Amelia set the two pies, one apple and the other berry, neither quite cooled to room temperature, on the table. Full as he was, when he smelled the deserts, Lonely Cricket licked his lips.

"My those look good," Dinah said.

"Amelia's pies is one of the reasons I stay around," Danforth said.

"Now, ain't that a thing to say," Esther commented. Lonely Cricket noticed that the coachman reached over and took the maid's hand.

"I didn't—" Danforth began.

"Oh, hush, Jerome." The maid used her free hand to playfully slap the coachman's shoulder. "You just hush."

Meekly, the man looked down at his coffee mug, reached for the sugar bowl, and heaped spoons of sweetness into his drink.

Sighing, the cook cut pieces of pie. "Apple or berry?" she asked Lonely Cricket. Before he could answer, she'd cut him two slices, one of each, and handed him the plate.

The youngster tried to resist. "No, too much."

"Now, you listen here, Harry—or would you prefer I call you by your Indian name?"

She turned to Dinah and asked, "How do you say that name of his?"

Listening carefully while Dinah said it twice, Amelia repeated it once to herself.

"Now you listen here, Lonely Cricket, I made these pies fer you and nobody else so you et up."

Amelia looked so stern that the young man didn't dare refuse. "I eat."

Danforth laughed. "I swear that woman's enough to scare anyone," he whispered to Esther.

"Hush now. Amelia wouldn't hurt a hair on any head."

"That is something my backside might dispute," Dorothea said. "She was quite strict when I was a child."

"And I still can be if I need," Amelia said as she smiled proudly at her daughter. She took a deep breath and then lifted a fork of berry pie to her own mouth. Chewing slowly, she sipped some of the now tepid coffee from the blue mug set to her right.

"This pie is good," Jerome said as he reached for the pie plate to take a second helping. "Did you enjoy it, Miss Dinah."

"Yes, thank thee. It was delicious."

The coachman held the pie plate towards her, but the young woman waved it off.

"I learnt my cookin' from my Momma and she learnt Louisa how to sew. You ever see them clothes she make?"

"No," Dinah replied.

"Yes," Lonely Cricket said at the same moment. "Miss Louisa make this shirt." He held his hand to his chest. "Give me. Give one Mose. We—"

"You know somebody named Mose?!" Esther interrupted. "Is he a colored?"

"He is and the best horse wrangler my father ever hired," Dinah answered. "Why dost thou ask?"

"Well, it's just … oh, I don't suppose …." Small tears appeared in Esther's walnut brown eyes. She dapped at them with a handkerchief and with a suddenly abrupt tone said, "I'd best get to the washing up."

The maid busied herself at the sink. Danforth hoisted himself onto his crutches and swung over to Esther. Placing one arm around her shoulders, he whispered in her ear. They stood there, at first quietly whispering, and then just stood.

"When we left home, Momma gave Louisa that brooch so's she could pass it on to her daughter. Since she never had no children, she wanted me to give it to you, Dorothea. I know your grandmamma Deborah would be bustin' at the seams to see you wearin' her brooch."

Tears ran down mother and daughter's faces.

"Seems to me that you're both very lucky," Dinah said. "I know my story. I know my father. But I'll never be as close to my mother as thou are to one another."

"I never knew my daddy at all," Esther said softly. Still standing by the sink, she was leaning on Danforth.

"Ain't you gonna do something with them dishes?" Amelia demanded.

"Never did know him at all … just his name. Momma say his name were Mose."

Chapter 38 ~ Some Folks Get Fortune and Some's Get Pain

It was well past dawn when Lonely Cricket awoke. Not used to heavy curtains on the windows, a comfortable bed, or a room far removed from the dawn-greeting rooster, he had slept late. The room was light enough that he could see Dinah—her back to him—lying on the far edge of the bed.

The night had not begun with such distance. They had reveled in the opportunity to share a bed, a real bed—not his cot in the barn. In a real room and not the thin-boarded space that might as well have been another stall in the Tideswell stable but with the sweet odors of perfumes and soaps—not the smell of horse and hay. Lonely Cricket had carried Dinah's bag from the second guest room while she busied herself at the full-length mirror. "Isn't this wonderful," she had exclaimed on seeing it. "Momma would have a conniption if she were here. 'Vanity's' what she'd call it. 'Vanity and sinful.'"

Dinah, arms outstretched, twirled about, laughed and plopped onto the bed. "I don't care if it's a sin or not, I just love it." She pressed the back of her hand into the softness of the bedspread. "What about you, Lonely Cricket, don't you just love this room?"

He kissed her on the side of her neck, bringing giggles to her mouth. "Love you. Love kiss you."

Turning from her image, the young woman had embraced him. Within moments, they were helping one another to disrobe and soon lay on the blue and yellow quilt coverlet naked except for the wrapping of the others' arms.

Love had been sweet that night. Once by the kerosene lamp and again in the dark. Exploring, touching, caressing, and penetrating.

In her room two doors down the hallway, Abagail Pirrip heard Dinah's moans and her cry of "Yes!" She heard Lonely Cricket's voice as well and understood the tone of ecstasy if not the boy's words.

Later, she had heard the harsher tones of the two young voices, but not their words. "What could they be arguing about?" the older woman had wondered. "Young love is so unpredictable. Still romance is best when it burns hot."

It was not an issue of their love or romance. After they had coupled. After their sweat and ardor had been shared. After the young man had come and the young woman, shuddering with excitement and desire, had climaxed, as they lay, her head nestled in the crook of his left arm, their bare skin touching and alive with needles of satisfaction, looking up into the darkness that was their ceiling, only then had Dinah made her comment. "What is wrong with that man? To do such a thing. It is iniquitous, a sin."

Lonely Cricket stirred, raising his head from the goose down pillow and—using his right hand—rubbed his neck where a stray shaft had irritated his skin. "Did I do wrong?" he asked with a plaintive note.

"Not you. That man Danforth."

"What he do? Nice man. Good with horse. Good to Esther. I like."

"That's just it. Esther. Obviously, they are having relations, doing what they should not. How can a white man be with a colored woman? It goes against the law and the Bible. I can't believe Miss Pirrip knows. A nice lady like she would never allow—"

"Why matter what color skin. People all the same."

"I swear, Harry, sometimes thou knowest nothing. If her neighbors thought Miss Pirrip allowed such miscegenation, they would burn the house down and run her out of New Albany … why out of Indiana altogether."

That had been the moment when she had rolled away from him. Twice Lonely Cricket had gently called her name to no response. Only her soft breathing which eventually took the tone of sleep.

Staring into the blackness he, too, had fallen into an uneasy slumber.

ΩΩΩΩΩ

When the Bear Men came among the people with their thunder sticks and their symbols and strange words, with their long hair covering their faces and wearing the fur of the great soosh, Tall Pine said, "Let us trade with these strange men who are so covered with hair. They want the hides of animals but of which they do not eat the meat like the beaver and the fox. In return they give us sharp knives with which we can cut the meat of the deer and elk and can clean the fish we catch in the great lake.

In those days, the people did not know of the White Man except the stories that had been told by our trading partners from the direction of the rising sun. "Beware of the White Man," our friends told us, "because they wish to kill the great spirits.

"They bring good things for your people, shiny things in which you can see yourself and beads from far away that your women can wear in their hair and your men around their necks. They bring such things as you do not know, but they also bring their god whom they say is greater than Ma-Ona and brought even the sun and moon into being."

When the Bear Men came, they brought all those things and more," Tall Pine said, "The people should have these things that the White Man brings us. We will trade with them and give them the hides they wish, and we will have those good things."

Falling Rock, who was a maker of great medicine, did not agree with Tall Pine. He said, "You are a great warrior and I would follow you into battle, but you know nothing of these men who have come from the Trickster. They do not come in friendship for they would kill animals and leave their meat for the vultures. Are they not also scavengers that will eat the body of men?"

For days, the men of the village sat at the council fire while the argument continued. All this time, the Bear Men were busy giving the women beads and other things. They spoke soft words and did gentle things until the women thought of them as friends and more.

Among the women who befriended the Bear Men were the wives of Tall Pine and Falling Rock. While their men argued, the two women made love to these strangers and began to carry their children.

When the men of the village learned that their women had made love to the White Men, they were angry. But, what could they do? If they drove their women from the village, then they would be without wives. If they killed the Bear Men and took their thunder sticks and other possessions, their wives would be angry and would no longer make their food or try to please them.

In the end, the people decided they would raise the children of the Bear Men as if they were of the people. "We will not drive them away," said Tall Pine. "Our land shall be their land and our people shall be their people."

"It is better to accept what has happened," Falling Rock agreed. "We cannot allow our anger to drive away the spirit of love."

ΩΩΩΩΩ

When Lame Bear had finished telling this story to his son, Lonely Cricket nodded with the grave agreement that young boys give their fathers' words.

"Now, my son, there is work to do."

That had been two days after Talking Mountain had spoken once more before the council of the Ho-Chunk. When everyone was seated around the fire and when Tall Grass had called on the spirits to give them wisdom, Talking Mountain spoke against the White Men. "They have no right to this land. We should drive them from here. They will take the best of everything and leave little for us. They will steal our women and drive away the game which we hunt."

All the men had spoken. Even Flying Cloud had shared his words. "The White Men bring their own women. If they want to make babies with the women of the Ho-Chunk, then their women shall bear our children inside their bellies. In the end, we will all be one people. If that is the will of Ma-Ona, then all people will be of one tribe."

Lame Bear had whispered to his neighbor in the council circle, "I do not know if this jester speaks true words or makes a joke."

"That only the creator knows. What is in your heart, Lame Bear?"

"In my heart is the love I carry for my wife and my children. In my spirit is the wish that in this Nebraska place all—the People and the White Man—will find contentment and live with peace inside our hearts."

In the end, the council had agreed to a path of peace, that the Ho-Chunk would live in peace with their White neighbors. As Tall Grass said, "We cannot fight the flow of a great river. The White Men will keep coming until there are no more People left to stand against them."

"Talking Mountain, will you agree to the decision of the council?" Tall Grass had asked.

Angrily, Talking Mountain said, "I will do as the Ho-Chunk wish. However, never will my heart accept the White Man."

***

In the yard beyond the kitchen door, Esther grabbed a bird and tucking it tightly under her arm, headed for the block.

Seated at the table, Lonely Cricket turned his attention back to his breakfast.

"Lord, child, don't you want more to eat?" Amelia had asked after he had helped himself to coffee and some bread left from the evening's meal.

"Eat too much last night." The young man didn't want to share the real reason for his suppressed appetite; he couldn't get his mind off of Dinah's words that morning. "I have no stomach for food this morning, Harry. Please tell Miss Pirrip and Amelia that I shall be down later."

Without looking in the mirror, Lonely Cricket had pulled his hair back and tied it with a leather thong. "Umm," he uttered as he opened the door; "I tell."

"She's a lot faster than me," Jerome Danforth said.

"What?" The young man was suddenly aware that the coachman—propped on his crutches—was standing behind him.

"Esther can catch them birds fast as a cat." Danforth laughed.

"On Tideswell farm cat catch rat not chicken."

"Rat or chicken that girl is fierce. She's needed to be, and that's a fact."

"You gonna splain that to the boy?" Amelia asked; "or is you gonna leave it hang there like a nest o' bees?"

"I'll tell the story, woman, but not here, not where she can hear. I'll tell him the same way I told you and Miss Pirrip. Folks don't know something they start wondering. They wonder and they get to making stories and fixing blame. I figure him and Miss Dinah are already at that wondering part, wondering what a one-legged white man is doing with a colored girl who looks so pretty."

"No wonder;" Lonely Cricket said; "you and Esther friends. Dinah and me friends. That life."

"Not if you's talkin' a white man and a colored girl livin' under the same roof. Not nowhere, not even in Indiana nor no other Yankee state," Amelia banged a pot onto the stove.

"Nope. And especially not in St. Louis, Missouri, where Esther and I done met. Me coming back from fighting them Apache and not having no leg and her...well, her doing what she had to to live."

"Not need know," the young man replied. "Not my business."

"Maybe not, but if you're gonna be living here, you'd best know the story case anyone ask, 'specially if a son-of-a-bitch name of Duke Frazier were to come 'round." Danforth spat the name.

"Frazier? Tall man, scar on face?" Lonely Cricket drew his finger diagonally down his right cheek. "Miss fingers," The young man held up his left hand.

"Sounds like him. Meanest bastard ever crossed my path. You know him, boy?"

"Same man hit ear, make deaf."

"Sounds like him. How'd you happen to run into that dung-pie?"

"He one of White Men take to school on train. Mean man. Other man throw him off."

"Throw him off? Damn well should have killed the bastard." The coachman's mouth contorted into snarled rage.

"How you know Frazier?" Lonely Cricket asked.

"I don't. Not really. I saw him in St. Louis, but I didn't actually meet him. More like I heard about him...from Esther. What he done to her."

Lonely Cricket looked at the gnarled White Man and waited for him to continued.

Danforth plopped himself into the chair to Lonely Cricket's right, propped his crutches against the table, and said, "Amelia, I sure could use another cup of that coffee."

"Seems to me you can always use sompin' or sompin'," the cook replied even as she poured hot, black liquid into an enamel mug.

"Biscuit wouldn't hurt neither."

"Ain't no biscuits here. Piece of stale bread's all I got."

"Bread good," the young Indian commented.

"Glad you's like it, boy. Wish you'd let me make you a proper breakfast, you's bein' a guest and all."

"What about me?"

"You' ain't no guest of nowhere, Jerome Danforth," Amelia answered; "though you's sure don't do 'nough to earns your keep here or nowhere." Try as she would, the cook couldn't hide her liking for the man; it was clear in her voice and the wry smile that accompanied her words.

For his part, Danforth snorted and turned back to Lonely Cricket. "When Mr. Lincoln freed the slaves, sure didn't help Esther none. Weren't till the federals moved into the old plantation and throwed them rebs out that she was free. By then her momma were gone. So was that bastard Raymond that owned them. Dead at Sharpsville and good riddance from what I hear. Son-of-a-bitch beat her momma and beat her, too, even though Esther weren't nothing but a little girl."

Danforth's voice broke as he continued, "But her momma, she'd told Esther over and over about coming North and finding her daddy. 'He swore me we'd meet in the Promised Land, child." That's what her Momma would tell Esther; "Just you follow that drinkin' gourd and he'll be there waitin'.' So, when them Yankee soldiers showed up, she skedaddled. Took what little she had and headed north like her momma told her."

Lonely Cricket was hanging on the coachman's words. Neither of them were aware that Esther had entered the kitchen. The dead, partially plucked chicken hanging by its feet from her hands.

"Girl, you's gettin' that bird's blood all over my floor," Amelia complained.

"Your floor?! Ain't I' the one mops it?"

"Well yous need wash it again."

Ignoring the cook, Esther asked, "You tellin' Lonely Cricket 'bout me."

Danforth blushed and nodded. "He knows Duke Frazier."

"You a friend of that son-of-a-bitch?" she demanded.

"Not friend. He hurt ear when I come to Pennsylvania. Bad man."

"Now ain't that the truth!" Esther replied. "Worst day of my life when I met that sidewinder. Told me how he was gonna help me."

"Help you?" Lonely Cricket asked.

"To come North. To find my daddy. Told me he was just out of the army and goin' home. That he'd take me along." Tears sprung to the maid's eyes. She wiped them away before continuing. "He took me and that's sure 'nough. Took me to a brothel and sold me."

"He rape you?" Lonely Cricket asked.

"No, not him. Said I was too valuable. Worth money for the first time."

"I didn't want…" Choking back tears, the maid continued. "I argued with that woman. I begged her… They beat me. Not on the back 'cause that might show. Beat me on the legs, on the butt. I still said no, but there were this fat, old White Man didn't care if I said yes or no. They pulled off my dress while he watched and him smokin' on that big cigar and laughin' while I tried to squirm out of their hands.

"When they tied me, he climbed atop of me and done me like I were nothin' but an animal." She slammed the chicken on the table. "Like I weren't nothin' more 'n this chicken.

"When he finishes, he says to Frazier, 'That's how you do 'em, Duke. Just like breakin' a horse.' And that Frazier says, 'Yes, Sir, Mr. Mercier, you sure broke her right.' Like I's a horse? Who'd treat a horse that mean? Would you, Jerome?"

The coachman looked down and shook his head as Esther continued. "If somebody were to treat Bathsheba that way, Miss Abagail take a whip to 'em. Ain't that right, Amelia?"

"It surely is. Don't you know it. It surely is."

"That's when I met her," Danforth said. "I ain't proud, but I was sure lonely and nothing but one leg and a few dollars left. There she was and they says I can have her cheap she being so difficult an' all."

Taking Esther's hand, the one-legged coachman continued, "Well, she and me, we got to jawin' and that meant more to me than me not having no woman. I figured I was coming back home with nothing and no one and here's this pretty gal got it worse 'n me. So's were talking and I say, 'Why don't I takes you to Indiana with me.' And she asks, 'Where's that?' When I tell her it's up North, she starts talking about her daddy and following that north star and all.

"Had to sneak her out the window 'cause them bastards weren't going to let her go no way less they get paid and I didn't got no money. So, we lit out in the middle of the night like we was a couple of thieves." Danforth paused to scratch his nose and take a slurp of coffee. "Maybe we was … thieves I mean. I guess they figured they owned her. Me, I figured that was what the war was all about, 'bout nobody owning nobody."

"When we came here to New Albany," Esther continued the story; "Miss Abagail give us work. I guess that ways we's lucky. She done needed somebody for the stable and a girl for the house and I don't know as she cared whether we is Black or White long as we does the job and don't make no trouble."

She leaned her slender frame against Danforth's side. "I guess I's lucky to have this, but it sure pains me when I think on what done happen, 'specially when I think on my daddy and if I's ever gonna meet him.

"Damn thing is, that Frazier fella comes from here abouts," the coachman added. "Seen him in town a few time, mostly when there's racing at the Fairground."

"That's why I sleeps with this hatchet under the bed, just case he show up here," Esther took her hand from Danforth's and picked up the chicken-blood-dripping hatchet from the table where she had lain it. "That's how it is in life. Sometimes it goes good and most not. Some folks get fortune, and some's get pain."

Chapter 39 ~ No Have Son

"Bathsheba good horse but grow old."

"Don't we all?" Abagail Pirrip mumbled to herself. More loudly, she said, "Then you'll go with Danforth to the horse sale?"

"You sell horse?" Lonely Cricket asked.

"Sell? ... Sell horse? ... Oh, you mean Bathsheba. No, no, boy. I wouldn't do that. It should be cruel indeed to hitch that poor animal to some hackney; and how long before her legs gave out altogether? No, no, indeed. She shall pull my carriage to church on Sundays, at a slow and dignified walk if I may say. 'Danforth,' I'll say, "bring oats and a brush to curry her whilst I pray.' Oh, no indeed. However, I shall need another horse, an animal more sound for day to day, don't you think?"

The old woman pulled the blue wool throw closer and motioned for Lonely Cricket to sit on the scroll-backed chair with gold satin cushion which stood opposite and identical to her own.

"Fire warm," the youngster observed. The fireplace grate was piled with red-glowing coal. "Not need today. Warm day."

"Perhaps for you young people, but my bones have grown old alongside Bathsheba's." Pointing her finger at Lonely Cricket, she added, "Danforth has her blanket on, has he not?"

"Horse have blanket. Better to not. But, Jerome tell, 'Miss. Abagail say horse must have blanket until summer come.'"

"You don't approve, Lonely Cricket? Do you think I am spoiling the animal?"

"Bathsheba good horse but old. Spoil, not spoil; she old legs weak."

"Why then, I suppose I shall go right on as I always have." She punctuated her words by folding her hands in her lap. "But you will go with Danforth to the sale tomorrow and find me another good animal?"

"We go. Find best horse we can for Miss Abagail."

Without touching the armrests of his chair, Lonely Cricket started to rise.

"Oh, no, please sit," the woman said. "That wasn't the reason I asked to speak with you. Of course, I am glad that you concur with Danforth about the animal and that you shall help find me another. However, there is something else."

Although she was already of rigid posture, the older woman sat even more stiffly and straight in her chair. "It's about your home."

"Home? Go back Nebraska soon."

"Yes. Yes! Of course, you shall. To Pierce I believe you said. Pierce, Nebraska, isn't that so? You and Dinah will be going there soon." The woman's voice quavered.

"Yes. Pierce."

"Do you see those pictures?" Her chicken-foot thin hand gestured towards a group of daguerreotypes and photographs hanging on the small stretch of forest green papered wall between the two bay windows of the sitting room.

"I see."

"They are as dear to me as that brooch you brought to Amelia. I inherited this house, everything in it;" she thumped down on the arms of her chair; "even the furniture from my family. But it is those pictures that are most…most dear to me. My parents, my brother Theodore, Teddy we called him. That's he when he graduated. And, there, my debut."

Stabbing forefinger gestures meant to indicate one from another clarified little. However, Lonely Cricket understood easily enough.

"That one on the bottom of Teddy and Willa on their wedding. What a celebration we had that day! We danced late into the night. Well, I didn't dance. I was sent to bed by midnight. I was only a child when they married and scarcely more when my nephew Theodore, Jr. was born. Named for his father of course; we called him TJ. Willa was a wonderful mother: always attentive, always playing with the boy, encouraging him. Took such care of little TJ.

"And then…"

Miss Pirrip's eyes took on a sad and faraway look as she continued. "It was horribly cold and storming that night. We were playing hide and seek. It was TJ's favorite game. He was the devil's own to find."

Thinking of Many Fish, Lonely Cricket said, "Little boy like hide."

"Willa was it," Abagail Pirrip continued. "She couldn't find him. I was hiding in the kitchen under the great table, the one at which you have eaten. She found me and then we both looked for him. When we still couldn't find him, she began to panic. 'He must have gone out,' she said and once that idea was in her head, there was no other course indeed. Willa insisted on going outside to look for him.

"Eventually, I did find him. He had gone into the attic and found a spot in the rafters. What a clever boy he was. But Willa had not yet returned."

"Mother still look for son in storm."

"Yes, exactly. She was terrified that he would … Eventually, Willa came back to get Teddy and father to help her look. "There we were, all of us sipping chocolate and wondering when she would return. Oh, we were worried so for her, Teddy wanted to go out and look for her, but father dissuaded him. 'Don't worry, son, your bride will return and then...why it will my turn to go off and look for you.' So, as worried as we were, we hid it for the boy's sake, singing silly songs and sipping that chocolate. TJ laughing how he had fooled Momma and Auntie Abgail as he called me. And, we wondering if she ... You know I've never liked chocolate, not since."

Lonely Cricket broke the long pause. "Mother must be happy boy safe."

"What? Oh, yes. She held him and hugged him until he said, 'Mommy, you're all wet and cold.' I don't know that she had even thought about how cold she was until that moment. She was just so happy...

"The next day, Willa didn't come to breakfast. She had taken sick and was slow to recover. The doctor came, but there was little he could do. Eventually, finally, she could come downstairs for meals and read. Oh, she loved to read. But she was not well, not really well. The doctor said to give it time; that she would recover with time."

Abagail Pirrip wiped her eyes with a lace-bordered handkerchief. "She didn't... You know... Within the month, she was gone."

"Sad story." Lonely Cricket shifted his gaze from the woman's face back to the pictures.

"Oh yes, very sad indeed. The saddest thing was how it changed the boy; he was never the same. Never happy. His grandmother and I tried as best we could, but I don't suppose he ever got over the loss of his mother. His father didn't help matters. I think Teddy always blamed TJ for his mother's death. Not a day went by they didn't argue.

"When the war came, it was the same. Teddy enlisted. So did TJ, but on the other side. In the drawer." Abagail motioned towards the small walnut table that stood under the photographs. "I have pictures of them both. Teddy in his blue major's uniform and TJ ... He went down the Mississippi to New Orleans to join up. He had no truck with slavery, and I don't suppose he cared about the rights of states as much as he did his own right to be rebellious. We didn't hear much after that until... He sent me one letter. That was from your home, from Pierce. The war was over. But he hadn't come home. Maybe if he knew Teddy was dead ..." Abagail Pirrip sobbed. Lonely Cricket silently stared at the red coals in the fire grate.

Sniffling back her tears, the woman continued. "The letter is there, too." She again pointed at the walnut side table. "He had married someone whom he met in New Orleans, a Papist, a woman he knew his father could never accept. Perhaps he loved her. Perhaps it was another act of rebellion.

"She was pregnant, and they stopped there for her to have the child. It was a boy. The mother died giving birth."

"That sad. Many tears in family."

"Oh, yes, Lonely Cricket, many tears indeed. And they don't end there. There was no preacher who would bury the mother or baptize the boy Catholic, so TJ did them both himself. He put his wife in the ground and christened their son all on his own and wrote me that letter.

"TJ knew he couldn't keep the boy nor raise him on his own, so he gave his son, my grandnephew, to the local Indian agent, a fellow named Ezekiel Jones to bring up, to adopt. He'd be about your age. I don't know if this Jones fellow and his wife kept the name TJ gave him or gave him another, but he was baptized Theodore after his father and his grandfather. I have been hoping you could tell me... It must be a small town this home of yours?"

"Pierce small."

"Do you know the boy? Do you know my grandnephew?"

"I know Agent Jones. He take me to train go school. I know wife. They not have son. Not have child."

"Are you sure?" Abagail Pirrip almost yelled. "You must know him. You have to..."

"Not know. Perhaps father change mind. Perhaps boy die like mother. Mr. Jones, Mrs. Jones no children."

The older woman closed her eyes and slumped in her chair.

"Miss Pirrip, you want I get Esther?"

Without opening her eyes, Abagail replied, "No. No. I'll be fine. Why don't you go downstairs? I'm sure your friend would like to... Thank you, Lonely Cricket. Thank you for taking time to talk with a lonely old woman."

Abagail Pirrip allowed her head to slip to one side.

Without another word, the young man rose. Before he closed the door behind himself, Lonely Cricket whispered, "Miss Pirrip have much sorrow, but Mr. and Mrs. Jones no have son."

Chapter 40 ~ Speakers of Sacred Words

ΩΩΩΩΩ

When the first people emerged from below and walked upon the Great Tortoise, they were grateful for the abundance of the earth. They were thankful for the many animals and the fruits and berries and the plants which they could eat. For many days they were happy, and they celebrated.

Then the Great Spirit sent an Eagle to speak to the people.

ΩΩΩΩΩ

Lonely Cricket remembered Lame Bear standing and waving his arms up and down to imitate the eagle as he danced—hopping from foot to foot—around the cabin. Lonely Cricket and Happy Turtle always laughed when their father acted out his stories. Often, as on this day, when they laughed too hard and giggled too long, Yquili Sparrow would admonish them. "These are the stories of our people. Your father tells them to you so you might learn our ways and the wisdom that has guided us."

Meekly, the children had resumed listening although Happy Turtle could not help but cast a glance and smile in her brother's direction, and he remembered giggling once more before settling back on the soft buffalo robe.

"What did Eagle tell the people?" Happy Turtle asked.

ΩΩΩΩΩ

"It is good that you celebrate the wonderful place Ma-Ona has given you," the Eagle Messenger said. "However, it will not always be this way. There will come a time when the sun will hide and the air will be cold, when the animals will hide, and the plants die. You must make ready for the hard times. And, you must learn how to summon the sun to come back to warm the back of the Great Tortoise."

Still, life was easy, and the people did not listen to the Eagle Messenger. Not even their chief who was called Finder of Pathways listened. Instead, he lay on the soft grass and watched the cloud spirits wander the sky. At night, he and all the people slept beneath the trees and watched as the Teller of Tales filled the firmament with dreams.

One morning when the people woke and welcomed the day, the sun did not warm them. They shivered in the cold and complained among themselves that the Great Spirit had forgotten them. Taking pity on the people, the Eagle Messenger came back among them and led Finder of Pathways to the Great Bear. The Great Bear said, "You must wear a coat against the cold wind."

Finder of Pathways listened to the Bear's teaching and taught his people how to make warm blankets from the hides of the buffalo and the other animals. The men of the people went on a great hunt and killed many buffalo to make robes. Then the women cured the hides and sewed robes and blankets. When everyone had a buffalo robe, the people rejoiced to have such warm clothing. "You are a great leader," they said to Finder of Pathways, and they sang his praises. And because of what the Great Bear had taught them, the people honored his kind.

One night, the people went to sleep beneath the tree and covered themselves with their buffalo robes, but in the morning, they were covered by the white rain. Once more they shivered in the cold and in the wet. Once more, they complained among themselves that the Great Spirit had forgotten them. Once more, the Eagle Messenger took pity on the people and led Finder of Pathways to the Diligent Beaver who said, "You must build a shelter to keep out the white rain."

Finder of Pathways listened to the Beaver's teaching and taught his people how to make tepees from the skin of the deer and other animals. The people worked hard. Soon tepees were erected and lodges built. The people rejoiced to have such a dry place. "You are a great leader," they said to Finder of Pathways, and they sang his praises. And because of what the Diligent Beaver had taught them, the people honored his kind.

The days grew shorter and shorter. Even though they had a dry place to sleep and warm robes with which to cover themselves, the people were again unhappy. Once more, they complained among themselves that the Great Spirit had forgotten them. Once more, the Eagle Messenger took pity on the people and led Finder of Pathways to the Wise Owl, who said, "You must learn the sacred words that will summon the sun to return to the world."

Finder of Pathways listened to the Owl's teaching and taught his people the sacred words and rituals. He taught them to build great mounds of earth that they could recognize the sacred day on which those words should be said and those rituals should be performed. And when the people said the sacred words and performed the rituals, the sun came back to warm the world and the days again grew long.

The people rejoiced to have the sun return. "You are a great leader," they said to Finder of Pathways and they sang his praises and called him "Speaker of Sacred Words". And because of what the Wise Owl had taught them, the people honored his kind.

And the people took upon themselves the remembering of the sacred language, which is why we are called Ho-Chunk.

ΩΩΩΩΩ

Lame Bear had sat between his children and wrapped them in his arms. "We must never forget that no matter how good the things of this earth are, no matter how kindly the spirits are to us, those things can disappear and leave us. That is why we must learn the lessons of this world and the sacred teachings of the spirit world so we can be ready for what will come."

The memory had come unbidden but most welcome as the young man sat on a green straight-backed, woven-straw seated chair on the porch of Abagail Pirrip's home. The air was redolent of spring: the bushy wisteria, the acrid lobelia, the sweet, weed-like Joe-Pye, and the modest, nutty scent of sunflowers. Lonely Cricket was waiting for Dinah. They would walk into town. "We must buy presents for your family," she had insisted after a lunch of ham sandwiches and preserved apples. "I cannot show up at your home with nothing in my hands. It would be shameful manners."

"Want buy for Mrs. Cook and Sapphira, too," Lonely Cricket had replied. "We go stores."

"Not looking like this," the young woman replied. "What would people think? What will they think of Miss Abagail, us being her guests and all?"

She had dashed upstairs before she could hear Lonely Cricket's reply: "No understand."

"Bein' a man yous wouldn't, now would yous?" Esther had scoffed. "Set on that porch and wait on her. Your gal will be down when she's good and ready."

After his first impatience, Lonely Cricket thought about his conversation with Abagail Pirrip, about the sadness of her family and of the dreadful snowy night that had so altered the Pirrip family's life.

"Yes," he thought as his thoughts went back to his own childhood; "bad things can happen, and we must be ready."

"Are thou coming or not?" Dinah's voice cut through the haze of reverie.

***

"I must buy a new bonnet, not this simple thing I'm wearing, it's meant for First Day meeting not real life," Dinah had said to Amelia and Esther at breakfast.

Lonely Cricket and Jerome Danforth had already eaten and were in the small barn at the back of the property where they were examining Bathsheba's aging legs so Dinah felt free to talk of more womanly concerns. "Yesterday, whilst we walked from the train depot, I thought every woman was staring at me and thinking. The young woman tried to alter her voice to sound more mature. 'What a rube this child is! Look at that bonnet: straw no less. She must be fresh from the farm.'"

"It ain't so bad," Esther said.

"Wellington's Millinery sure is the finest in town," Amelia replied. "My Dorothea buys her hats there."

Quickly Esther gave directions to Market Street. "Next door to that bonnet shop there's Miss Brownstone. She done sell cloth and thread and all the stuff you needs fer makin' clothes."

"Perfect. I shall suggest we go there. Harry will want to buy presents for his mother and that precious sister of his. Then, I shall say, 'I wouldn't mind a nice, new bonnet for myself.'" This time she used her most seductive voice.

"I don't knows yous needs to figure nor talk no ways like that," Esther said. "That boy'll dos what yous want just 'cause."

Amelia hushed the maid. "You let the girl handle her own man."

Esther huffed off to her chores as Dinah took small bites of a warm biscuit dipped in bacon grease, took sips of sweet white coffee, and dreamed of the blue satin and beribboned hat that she would buy and how she would maneuver Lonely Cricket into spending money, something to which he was so averse.

***

A ten minutes' walk brought Dinah and Lonely Cricket to Market Street. As busy as they had thought the city of New Albany on their arrival the previous day, the two young people were unprepared for the rush and flow along the town's main thoroughfare. They walked along the north side of the street squinting into the sun. The two stopped time after time to peer into shops and marvel at the variety of things offered within. Fascinated as she was with the town's commerce, Dinah was more taken by the other women—many with a basket over one arm—and their clothing. "Why look how fancy she is," the girl whispered hoarsely more than once.

Each time, Lonely Cricket grunted an acknowledgement and hopefully asked, "Cloth store near?"

"How would I know?"

"Maybe ask."

Approaching a police officer, Dinah nervously asked after the draper. "One block on the other side of the street. Right 'cross from Morgan's hard goods and leather."

"And the milliner?" She asked this in a whisper so Lonely Cricket might not hear.

"Aye, Wellington's. Fancy hats for a pretty lady, I reckon. Right next door."

"Have hat," Lonely Cricket pointed to Dinah's bonnet.

"Oh, don't be so simple, Harry. I need a new one, one fit for meeting people, not for going to meeting." She pulled determinedly forward, and the young man followed.

The two shops, draper and milliner, stood so close that a man would be hard-pressed to wheel a barrow down the alley between them. Crossing Market Street, Dinah stopped to admire the signs hung above each shop. Lonely Cricket advanced one more step before he, aware of her, stopped as well. A passing cyclist yelled, "Look out!" as he swerved his way past the two young people. "Get out of the road," a teamster hollered as his wagon loaded with furnishings and going in the direction opposite the cyclist spattered a clod of dirt at Dinah's dress.

"Come. Not safe to stand in street," Lonely Cricket scolded.

"Oh, Lonely Cricket, didst thou ever see such marvelous emporia?"

"What emperor do with New Albany? No emperor in America."

"What am I to do with thee?" Dinah laughed. "Emporia, emporia. Hast thou ever seen such wonderful shops. Why one to buy only hats and bonnets and the other for fabric and notions. I declare this the most wonderful of cities. Will we ever find such a place in Nebraska?"

"We not get Nebraska if Dinah stand in road." He tugged on her arm.

Dinah's inclination was to head for the milliner. "Where go? Cloth for presents in this store." Lonely Cricket pulled her to their right and towards the door of the draper.

"Harry, thou canst be so difficult. I swear thou and my father are like peas in a pod. Practical and purposeful are all well and good, but I shall live this once and make the most…" Her words were cut off as she stumbled against the raised plank sidewalk.

Lonely Cricket grabbed Dinah's arm in time to prevent her falling. "Watch step." Before Dinah could say another word, the young man had pulled open the door of Miss Brownstone's Draper and Notions. Grimacing in frustration, Dinah followed him into the shop.

The overhead bell clanked and clunked as Lonely Cricket closed the door. The sound distracted him so he couldn't see the expression of the young woman clerk who stood behind a long counter on which a bolt of cloth was laid out.

Shears in hand, the clerk was assiduously working on a customer's written order. However, that concentrated effort had not stopped her from instantaneously recognizing the young man who entered. It had been a few years since he had left Pierce for school in Pennsylvania, but surely it was.

Sapphira Cook's heart raced.

"Oh, my God, Lonely Cricket?!" she said to herself.

Her hand jumped leaving a jagged cut in the expensive fabric. "Oh no!" she said much more loudly than she intended and dropped the shears clattering to the floor. Whether her reaction was to the ruined cloth or the sudden appearance of somebody whose presence was so unexpected, so fortuitous, and so horrible: that was a question she would ponder later when she lay on her cot in the attic of her mother's cousin's home, trying desperately to understand the workings of fate.

For the moment, Sapphira was dumbstruck.

Chapter 41 ~ So, Thou Art Sapphira Cook

Elisabetta Brownstone helped her shop assistant up from the floor behind the sales counter. Tsking quietly, she picked up the shears and folded the cloth that Sapphira had been cutting when Lonely Cricket and Dinah had entered the shop. Having made sure everything appeared in order, she took charge of the situation. "Who are you?" she demanded of the young couple who had entered her establishment. Then to Sapphira, "Who are these people?"

Sapphira cook blinked her eyes into focus. "I don't know her, but he..." she pointed at the young man whose own mouth was agape. "That is Lonely Cricket... from Nebraska... We..." She clutched the counter to keep from again dropping to the floor.

Miss Brownstone turned to the young woman, "And you are?"

"I am Dinah Tideswell of Pennsylvania." She curtsied. "Lonely Cricket and I..." Dinah bit her lip for a moment, turned to Lonely Cricket her eyes ablaze, "What's going on, Harry? Just who might these people be and how does this woman know thee?"

"This Sapphira Cook."

"This is Sapphira Cook?!" Dinah's voice raised in pitch and volume.

"My," said the shopkeeper. "Perhaps, Sapphira, you ought take your visitors into the office." Turning towards Dinah and Lonely Cricket, she added, "I'm sorry we cannot offer you a refreshment. Sapphira, perhaps a glass of water would be—"

"Not thirsty," Lonely Cricket interrupted. "Surprised to find Sapphira Cook in New Albany."

"I daresay you are," Elisabetta Brownstone replied. "I'm sure she can explain her presence more adequately than I; however, as you can see..." She waved her hand to take in the three women who were examining fabrics and notions and the fourth who was rummaging through a pile of dress patterns. "We have other customers and this conversation might be more privately held."

Dinah wondered how disappointed the other two customers in the shop, who had stopped their rummaging to better listen, might be to have the conversation removed from their hearing. Dinah had no doubt this encounter with Saphira Cook could well lead to titillating gossip more diverting than the selection of fabric. "If only I had a new bonnet for their gawking," she thought.

Aloud, she said, "Thou art most kind, ma'am."

***

Crammed in the office to which Sapphira had shown the other two, the three young people sat in silence until Dinah spoke. "So, thou art Sapphira Cook?!"

Sapphira bobbed her head in answer.

Dinah Tideswell scrutinized the young woman sitting diagonally from her. The girl's blonde hair put up in artless curls, her hazel eyes, the ill-fitting counter girl white smock which emphasized rather than concealing her full breasts. "Harry, I thought you told me that Sapphira was a girl, not a young woman."

"Has Lonely Cricket spoken of me?" Sapphira fought to keep her soft mellifluous voice under control just as she struggled to keep her composure, to remain seated on the stiff-backed chair. How she wanted to jump up, scream her sorrow, and run from the small office made even smaller by the cases of notions, piles of patterns, and books of sample fabrics that Elisabetta Brownstone stored there.

Ignoring Sapphira's question, Dinah continued. "Harry, thou toldest me she was a child, a play fellow. Thou never mentioned a woman."

In Dinah's tone, Lonely Cricket heard the iron anger of Rachel Tideswell when she would scold Dinah or remonstrate with the other young men on the farm for tracking dirt into the house at meals. Seldom had that scolding voice been turned on him, only after Dinah declared her intention to go with him to Nebraska.

"In my home! Behind my very back! How darest thou, thou heathen. And, I thought thou hast accepted God's words. The sooner that we are shut of thee the better." Lonely Cricket had not been sure if Mrs. Tideswell was addressing those words to him or to her daughter.

"I'm hardly a child, Miss Tideswell. However, this is now. I haven't seen Lonely Cricket for some years. I'm sure I am not as he remembers me, and he is certainly not as I remember him."

"Sapphira change much. But—"

"I notice that you call him Harry, why? His name is Lonely Cricket?" Sapphira asked before he could say more.

The intense staccato of Sapphira's words startled Dinah, who nodded in response.

"School make Indian take Christian name. I take Harry."

"Why Harry, Lonely Cricket? Why did you choose Harry?"

"Harry Cook good man. Your father. They want call me something from Bible. I say, 'No, Harry.' I say, 'I know man Harry Cook.'"

Sapphira paled. The dam she had worked so hard to build against her emotions burst. First a trickle from her eyes and then a torrent.

"Sapphira, why cry?" Lonely Cricket's question elicited even louder wails.

Turning to Dinah, the young man asked, "What do?"

"How would I know. She is thy friend." The last word filled with anger and other feelings that Lonely Cricket could not understand any more than he could comprehend the moans and sobs of his childhood friend.

"When we were little and she barked her shin, her father sang," Lonely Cricket recalled. "Perhaps, if I… What was that song? 'Oh, my lady, let's be… Oh, my lady, let's be merry.' Yes, that was it."

In a soft, tenor he sang the words aloud. "Oh, my lady, let's be merry let us sing and play this day so tonight when we are weary and in our feather bed we lay we shall have those dreams so merry that we shall ever want to stay."

For a moment, Sapphira smiled through her tears before becoming even more disconsolate. Through her sobs, she gasped, "I'm so sorry. It was my fault. I didn't want to leave. Oh, Harry, what have I done? I'm so sorry. I feel so guilty."

Her utterances made no sense to the young man, who now knelt beside her, rubbing her hands and mumbling reassurances.

"Sapphira Cook, indeed! Harry, thou toldst me her name but not the truth. I thought her thy playmate, a friend from thy childhood, not thy guilty lover. And thee, thou art, as my mother says, a savage. How dare you?!" With those angry words, Dinah pushed back her chair so abruptly that it fell backward against the crowded table behind her knocking a piece of chalk shattering to the ground where it was followed by a box which opened spewing small straight pins across the floor.

Lonely Cricket stared at the minor mayhem on the otherwise clean floor as if somehow the answer to his confusion might lie among those bits and pins. "Not understand why Dinah angry," he said. Then he turned his attention back to the sobbing, gasping Sapphira. "Not understand why Sapphira sad."

"Ohh, thou art just like a man!" Dinah—her jaw jutted forward, her nose upturned—stomped from the room.

For the moment, Lonely Cricket started after her and then, without thought, turned back and again knelt by Sapphira's chair. "Did I sing song wrong? It make you laugh when Harry Cook sing. Now, it make you sorry and make Dinah angry. No understand women."

Soon after Dinah slammed it behind herself, Elisabetta Brownstone came through the office door. "What in tarnation…" Crossing the distance to the desk chair where Sapphira sat—her head sagging to her breasts—sobbing and moaning, the older woman said, "I was afraid of this. Had I known you were in town, I would have closed the shop and kept her and myself to our beds until you were gone. She has told me everything. I cannot imagine how you feel, but—"

"Feel confused. Not understand women. Not understand Dinah angry. Not understand Sapphira cry. Can Miss Brownstone explain?"

"You don't know?!"

"Know? Not know what to know."

Elisabetta Brownstone blanched. "Goodness, oh my goodness. I'll close the shop and then the three of us must have a long talk."

Through the open door, Lonely Cricket could hear the proprietress shooing customers from the store. As each left, the bell clunked and clanked. Then he heard her throw the lock. "What if Dinah come back?" he thought, but that didn't seem to matter as much as the questions that came to his mind with each sob and gasp from the young woman next to him. "What make Sapphira unhappy? What wrong?"

Again, he rubbed Sapphira's hand.

***

"Nathan Wainright marry Happy Turtle?" Lonely Cricket stared emotionless into Sapphira's face.

She shook her head. "No."

He could barely hear her voice.

"Where he go?"

"We don't know. He stayed in town for a while, then drifted… I guess wherever he could find a bottle."

"Lame Bear no go after him?"

Sapphira shook her head and looked towards the floor. "I don't think he could. Being an Indian and Nathan…" The young woman took a sip of water from one of the cups Elisabetta Brownstone had brought in and set on the desk.

"I'll leave you to talk," the shop owner said. "There's a lot that needs discussing."

"Words not help," Lonely Cricket's responded. Still, he listened to the story.

"I kill Wainright."

"Lonely Cricket, you can't. Even if you found him, they'd hang you."

"Older brother must avenge sister. That Lonely Cricket's job."

"How will that help her? How will it help the baby?"

"Baby?!"

"When we left, when my parents headed for Butte, for the mines. I'm pretty sure Happy Turtle was with child."

"And Wainright not come back?"

"No." A look of terror passed across Sapphira's eyes. "Oh, that would be horrible—if he were to come back. That's the last thing Happy Turtle would need, a drunk, no-good to take care of along with a baby."

"I go back Pierce and help sister. I go back Pierce and help take care of child. I go back Pierce and kill Nathan Wainright."

"I felt so awful leaving. Lonely Cricket, I tried to tell my parents we should… I wanted to stay, to help." Sapphira wrung her hands, reached for the piece of white linen her cousin Elisabetta had given her to replace her already soggy handkerchief and wiped her eyes. "They said we couldn't, that we mustn't. They said it would be too painful for your family. So, we told Mr. Jones that Lame Bear was to have our place. 'You let him hold onto it so that young gal got something for herself,' my papa told Mr. Jones. Then, he climbed back in the wagon, snapped the reins, and off we went. I cried all the way … wanting to go back to Pierce … wanting to be there for your sister, for your family, and—when you came back …"

"I help find horse for Miss Pirrip then go Pierce."

"Will Miss Tideswell go with you?"

"Dinah go. You come, too?"

"Would that … Would your parents … Would that be … Lonely Cricket, would you take me with you?"

"Sapphira Cook want come to Nebraska, she come."

Her emotions launched the girl from her chair and at the sitting young man. Wrapping herself around Lonely Cricket with such force that she almost tipped him backward, she exclaimed, "I want to. Yes, I do so want to!"

Chapter 42 ~ A Cab for Miss Dinah

A mix of odors welcomed Dinah to consciousness. For the moment, she could not remember where she was. "Momma." Her voice weak. Then again, louder, "Momma!"

"Easy there, Miss Abagail." The tall, thin man smirked at his own joke.

Where had she heard that voice before? She blinked her sight into focus. The man stooped over her was familiar, but there was no recollection of a name.

"My name's not Abagail."

Jim Wickham laughed. "Don't you think I know that, Miss Dinah? I was just making light." His smile turned grave. "Are you all right then? You had a nasty fall."

"Where am I?"

"On the ground."

"I know that. On what ground? Where is my mother?"

"Far from here, and that's a fact. Do you not remember?"

"Are thou not the cabby?" Slowly Dinah regained her faculties. "Thou wanted too much money to torment thy sadly horse into carrying us."

"Aye, Jim Wickham at your service, Miss Dinah. I fear you've taken a tumble, hit your head, and given yourself a lump in the bargain." He touched her forehead just below her hairline.

"Ouch. Don't!"

He pulled his hand back and frowning, examined the blood on his fingertips.

"All apologies, Miss. Allow me to help you up." He held out his left hand, which she took in her right. As she put weight on her right foot, Dinah again cried out in pain. "My ankle."

Quickly, the cabby moved to her side and put his left arm around her. "Lean on me and let's hop you to the sidewalk."

"This is the alley next to Miss Brownstone's establishment?"

"Aye, and that's a fact." Suddenly, Wickham hoisted her into his arms and stepped onto the raised wooden walkway. "Sorry about that, Miss," he whispered, "but I think it would be best to have you on that seat than on the sidewalk." He stepped towards a simple bench that ran before the millinery shop. Having deposited her on the bench, he knelt and ran his hands up and down Dinah's ankle.

"What dost thou think thou art doing?" Dinah demanded as she brushed fiercely at her skirt.

"Why, what I would do for any horse, and that's a fact. There don't seem to be a break, but I don't think you'll be walking on this foot for a while. It's already swelling, and that's a fact."

"Fact or not, I don't... Oh, this is infuriating!"

Glancing again at the lump and oozing blood on her forehead, he pulled off the checkered scarf knotted around his throat. "Let me." He dabbed at the crimson seepage.

"Don't! It hurts."

"Then do it yourself, but that blood needs staunching and that's a fact." He handed her the kerchief, which she wadded into a ball and pressed gently to her head.

"You want me to fetch that Injun friend of yours? You know where he's at?"

"Harry?! I should say not. The last thing I need is him prattling on about that girl."

"What..." The cabby gave a fleeting smile and tried a different question, "I could take you where you need. Just take me a minute to get old Twister."

"I suppose I have to go back to Miss Pirrip's house."

"I'll get my wagon."

"And charge me a fortune for a short ride? I should think not." Grimacing, the young woman pushed against the deep red clapboard building to rise.

"Short ride or not, you can't do it on foot."

"Then I shall sit here until I can."

"You sure are a stubborn filly. Tell you what, I won't charge you a penny. Just take you there and help you in. All you need do is thank me. A sweet word from a beautiful lady will make my day more than a dollar, and I swear Twister will be happy for the chance to show you how well he does. I swear you folks hurt his feelings; old Twister's got a ways to go before the knacker, and that's a fact."

Chapter 43 ~ Saturday

The clock sounded ten as the two men struggled to move Miss Abagail Pirrip's dark maroon brocade and mahogany fainting couch to the porch. Esther stood waiting with two pillows and a tri-colored afghan—red, white, and blue—which Abagail Pirrip had crocheted in celebration of the Union victory at Gettysburg.

"My Dearest Brother," Abagail had written in her diary on August 6, 1863. "Old Abe has declared this a day of thanksgiving. I fly our union's flag and start an afghan in your remembrance. These victories come at such a cost it is difficult for me to find thanks in my heart, but in your memory, I shall do as the president requests. If God sees fit to end this war as we all pray, he might and free the darkies whom the south enslaves, perhaps it will someday seem worth the horrible price. I pray for your soul and for your son on whatever battlefield he may be."

It had taken months to finish the afghan only to camphor it in a mahogany chest. Carved with a likeness of the friezes of the Parthenon, the trunk had been their father's. Only months later, when Esther and Jerome Danforth had found their way to her employ, did Abagail allow herself to remember that throw. "This will give you warmth," she'd said and meant that it would give purpose to her brother's death.

Days of hanging in the yard rid the reek of camphor. Even then, Esther and Jerome could not bring themselves to use the afghan on their bed. "It ain't right with her makin' it for him," Danforth had said.

"Seems like it's fer the dead. Gives me the shivers to think," Esther commented.

Never mentioned again, the afghan had been moved to another shelf to await someone who did not know its story.

"Couch heavy," Lonely Cricket said as he pushed and grunted.

"Not so easy with one leg neither," Danforth added.

Progress was slow; Danforth would hop back a step, balance with one crutch, and lift his end. Then Lonely Cricket would move forward, and both would set the couch down, take a breath and ready themselves to repeat the maneuver.

"Don't keep me standin' here all this day," Esther remonstrated. "There's work and more to do fer tonight's dinner."

"At least you can stand on your own," Danforth muttered as he took a deep breath and bent once more. "Don't know the why of this. Seems more work than it's worth."

"Stop 'plainin' and get that thing moved. I'se gots lots more to do. Amelia wants two chickens fer dinner and Miss Abagail say I'se best make that dinin' room shine."

"They all comin'?" Danforth asked.

"Sure is. Everybody done comin'. I'se don't mind Miss Sapphira none. She ain't like no guest, just like she's part of the family. And I reckon that Miss Wellstone, she be a proper guest. But that Wickham actin' like he's somebody and he ain't much mo than dirt."

"What's he comin' round fer anyways?" Danforth asked.

"Men! I declare." Esther stomped her foot in frustration. "God gave you heads but all youse do with 'em is act like they's empty."

"Dinah say same. Say Lonely Cricket brain only good for horse."

A nicker from the street interrupted. Without looking, Lonely Cricket said, "Wickham here now."

"I swear you can tell every horse in New Albany just by their whinny," Jerome Danforth commented. "How you know horses so damned well, I don't have a clue. I have to say, I never seen a horse train up so quick as Miss Abagail's new mare. How'd you know Princess would be be so damned-near perfect?"

"Horse tell if listen."

"You fellas look like you need a hand, and that's a fact," Jim Wickham called from the street.

"That we could," Danforth replied; "leastwise that or another leg."

Tying Twister to one of the ornate metal hitching posts outside the gate, Wickham swung open the squeaky entrance, walked jauntily across the yard, and bounded up the steps.

"Here, let me." Shouldering past Danforth and taking hold of the foot end of the couch, he added, "Come on then, Harry, let's get this out of the way so's I can go up."

"Go up?" Lonely Cricket asked. "Why go up?"

"Why, to see my lovely patient as if you didn't know."

"When did you'se become a doctor?" Esther asked. "And if you was, I wouldn't let you tend a chicken 'fore I wrung its neck."

"Esther, that wouldn't matter to me none long as Amelia cooked it, and that's a fact." Jim Wickham laughed and grunted at the same moment.

"Thou art in a good mood today, Jim." Leaning on Amelia, Dinah hobbled onto the porch.

"So, you've decided to get up and about." Wickham's grin broadened. "Glad to see you're recovering." He moved closer, peered at her forehead, and added; "that bump is going down as well."

"How horse legs?" Lonely Cricket turned his attention to Wickham.

"Harry, I swear thou wouldst give me more attention were I to nicker and whinny," Dinah said.

Jim Wickham said to Esther. "You may not want to admit it, but my patient shows my skill."

Dinah laughed. "Doctor, I think thy patient shows that she is young and healthy."

"That, too," Wickham agreed. "And beautiful," he added in a whisper meant only for Dinah's ears.

The young woman blushed as she settled on the fainting couch, Esther fussed at the pillows and afghan. "Oh, I'm fine, Esther. I'm sure thou hast better things to do. Jim will help me if I need."

"There's work needs doin' and that's true," Esther replied. "Ain't that so, Jerome?"

"I sure s'pose there is what with gettin' ready for this here dinner party. Hand me my second crutch from inside the door, and I'll be doin' it."

"And what about thee, Harry?" Dinah asked. "Dost thou not have work to do? Perhaps thou needs tend to Jim's horse."

"Lonely Cricket not tend horse. Go Miss Wellstone store unload wagon."

"What wagon's that?" Wickham asked.

"Cloth women sew. I ask Miss Abagail I needed here. She say, 'No, be in way.'"

"And Miss Cook will be there, too, I reckon; and that's a fact."

"She still help store."

"Then go on!" Dinah almost shouted. "Thou must not keep thy Miss Cook waiting."

"Why is Dinah angry when we talk about Sapphira?" Lonely Cricket thought as he closed the gate behind him and stopped to pat Twister's muzzle. "I never understand woman."

***

This Saturday's supper was as close to formal entertaining as Abagail Pirrip had done in some years.

"It's almost as it was when I was a girl," Dorothea said to her mother; "when Mr. Theodore and Mrs. Willa would entertain."

"Weren't them some lovely dinners even if I did have to cook and cook and cook," Amelia replied. "Now, put these here pies in the window to cool while I see to the roast." The sweating cook had been working all day.

Esther and Danforth had been working as well. The dining room table had been extended and the extra chairs pulled from their places along the walls. A vase of wisteria had been placed in the middle of the table, which was covered with a lace cloth somewhat tinged with age and set with the Pirrip family's finest china and silver. As evening fell, they filed in; Abagail Pirrip leaning on Jerome Danforth's arm in the lead. The room was festively lit by beeswax candles and redolent of food and flowers.

Elisabetta Brownstone wore a green linen décolleté dress with full skirt. Lonely Cricket held her chair as she took her place opposite their hostess. The young Indian, dressed in his school uniform, his hair tied carefully in a black band so it fell in its curly way over his ears and down his neck, sat to Abagail Pirrip's right. Next to him, Sapphira Cook sat primly, her hands finding the lap of her modest ecru dress between every bite but a smile beaming.

Dinah sat across from Lonely Cricket and to her left was Jim Wickham. Jim's concession to the occasion was substituting a blue cravat for his checkered scarf; and—to the relief of some—he had taken a bath and splashed himself with a lotion of rose and lemon. If the resulting odor was more appropriate to the ladies at the table than to a young man, it was at least not unpleasant.

Amelia sat beside Sapphira except when she was jumping up to fetch the over-laden dishes. Hens, roast, chops, vegetables, potatoes—white and yam, and three kinds of bread: white, corn, and biscuits. Wine, beer—some even from far-off Milwaukee—and milk were all on the sideboard, from which Esther, who sat next to Wickham, kept fetching them to refill everyone's glasses.

Dorothea, dressed in startling cramoisy, had the place at Miss Brownstone's left. "Your daughter's a schoolteacher," Abagail Pirrip had clarified the placement to Amelia. "She can discuss books and events with our guest of honor."

Across from Dorothea, sat Danforth, his crutches balanced against the wall behind and within easy hopping distance.

Between Danforth and Esther was an empty chair with a place laid before it. "For your father," Abagail had explained as she instructed her maid on the setting of the table. "Although Mose is not yet here, assuredly he will soon come."

The letter from Mose had arrived on the seventh day after Dinah's fall. The postman handed Esther the small pile of correspondence, and she, in turn, took it to her mistress. "Why this one's for you, Esther," Miss Pirrip exclaimed. She studied the markings. "It's from Pennsylvania. Would you—"

"Please, can youse done read it fer me?" Esther held on to the back of a chair in fear of the rejection that might be contained or perhaps worse the excitement of a positive response. "Must be 'cause of Lonely

Cricket writin' him. What might...Do yeh s'pose...Oh, Miss Abagail, I is ready to die not knowin'."

"Then hush and let me read it." The mistress of the house settled her spectacles on her nose and carefully unfolded the paper. "This handwriting... He must have written it himself." Abagail squinted and moved the paper closer to her face.

"'My dearest Esther,'" Miss Pirrip began. "'I don't know as you is my daughter or no. Sounds as you might be. I've dreamt years of finding you. I told Mr. Broadmore Tideswell for who I work I got to be certain. So, he says I can come to New Albany, where I've never been, to meet you and learn if you is or isn't. I'll be taking the train soon as I can arrange. Got to make sure Mr. Broadmore's got nuff help before I leaves, but he's a good man and wants I should go right off.'"

The older woman took a deep breath. "Sounds to be a good and responsible man," she commented so softly as to make her maid strain to hear.

Then Miss Pirrip continued, "In the meantimes, he asks you to say hello to Harry and give his best to me and mine. And, to Miss Dinah, too. I reckon he'd want you to give his love e'n though he can't say it hisself."

Esther broke in, "How soon he gonna be here?"

"I'm sure I don't know," her employer answered. "Let me finish reading your letter; perhaps it will say."

Once more adjusting her pince-nez, Abagail continued reading, "'If you be my flesh and blood, that will make me proud and happy. Harry says you is a fine woman and I take his word. He says you also got a man who loves you. I knows how important love is, so I is glad for that. Knowing that soon we will meet and sure that once we do, we will know what is true. With hope, Mose"

Each morning since Mose's letter had arrived, Esther asked her employer, to read it again. After each reading, she asked, "Miss Abagail, you think Mose will come today?"

To which the elder woman would reply, "That is in God's hands. In God's hands and the railroad's."

At every meal including this Saturday supper, Esther had set an extra place for Mose, and Amelia made sure there was enough food just in case the old man might arrive in time to eat.

"Are you well enough to go to church tomorrow?" Amelia, who was once again circling the table offering food—this time a strawberry pie in one hand and apple in the other—asked Dinah. "Dorothea and I would sure be happy to have you and Lonely Cricket join us."

Exchanging a quick glance and smile with Wickham and then taking a small piece of apple pie, Dinah replied. "I thank thee for the kindness, but we members of the Society of Friends do not attend such churches. Our meetings are without ritual or sacrament."

"I told you, Mother." Dorothea's hoarse whisper could be heard and at the same time denied by all.

"I'm not a churchgoing man and that's a fact," said Jim Wickham—his mouth filled with apple pie; "but if you want me, why I can find out if there's one of them Quaker meetin's here in New Albany and escort you there myself. Of course, you'll have to instruct me proper in the kneelin' and singing and all. I ain't been ta church in a coon's age and more, and that's a fact." His words were accompanied by a quick wink and smile.

"There is nothing of that kind at our meetings, only silence. People speak when the spirit moves them and everyone knows that god can be heard in every voice."

"That sounds most poetic," Elisabetta Brownstone took another bite of strawberry pie and dabbed the corners of her mouth. "Amelia, I swear this pie is the best I've ever tasted."

"Thank you for the kind words, but it was my Dorothea brought them berries."

"Wheres yeh find 'em?" Esther asked. "They's right good. Sweet as sugar."

Dorothea nodded her thanks for the recognition. "My friend has a few acres across the river. She doesn't work the land but takes the bounty it gives."

"Well, you must thank your friend for us," Abagail Pirrip said.

"And where do you folk go to church, Miss Brownstone?" Amelia asked after carefully swallowing.

"Like Miss Tideswell, Sapphira and I go to a meeting, but ours is not of the Quaker friends. We are universalists."

"What in tarnation's a universalist?" Crumbs of pie sprayed from Danforth's mouth. Turning as red as the strawberry filling, the groom tried to pick them up—one by one—and return them to his mouth.

"We believe in god, but he comes in many forms and faiths. Jesus spoke for him as did Moses and Muhammad and even the Hindu priests."

"Creator take many shape," Lonely Cricket observed.

"Exactly," Elisabetta Brownstone responded. "I imagine an Indian such as yourself would be quite at home in our meeting."

"Go White Man church in Pennsylvania. Go church at school. Go church when live with Tideswells. Sing good. Listen sermon, read holy book not so good. Minister good man. That best part."

"Perhaps you'd like to come to our meeting," Sapphira offered. "You're all welcome to join us." Her words were inclusive, but her eyes and smile fell only on the young man to her left. Reaching under the tinged white tablecloth, she took his right hand in her left and squeezed.

Twice he squeezed back. "Sapphira," he began.

"Oh no!" She feared he would share her secret touch.

"I go meet with you and Miss Brownstone. Dinah come, too?"

"No, thank thee, Harry. I will take Jim up on his offer." Her foot touched Wickham's and the cabby smiled again, allowing the grin to linger on the corners of his lips.

Lonely Cricket could not put words to his emotion, but it did not sadden him that Dinah had declined. No matter what god of the White Man might inhabit the meeting to which he and Sapphira would go, the young Indian was sure he would be a spirit of great happiness.

"For myself," Miss Pirrip announced, "I will spend this Sabbath morning as I sometimes do, writing in my diary where only God and my dear brother Theodore can read them.

"Jerome, you and Esther may take the curricle to church. I know Bathsheba will be happy for the service. She must be in want of exercise with Princess so often in the traces."

Jerome Danforth flashed a quick smile to Esther before replying, "If you wish, Ma'am; then thank ye very much."

As the mistress of the house knew full-well, the couple would not be going to the Anglican church to which Abagail ordinarily went with them in tow. No, they would take a Sunday morning ride, perhaps to the fairgrounds where Danforth had friends among the horse handlers or perhaps along the river where privacy and love conjoined.

"Miss Pirrip brother dead," Lonely Cricket whispered to Sapphira.

"I figured that," she whispered in return. In a louder voice, she said, "It must be very lonely in this big house without your family."

"Worse than lonely, young lady. If God has made a Purgatory in which sinners wait for eternity, I surely dwell there. However," she swept her arm to take in the table of diners, "you have all eased my pain this evening. And you, Lonely Cricket and you, too, Dinah, you have made the last twelve days happier than any time I have known for years."

"Thank thee for allowing us to stay, 'specially with my ankle being sprained and not being able to help. Thou hast all taken such good care of me." Dinah took a moment to nod acknowledgement to each member of the table. "I can hardly thank thee enough." She finished with another bob of her head toward Abagail Pirrip before again smiling at Jim Wickham.

"You kind lady, Miss Abagail. When I get Nebraska, I write." Lonely Cricket added.

A tear crept to the corner of Abagail Pirrip's eye. "Yes, thank you. You'll be sure to write?"

Later, Dinah and Lonely Cricket went upstairs—she to the best guest room, which had become hers alone because of pain. She asked, "What will thou write her about?"

"She ask question. I not sure answer."

"What question?"

"Not important. About government agent."

Once the door was closed behind her, Dinah muttered, "He's damned near impossible. He's supposed to love me, but try talking… like being at meeting, nobody saying a damned thing… nothing that matters to me."

Later, lying in bed, she rolled the name over in her head, "Jim Wickham, James Wickham, Mrs. Wickham, Mrs. James Wickham."

Chapter 44 ~ By the River

Even though the day was sunny, it was chilly by the river. The breeze, on which children—free from church and ready for action—were gleefully flying kites, made it feel even cooler. Still, it seemed to Lonely Cricket that the entire world was on its banks. "Many people live New Albany."

"And it's growing," Sapphira replied as she settled next to him. The chestnut tree against which they rested was in bloom, white candles of flowers.

The tree's smell—rank yet tinged with life—reminded the young Indian of the day he, Sparrow Yenri, and Twisted Rock had wandered along the stream near their homes in Nebraska. Rounding a copse of willow, the three boys had heard singing. It was Charging Buffalo.

Lonely Cricket and the other boys admired Charging Buffalo, not only because the older boy could hunt and could speak at the council fires and be listened to by men, but also because he would admonish Shadow Fox when he was cruel. Often Charging Buffalo would stop to talk to the younger boys. If Charging Buffalo heard Shadow Fox call Lonely Cricket "Bird Head" or "Ghost Boy," Charging Buffalo would say "Are you afraid to be a man, Shadow Fox? Why don't you stop bullying the younger boys and come hunt with us?"

Each time this happened, Shadow Fox slunk away like a dog that had been beaten. But, later, when Charging Buffalo had gone, Shadow Fox would come back to torment Lonely Cricket again.

On this day, Charging Buffalo was not hunting or fishing. He was looking carefully at the branches of the trees and singing a song which the boys had never heard.

"Let's ask what he is doing?" Twisted Rock suggested.

"No, let us listen to his song first," Lonely Cricket replied.

"I search among the gentle trees for a flute that will play the song of our love," the young man sang.

As they crept closer, the boys watched Charging Buffalo search among the willow branches. Using a hatchet, the man cut a small limb from one of the smaller willows and—sitting, his back against that same tree—took out his knife and started to work on the wood.

The three boys stood up and walked towards Charging Buffalo. "What are you doing?" Lonely Cricket asked.

"I am making a flute to play for the woman I love."

"Who is that?" Sparrow Yenri asked eagerly. The boy always loved to carry stories.

"I don't know," Charging Buffalo answered. "When I play the flute, I will know for whom I play it."

"Will you show us how to make such a magical flute?" Twisted Rock asked.

"No. You can sit and watch, but it is for your fathers to teach you how a flute is made. It is for your fathers to teach you the ways of love."

"Did my father make a flute to find my mother?" Lonely Cricket wondered, but he knew that Charging Buffalo would not know the answer; he also knew it was a question that he should not ask Lame Bear.

"If you wish, I can tell you the story of the first flute maker and how the people learned to make flutes."

Carefully, gently, Charging Buffalo worked his knife to split the section of willow branch into two even lengths. The boys inched closer, sat down, and waited to hear the story that he would tell.

ΩΩΩΩΩ

Long ago, before the people climbed to the surface of the world, there were no men and no women. All the people were of two spirits.

One day a man appeared outside the village of the people and said, "Why have you no women here? Who will bear your children? Who will raise your crops?" He was a tall man. A light so bright that it must have come from the sun followed his gaze. With long strides—longer than those of any of the people—the stranger walked around the village staring at everything and at everybody. When he looked in their direction, even the bravest of the people looked away, for they knew this stranger had been sent by Ma-Ona.

Why would we want to carry children?" one of the people asked. "We are enough and do not need more."

"Why do we need to raise crops?" another asked. "There are fruits and nuts and berries everywhere we turn."

Then the stranger stopped his walking and spoke again, "Why have you no men here? Who will defend you against your enemies? Who will hunt game and catch fish for your food?

"Why do we need warriors to fight when we have no enemies?" one of the people asked.

"Why do we need to hunt and catch fish when the animals of the land, water, and air are tame and come to us when we have need?" yet another asked.

"It will not always be thus," the stranger said. "The world for which you have been created is one in which people will die and so you will need children to take their place. The world for which you have been created is one in which it will not be sufficient to gather fruit and berries but also there you will be able to eat things that will be new to you, foods that you do not yet know, foods that grow in the earth and bring strength. The world into which Ma-Ona will send you is not a place of friendship but a place in which some will want what you have and will take it from you if you allow them. The world in which Ma-Ona has decreed that you shall live is filled with animals, birds, and fish that you do not yet know, but they will try to flee from you.

"This will be a different world than you have known. In this new world, you will need to be man and woman so you can survive. You will need to be a man to fill the woman with seed so she can produce children. You will need to be man so that you can hunt and fish. You will need to be woman so you can bear children within you. You will need to be women so you can raise the crops that you will need to survive."

When he was done speaking, the tall stranger took his lance from his shoulder and pointed it at the people. When he did this, a bright flash of lightening came forth from the lance and broke the people into two parts, and men and women were separated.

The people wandered around, for they were dazed by what had happened. And the male parts and the female parts of the people became lost one from the other, the man from the woman. Many of the people became frightened and they called out, "Ma-Ona, tell us what to do that we may find the other part of ourselves." They said this because they realized this was not some strange man who stood outside their village but the Creator himself.

The stranger went to a tree that grew nearby and cut a branch from it. He sat on the ground and did as I do now; he made a sacred flute. And, as he crafted his flute, the man sang, "I search among the gentle trees for a flute that will play the song of our love. I ask the tree to give me sweet music to attract my love to me. I shall play the song of my love on the sacred flute. I know that its sound will bring my love to my side."

ΩΩΩΩΩ

As Charging Buffalo sang the song, he carefully worked the length of branch which he had cut.

"How long will you sit here and work on this flute?" Sparrow Yenri asked.

"I will stay here, sitting with my back to this tree until I know that the flute I have made is ready to play for the woman I desire."

When Lonely Cricket returned home, Happy Turtle and her best friend Quiet Raven were stripping reeds they had collected by the stream. "We can weave baskets for Jedadiah Jacobs to sell in his store," Quiet Raven had proposed; "then we can use the White Man money to buy things."

Lonely Cricket sat next to his older sister and told the young women about meeting Charging Buffalo. "He was making a flute to play for the woman he loves."

"Did he tell you her name?" Quiet Raven asked.

"No. He said that when he plays the flute, he will know for whom he plays it."

"Perhaps one day, Charging Buffalo will play his flute for you," Happy Turtle teased her friend.

"Or perhaps he will take you," the deep-green-eyed Quiet Raven replied.

"No, I think that Small Deer has claimed me and his friends will not compete with him. They will not come in the night to play their flutes for me."

"And has Small Deer come?" Happy Turtle's friend asked.

"No. Instead he brings me moccasins and plays with Many Fish, who laughs and toddles after him. My mother laughs and says that Small Deer will be a fine father to our children."

"And what does your father say?"

"Lame Bear does not speak of these things. He is too busy working with our white neighbor. He is too busy teaching my older brother how to be a farmer. I do not think my father cares who will play their flute for me. But Lonely Cricket cares a great deal." She paused to touch her brother's arm and smile at him. "He asks me if I love Small Deer. When I say, 'no,' he makes a face and tells me that Small Deer is a good man but that I should have a husband whom I love. He says that our neighbor Sapphira Cook tells him stories of love, of great White people who have found their lovers, of great warriors who have killed horrible beasts to save their women. Lonely Cricket says I should have such a great warrior."

"Well, Charging Buffalo will certainly become a great warrior; he is very strong," said Quiet Raven.

"Yes, and very handsome," Happy Turtle added.

The two young women giggled.

As the girls continued working on their reeds, Lonely Cricket walked towards the barn where he could hear his father working.

"I wonder if Small Deer will play his flute for Happy Turtle," Lonely Cricket thought. "I wonder if I will someday learn to make such a flute."

***

At school, Plenty Horses had carved a flute from an apple tree that stood not far from Major Pratt's office.

"That's fine carving," the major commented when he heard Lonely Cricket's friend first try playing the flute.

The young man had thanked the school's senior officer and even offered a small salute.

That night, when the young warriors had gathered at the abandoned farm, Plenty Horses laughed at the White Man. "Major think he know Indian," Samuel said when Plenty Horses had shared his story.

"Maybe must speak English at school, but we still think Indian," Plenty Horses added.

"Which girl you play flute?" one of the other young warriors asked.

"I play Running River."

"She like you?"

"No matter. She will like flute."

The others laughed. Lonely Cricket, not understanding the joke, forced himself to laugh with them.

Now, sitting beneath that chestnut tree, Lonely Cricket understood. "I want to carve a flute and play it for Sapphira," he thought as he took her hand in his.

"I never wanted to carve one for Dinah," he thought; "perhaps there is a difference between love and love." He gently rubbed his thumb over Sapphira's knuckles.

Slowly, without speaking, they inclined their heads towards one another. Their lips touched. It was a soft kiss, no forcing of tongue, no insistence, only the gentleness of a desire to join as one.

"Someday, I play flute for you," the young man said.

"Do we have to wait for someday?" Sapphira replied.

"This good day."

They kissed again.

***

Dinah and Jim Wickham had not looked for a meeting of Friends.

"It's such a lovely day, let's ride into the country," the cabby had suggested when he came to the Pirrip house to collect Dinah.

"What will we do there?" Dinah asked. "Perhaps we could find a place to picnic."

"That would be grand."

The young woman tried to run as she hobbled into the kitchen to scrounge for the making of their meal. With no thought of the picnics she had despised in Pennsylvania, she found a basket and filled it with food and beer.

"Slow down, Sweetie," Wickham said. "I don't want that ankle to give way and ruin our day."

"Then thou must help me and find some plates, glasses, and …," searching the icebox she found a large hunk of cheese, "and a knife so I can cut this." She smelled the cheese, wrinkled her nose, and said, "This will go nicely with that beer and some apple pie."

"Apple pie, cheese, and beer, now there's a treat, and that's a fact."

Carrying the well-laden basket in his right hand, Wickham offered the left to Dinah.

Tucking her arm in the cabby's, Dinah yelled up the stairway, "We're going to have a picnic after meeting, Miss Abagail. Please tell Amelia that we won't be here for lunch."

"Of course, my dear," the older woman called back. Allowing herself a chuckle, Abagail mumbled so only she could hear, "After meeting indeed. What need to tell me such fibs?"

"There's a lovely grove of sweet-smelling sycamore in bloom just up the river a bit. Quite the place for a picnic and that's a fact."

"That would be lovely if thou wishes." She laughed gaily and took a deep breath of the spring breeze. "It's so nice to be out of that old house. I know they were all concerned for my ankle, but I could hardly breathe for their hovering."

"Then we shall enjoy nature as God intended." Wickham snapped the reins and Twister broke into a trot.

"Poor Twister," Dinah said. "Perhaps thou shouldst pity his legs and slow thy pace."

"Poor Twister indeed. Why not poor Jim? Hasn't he slowed his pace all this time you've been an invalid? Would you ask me to delay another moment?" Wickham reached over and touched Dinah's breast.

Pressing his hand against her, Dinah replied, "Only for Twister's sake, not for mine. Were it up to me, we should be there already."

By the time they arrived at the spot Wickham intended, the horse was sweaty and favoring his left front leg.

Swinging Dinah down from the wagon, Wickham said, "Lunch can wait, but I can't." Taking her hand in his, he pulled her towards the shelter of a clump of bushes.

"What about thy horse?"

"Twister can wait as well. There is no time for dallying. If I do not have you right now, I shall go quite mad."

"But, what of Harry?" she said.

"What of him when you have me?"

"Well, I don't suppose I shall be going to Nebraska with him."

"Does that mean you will be staying here in New Albany?"

"If thou wantest me to."

"Course I do, and that's a fact." He ducked around the branches of a bush and Dinah followed after.

***

"My, my! Girl, ain't you a sight?" Jerome Danforth's eyes widened, and he rubbed his hands together as Esther walked toward him. "Now, where did you get that dress?"

"Ain't it beautiful?" She whirled around so he could admire the yellow, lacy Cassandra-dress. "Dorothea done boughts it for herselfs but says the school won't 'low her to wears it. So she done give it to me."

"How come I ain't seen it before?" He rubbed his chin, fresh shaved that morning. "My goodness, a dress like that you could get up on stage and sing like Lillie Langtry. My goodness in—"

"Been savin' it for a special time when youse and me could ..." Esther sashayed about and blew a kiss.

"Come on and get up here and let's get to goin'." He held out his hand to help her mount the two-wheeled carriage. Using his arms to compensate for his missing leg, Danforth climbed up next to her, the groom clicked his tongue and gently slapped the reins against the rumps of the two horses. "Move on."

Dust blew this way and that, swirling about the curricle as they came to a stop at the county fairgrounds. Princess stomped impatiently. "Easy, girl," Jerome Danforth said as he wrapped the reins around the brake, dropped from the seat, and moved to the horses' heads. "Easy, 'tis just the wind. It'll not hurt you. Just listen to your sister." He held his hand beneath the younger horse's muzzle and let her lick the salt from his callused hand.

A speck of dust landed in Esther's eye. She blinked and rubbed. "Help me down. I'se needs to find a place to squat."

Jerome surveyed the scene as he helped his lover to the ground. "Looks like folks are arriving early."

"You gots nuff money for thems horses that wins and folks come runnin'."

"Ain't that the truth? Gonna be a good meet."

"That what you'se call it? I'se call it wastin' money you ain't got bettin' on them horses."

"Well, it ain't our money, Esther my love. Even if I come out to watch, you know I don't bet no more'n a couple of bits. Someday, we'll need money so as we can buy our own place. No need giving to no bookmaker."

"You says that now, but I knows you'll find a horse just gotta win, Jerome Danforth. Ain't that why's we's here?"

"You know better than that. Now go find yourself a place you can relieve yourself and I'll see to the horses. Then we can go socialize."

The fairground—populated as it was with grooms, roustabouts, and dollymops—was one place the couple could move about without criticism. Even the occasional preacher come to save the marginal population who lolled about the grounds taking care of animals, setting up events, and selling their wares as best they might in the woods and under the wooden stands would not single them out for the difference in the skins. Blacks, whites, even a Chinese or two could be found this Sunday.

"Heathens," Amelia would have called them. Her daughter, Dorothea might have used a stronger term, but to Jerome and Esther this flotsam of New Albany were the folks with whom they could share a drink, some gossip, and a joke.

To grease the wheels of intercourse, Jerome brought bottles of corn liquor—the kind of cheap drink that Abagail Pirrip would never allow in her home—to share with what passed for his friends while Esther sipped sherry with the women.

All the while of such a Sunday's pleasantries, men from town and neighboring farms dropped in to check on the livestock that was to be sold or raced and to spend time in ways their women at home would not abide. For them, liquor was served from a Conestoga wagon with nowhere else to roll.

Hanks, the burly, bearded keeper of the bar, remonstrated with the groom about the bottles Jerome had tucked under his army tunic.

"I'll not be wasting money on your bottles, sir," Danforth replied. "Why it's no better'n water and you know that as good as I. Steal from thems that has the means. For me and my friends, you'll not get a penny from me."

"If you weren't a veteran and a cripple, Danforth, I'd knock your block off." Hanks knotted and unknotted his hands in the frustration of sales to be lost.

"And what are they doing over there?" Jerome Danforth pointed to a group of roustabouts who were tugging ropes into place.

"You ain't heard, Danforth? We're to have a demonstration of the manly art of pugilism."

"A fight, is it?"

"Not just any fight, but a prizefight with bare knuckles and broken teeth." Hanks grinned.

"You looking forward to blood?"

"The hell with the blood. I'm looking to the thirsty folks gonna come out here this afternoon. Nothin' makes for a better thirst than watching two grown men go at one another like rutting bear." The keeper of the portable canteen laid his hands flat on the roughhewn plank set on sawhorses that would serve as his bar. "Course, you want to make some cash selling your booze, I cain't stop you. But, tell you what. You put them bottles away and help me tend my customers and I'll make it worth your while."

Jerome Danforth slowly shook his head. "I weren't plannin' on selling nothing. Just brought some drink to share with friends. Tell you what, I'll ask my lady friend. If she's a mind to stay round, well I'll drink my hooch and sell yours."

"I know yous fer the beast you is, Duke Frazier. Take your fuckin' hand off-en me." Esther's voice cut through the stir of voice and sound.

"I'll do you as I damn want, you fucking whore, and you'll be glad for it. No Black gal never didn't complain after Duke Frazier been inside her. Better'n any nigger and bigger." Frazier had grabbed Esther's shoulders and held her facing him while she struggled to free herself.

"You son-of-a-bitch," Danforth screamed. "I'll kill you where you stand." He propelled himself in the direction of the struggling couple.

"Now, ain't this sweet. A nigger whore and a one-legged nobody. And how are you gonna kill me, soldier boy? Gonna beat me with one of them crutches?" Frazier let loose a nasty cackle.

"What de matter here?" An enormous stranger stepped out of the knot of men who were gathering around the ring.

"And who the fuck are you?" Frazier demanded.

"I am King Louis of France," the man replied. "I fight in ring. Knock down everyone. Take prize money in every place. And, you, who are you and why you have girl 'gainst her will?"

"That ain't none of your business Frenchie Freak. She's a whore and I'm planning to have my pleasure. You got a problem with that?"

The giant replied, "I got problem man treat woman bad. Lady, you whore?"

"No, she ain't," Danforth shouted from behind the Frenchman. "She's my wife and this man's a piece of god-damned shit."

"Your wife?" The Frenchman turned slightly to see Danforth crutching toward them. "You fight for wife?"

"Damn straight I will."

"You cripple."

"I may be, but I'll kill that son-of-bitch."

The big Frenchman turned his attention back to Frazier. "You let woman go."

"Hell, I will."

"You let go or Louis of France take off head like guillotine." Grabbing Esther, who was still struggling, around the waist, Louis pulled her out of Frazier's hands.

"You arse-hole, what do you think you're doing?" Frazier reached for the Colt revolver that was tucked in his belt.

Louis was fast, much faster than would have been expected from his size. Pushing Esther to one side, he reached for the revolver, plucked it from Frazier's hand, and threw it to the ground. "You want fight; we fight fair. No gun. Hand to hand. Knuckle to stupid head."

Esther—suddenly freed from the resistance of Frazier's restraint and propelled by the Frenchman's push—stumbled. "Jerome," she called out as she fell.

Esther's call distracted Louis for a moment, an instant long enough for Frazier to seize his knife from its sheath and plunge it into the stomach of the bigger man.

As Danforth helped Esther from the ground, King Louis sank towards it. Clutching his stomach from which blood flowed, he said—his accent now Kentucky rather than French, "Ain't you a no-good cheatin' bastard."

The big man slumped forward. Somebody screamed, "Murder." Another voice yelled, "He killed the big guy."

As people ran in toward them, Frazier bolted in the direction of the river. "I didn't do nothin'. I had to defend myself."

Pushing his way past the two young men who were standing on the bank, he untied one of the rowboats they were offering for rent.

"Hey, mister, that's our boat."

"Screw yourself," Frazier shouted. He grabbed the oars and rowed toward the opposite bank.

Having regained her feet, Esther went to the dying giant and dropped to her knees beside him. She held him as he gasped the last of life.

"Esther, sweetheart," Danforth said as he helped Esther to her feet; "I fear he's gone."

"That Frazier ain't nothin' but a murderer and a coward," the woman yelled. "He deserve ta rot in hell."

"Your dress," Danforth said.

"What 'bout it?"

"It's covered with blood."

"Ain't ev'ythin'?"

Chapter 45 ~ Things Spoken and Not

"No!" Esther's scream broke the night like a sharp clap of thunder. She sat up, shuddered, and dropped back to the pillow moaning, "Help me, Jesus. Lordy, help me, Jesus."

"My darling, what on earth's the matter?" The iron bedstead groaned as Jerome Danforth rolled over and protectively encircled Esther with his left arm.

"I didn't means ta wake ya."

"Were you having a bad dream?"

"Just seein' his face and that claw of a hand reachin' fer me. Nothin' I ain't dreamed afore."

"Well, Frazier's gone, and I don't think he'll be coming back to New Albany, not with the hangman chasing him."

"Hope he catches him," Esther answered. "Now yous go back to sleep. We's got a might load of work needs doin' tomorrow."

When Danforth woke to the rooster's crow, Esther was still staring wide-eyed at the raftered ceiling of their bedroom. Below them, in the barn, the two horses were stirring, calling to one another. "Reckon they need feeding," the groom said. "You all right?"

"Right as I's gonna be."

"More bad dreams?" He reached over to run his fingers gently down Esther's brown cheek. "Frazier, he's gone."

"Not no Frazier and not no dreamin', just thinkin' on all them sorrows." She patted his reassuring arm with her right hand. Her hand made a blotch of darkness against his bare white skin.

"What sorrow is that? We got a lot more happiness than pain these days." Danforth gently kissed Esther's neck. "Course it were a shame King Louis being kilt and all, but mostly these are good times."

"It were my fault that man he's dead."

"It weren't nobody's fault except Duke Frazier's. If he hadn't run off, there'd be a hangin' sure as God's love."

"If I'se hadn't been there. Maybe, ifen I'se wore a different dress so's he didn't look so hard."

"Maybe, maybe, maybe? Hell and tarnation, woman, that man was bad. I reckon from the day his momma dropped him into this world he was plain evil, and he'll be the same the day the Good Lord takes him out of it."

Esther sobbed deeply. "Sayin' he a bad man don't bring the good un back. And it don't make nothin' else right neither."

"Nothing else? What else needs putting right?"

"Where my daddy at? Tell me that, Jerome Danforth." Esther dug her fingers into his arm. "He done writ he was comin', but he ain't here."

Danforth rolled over and lay on his back. Once more reaching out with his hand to find hers, he replied. "I imagine he'll be here any day. He did say he'd have to make sure that Tideswell fella got the help he needs first. I'm sure Mr. Mose is as eager to set his eyes on you as you are to see him."

"And if he ain't my daddy?"

"That'll be right sad, but no sadder than things were. Not like you knew where your pappy was then, now maybe you do. Seems to me that's better than not having no idea."

"You's got words for ev'ythin', but you'se don't know nothin'."

"You women folk always think you know more'n men, but we know plenty." Danforth snorted, wiped his nose, and added, "What is it I don't know nothing about anyhow?"

"Them young folk."

"You mean Lonely Cricket and Dinah?"

"Part them and them others."

"I know you'll be sad to see them leave, but it's sure time fer them to—"

"Where's you gettin' them? They ain't a them no more."

"What in tarnation? What are you going on about?"

"Men. What you'se don' know 'bout life and 'bout love is 'nough to fill this room."

"I may not know much about life, but I know all I need to about love. I know I loves you and you loves me. Nothin' ever gonna change that. Not while I got breath left in me."

"Yes, Jerome Baby, I knows you's is lovin' me."

"Ain't that enough?" He pulled her towards himself. "Ain't it?"

As she snuggled her face against Jerome's collarbone, Esther said, "I sure wish that Frenchman didn't get hisself dead."

He kissed the top of her head.

***

"Frazier bad man," Lonely Cricket responded when he heard the story of King Louis's death at breakfast.

"That all you got to say?" Danforth demanded.

"What more say?" The young Indian asked as he waited for Amelia to finish slicing the pork to go with the biscuits which she had laden with honey. "Someday meet Frazier again. Someday make pay for ear, make pay for Esther, make pay for King man." Amelia handed the platter to Lonely Cricket. "Nathan Wainright, Duke Frazier—they bad. Life not always good." He sat down and set his plate on the long plank table. "Not good such men live."

"Well, I sure would like to get my hands on him."

"And you's would do what?" Esther demanded.

"I'd ... I'd ... oh, tarnation, woman, I don't know what I'd do."

"I'd make him a pie. That's what I'd do," Amelia said as she busied herself with the morning's biscuits.

"You'd what?" Danforth slammed his fist on the table.

"You heard me, Jerome Danforth. I said I'd bake that man a pie. Course, I didn't say what I'd be puttin' in it. Guess what he didn't eat I could feed to them other rats I hear scurryin' round in the basement."

Esther laughed. "Almost good as whackin' his head with my hatchet."

"Esther take Frazier scalp? Least they not say Indian do." Lonely Cricket chewed thoughtfully on a piece of pork. "Some men help world when die."

"They surely do," Amelia responded. "I say amen and they surely do."

"Say, Cricket, you ever lose anybody? How does you Injuns bury folks?"

Lonely Cricket took a deep sip of coffee before answering the groom. "Friend Standing Oak die at school. Bury like White Man. Put in box. Sing songs. Preacher words. Say Standing Oak go live forever with Jesus."

"No different than us," Amelia observed. "Guess he deserved heaven much as anyone."

"Same as White Man," Lonely Cricket replied. He wondered if Amelia and Esther would see anything strange in his words. He knew they would find his thoughts difficult to understand. Those he would not share, not even with Sapphira when they would talk about King Louis and the fact that Duke Frazier was there in New Albany.

Eating slowly, the young man allowed his mind to drift back to the Indian School in Carlisle, back to the root cellar hideaway in which he and the other young warriors would meet late at night.

"Why would Standing Oak want to be in box, live forever with Jesus, not with family, not with clan, not with village?" Plenty Horses asked when the young warriors had met that night after the younger boy's White Man funeral. The tall Dakota teen had led the solemn procession away from the school to the deserted farm. The shadows cast by the kerosene lantern he carried had filled the woods with ghosts and spirits.

"White Man not understand," Samuel replied. "They think we not people. They think our creator is not god, that our soul's worth nothing without their Jesus."

Lonely Cricket had said nothing. As one of the younger boys in the group, he seldom gave tongue to his thoughts. When the boys chanted and danced to say that Standing Oak would be joining the world of spirits, he joined with them. When they buried the dead boy's belongings and placed a small bow and arrow with his blanket so that he could hunt in the world to come, Lonely Cricket wished his friend good hunting.

When it was time to place Standing Oak's drinking cup with the other objects in the hole they had dug, another of the many among the stray plant remnants of the garden behind the ruins of the farmhouse, Plenty Horses handed the mug to Lonely Cricket. "You were best friend. Make opening in bottom of cup so Standing Oak Spirit not be trapped."

Lonely Cricket did as he was told and added the cup to the pile. As they took turns covering the dead boy's possessions, the young men sang. It was a song to summon Father Sky and Mother Earth to witness that the spirit of Standing Oak was pure. When the hole was filled with dirt, the young warriors cut locks of hair from their heads to show that they mourned the younger boy.

Walking back to the dormitories, the young men did not speak, just as Lonely Cricket didn't speak of that night to Danforth, Esther, and Amelia.

Rising from the table, the young man carried his plate and cup to the sink, poured some scalding water from the kettle that sat to one side on the cast-iron stove, added cold, and set to the washing up. "No need you doin' that, Boy," Amelia said.

"Need do something," Lonely Cricket replied.

***

Twister's iron-shod hooves clopped unevenly and the steel wheels of Jim Wickham's wagon ground on the gravel as they turned onto Crandle Street. Elisabetta Brownstone sat next to the cabby on the front seat. Sapphira Cook sat behind her cousin and her bags were loaded in the back.

"I can take Lonely Cricket and Miss Dinah to the station easy enough," Jerome Dansforth had offered two days earlier when the plans had been made. "You just bring Miss Sapphira and meet us there."

"Can't see Miss Abagail, Amelia, Esther, all getting in your little carriage long with them bags and that's a fact," Wickham had pointed out.

Before Danforth had been able to think of a response, Dinah had added. "It'll be easier all round to do the goodbye saying here. Besides, I imagine Miss Brownstone will want to visit with Miss Abagail and the railroad station's no place for that. We'll say our goodbyes here and thou canst take Miss Brownstone back to her shop if thou wouldst."

Jerome could offer no answer to the arguments. "Guess, you're right," he replied casting his eyes to the ground like a boy caught red-handed in mischief. "Just thought it would be nice you and Lonely Cricket knowing we all wanted to—"

"Harry and I know thou carest about us." Dinah moved closer to the groom and gave him a peck on his whiskered cheek. "Thou art a good man, Jerome. Esther is lucky to have thee."

Danforth blushed and ducked his head. "Tarnation!"

"I wish I could say Lonely Cricket were as lucky with havin' you," the groom thought, but held his tongue.

Wickham's wagon crunched to a stop in front of the Pirrip house. The cabby jumped down, tied his already weary horse to the post, and offered his hand to Miss Brownstone, who climbed down from the wagon and walked towards the porch.

Next, Wickham offered a hand to Sapphira, but she ignored his assistance and hopped down on her own.

"Where's Lonely Cricket at?" Wickham asked. "We'd best get movin', there bein' a train to catch and that's a fact."

"The bags are ready in there," Danforth replied. "I'll help best I can."

"I can grab a bag's well as you," Esther echoed.

"Good, thou art here, Mr. Wickham," Dinah said as she strode across the porch to greet the young cabby.

"Good morning, Miss Tideswell," the cabby said touching the brim of his tall hat and winking in Dinah's direction. "It's a lovely day for travelling and that's a fact.

"What's they playin' at now?" Esther looked questioningly to Jerome, who squinted in response.

"Don't know if that nag of yours'll get these folks to the train in time," Jerome Danforth commented.

"And, don't you go knockin' my Twister, Old Man. He's brushed and fed right proud this morning. Knows it's an important day and that's a fact." Jim Wickham touched his cabby's top hat in mock respect for the older groom.

"Lonely Cricket's upstairs saying goodbye to Miss Abagail," Amelia said. "Oh, the lunch. I'd almost forgotten," she added as she rushed inside. The cook would never admit—except perhaps to her daughter Dorothea—that she had risen an hour early to prepare a trove of breads, meats, and fruits for the three travelers. She'd never tell even Dorothea that she had cried the entire time. "It ain't Miss Dinah I'll be missing," she had said to the empty kitchen; "or Miss Sapphira, but that boy, now ain't he somethin' special?"

Minutes later, having once again promised to ask about Theodore Junior and to write with all the information he could learn, Lonely Cricket came slowly down the stairs. "Of course, want to go home," he had told Sapphira the day before; "but see Happy Turtle not easy."

"Nor will it be for me."

"New Albany good place."

"Yes. Cousin Elisabetta has been very kind to me. Certainly, nobody can say anything but the very best about Miss Pirrip. I will miss them."

"Miss Abagail family good, too."

Sapphira laughed. "They aren't exactly her family, but yes, they are good, too."

"Family who make love."

"I suppose so," Sapphira replied. "Maybe that's why I feel that you are family," she added to herself.

***

Lonely Cricket grabbed one of the bags from the back of Wickham's wagon and set it on the ground.

"You got the tickets?" Jim asked.

"Sapphira go but. I help bags."

"Maybe thou should go with her," Dinah suggested. "This is not a place a young woman should be on her own."

"You think Sapphira need help?"

"Not help but—"

"Protection." Wickham interrupted. "Pretty young woman in a place like this needs lookin' after and that's a fact."

"We'll take care of the bags," the cabby called after Lonely Cricket.

When Sapphira and Lonely Cricket returned with three tickets in the young woman's clutch, some of the bags were still in the back of the wagon. "Need get bags," Lonely Cricket said, mounted the running board of the wagon, and reached up. "Not those," Jim Wickham said. "Them's Dinah's and she ain't goin' and that's a fact."

"Dinah not go?"

Sapphira looked away lest one of the others see her smile at Lonely Cricket's surprise.

"Nope. She's stayin' here."

"You go back Miss Abagail?"

Dinah shook her head.

"Not back to Miss Amelia's. She's goin' ta live with me. Share my place and that's a fact."

"This what you want?" the young Indian asked.

Sapphira grabbed Lonely Cricket's arm and pulled him close so she could whisper in his good ear. "I think they've been planning this all along. This way nobody's here to tell them what they don't want to hear."

"This what you want, Dinah?" Lonely Cricket asked again but in a softer voice.

"I don't mean to hurt thee, Harry; but I do not love thee, not anymore."

"And you love Jim," Sapphira said, her voice a simple declaration. Dinah busied her hands primping her hair. "I never did live in a city before. Never had a life of my own. I don't mean to hurt thee, not either of thee, but I have no wish to live on another farm."

"Wait a minute." Wickham reached out towards Dinah. "What about me? Ain't you stayin' to be with me?"

"Of course, I am," Dinah crooned. "I couldn't hardly stay if thou werenst here."

The young cabby preened at her answer and doffed his top hat to nobody in particular.

Lonely Cricket bent down and picked up Sapphira's bag, his own, a third bag holding the few gifts he had finally purchased for his family—a jumping clown on a stick for Many Fish, a knife for Lame Bear, and cloth and notions for Yquili Sparrow and Happy Turtle.

"You don't have to pay for that cloth and them notions," Elisabetta Brownstone had said when he and Sapphira had picked them out.

"I give. I pay."

"Well, how would it be if you pay what it cost me. I have no wish to make a profit on family."

"That good. I pay what cost."

Even then the shopkeeper had undercharged, winking to Sapphira as she totaled the young man's bill. Sapphira Cook picked up the one remaining parcel, the box of food that Amelia had prepared.

"You look out fer him," the cook had instructed Sapphira when she had given her that box at the Pirrip house. "That boy needs takin' care of."

As Sapphira replied, "I guess he'll take care of me, too," the cook was turning away to wipe her eyes.

Lonely Cricket started to walk away from the wagon and towards the train platform.

"Ain't you gonna shake goodbye," the cabby called after him.

"Hold on a minute, Cricket," Sapphira said. Digging into her purse, she pulled out one of the train tickets. "This one's for you," she said as she handed the ticket to Dinah. "I guess you can keep it in case you change your mind or … I suppose they'd give you the money."

Dinah took the ticket without a word and slipped into her own purse.

"Guess we got paid for takin' them to the station," Jim said with a chuckle. "Always knew I'd get some of Harry's money."

"Sapphira Cook, we need go," Lonely Cricket said.

"I suppose we do."

"Are thou not going to say farewell?" Dinah asked.

"Mind horse's legs. Twister leg not good."

"Guess that's as good a goodbye as we're gettin' and that's a fact," Jim Wickham muttered to Dinah as he helped her back onto his wagon.

***

The train lurched forward. Lonely Cricket, leaning over Sapphira, looked out the soot-gray window.

"Did Dinah and Jim stay to wave us off?" Sapphira asked as she adjusted her blue dress and surveyed the car, which was half-filled with passengers.

"Not stay." Lonely Cricket pulled at the earlobe of his partially deaf ear. "Not understand."

"What's that, Lonely Cricket?"

"Why Dinah stay New Albany."

The young woman chuckled. "You really don't understand, do you?"

"What funny?"

"You. Men I suppose." Sapphira gently touched his hand which propped him against the sill. "Do you mind? That Dinah didn't come with us; do you really mind?"

"Want happy. If Dinah stay in New Albany happy, that good."

"Do you think she'll be happy?"

"Think Jim Wickham not take care Twister legs; not take care Dinah."

Sapphira couldn't help chuckling as she added, "And that's a fact."

"Hey, Mister." The boy was bouncing up and down the railroad car's aisle grabbing bench backs to keep from toppling with each lurch of the train as it gathered speed.

"Skadedjur, don't disturb gentleman, lady," A woman called to him in an accent that Lonely Cricket didn't recognize. Blonde haired and holding a younger child in her arms, she was seated four rows and across the aisle from them

The young Indian turned in the woman's direction. "Boy not disturb."

"So your name is Skadedjur?" Sapphira asked.

"No, my name is Skirmer. My mother call me skadedjur because yoke. That my sister. Her name is Hilda." The boy pointed to the baby in their mother's arms.

"Yoke?" Lonely Cricket's voice conveyed his confusion. "Boy not big enough pull plow," he whispered to Sapphira.

"I think he means joke," Sapphira explained.

"What joke?"

"I suppose we'd have to speak their language." She turned to the boy, "Where are you from?"

"New York City. We go to Pappa in Nebraska."

"We go Nebraska," Lonely Cricket echoed.

"Pappa buy farm. We join him and have new home." The boy looked down wistfully. "But I miss our old home."

"In New York City?" Sapphira asked.

"No, before. In old country."

"Skirmer, come here; sit down," the boy's mother called to him.

"Where old country?" Lonely Cricket asked as he straightened himself back into his side of the bench seat.

"Far away," Skirmer said. "We come Sveeden. You know where is?"

"Yes, in Europe," Sapphira assured him. "I've never been there, but I'm sure it's very beautiful."

"Is Nebraska beautiful?" the youngster asked. "Have you been there?"

"We grew up there in a little town called Pierce," Sapphira explained. "We've been away a long time, but now Lonely Cricket and I are going home."

"Why mother call you joke?" Lonely Cricket asked.

"Momma," the boy cried out; "they're going to Pierce. Isn't that where we're going, too?"

"That place Papa buy farm. Say it good place. Cabin is built and farm plowed. Buy from man named Nathan Wainright. Man said his family go away so he has no reason stay. You know him?"

Sapphira blanched. "It can't be."

"How he sell Cook home?"

"I don't know, Lonely Cricket. I can't imagine. My father gave that place to Lame Bear. I ..."

"Skirmer," the boy's mother insisted, "you come sit. Eat smörgås."

"But—"

"Komma! Not argue. I tell Papa you argue" She fished in the large box that sat on the floor in front of her seat. "You eat, too?" she asked and held up a loaf of bread.

"No, thank you," Sapphira replied. "We have … I don't know what could have …" she mumbled. "Why don't we share," she said more loudly. Amelia made us some nice cakes. I'm sure the children would enjoy them."

"Get the cakes down," she told Lonely Cricket. "We might as well be sociable. Whatever Nathan has done, it won't help us getting angry and aggravated with these nice folks. It's not like they know anything about him or Happy Turtle."

"White Man not want know," the young Indian replied.

"Can I have a piece of cake, Momma?"

"First, eat bread and meat, then you have cake," the woman answered.

Part Four ~ Haunting of the Spirit World

Chapter 46 ~ Homecoming

"Hey you. Yeah you, young buck," Abner Banner yelled. The bald, heavyset man lurched drunkenly out of Miss Birdie's Rooming House and Sumptuous Parlor—of which he was part owner and frequent customer—and up the muddy street, which led out of Fayette in the direction of Pierce. The suction against each step threatened to send him toppling. The man's whiskey-loud voice jolted Lonely Cricket to a stop.

Lonely Cricket took a deep breath, looked up to the cloudy sky and muttered a reminder to himself, "Today not good day to fight White Man."

In Pennsylvania at the Carlisle School, Samuel, the Chiricahua who so despised the white Major Pratt, had taught the young Ho-Chunk to say those words. "Someday, great spirit give all Indian time to fight. Today not good day fight White Man." Swallowing his pride, Samuel had acted as the major's driver and orderly.

"When will be good day?" Plenty Horses had asked Samuel many times.

"Spirits show way. Send messenger. Wait for call to great war dance," had been Samuel's answer.

"Major Pratt think Samuel friend," Singing Wolf had said one evening when the young warriors had gathered in the abandoned root cellar they had commandeered as a meeting place.

"Yes, White Man think Indian friend then Indian surprise him," Samuel had concurred. "Geronimo say White Man never see ambush."

"Afternoon, sir," Lonely Cricket said as he turned towards the voice. The young man stood at attention the way they had been taught in the White Man's school.

"What do you think you're doing sashaying down the street with a pretty white woman, boy," Banner demanded.

"Go Pierce with Miss Sapphira," Lonely Cricket replied. "We just from train."

"Travelling together, are you? Now, don't that beat all."

"We both grew up in Pierce," Sapphira started to explain her voice quavering. Abner Banner had accosted Happy Turtle years earlier, and Sapphira had watched John McCabe rescue her friend.

Sensing her companion's tension, she pulled on Lonely Cricket's arm and whispered, "Don't get into an argument with him. The folks here will lynch you quick as they'd squash a bug."

"Not worry, today not good day to fight White Man," the young man whispered in reply.

"Go Indian school in Pennsylvania," Lonely Cricket said to Banner. "Stop in Indiana on way home. Miss Sapphira work store. Remember me from childhood. Ask Harry help to carry bags return home."

"That your name, boy—Harry?"

"That name Major Pratt give," Lonely Cricket replied. "You know Major? He famous Indian fighter."

"Hert of 'em. Whopped them Apach didn't he?"

"Yes, Sir." Lonely Cricket pulled himself into an exaggerated attention and clenched his hands to hold back his building anger.

"So, you one of them good Injuns?" Banner was now playing to the small crowd that had gathered around them.

A few of the men laughed in anticipation. "The only good Injun's a dead Injun," one of the men muttered to his companion.

"Yep," replied the other man.

"Is he gonna kill the boy?" a woman asked no one in particular.

The big man spit tobacco juice in Lonely Cricket's direction, reached inside his tobacco-stained white duster, pulled a revolver from his waistband and cocked it. "Well, let's see you do one of them Injun dances." He fired a shot near the youngster's feet. Dirt sprayed up.

Dropping the bags he was carrying, Lonely Cricket jumped up and down, flailed his arm, and whooped the way he'd seen foolish White boys do when they were trying to act like Indians.

The man fired again. "Faster!"

Lonely Cricket jumped and whooped more. He tried to not look in Sapphira's direction but couldn't help noticing the tears forming in the corners of her eyes.

Just as the bully was about to fire yet another shot, a deputy marshal hurried up. "Sorry to break up the fun, Mr. Banner, but Miss Birdie sent me along to find you. Seems there's one of them gals been holdin' back and she wants to know what to do. Said I should fetch you a'fore she does nothing she ought."

"Damn," the big man muttered and jammed another plug of chaw into his cheek. "Man can't have no fun without business getting in the way."

"No, sir," the deputy replied.

As Banner stomped back the way he had come, his boots spraying mud and manure in every direction, the lawman turned to the crowd. "You folks move along, now."

As people dispersed, some muttering about the damned marshal interfering with their fun, the deputy turned to Lonely Cricket and Sapphira, "You young folks get out of town while you can. When Banner finds out there weren't no message fer him at all, well I reckon he'll be back here looking for you."

"Thank you save us," Lonely Cricket said.

"I didn't do it to save you. Let that crowd get lathered and we'd have a real mess to straighten out, boy." Turning to Sapphira, he added, "I don't know if you're from these parts or not, but one thing you have to know right off, no white girl walks around with an Injun, not even if he's carryin' her bags. Folks around these parts just don't like it."

"But—"

"Ferget them buts. Worst thing, before they was done what they would of done to you. Hell, the boy here would be dead, but you'd be wishin' you was. Do what you folks like, just not 'round Fayette."

Lonely Cricket picked up the bags he had dropped. "All right we go Pierce?"

"That mays be but go 'round that way." The lawman gestured. "That motherfucker sees you folks going by Miss Birdie's, just as likely to shoot you as spit."

ΩΩΩΩΩ

When the people reached the outer layer of the world and found their place upon the great tortoise, the dwellers of the spirit realm worried at what Ma-Ona had done. "Does he mean for these humans to find their way into our world? Does the Great Spirit mean for man to dwell among us?

They went to the Great Father and spoke of their concerns. The Raven and the Owl spoke. The Coyote, who is the Trickster spoke. Even the Eagle, who flies in solitude above the clouds, spoke. The Moon and The Sun, too, shared their concern about these humans whose bows and fires, whose knives and canoes gave them so much power among the creatures of the earth.

"If we do not control these men, they will make war on us," said White Buffalo Woman. The other spirits all agreed.

"Go among the humans," Ma-Ona told Coyote, "and learn if they would make war on the Realm of the Spirits."

Coyote went among the humans and listened to their songs. Coyote learned the dances of the people and heard their stories.

When he returned to the Spirit Realm, Coyote said, "The humans do not plan to make war on our world, but neither do they know their place. They are adventuresome and brave. They are curious and willing to take risks in their explorations. They are envious and mean-spirited as well. It is likely that they will find their way to our world just as they have climbed through the levels of theirs until they have reached the shell of the great tortoise. And, when they do, it is likely that they will make war against us."

Ma-Ona called a great council fire among the spirits to discuss what should be done about the humans. Some wanted the people destroyed. "Send fire to consume them," said some of the spirits. "Send floods to drown them," said others. "Send ice to freeze them," was yet another suggestion.

Finally, it was time for Coyote to make his suggestion. "Let us teach them different languages and different songs each from the other," the Trickster counseled. "Then they will make war on one another and forget to strive to enter the realm of the spirits."

"This is wise advice," Ma-Ona said, and the other spirits agreed. "Go back among these humans and teach them to be different, one group from the next. Then they will make war one tribe against the other."

"What if they someday make peace among their tribes?" asked Owl, who always thought of the things that might happen.

"What will we be able to do then? Will we be able to keep things from going wrong?" asked Raven, who always worried about things going wrong.

Coyote spoke again. "Ma-Ona can create new humans to fight those that have made peace. He can give them a new language and ways of dancing. He can give them new weapons. He can give them new hatred."

White Buffalo Woman said, "It will be sad if the new humans hurt the people who know us."

"Yes, it will be sad," agreed Ma-Ona, "but the direction of sadness is often the best path."

ΩΩΩΩΩ

When Singing Wolf finished telling the story, the young warriors pulled their blankets tight, lit their kerosene lanterns, and walked back to the school. Lonely Cricket was among the last to leave the abandoned cellar. "Why White Man come to our land?" he asked Singing Wolf.

"Story true. Now people decide what happen."

"What do?"

"Not know. Maybe kill White Man. Maybe White Man kill Indian. Maybe all friends."

"Not all White Man bad," the young Ho-Chunk said.

"No. Not all bad. Not all Indian good."

The two young men had walked together. Overhead the quarter moon hung in the crisp air. It was the Moon of the Sleeping Fish.

***

Sapphira Cook slipped to the floor of the cabin.

Rushing to the young woman's side, Ebba Anderson knelt and rubbed Sapphira's face and hands, and barked at her husband and son. "Lars, get her some vater. Skirmer, quickly a kudde for her head. A filt, too, to keep her varm."

Sapphira slowly woke and focused her eyes. "What happened?"

"You faint, too much valking," Lars answered as he held a glass to her mouth.

"Not from valking. From in here." Ebba stopped rubbing Sapphira's brow long enough to hold her own right hand over her heart. "Hard coming home. Especial when home no more hers."

Lonely Cricket opened the cabin door. Behind him came the crepuscular sounds of Nebraska. "Horse fed in barn. Now he is calm. Not want work but want plenty hay."

Then he saw Sapphira slumped against the cabin wall. "What happen? Sapphira, she all right?"

"She faint from heart," Skirmer said as he tried to hand his mother the heavy, bright red blanket which was decorated with yellow horses and blue floral designs. It was one of Ebba's treasures from the old country, one of her dearest possessions that she had brought in the three heavy trunks the porter had helped stow in the pile of passengers' baggage that had taken up a good portion of the railroad car.

At Fayette, when they were exiting the train, the porter—realizing that this foreign woman with her long blue skirt, red-vested bodice, and elaborate belted sash would know nothing of tipping—had toppled the first of those trunks out of the door and onto the platform.

"Min porslin. Min porslin," the Swedish woman clutched her baby to her breast and cried out.

Quickly, Lonely Cricket had run to the back door of the car and offered his help.

"Tack! Tack," Ebba had clucked as the two remaining trunks were gently deposited next to the first.

"How far is it to Pierce?" Ebba asked the two young people once their bags were all accounted for.

"Too far for you to be carrying those chests. In fact, I doubt you could drag them down the street," Sapphira said.

"Four, five hours if walk fast," Lonely Cricket answered.

"How do ve get there? You have vagon?"

"No, ma'am. We're on foot same as you. Course, Lonely Cricket and me, we don't have so much to carry."

"Someplace ve can rent vagon?"

"I don't know about that. Probably."

"So, you and boy maybe rent vagon med us?"

"I don't think so, ma'am. First off, whilst you're nice enough and all, well, it doesn't feel right. Not with your husband buying my family's cabin from Nathan Wainright. Besides, nobody here will rent any wagon or anything else to Lonely Cricket."

"Vhy not?"

"He's an Indian. White folks here don't—"

"Me Ho-Chunk. White Man no like Indian. No trust we not steal horse. They say we all go to hell. They steal land. Now, they steal Harry Cook land give to your man."

"My father didn't steal nothing," Skirmer shouted. "Ain't that right, Momma? He pay proper, don't he?"

Holding Hilda with her right arm, Ebba Anderson wrapped her free arm around her son. "Your papa, he never cheat no one," she reassured the boy. The woman turned to Sapphira. "I'm sorry your papa's cabin sold, but my Lars vould not steal." She patted her son on the head. "Lars not cheat and he not hate Indian. He good man, vork hard, good farmer."

"That may well be, but I reckon we'll be walking to Pierce. Good luck to you finding a wagon." Sapphira bobbed her head and picked up two bags. "We'd best be going, Lonely Cricket."

As the two trudged away, a heavyset man with a long mustache and eyes that glinted steel approached Ebba, "Did I hear you is in need of renting a wagon?" I got me one and a good horse to pull it. Even help you get them bags loaded and help you on your way." He paused to look at the woman. She stared back, her eyes unblinking under the wide white of her bonnet. Only when the baby burped did she glance down and then lifted her own blue eyes back to stare directly at the stranger.

The man gestured down the road in the direction in which Lonely Cricket and Sapphira had walked a few minutes earlier. "That's long as you ain't taking no damned Injuns with you. Don't trust them."

"No, Indian not going med us. Not going to hell neither, but not go med us."

Having overcharged the woman by twice, the man was true to his word—driving the swaybacked gray and the splintery, cobbled-together wagon to the edge of town. "You keep right that way and you'll come in Pierce. Ask anyone from there. I don't know no Wainright place, but them folks'll know it sure. Tomorrow or the next day, have your man bring my horse and wagon back. I'm always 'round the station. Just tell 'im ask for Jim Brodie. Folks all know me. He brings back my horse and wagon and I give him back that twenty-five-dollar deposit just like I promised."

Brodie climbed laboriously down from the wagon bench. "Don't you go beating on my horse none, neither," were his last words as he headed back into Fayette.

The horse and wagon creaked in one direction and Brodie in the other. About fifteen minutes had passed—at least as best as Ebba could figure—when the horse took it into his mind to veer off the road and sample the tempting, green vegetation.

When Lonely Cricket and Sapphira Cook—having doubled back to take the alternate road out of town, the one that didn't go by Miss Birdie's Rooming House and Sumptuous Parlor—had arrived on the scene, Skirmer was pulling to no avail on the nag's bridle. His mother sat on the wagon bench, the reins draped worthlessly in one hand while the other hand tried to comfort the squalling baby who lay next to her.

"Please, you help?" the woman asked. "You know how to make horse go?"

"We can't leave them out here," Sapphira whispered.

"No. Not want to carry bags all way to Pierce," Lonely Cricket replied.

"Besides, they don't seem like bad folks."

"No, not bad, but take Cook farm." In a louder voice, Lonely Cricket said, "We help. Wagon carry bags and we help get wagon to Pierce."

***

"Sure, you can borrow lamp. Bring it back tomorrow. But is a long walk to your papa's cabin," Lars Anderson answered Lonely Cricket's request.

"Not far. Just through field. I walk many times."

"Used to be easy. Now, you must go on the road. Your papa, Lame Bear, he put vire med barbs to make a fence. Plant crops next to fence, so not a field no more. Not can valk, not even in day."

"Why did he do that?" They young Ho-Chunk shook his head in disbelief.

"Ven Agent Jones say I buy farm. He say, 'Indian not own land. Only white man can own. That vhy Nathan Vainright have right to sell land and papa cannot keep.'"

"But Lame Bear does own land. He has his own farm."

"Yes. He has vhat Mr. Jones call allotment. Papa can use. You use vhen he die. But he not own. Not sell. That because he is Indian."

"So, if my father had kept it in his name instead of giving it to Lame Bear?" Sapphira asked.

"Then, Lame Bear be farming Mr. Cook's land. That be fine. Or, if your papa had given land to you, that fine, too. You White so you are person even if you are voman. But Indian not person. Mr. Jones even say if Lame Bear had white son adopt in family, boy could own farm. But Indian not can own."

"What?" Sapphira asked.

"That what Agent say. White people can own. Even Black people can own. Not Indian."

Flabbergasted, neither of the two young adults could think of anything more to say.

"You vant lamp?" Ebba asked. "Skirmer you get lamp for Lonely Cricket."

"Yes, Mama." The boy ran to fetch one of the two precious kerosene lanterns that stood on the mantle.

"You velcome to take," Lars said. "But long vay in dark. You velcome sleep in loft. Skirmer sleep med oss. Yah, Skirmer?"

"Yah, Papa." The boy turned back from the mantle.

"I think that is good idea. This boy's first night in new house. He sleep better in room with his papa and momma," Ebba added. "Ve put Hilda's vagga next to bed. She sleep better next to oss, too." Ebba pointed at the ladder that went to the loft. "Is that where you sleep as girl?"

"No. I slept by the fire. Nathan Wainright, my cousin, he slept up there."

"You vant sleep by fire?"

"No thank you, Mr. Anderson. The loft will be fine."

"I make comfortable for Skirmer. Mattress and filte to keep varm; kudde for make head soft."

"Not sure we stay," Lonely Cricket began. "Maybe, we go long way to Lame Bear and Yquili Sparrow house. Want see parents and sister. Want to see younger brother."

"Your sister ain't in house, boy," Lars said. "Guess you ain't heard. She gone off with a White man."

"She go with Nathan Wainright? She marry him?" Lonely Cricket slammed his hand against the log wall of the cabin. The thud woke Hilda who was sleeping in her mother's arms. The baby whimpered twice and then burst into tears.

"Don't vara rädd," Ebba whispered into the baby's ear. When her words didn't stop the child's fear, Ebba held the infant to her breast and gently worked the teat into the little mouth.

"Careful, Cricket. You'll hurt yourself." Sapphira rushed to the young man's side. He was already shaking his hand.

"I not hurt. Just angry. Why Happy Turtle go with that man? He not even good to horse."

Sapphira could not help laughing. "You still remember Maggie?"

"Of course remember. Way man treat horse same as way he treat other man."

"True enough," Lars commented. "Anyway, it not med Vainright she go. She go med man from town. Vork in saloon for Old Man."

"What was man's name?" Lonely Cricket demanded.

"Not sure. John, I think, but not know rest."

"John McCabe I'll wager," Sapphira said. "I remember him. Good looking. Light brown hair. Tall but a little stooped. Always said hello to everybody. When we were in town, he was nice to Happy Turtle. I recall—"

"Where they go, Happy Turtle and this John McKay?" Lonely Cricket demanded.

"I ain't sure vhere they go. Somebody say far away."

"He helped her. The horrible man was … the one this morning … and John McCabe went and fetched her before he …" Sapphira continued, her trembling voice ignored by the rest.

The young man cupped his hands to his eyes. The right hand was already swelling.

"Cricket, I don't think we should go to your folks tonight, not with that hand needing tending." Gently, Sapphira tried to take the young man's hands away from his face.

Unable to summons the strength to resist, Lonely Cricket allowed Sapphira to wrap his hand in the cloth bandages that Ebba provided and then to lead him to the ladder.

It was only when they were in the loft, hunching over to avoid hitting their heads on the sloping ceiling of logs chinked with sod that he spoke. "I not sure we should come home. Not sure what say to Lame Bear, what say to Yquili Sparrow. Maybe we go back Indiana."

"That isn't like you, Cricket. That isn't like you at all. Since when do you run from things?"

"Not run from things. Not know what say."

"That you can figure on tomorrow. Tonight, let's sleep."

Taking off their clothes until they were only in their undergarments, the two young adults lay down on the mattress that Lars Anderson had put on the loft floor for his son. There was barely room for them, but they fit their bodies together in a comfortable spoon.

"Tonight, let's sleep," Sapphira repeated. But they didn't. Instead, for the first time they allowed themselves the full expression of their cravings. In the dimmest of starlight that found its way through the chinks of the cabin walls they held one another close. Their bodies came together, hip to hip and thigh to thigh. The rhythm of their desires danced in the faint shadows. With whispered moans they declared passion and love.

In the room below, Lars Anderson heard the young lovers, smiled at his thoughts, and reached for his wife.

"Nej, pojken kommer att höra." Ebba pushed his hand away.

"If he hears, he hears. Skirmer vill know his papa and momma in love."

"That not bad thing," Ebba replied, her voice unsure.

"Not bad thing," Lars squeezed her hand.

Chapter 47 ~ Breasts

Yquili Sparrow sang as Many Fish sucked deeply at her breast. "Náni Atina, watch over my children. Protect them from the darkness of the spirit world. Protect them from the darkness that is in men's hearts. Protect them as I nurse my son on the milk that you have given me."

"Why do you sing that song, Mother? Why do you sing to Mother Atina?" Happy Turtle asked.

"Listen to it carefully that you will know what to sing to your own child when that time comes," the older woman replied. "Learn the sacred song and I will tell you the story of the rabbit and the hawk."

Yquili Sparrow held the small boy to her shoulder and patted his back. Many Fish's loud burp brought laughter to the lips of his older brother and sister.

"Tell us the story," Lonely Cricket begged.

"Yes, Mother," Happy Turtle echoed.

Their mother looked to her husband. "It is a good story," he said.

The two youngsters settled onto the buffalo hide that covered the cabin floor as their mother began to tell the story.

ΩΩΩΩΩ

One day, Mother Rabbit and her two baby bunnies were in the fields eating the tender shoots and roots of the grass.

Mother Rabbit pointed her paw at one plant and said, "Eat this root because this is the grass that will give you strength."

She pointed to another plant and said, "Eat this shoot because this is the grass that will give you speed."

Then she pointed to a third plant and said, "Eat this plant because this is the grass that will give you good thoughts."

As the three rabbits ate, Mother Hawk flew overhead. Seeing that the rabbits were so interested in the grass that they were not watching out for her, the hawk swooped down and seized the mother rabbit in her talons which were as sharp as knives and as hard as the wood of the hickory tree.

"What are you doing?" Mother Rabbit asked as the hawk flapped her wings in order to carry her prey away.

"I am taking you to my nest so that my chicks can eat," Mother Hawk replied. "I have little ones who are freshly emerged from their eggs and are hungry for their dinner."

"But, but, but," Mother Rabbit stammered, "if you take me off so you and your hatchlings can dine on my insides, what will happen to my children? They will die without me to teach them what to eat."

"What do I care if your babies live or die?" Mother Hawk replied. "I only care about my chicks. If I do not pull your body apart and allow them to peck at your heart and stomach, they will perish."

"But," Mother Rabbit, who was very quick to think, replied, "if my babies die then there will be no more rabbits for your sons to catch when they are hungry. Then they will die, too."

The hawk stopped digging her talons into the rabbit's hide and thought about what she had said. "Well, what do you propose?" the great bird demanded.

"Why, isn't it obvious? You should let me go."

"And what would my sons and I eat in your place?"

"I could happily teach you how to choose the best grass and where to find vegetables to your liking."

"That would be of no use to us. We are eaters of meat, if you please, and carnivores, if you don't please." The bird thought. When she did so, she turned her head from side to side so that her sharp eyes could consider everything about her.

"I have it," Mother Hawk announced. "I will take one of your children instead. That way, I can hunt the other another time and then finally I will let my children capture you."

The hawk laughed and the high pitch of her voice filled the rabbit with fear.

"Now, you must choose," the hawk continued. "Choose what?" Mother Rabbit squeaked in a voice that was filled with terror.

"Why, which of your children I shall eat today and which I shall eat tomorrow."

"That is a choice I cannot make," Mother Rabbit replied. "Could you choose which of your chicks should live and which should die?"

"Yes, it is difficult," the hawk replied, "but you must make the choice, or I will take you now and not worry about tomorrow."

"Please, I need time to consider," the rabbit pleaded. "Can you wait until tomorrow? Surely, your chicks will not die if they do not have this night's supper."

Mother Hawk agreed to the rabbit's request. "You must swear by the great spirit creator that you will come tomorrow and tell me which of your children you will give me."

Mother Rabbit swore, and the hawk knew that the rabbit would keep the oath for none of the creatures of the earth except man would take such an oath and then not keep it. So, the hawk lifted her feet from Mother Rabbit's body. The small beast shuddered in pain when the hawk's sharp talons withdrew from her side, but then she sighed in relief.

That evening, when the moon shed her soft light on the rabbit's sleeping babies, Mother Rabbit prayed to Atina, for Atina blesses the harvests of the earth and makes sure that all creatures have enough food. "Atina, who brings forth the crops of the earth, the three sisters whom the humans eat and the grasses and grains that nourish rabbits, help me. Tomorrow, I must keep my oath to the Great Creator and give one of my children to Mother Hawk, but how can I do such a thing? How can I sacrifice a child of my body, a child who has nursed at my tit? Help me, I pray."

Atina heard Mother Rabbit's prayers and told her what to do.

In the morning, Mother Rabbit and her two children went to woods and found a young squirrel who was looking for acorns. The squirrel darted this way and that in confusion, for squirrels are often too confused and distracted to remember what they are doing and where they have left the nuts which they have gathered.

"Little Squirrel," Mother Rabbit said; "I know where there are many acorns and other nuts. It is not far from here, and my children and I will gladly take you."

The squirrel was excited by the prospect of finding so many nuts. "Please, please, take me," he begged.

"Of course, there will be some who wonder why you, a squirrel, are traveling with a family of rabbits," Mother Rabbit said. "If anybody asks, tell them that I am your mother, too. They will be confused, but at least they will let us pass without an argument.

"Now, who am I?" she asked.

"You are my mother," the squirrel answered. Since he was all alone in the big world, the little squirrel was even happier now that he had a new mother. He was so happy that he tried to bounce and jump like the baby bunnies instead of scampering like a squirrel as he and the two little rabbits followed Mother Rabbit out of the woods and into the field.

Soon they were at the place where Mother Rabbit had promised to meet the hawk. That great bird sat high in a nearby hickory tree. Seeing Mother Rabbit, the hawk flapped down to the ground and said, "I see that you have kept your word. Now, which of your little ones shall I take home for my chicks' dinner?"

Mother Rabbit pointed to the small squirrel. "Take this one."

"That is not one of your children," the hawk replied.

"Of course, he is. Ask him yourself."

"Who is this rabbit?" Mother Hawk asked the squirrel.

"She is my mother," the squirrel answered as he searched for hickory nuts.

The hawk jumped on the squirrel, dug her talons through his fur, and flew off to her nest.

"Come, children," Mother Rabbit said, "we should go someplace else to find our dinner."

ΩΩΩΩΩ

"Mothers always fear for their children," Yquili Sparrow said, "so we pray to the spirit of Atina that she will give them food and keep them safe.

"Now, go and do your chores while I feed Little Brother." Again, she held Many Fish to her breast.

***

"What is wrong with them?" Sapphira moaned. "Why don't you love me?" The young woman sat with her back to Lonely Cricket, her voice so low and choked with tears that he could not hear her words.

"What is matter?" He sat up and reached out his right hand to touch her trembling, naked shoulders.

She turned to him. "Last night you did not kiss me. You didn't even touch me."

"I not understand. I kiss you many times. I touch you. We make love."

"I don't mean anywhere, everywhere. I mean there." She cupped her right hand under her breasts. "On my breasts. It's as if you don't see them, as if you don't want me to have them. When I was little, when we played together, I dreamed of having breasts like my mother, like Happy Turtle. Now I have them. I want you to tell me they are beautiful, that I am beautiful."

"You very beautiful, Sapphira."

"Then why don't you look at them? Even now you are looking away. What is wrong with my bosom? Tell me. Is it something—"

"Nothing wrong." The young Indian forced himself to gaze at her exposed breasts and quickly looked down.

"You did it again."

Lonely Cricket could hear the irritation in her voice. "Not supposed to look at woman breasts. Not right to look."

"Who told you that?"

"At school they hit boy look at girl not dressed. And, Dinah say it wrong to touch. Say Elder at meeting touch breast make her feel shame. Make me promise never touch."

Suddenly, Sapphira laughed.

"Why you laugh?

"Do you think Jim Wickham abides by such a rule? Nor many other men Dinah might meet either. She'd best get over that or find herself another man as good as you. I wager she never will."

"Me not good but try respect Dinah wish."

"Then how about respecting mine? I want you to touch me. I want you to love me. I want you—"

The ring finger of Lonely Cricket's right hand softly touched her left breast. Slowly, he followed the line of her areola.

Sapphira's nipple stiffened at the touch. The young man bent over and gently kissed it. Only then did he allow himself to open his eyes. "You beautiful," he said and kissed her breast again.

"As beautiful as Dinah Tideswell?" she asked with a smirk.

"More beautiful than Dinah." He pulled her towards him.

Downstairs, Ebba Anderson was preparing breakfast. Her husband was already out in the barn feeding the animals. Hilda, sated by her morning feeding, snored gently in her cradle, which Ebba had carried from the bedroom and placed near the wood-burning stove on which she was tending a skillet of pannkator.

Skirmir, waiting impatiently for his meal, looked up when he heard the groans coming from the loft. "They make same noise last night. Vhy they make so much noise, Momma?

Ebba reddened. "That is something you understand vhen you get older, Skadedjur."

"I am not pest," Skirmir insisted.

"Then stop ask so many questions."

***

The sun had climbed halfway to the top of the world by the time the two young people were ready to leave the Anderson home and walk to the cabin where Lonely Cricket had grown up. "You help good med animals," Lars said to Lonely Cricket. "Things not go good vith your papa, you vant come back vork for me. You and Sapphira live med us."

"You can sleep in the loft. I share bed vith Papa and Momma," Skirmir added. "That not so good," Lars said with a laugh. "Ve make you room in barn."

"Thank you for offer." Lonely Cricket held out his hand. "I will come back. Help bring horse and wagon back to Fayette if you want."

"That vould help us much." Lars answered taking the younger man's hand in his own.

"I not vant you to leave," Skirmir yelled after them.

"We have to," Sapphira explained once more. "Lonely Cricket has to see his parents. He misses them so much. I have to see them, too. I have to apologize."

The young woman started to cry. Ebba put her arms around Sapphira. "Shhsh. Shhsh. You not should cry. Everything all right. You see. Everything be good."

Lonely Cricket picked up two of their lightest bags and handed them to Sapphira. Then he picked up the rest.

"Need help carrying those?" Lars asked. "Not far," the younger man replied. "Many years but not far."

***

"White Man not want here. Go 'way," Many Fish said loudly in English. The boy, dressed in a deer hide breechcloth and rabbit skin moccasins, nocked an arrow and aimed at Lonely Cricket.

"What's wrong with you, Many Fish? Don't you know your henehare-ah?"

"I do not have an older brother. Gentle Hawk passed into the spirit world before I was born. There was a snowstorm in the place where our parents once lived.

"And you are not a Ho-Chunk; you wear the clothes of a warrior of the White Man. You wear hair of White Man. Your skin is not the color of the earth of the Ho-Chunk."

"These are not the clothes of a warrior. They are my school uniform. I've been—"

"How do you speak our language? Does the White Woman also know our words?" Now, the boy aimed the arrow at Sapphira.

"No. She is a White Woman," Lonely Cricket answered. His voice shook with confusion and irritation. "But I am your henehare-ah; I am Lonely Cricket. Do you not remember me?"

"Lonely Cricket is not my brother. He is not a Ho-Chunk. He is a mauhehetta."

Lonely Cricket's mouth opened in astonishment.

"What's he saying?" Sapphira whispered hoarsely. "And, why is he pointing his bow at us?"

Lonely Cricket shrugged his shoulders. "I not understand. Bad thing happen. I go away. Happy Turtle rape. My brother think I become White Man. Confuse. Not understand."

"Many Fish," Sapphira said, "don't you remember me? I'm Sapphira. I lived—"

The boy gestured with his bow in the direction of the cabin from which Lonely Cricket and Sapphira had come that morning, the cabin which now belonged to the Andersons. "Your brother rape sister. Make her with child. She run 'way to old home. Have baby there."

"He isn't my brother. He's my cousin ...." Tears choked off Sapphira's voice.

"Happy Turtle have baby?" Lonely Cricket said to Sapphira. "Sister have baby and I not there for naming." His legs felt weak, his shoulders stooped.

It took a moment for the young man to recover. Once he could focus his thoughts, he peppered questions at Many Fish. Sometimes, Lonely Cricket had to stop to think of the Ho-Chunk words that he had not used for years. Still the questions came. "Did our sister have a baby? What do you know of Happy Turtle? How is the child? Did she have a son or a daughter? What is the child's name? Where is our sister now?"

Many Fish gave no answers. Instead, he directed his gaze at Sapphira. "You go now. White Man not good. No want here."

"That is not up to you," Lonely Cricket replied. "Where is our father Lame Bear? Where is our mother?"

"They are not your father and mother. They are the father and mother of Gentle Hawk who is with the spirits. They are the father and mother of Happy Turtle and of Many Fish, but they are not the parents of Lonely Cricket. You are mauhehetta. Shadow Fox told me you are a White Man. Lame Bear, too, has told me that you are a White Man."

"I don't know what lies Shadow Fox has told you, but you have not understood the words of Lame Bear, sonkhare-ah. I have been at the White Man's school far away. Shadow Fox was there with me for some moons. Then he left and I stayed to learn more. I have learned the ways of the mauhehetta, but I am Ho-Chunk."

Lonely Cricket moved forward slightly. "Put away your bow and take me to our father. I am eager to greet him and tell him of what I have learned."

He turned to Sapphira. "You stay while I talk with father. Maybe you show Many Fish present we buy him." He put down the bags he had carried from the Anderson cabin. "Presents in that one." He pointed to a brown carpetbag

Sapphira nodded. "Do you think it's true? That Happy Turtle has a child?"

"Yes, that true. Many Fish would know."

Many Fish having heard Sapphira's words said, "I not lie."

Ignoring the youngster's anger, she went on. "But, why would he think you're a White Man? Doesn't he understand—"

"I not know. Need speak Lame Bear and Yquili Sparrow. They tell." He moved towards Many Fish.

"Cricket," Sapphira called after him; "who is Gentle Hawk?"

"I not know."

"He brother of Many Fish," the boy answered at the same time.

Ignoring Many Fish's bow, Lonely Cricket walked towards the barn. "Lame Bear," he called, "I have come home."

Sapphira opened the carpetbag and moved the gifts around looking for the knife that Lonely Cricket had bought for his brother. "It's one of the best in the store," the shopkeeper in Albany, Indiana, had insisted when Lonely Cricket and Sapphira had gone shopping for presents. "See that silver detail, the genuine stuff." He rubbed his finger on the "German silver" and smiled at his lie. "I'm selling it to you cheap. Should just take her home for my own boy. But, since you picked her, guess I got to sell it to ya."

Lonely Cricket had counted out the dollar and three bits.

"That brother of yours is gettin' something every boy would want and at half the price," the shopkeeper said as he pocketed the money. That night he would bring home a candy for his son. In business even small victories were always to be celebrated, especially when they involved stealing from a heathen.

"No want White Man gift," the boy said.

Sapphira looked at him and could not see the little boy she remembered in his unforgiving stare.

Chapter 48 ~ The Past Begins

Sitting on the bench, his knees almost touching his chin, Lonely Cricket remembered his first meeting with Major Pratt at the Indian School. The young boy had squirmed with discomfort sitting on the hard, wooden chair opposite the Major's desk. His new uniform scratched and itched. The shiny shoes pinched his feet.

Lonely Cricket remembered the sound of the officer's voice, but not the words. Of those, he had understood only a few, and that more than most of the boys.

They had marched outside to have photographs taken. Samuel, the major's Apache aide, showed them where to stand.

"This White Man say too many words," Standing Oak whispered to Lonely Cricket.

"Why does the White Man want to steal faces of Indians?" Shadow Fox complained in Ho-Chunk and simultaneously signed to the Apache.

"Not hurt," Samuel replied and made a sign of reassurance.

"Not afraid," Shadow Fox signed back. "Not trust White Man."

"Hey, you injuns better be talking English," Langdon said. "None of yer heathen talk here."

"Sorry. Sir," Samuel answered.

"What does 'sorry' mean?" Standing Oak asked. "It means you did something wrong," Lonely Cricket whispered.

"What did Samuel do wrong?"

"We must speak the White Man's tongue."

"But—"

"Speak American, boy," one of the White Men standing on the lawn said.

Standing Oak made no reply.

"You deaf?"

"Him not speak White Man language," Lonely Cricket spoke up.

"Well, he damned well best learn."

"You sorry," Lonely Cricket signed the word "speak" to Standing Oak.

"You sorry," came the younger boy's hesitant response.

The White Man laughed. "Guess the boy will learn."

"That why we come school," Lonely Cricket replied.

"I have learned much of the White Man," the young man thought as he waited in the agent's office. "I know that White Men are not like Indians. White Men do not wait to be asked what they want. They do not wait to be told the truth. I will not wait for Jones to answer my questions."

Lonely Cricket looked up as the door that connected the agent's office to his house opened. It was not Ezekiel Jones who stood there, it was his wife.

Sarah Jones walked into her husband's office. She was followed by the housekeeper Mrs. Ferguson who wore the same food-stained apron she had worn when Lonely Cricket had knocked at the kitchen door.

"Want speak to Agent Jones," the young man had explained before the housekeeper could ask.

"Harumph. Is that what you're wanting. Go 'round to the office and wait," the woman had said. "When Mr. Jones gets back, he might just—"

"This important," the young man said. "I wait, he come." He knew that the housekeeper had meant for him to wait on the splintery bench that stood in the sun near the office door, but Lonely Cricket had decided to go in. "If I go into the office, they cannot ignore me and just wait for me to go away."

All the Ho-Chunk knew the trick. Few of them got to see the Indian Agent unless he had sent for them. Some had sat on that splintery bench for days before giving up. To the best of Lonely Cricket's knowing, none had ever gone inside.

Now, Mrs. Jones stood near the doorway and stared at Lonely Cricket.

"I come speak to agent," Lonely Cricket said as he stood up. "Mrs. Ferguson said you say it's important."

"That true."

"My husband's not here."

"Uh."

"My husband's not here," she repeated. "He's in Fayette on business." She moved forward.

"Not on business," the young man thought. "He is at Miss Birdie's. Mrs. Jones knows where her husband is, but she does not want to say. Perhaps, she does not want to admit it to herself."

"Then need speak to you. My father Lame Bear say agent and agent wife know truth. Say they tell truth."

"The truth about what?" "Truth about parents."

"I don't understand."

"They say I not Ho-Chunk, that I mauhehetta. They say agent and wife know truth. Miss Pirrip say I speak agent, too. She say nephew write letter. Say agent and wife know truth. Want Lonely Cricket ask."

Sarah Jones whitened and stepped back. Ruth Ferguson reached out to take her employer's arm and guide her to the agent's chair.

Collapsing into her husband's swivel chair, Sarah Jones fought to catch her breath and to gather her composure.

"You know Abagail Pirrip. How is that—"

"Meet in Indiana. Return brooch and she there."

"I-I-I don't under ..." The last of the color drained from Sarah Jones's face and she shrank into the desk chair.

Ruth Ferguson said, "Stay with her, boy. Don't ... I'll be back with the salts."

Soon the housekeeper returned with a metal tin, which she opened to release an odor that brought tears to Lonely Cricket's eyes.

Sarah Jones stirred in response to the noxious odor.

"You'd best go lie down, Missus," Ruth Ferguson suggested.

"No, I think it better if I stay and speak to this young man. What did you say your name is?"

"My name Lonely Cricket, but White Man call Harry."

"I fear that neither is your name, not the name you were given. Your father, your real father called you Theodore, which was his name as well. Theodore Pirrip. He Christened you himself for there was no one about who would do it for him. "Jeb Ludlow could have if he were not such a heathen. Wouldn't bury your mother nor christen you and still calls himself a preacher." Sarah Jones's voice rose in anger.

"I guess that's what your father was talking about and what Miss Abagail Pirrip wanted to know. I never did expect to hear her name again. I couldn't bring myself to ...," Sarah gulped and continued, "to write her and then after ... after we gave you up there was nothing I could think to say if ... I don't know if you can understand, Theodore. Do you mind if I call you Theodore? I have always thought of you that way."

"Not matter what name you call, but my name Lonely Cricket. White man call Harry at school."

"I understand, but Theodore was your father's name—though we called him Ted, him being grown and all. Anyway, it were the name he wanted passed to you." She took out the frilly handkerchief which was tucked in the cuff of her blouse and wiped her eyes. "I promised him that we would call you Theodore even though Ezekiel wanted to name you after my cousin, Senator Arnold. 'Butter the old boy up a bit,' was how Ezekiel saw it."

"Not understand. Who Senator Arnold? What mean butter? We eat butter on pancake at Tideswell farm. Butter good, but not use on people."

Suddenly, the woman started laughing. She laughed and laughed while the young Indian waited patiently for her to stop.

The housekeeper left the office and came back with a glass of water. "Drink this, Missus," Ruth Ferguson suggested.

"Do you think all the water you can pump from that well will wash away my sins, Ruth?"

Still, Lonely Cricket waited. Questions burned in his heart. "Who am I? Am I Miss Pirrip's great-nephew?" And, the biggest question of all, "Am I Ho-Chunk or am I a mauhehetta?"

***

"It was all because of Josey," Sarah Jones began. "Actually, your mother's name was Josephina. Named after the French empress she told us. 'If I had been a boy, my mother would have called me Napoleon,' was how she put it. Her mother was so proud of their French blood. Maybe, that was because of the other."

"Other?" Lonely Cricket asked.

"Shhh, boy," Mrs. Ferguson commanded. Let the missus tell the story. You want the truth, and you'll be hearing it from her."

Lonely Cricket sat back into the comfortable, if worn, chair. Threadbare as it was, the parlor of the agent's house was far more comfortable than his office. No flags or banners, but a few daguerreotypes, stitched samplers, and one painting of a man dressed in a parade uniform. The chairs had seen better days and the tables were scratched and showed rings from past abuse. The fireplace offered no mantle, and the andirons looked as if they had been made by a local farrier. "The other blood," Sarah Jones continued. "She was mulatto. Do you know what that means?"

"Not know."

"It means she was part African. They call such people mulatto because it's Spanish for mule. A mule—"

"Is the child of horse and donkey," Lonely Cricket interrupted.

"Exactly, two different species. Well, those folks who use such a word think a Black and a White are two different species, too, like a horse and a donkey."

"Color of skin not make different animal."

"True enough, but there are some .... Anyway, Josey's mother was proud of her French blood and hated her negra. That's why she called her daughter, your momma, Josephina, after the empress of France."

"I thought Louis King of France."

"Well, he was, but Napoleon Bonaparte was the emperor. I guess, I'll leave you to study that on your own."

"Will ask Sapphira. Maybe she know."

"Who's Sapphira?"

"Sapphira Cook friend. She help understand White Man."

"Ah, you have a girlfriend."

"Sapphira good friend."

"Yes, I'm sure she is." Sarah Jones paused for a moment and scratched her head. "Cook … I remember that name. Something about an allotment for sale."

"You'd best tell him the rest about his mother," Ruth Ferguson reminded.

"Yes, yes, I'd best." Sarah Jones took a sip from the glass of sherry that sat on the scarred end table. "Are you sure you don't want something to drink?"

"Sure not want." Lonely Cricket forced himself to not stare at Sarah Jones. Impatient and uncomfortable as he felt, he knew that the conversation was even more difficult for the woman sitting opposite.

"Josey worked for me, that was before Ruth." The woman gestured towards her housekeeper. "But she was more than just help, she was a friend, a dear friend."

"Not that you aren't, Ruth," Mrs. Jones hastened to add. The housekeeper nodded in recognition of the sentiment.

"She was so happy that she was pregnant. And they were so much in love, she and your father." This was followed by another sip of sherry and a long pause during which Sarah Jones allowed her eyes to drift towards a daguerreotype of two people, a man and a woman, looking at one another.

"That my parents?" Lonely Cricket asked, his eyes widening.

"Yes, boy, they are. Can you see—"

"Ruth," Sarah Jones interrupted herself. "You wrap that picture up. By all rights, it's Theodore's, don't you think?"

"Yes, ma'am."

"Picture not bring them back. You keep. Picture keep memory for you."

"Memories? Yes, I have many memories. They were happy times, Theodore. The war was over. Nebraska was just become a state. Ezekiel had this new job and we thought there would be more, better jobs. Harmon had promised, and he was a rising star in Lawrence."

Lonely Cricket turned to the housekeeper. She saw the look of confusion on his face.

"I don't think the boy understands," Ruth Ferguson said.

"No, of course. I was just …. What do they call you?" The tone of her voice suddenly tuned to her own confusion. "Name Lonely Cricket." He paused for a moment. "If easier, call Harry." Another pause, "You can call Theodore if want."

"Yes, Harry. You see, we were expecting great things in our lives. So, when your parents came to town looking for a place, hoping for a homestead and her willing to work to help, why it seemed a godsend. Not many women hereabouts know how or are willing to keep house for another. Especially, when there's nice things."

Sarah Jones gestured to take in her living room. "It may look over-worn now, but in its day, this was as fine a room as you'd find in Omaha. Ezekiel insisted on it, said we had to bring class to Pierce so the Indians could see what the White Man's life was. Harmon agreed. Got the War Department to provide a thousand dollars for furnishings. Why, I felt like I was Mary Lincoln herself."

Having taken another sip of sherry, the woman shook her head. "Waste of money. Don't think five Indians have been inside this house since it was built. Of course, Washington doesn't care. They waste more than that on brandy for their generals every month."

Laughing at her own joke, Sarah Jones shook her head once more and then continued. "Josey was used to keeping house. She'd worked for some rich fellow in New Orleans, said he bought corn and liquor that came down the Mississippi and shipped it to France. Claimed he'd even done business with Old Abe one time. Of course, I wouldn't be surprised if every trader in New Orleans didn't claim the same.

"When the war came, times got hard for the family. She said it that way, 'the family.' Wouldn't surprise me if she didn't have some of the same blood along with some African."

"What do you think, Ruth? Do you think they were her blood?" Sarah Jones interrupted herself to ask.

"I wouldn't hardly know. I didn't really know Josey that well and only just before—"

"Anyway," Sarah Jones continued, "during the war she went to work for one of them rebel generals, fellow name of Lovell. To hear your father talk on it, that Lovell fellow was the one running things. Didn't do it too well, surrendered the city without a fight. That's when your daddy saw the writing on the wall. Knew the Union was going to win. Not that he minded one way or the other. He'd only gone South because your granddaddy went North."

She interrupted the train of her story to ask, "Did you study on the war at all?"

"Some. Major Pratt fought. He tell stories. Teachers tell stories. Mose tell stories."

Ruth Ferguson asked, "Who the devil's Mose?"

"He friend at Tideswell farm. He negra man. He tell us what do."

"Miss Sarah, do you mind if I help myself to a bit of that sherry?" Ruth Ferguson asked. "I'm getting a mite confused."

The mistress of the house nodded her acquiescence.

As the housekeeper took a chipped crystal glass from the tarnished tray and poured herself a splash of the tawny liquid, Sarah Jones continued her story.

"When Ted saw the end coming, he took off with Josey and some of that silver from that fancy house they was living in."

"Why he take Josey? He love?"

"Good question, boy. I doubt it. I don't think Ted Pirrip loved anybody but himself, but he was used to the comfort she gave. Knew she'd just end working for a Yankee officer, so might as well be him."

"Why she go if he not love?"

"Not sure of that, neither, but I guess she didn't know better. Of course, I'm no one to talk am I, Ruth?"

The housekeeper bobbed her head in response. "It ain't so easy for a woman, Missus. I reckon you know that as good as anyone."

"Yes, once the bed is lain." Sarah Jones drained the last of her sherry, "It's a mite easier to climb in."

"Maybe for the boy's mother but not for that no-account," Ruth Ferguson added.

"Well, let's just say that Ted and my husband shared a liking for the women."

"They go Miss Birdie's?" Lonely Cricket asked.

"No. They would have, but that place wasn't there, not yet. Went to another whore house, but what difference that makes I'll never know. The two of them thinking with their men's parts and never with their heads or their souls."

Ruth Ferguson's answer to the young man's question brought tears to Sarah Jones's eyes. "You like that, Theodore?" She asked. "You follow your lust, or you stay true to that gal of yours."

"Never go woman for money." Lonely Cricket felt the blush rushing to his cheeks.

"That's in your favor," Sarah responded. "Now, I know you got plenty of more questions, but I ain't got more answers, least ways not today. You come back tomorrow and bring that girl of yours and we can talk some more. For today, I'm tired of thinking on it. Tired of memories. "You take that picture with you," she added as she rose from her chair. "You were right about it being my memories and I can't say I want 'em around me." She picked up the daguerreotype, which the housekeeper had wrapped in a gray linen cloth worn and yellowed by time. "Like me," Sarah added as she looked at the cloth. "Maybe if I hadn't let them … if you …"

She pushed the picture toward him, and Lonely Cricket took it. "Come back tomorrow."

"Yes, and bring your friend. What is her name?"

"Sapphira Cook," Ruth Ferguson reminded her employer.

"Yes, you bring her with you." Turning quickly away, the Indian agent's wife strode out of the parlor, leaving her housekeeper to show Lonely Cricket out.

"So, I not Ho-Chunk?" Lonely Cricket said to Ruth Ferguson as they stood at the door.

She shook her head.

"I mauhehetta?"

"If that means a White Man, I reckon you are, least ways mostly."

He stepped off the stoop. "And Miss Abagail my family?"

"Yes, boy, it seems to be."

Lonely Cricket shook his head in bewilderment as he walked away from the agent's house.

"I don't know what more there is for Miss Sarah to tell you, lad," the housekeeper called after him, "but I'll be guessing you aren't going to sleep so well this night. Course, neither will she."

Lonely Cricket turned back and asked, "Will agent come back tonight?"

"Now, that isn't likely, not with him gone only two days. Don't you worry about it none."

"Not worry. Have questions."

Ruth Ferguson laughed. "Once the liquor's out of him, you can ask away. Not that anyone will ever get an answer worth hearing from him."

Turning back towards the road, Lonely Cricket strode off. If he hurried, he would be back at the Anderson's farm in time to help bed the animals. Later, in the dark, lying in the place they had set for themselves in the Anderson's barn, he'd share the day's strange turn with Sapphira. "She will help me figure this out," he thought. Then he added these words aloud, "White Man or Indian; Lonely Cricket, Harry, or Theodore. Lame Bear's son or Ted Pirrip's. Who I am, where I belong, that is what I must know."

A crow pecking at the remains of a hawk's kill, fluttered away as the young man came near. "Caw. Caw," the bird called.

"Not know what you say," Lonely Cricket responded in English. "Not know what I say."

Chapter 49 ~ What Fortune Guides the Lives of Men

"Josey told me this story the day before she died. I wrote it down just as she told it." Sarah Jones cleared her throat and began reading from the carefully creased papers she had taken from the back of her Bible. "Once there was a very fortunate king," she began.

Lonely Cricket cocked his head so he might hear each word clearly.

As Sarah began reading, Sapphira reached for Lonely Cricket's hand, taking it gently in her own.

The woman stopped. Dabbed at the corners of her eyes with her handkerchief and held the paper closer to the kerosene lantern, which was burning even though it was now close to midday. "My eyes aren't what they were." She dabbed again at the corners of her eyes and once more began reading.

"Once there was a very fortunate king. This king was lucky because he was handsome and he was rich and he had four wives, who loved him and did for him whatever he desired. However, the king was not happy for he had no children. He had no sons to lead his army and no sons to someday inherit his throne. He had no daughters to grace his palace and no daughters to marry to the sons of the kings of the nations that surrounded his.

"One of the king's wives, whose name was Fatima, wanted to please her husband so she devised a plan. She sent a messenger to the village from which she came. Her village was far away in another land, so the messenger had to ride for many days to deliver her letter. It was to her family. Fatima told the messenger to wait for a reply no matter how long it took.

"For three months, the messenger waited. Finally, the princess Fatima's father, who was the local chief, called the messenger to him and said, 'Go back to your mistress. Ride as quickly as you can.'

"The messenger asked if there was a reply to the message that he had brought. 'Your return is the only reply my daughter needs,' answered the chief. 'Ride now as the wind.'

"Away the messenger rode on the fastest horse in the chief's stable. When he arrived at Fatima's palace, he found she had packed for a journey. 'Tell my lord the king that I have gone to see my parents, that I have great need of my mother,' she instructed the messenger.

"The king, her husband, asked the messenger, 'Did Fatima say anything else?'

"'Yes, my lord,' the messenger replied, she said her return would be a day of joy for you.

"With the messenger's words the king was content. 'Fatima is with child,' he thought. 'Soon I will have a child of my own. I shall have a son to lead my army and to someday take my place or perhaps a daughter to grace my palace and to someday tie my house to that of another. I have only some months before Fatima's return,' the king thought. 'Therefore, I shall order preparations for the great day.' And, he ordered a nursery be built in Fatima's new palace, which was to be constructed right next to his own. And, he ordered that new coins should be struck of gold and silver with Fatima's likeness and his own. The king was now truly happy.

"Meanwhile, Fatima arrived at her parents' home where one of their servants had become pregnant by one of her father's grooms. This young woman was comely and pleasant and lacked the wiles of this world. 'We must take care of you and your baby,' the chief's wife had told her serving girl, 'for nothing is more precious than a new life.'

"The girl was given a suite of rooms in the chief's home and servants to wait on her. There was a guard to watch over her and two guards to escort her when she went for a walk in the gardens.

"The serving girl was very pleased with her new station even though she did not get to spend more time with the groom, whom she truly loved. Indeed, she could not even catch a glimpse of him. When Fatima arrived at her parents' home, the first thing she did was to visit the young serving girl in her suite. 'You are so fortunate to be having a child,' Fatima said. 'I am glad my parents are taking such good care of you.' The serving girl thanked Fatima and was particularly pleased that Fatima took the time to visit with her every day. 'The princess Fatima is my friend,' she said to one of the women who helped care for her; 'how honored I am.'

"'Indeed, she is a most kind princess,' the woman replied. "In time, as is the way of nature, the young woman gave birth to a child, a boy, healthy and full of the sound of life. When the midwife had placed the child to the serving girl's breast, the princess Fatima stepped forward and stabbed the girl, robbing her of life and robbing the baby of his mother.

"Quickly wrapping the infant in a blanket, Fatima was off to her own palace. 'Thank you, father,' she said as she left her parents' home, 'with this child I will now become my husband's favorite. I shall be queen of his domain. And, when the child grows up, he will look to me as his mother and I shall surely be the first in the land.'

"It was as the princess hoped. The king was delighted with the infant, whom he believed to be his first-born son. He showered the boy with gifts and honors and did the same to Fatima. There were many happy years.

"With time, the youngster led the king's army. And, when the king grew feeble, he appointed his son to the throne.

"From her place in heaven, the serving girl watched her son grow into manhood. On the day he ascended the throne, she rejoiced. 'Surely, my child has become great,' she proclaimed to the angels. 'What more can a mother wish?'"

The others remained quiet when Sarah had finished.

Sapphira tenderly squeezed Lonely Cricket's hand.

Ruth Ferguson rubbed her hands together, waited for her employer to say something, anything, more. When there were no words, she asked Sapphira, "Would you like more tea?"

"No … no thank you, but …" the young woman stammered in response.

Finally, Lonely Cricket stirred in his place on the sofa. "My mother tell this story?"

"Yes," Sarah Jones answered.

"May I look?" The young man held out the hand which Sapphira had been squeezing.

Sarah handed the papers to him. Holding them in his left hand, he looked at them carefully and gently ran his fingers over the letters. There was quiet as Lonely Cricket looked at the paper and repeatedly moved his fingers over the pages.

"She wanted me to read it to you when you were old enough …when I thought you were old enough to hear it. When Ezekiel and I thought you were old enough to understand … to under … that you weren't ours. I mean you would be ours but not …not by our having made you, only by our loving you.

"Father not write letter to Miss Abagail," Lonely Cricket announced suddenly.

Sarah Jones's face blanched. "How …" Her voice failed.

"Writing same." The young man held the pages out to Sapphira. "See, it same."

"I never saw the—" Sapphira began.

"You're right. Of course," Sarah stammered and gulped as she spoke. "I wrote it. He … he was gone. He'd left before you were … before Josey died."

"Fetch me some water, Ruth," Sarah instructed her housekeeper.

"Father not write letter to Miss Abagail, you write," Lonely Cricket repeated.

"Yes. I wrote it," Sarah continued after she took a sip from the china cup Ruth handed her. "I told mostly truth, how Josey had died leaving you. How you was christened Theodore. How the preacher wouldn't christen you, so it was me and Ruth gave you your name. Like I say, mostly true, but I made it like Ted was writing."

"Why?" Sapphira's voice was almost a whisper but harsh and filled with judgement. "Why didn't you tell her the truth?"

"Why hurt Miss Pirrip even more? Truth was Ted was long gone. He didn't really want to settle down and he certainly didn't want a child. Then, when Josey took sick and the doctor said he couldn't help, well Ted just said, 'You do with the baby,' and off he went."

"The truth is," Ruth Ferguson added, "there's no saying he would have stayed even if Josey weren't dying."

"That's true," Sarah Jones agreed. "There never were a more selfish man in this world." She smiled at Lonely Cricket. "At least I can see you ain't like him, not that way."

"Where father go?"

"We ain't sure," answered Ruth Ferguson. "He never wrote, did he, Missus?"

"No. Ted never wrote. But we did hear stories about him and the Dakotas. Looking for gold most likely."

"And women," Ruth added to her mistress's words.

***

"It wasn't a lie, not when I wrote it." Sarah Jones's words were directed to Sapphira Cook.

The chin band of Sarah's white indoor bonnet had come untied. Her left hand played unconsciously with the loose ribbon. With a sudden burst of anger, she pulled the cap from her head and threw it onto the nearby table. Worn smooth with years of washing, the cap didn't stop but slid to the floor. Lonely Cricket started to rise to retrieve it, but the Indian agent's wife resumed talking and he sank back into the sofa.

"When I wrote your aunt, I did plan on raising you as our own. Ezekiel was all for it. Said he'd been wanting a son. Said maybe having a boy would give him a reason to stay out of Fayette, stay away from them whores."

"What make change mind?" Lonely Cricket asked.

"There was a letter from my cousin. Harmon had got word what we was planning to do."

"Not much goes on in Nebraska that Harmon Arnold don't know about," Ruth Ferguson muttered.

"That's true, Ruth, but he doesn't usually mess in unless it has somehow to do with himself. How our raising you had to do with him I didn't see, but he sure did. Said if we claimed you as our own Ezekiel would rot here in Pierce the rest of his life. Said he wouldn't have no relation with tainted blood. Said the war may have freed the slaves but it didn't make coloreds human any more than Injuns."

The woman's small hands had knotted into tight fists. The right one slammed down on the armrest of her chair. "My cap seems to have .... Would you get it for me?" she asked no one in particular.

Ruth Ferguson was the first to react, picking the white fabric up and handing it to her employer. Sarah Jones examined it carefully. Finding a louse hiding in one of the seams, she crushed the tiny creature between the thumb and forefinger of her right hand. "Damned things," she exclaimed.

"Your cousin told you that you couldn't adopt Lonely Cricket?" Sapphira asked, her hand reaching out to touch his.

"Said we could raise him as he were the son of a dead servant but taking him as our own, that Harmon would never allow."

"So you give me Lame Bear and Yquili Sparrow?" Lonely Cricket sensed the mix of anger and sorrow in his voice. He felt Sapphira's soft, reassuring touch on his hand.

Sarah Jones shuddered before responding.

"No. I would have kept you even if." She busied herself tying the chin strap of the cap she had repositioned on her head. She tied a bow, untied it, and tied it again. Then yet another retying. The room was silent except for the woman's deep breaths.

Finally, Sarah took up her thought. "And, I wouldn't have said anything about no servant. I'd have raised you as my own. I was so proud of you, wasn't I, Ruth?"

"She was indeed," the housekeeper affirmed.

"Truth be told, it was Ezekiel. He didn't say anything, not right out. Said we could keep you, that Harmon could be damned. That's what he said.

"Next day he lit out for Fayette. Said he had business needed doing, supplies for the Indians. Didn't come back for more'n a fortnight."

Suddenly Sarah Jones was sobbing. Even as she moved to comfort her employer, Ruth Ferguson said, "That's Ezekiel, he says lots of good stuff, but in the end, he always goes back to his nature."

Sarah Jones put her hand on the housekeeper's arm, took a deep gulp of air and said, "I knew then he'd never be a fit father, not for you or any child. That's when I decided. But, you see, the letter to your great aunt, that had already been posted. It wasn't a lie, not when I wrote it."

Exhausted, Sarah Jones closed her eyes and let her head sag forward until her chin rested on her breast. "Might be best if you come back another time," Ruth Ferguson said.

Lonely Cricket wanted to know how this woman had chosen Lame Bear and Yquili Sparrow to be his parents and why they had agreed, but he knew there would be no more answers that day.

Chapter 50 ~ A Search Begins

The midmorning sun baked Lonely Cricket's naked shoulders. Back and forth he twisted, shuffling the length of the field before stopping to whet the scythe blade, take a sip from the sheep bladder sack slung over his waist, and turn to the next swatch of grass to be mown. The steady rhythm of the work calmed him. He thought of the pendulum in the big clock in Major Pratt's office. Seconds, minutes, hours: tick, tick, tick. Swish, swish, swish, his body twisting with the shearing of the scythe. Behind him, chattering away like a chipmunk, Skirmer tried to rake the long blades of switchgrass into windrows. The rake was far too long and heavy for the boy, who stopped often to rub his hands before rushing forward to catch up with the young man—each rush leaving hay ungathered.

"You work good," Lonely Cricket said to the boy after they had finished four passes the length of the field. "Father proud."

Skirmer beamed with pleasure. "I like to vork med you. Pappa say you are good vorker." He took another chug from the waterskin that Lonely Cricket had handed to him.

Lonely Cricket patted the boy's head. "Ready to do more?"

"Yah. I ready." Gamely, the boy rubbed his hands one more time and picked up his rake. "Did you vork with your pappa when you were a boy?"

"I work with Lame Bear," Lonely Cricket answered. "I thought he was papa but now not know. My real papa go away. Mrs. Jones give to Lame Bear, but not know why."

The boy nodded gravely and tried to understand the man's words. "So, your pappa not your pappa?"

Lonely Cricket scowled. "No. My name not my name. My people not my people."

"I not understand."

Shouldering the scythe, he strode towards the Anderson's cabin. "I not understand either," he muttered. "Must learn. Must find father. Must find why give to Lame Bear."

"Vait, Vait for me," Skirmer yelled as—dragging the rake behind him—he struggled to keep up with the man.

***

Sapphira sat on a stool, her arms plunged deep into the metal washtub. The strands of hair that peeked from the edges of her white bonnet shone in the near-noon sun. Sweat glistened on her brow. "Of course, you can use," Ebba had replied when the young woman asked if she could do Lonely Cricket's and her own laundry in the corrugated tub. "It belong to your parents. Come med farm. Vhen Lars buy house, he find tub and know I vould vant."

The two women had boiled the kettle many times to fill the tub, flaked soap from the large cake into the water, and added the clothes. Then Sapphira, straining with effort, had stirred the whole with a large wooden paddle. Now, most of the clothes lay in a wet heap on top of a large sheet. A few, having been rinsed in the clean water that had replaced the soapy, and then wrung as tightly as she could manage, were draped over ropes that Lars had helped the two women string.

"Good to have clean clothes," the farmer had commented.

Sapphira had offered to do the Andersons' washing as well. "No, I vill do it," Ebba had replied.

"Please, at least the little one's," Sapphira had pled. "She makes so many diapers."

"That could be a big help," Ebba had agreed. Sitting next to the young woman was her next chore, a large pot of diapers soaking in hot, soapy water. Sapphira eyed that next task and thought, "I wonder how many babies Harry and I will have? I would love to live in our own home and raise our children."

She could not fend off the thoughts that had whirled in her head since the truth of Harry's birth had come to light. Should they go back to New Albany and claim his name and birthright, or should they stay here in Nebraska, or perhaps go someplace else, maybe join her parents or look for Happy Turtle? If they went to New Albany, would Abagail Pirrip accept Harry as her great-nephew? Would they live in that wonderful house? How could Harry earn their living in such a place? In any place?

She wondered what he would he call himself: Lonely Cricket, Harry, or Theodore Pirrip. And what would he call her? Would he marry her? Would she be Mrs. Harry Lonely Cricket or what? She could accept whatever name and place. "But, if we go back to Indiana, if Dinah is there, will he ..." The thought of Harry being with Dinah overwhelmed Sapphira.

Wiping away the tears that had sprung to her eyes, Sapphira thrust her hands back into the tub and grabbed the blouse of Harry's Indian School uniform. Knotting it in her hands, over and over she wrung and squeezed to remove as much water as she could.

"Why you bother with that?" The sound of Harry's voice startled her.

"I'm doing the wash. Getting our clothes clean."

"I know you do wash, but why wash uniform? Not want to wear clothes from school. Not Indian boy. Not student. Me man." Tears sprung to Lonely Cricket's eyes. He grabbed the blouse and threw it to the ground. "I hate White Man. White Man hate me. Not want me for son. Nobody want son."

"I want you, Harry. I love you," Sapphira said, but Lonely Cricket turned away and walked towards the road.

"Where are you going?" the young woman called after him as she stooped to pick up the shirt from the ground.

"I go find truth. I go find my father."

Sapphira clutched the muddied shirt to her breast. Her shoulders heaved with the rhythm of tears. The shoulders of the young man she loved also heaved. They were two young lovers separated by his pain.

***

"Where you goin', Harry?" Ruth Ferguson demanded. "You ain't gonna torment Mrs. Jones no more, are you?"

"Have question need answer," Lonely Cricket replied. The woman stepped off the sidewalk into the street and stood directly in the young man's way. She carried a wicker basket over her left arm and a parasol, opened to ward off the just past noon sun, in her right hand. "You may think you're asking questions, but what you is really doing is sticking knives in that poor woman's wounds."

"Not want to hurt Mrs. Jones but need answer to questions."

"Well, why don't you ask them of me and maybe I can tell you straight." The housekeeper realized that the young Indian was paying scant attention to her words.

Hammer raised, another young man looked up from his father's anvil, took a moment to relieve his sinewy muscles—bare of shirt and greased with sweat—then glanced out from the forge and into the street.

"What you lookin' at, boy?" Angus Cooperman demanded. "You lollygagging whilst that iron cools and you've got double work to do!?"

"Just lookin' 'round," the young man said. "If it ain't Ruth Ferguson talking to one of them young Ho-Chunk bucks. Think she'd have better things to do."

"Them Injuns getting too free in this town. Ain't like a White woman can walk down the street without one of them taking liberties," the blacksmith replied.

Young Cooperman bent back to his father's anvil. Using heavy tongs to pick up the horseshoe on which he had been working, he plunged it back into the flames of the forge, removed it, and then the clang of hammer against hot metal. Sparks flew with angry energy.

The sound of hammer on iron startled Lonely Cricket. "What you say?" he asked the housekeeper.

Ruth Ferguson frowned. "I said we should talk." Her voice softened as she added, "Maybe I can answer your questions without you hurting Mrs. Jones."

"Mmm. Without Mrs. Jones hurt me."

"I suppose that's true, too."

They moved towards the shade of one of the few beech that had escaped the saws and axes of the town's creators. His head tilted to one side to better hear, Lonely Cricket absentmindedly traced the letters carved in the mottled gray-green bark: "J McC & S H" Having traced the letters over and over as if committing them to memory, he ran his finger over the rough heart that surrounded them.

"So, what do you want to know?" Ruth Ferguson asked sternly.

"Want to know why if Mrs. Jones not keep she give me to Ho-Chunk not to White Man?"

"Now that's an easy one, same reason as you weren't baptized proper. That so-called preacher Jeb Ludlow." She swept her right hand, which still held the parasol—now closed— in an arc and pointed up the road towards two small, white, wooden buildings that stood side by side and out of the way of daily commerce. The roof of one sported a cross, on the other was a bell. "Said no mixed-blood heathen would be welcome in his church or his school. Says coloreds was descended from Ham, you know in the Bible, and not fit to be in the presence of the Father. Same as Injuns 'cause them comin' down from Ishmael, and his momma being a slave and all. Anyways, that's how he preaches and it's how folks hereabouts believe. I guess Mrs. Jones figured it would be better you being raised by people who could see beyond skin and blood."

"I taught in school Christ love all men."

"Maybe Christ does, but Jeb Ludlow sure don't. Like a-lot-a-men, he only cares 'bout himself. Anyways, that was why Mrs. Jones asked Dreaming Woman to take you and give you to a good family."

Lonely Cricket, surprised by the housekeeper's answer, asked "How she know Dreaming Woman?"

"Every woman knows about her. If the men would allow it, she'd be there for every birthin'. Certainly, could have gone better for your mother if she'd been there. Least, by the time young McCabe ridden over and brought her back, you was still alive. Barely, but alive. Pale, not breathin' enough to be alive and not stoppin' enough to be dead. Course, Ezekiel weren't around. 'Off on Indian business.' That's what he'd say 'fore he'd go off to Fayette and his whorin'. Never fooled the missus nor me, but we'd always make believe. No sense arguing with a man who's lettin' the wrong head do his thinking."

Lonely Cricket tried unsuccessfully to follow the woman's flood of words. He heard the bitterness in her voice and wondered if Ruth Ferguson was ever at peace.

"So, Dreaming Woman come after mother Josey die?"

"That's the short of it. Lucky for you, though. She has herbs and powders and spells no White doctor got. Used them to save your life. Conjured you right back from the dead. Then, that woman asked the strangest thing." Ruth Ferguson took a step backwards as if that strange moment was reoccurring. "She asked for your cord. Said it needed proper burying."

A picture flashed through Lonely Cricket's mind. He saw the morning of Many Fish's birth and the medicine woman burying something in the garden by their family cabin. "Need bury in garden," he said so softly that the White woman could not hear.

"When Sarah realized she couldn't raise you and that no White family would take you 'cept as a servant, well, she asked Dreaming Woman to find you good parents."

The woman opened her parasol. "Now, I got some buying to do at Jedidiah's, so you go on home and leave Miss Sarah be."

Lonely Cricket grunted in response.

"Not need talk with Sarah Jones now," he thought. "Now, need talk with Dreaming Woman."

Moving away from the beech trees, Lonely Cricket moved in the direction from which he had come that morning. Little devils of dust danced along the street. He tasted the grit of sand and felt the sting as it abraded his bare torso.

"Look, Small Deer, isn't that Bird Head? Has he come back from the White Man's school?" Lonely Cricket heard Shadow Fox's voice and cringed as he had so often done when still a boy.

"Yes, it is Happy Turtle's brother," Small Deer replied.

Turning in the direction of the voices, Lonely Cricket saw three young men, a few years older than himself, sitting in the alley behind the saloon. They had a bottle of the White Man's liquor which they were passing among themselves.

"Come join us," Morning Spring gestured with the bottle. "It is a good day to drink the White Man fire."

ΩΩΩΩΩ

Winter Woman was looking for berries that she might dry to decorate the basket she had woven from strips of black ash. She would use her new basket when she gathered nuts and other food for her husband, who was the war chief among The People. "If I find him good things to eat, perhaps Buffalo Warrior will still love me even though I have not borne him any children," she thought as she waded through the marsh on the edge of the great lake.

There were many plants, and Winter Woman worked carefully. Taking only a few clusters of flowers or berries from each plant and only after thanking the plant for its gift. She knew that the spirits of the plants could aid her when she was foraging but that they would only do so if they knew that her heart was pure.

"Thank you, cranberry, for your gift," she said. "Your berries will help the food I gather to be fragrant."

"Thank you, thistle, for the purple flowers you have given me. They will help the food I gather to look bright and fresh."

"Thank you, sedge, for ..."

"What is that?" Winter Woman interrupted her thanks to the sedge plant from which she had taken three yellow spikes. She moved closer to the object she had spotted floating among the reeds. It was a basket, not one made like those of the People—not made of strips of ash wood but of reeds and twigs—but nevertheless a basket.

Using a long stick, Winter Woman pulled the basket towards herself. As she drew it closer, she could hear a sound coming from within the basket. It was a soft sound like the cry of a small animal.

When Winter Woman had pulled the basket close enough so she could bend down and look into it, she saw that it held a small buffalo robe decorated in the manner of the Arapaho. Wrapped in the robe was a baby boy. It was the child's voice that Winter Woman had heard. He was so weak that he could barely make a sound, but still he cried.

"He must want his mother," Winter Woman said to herself. "And, he must want his mother's breast."

Her first reaction was to pick the child up and hold him. "Has Goddess Atina heard my prayers?" Winter Woman asked herself. "Is this child to be mine? Should I bring him to Buffalo Warrior and say, 'This is your son'?"

Carrying the child clutched to her breast, Winter Woman went to seek the advice of the Medicine Man.

The Medicine Man said, "Clearly the Goddess Atina and the Great Spirit have given you this child. Even though he was born an Arapaho, it must be their wish that he is to grow up among the Ho-Chunk and be the son of Buffalo Warrior.

With the blessing of the Medicine Man, Winter Woman brought her new son to the bark-covered wigwam of Buffalo Warrior. The war chief welcomed the little boy into his home and into his heart. He taught the boy the way of the Ho-Chunk and called him Comes From the Water.

From the Water was a good child, brave and dutiful. He watched everything that Buffalo Warrior did. "I would be like my father," he explained to the other boys when they asked him to play their games.

"I would be like my father," Comes From the Water would say when the other young men would slip out of their parents' homes to play the flute for the young women of the tribe.

"I would be like my father," he would declare when other men suggested they drink the White man's drink

Even though the People knew that Comes From the Water had been born an Arapaho, they came to trust him and to know that he was a good Ho-Chunk and a speaker of sacred words.

ΩΩΩΩΩ

"That was the story Tall Grass told us when Dreaming Woman brought you to live among our people," Morning Spring said. "Isn't that so, Small Deer?"

Small Deer took a drink from the bottle that was being passed around and grunted his agreement.

"Then you all knew?"

"Knew what, Lonely Cricket?" asked Small Deer.

"That I was born a White Man. That I was—"

"Yes, we all knew," Morning Spring affirmed. "We all knew. Tall Grass told everyone at a great council fire. He said that you had been born to the White Man but that now you were Ho-Chunk. Then he told us the story of Comes From the Water and said that we should all welcome you."

"But you, you did not accept me," Lonely Cricket stared at Shadow Fox.

"No, Bird Head, I did not accept you despite the words of Tall Grass."

"Why?" Lonely Cricket's question was asked so softly that it could barely be heard over the creak of a passing wagon. "Why Shadow Fox did you not accept me?"

"It was my parents who were to take you," Shadow Fox answered. "It was my home in which you were to grow up. My father had told Tall Grass that in his heart I was not his son. That I did not have a place in his cabin. That I was not good enough to be his. He hated me and that is why I hated you. That is why I hate you now. What son does not want his father's love? What son wants his father to choose another?"

Shadow Fox reached for the bottle, which Morning Spring held. He held it to his lips, tilted his head back, and drank until there was no more drink. "Need another bottle," he said in English. He stared back at Lonely Cricket. "You buy and we talk more."

"White man's liquor is not good. We shouldn't—"

"You buy and we talk more," Shadow Fox repeated. "You still have money from White Man school?"

"I have a little."

"You buy and we talk more."

Reluctantly, Lonely Cricket went to the back door of the saloon. When he returned with another bottle of cheap drink, he handed it to Shadow Fox. "If I was to live with Talking Mountain —"

"My father says that I am not worthy. He says that I should never have been born. He wanted you to take my place. I hate him and I hate you." Taking a deep draught of from the bottle Lonely Cricket had bought, Shadow Fox coughed and then slipped onto his side. "You leave Shadow Fox alone," the young man stammered as Morning Spring reached over to grab the bottle before it slipped from his hand.

"If Sparrow Yenri was not born, Talking Mountain would have adopted you, Lonely Cricket," Small Deer said. "He wanted a son of whom he could be proud. Though it is a sad story, Talking Mountain never accepted Shadow Fox, never called him his son. Once, I heard him say that the boy's name should not be Shadow Fox at all but Hiding Rabbit because he was so frightened by everything. But when it was known that his woman would soon have another child and when Dreaming Woman said it was sure to be a son, then Tall Grass told Dreaming Woman to pick another home, one that did not have a son, for soon Talking Mountain would have a son of his own who would be worthy."

"So, she gave me to Lame Bear?"

"Yes," answered Mountain Spring; "she gave you to Lame Bear. He was to be your father, and we were all to be your brothers."

"You have been good brothers," Lonely Cricket responded. "Even Shadow Fox, although he has hated me. I cannot blame him for his anger." Thinking of the pain he now suffered because Lame Bear had rejected him and would not speak with him and thinking of the White father who had never held him, the young man added, "He is right. What son does not want his father's love? What son wants his father to choose another? Why did my father not want me?"

"There is more to the story." Shadow Fox had jolted out of his drunken slumber. "Falling Cloud told me how the story ends."

"What would a Heyoka know of such things?" Small Deer tried to interrupt.

Shadow Fox talked over the interruption. "Do you want to know what happened to Comes From the Water?"

"Yes," Lonely Cricket answered. "What happened to him?"

ΩΩΩΩΩ

Even though the people trusted him, even though Buffalo Warrior called him son, Comes From the Water was not happy living among the People. Even though many of the young women of the tribe wished him to take them into his lodge, he wanted none of them. He wanted to find his own people. He wanted to know the nature of his own heart.

One night, he gathered together his clothes, his blanket, his buffalo sleeping mat, his bow and arrows, his knife and eating bowl. Everything that was his he gathered. Then, when Winter Woman was sleeping, and when Buffalo Warrior was sleeping, and when all the members of the village were sleeping, Comes From the Water left the People and went in search of his own, his real family.

ΩΩΩΩΩ

That is what Falling Cloud told me. That is the rest of the story. With a great snore, Shadow Fox once again disappeared into the fog of drink and sleep.

Chapter 51 ~ Sorrows and Promises

ΩΩΩΩΩ

When Crying Birch entered this world Ma-Ona blessed her eyes with darkness that she might better see the things of the spirit. At night, when the people slept, Crying Birch would fly to an owl's perch high in the sycamore. There she could hear the whisperings of the world, the cries of dreams, and the messages sent to mankind. It was to Crying Birch and to no other that the secrets of life and death were first revealed.

"Stay in your perch and watch," Ma-Ona instructed. "There you will learn to see what others cannot."

On the first night, Crying Birch flew to her place in the sycamore and waited and watched. When the night was darkest, she saw a being pass beneath her perch. "Whoo are you?" Crying Birch demanded. "I am the hope of wañgrá," the being replied. "And what does the hope of man seek in the night?"

"I seek the praise of my father that I have led the life of a true warrior," the being replied. "May your search be successful," Crying Birch answered as the being continued down the path.

"Ah," she thought, "a son needs the praise of his father. That is worth knowing."

On the second night, Crying Birch again flew to her place in the sycamore and waited and watched. When the night was darkest, she saw a being pass beneath her perch. "Whoo are you?" Crying Birch demanded. "I am the dream of hinugijá," the being replied.

"And what does the dream of woman seek in the night?"

"I seek the love of my children that they may follow in the path I have shown them," the being replied.

"May your search be successful," Crying Birch answered as the being continued down the path.

"Ah," she thought, "a mother needs the love of her children. That is worth knowing."

On the third night, Crying Birch once more flew to her place in the sycamore and waited and watched. When the night was darkest, she saw a being pass beneath her perch. "Whoo are you?" Crying Birch demanded.

"I am the navushieip of mankind," the being replied.

"And what does the soul of mankind seek in the night?"

"I seek the way from the surface of the great tortoise to a higher place of existence. I seek the rainbow bridge of passing for I fear being trapped in this world."

"May you find a guide to lead you," Crying Birch answered as the being continued down the path.

"Ah," she thought, "the spirit of mankind fears being trapped in this world. Such fear is a terrible thing. That is worth knowing."

On the fourth night, Crying Birch flew yet another time to her place in the sycamore and waited and watched. When the night was darkest, she saw a being pass beneath her perch. "Whoo are you?" Crying Birch demanded.

"I am an heyoka searching for souls that are lost in this forest," the being replied.

"And why does the clown seek the souls of the People in the middle of the night?"

"I seek to lead them to the rainbow bridge that they might pass from this world of illusions and find peace in next world."

"Have you been sent by the Great Creator to show us the way?" Crying Birch asked as the heyoka walked backwards down the path.

"Yes, for once I, too, lived in this world," the clown replied. "Then, when I had had enough of its foolishness, I crossed the bridge into a better place. But, Ma-Ona told me that I must return to lead others to that place. And, so, I am here once more."

"Ah," she thought, "there is hope in the foolishness of the heyoka. That is worth knowing."

"Though you travel up the worlds of existence until you reach this the uppermost level of the great tortoise," the heyoka continued, "you must realize that you will someday leave this earth on which you dwell and travel to another world. When that day comes, you may bring nothing of this worldly existence with you. If you try to bring so much as one piece of wampum or even an eagle's feather, it will weigh you down and you will be trapped in this world forever. You will be a ghost left to haunt the people of your village, moaning in the night and praying for them to free you, but they will never be able to do so. Therefore, do not hold too tightly to the things you possess but, rather, ready yourself to pass over the bridge between this world and the next."

"Whoo passes?" Crying Birch asked. "Whoo passes from this world into the next?"

"All people of pure soul pass. When the rainbow is in the sky, the souls of the pure walk across it into the new world."

"What about the White Man? He steals our land and kills our game; does he too cross the rainbow bridge?"

"Those who are without selfishness and greed, no matter what tribe no matter what skin, are allowed to pass."

"But, but whoo keeps the White Man and the Red from fighting in this next world?" Crying Birch asked.

"One day a prophet will come, and he will tell the people of the ceremonies to be performed in this world and the next. When the people listen to his sacred words, they will know what they must do," The clown answered her, and Crying Birch knew that it was Ma-Ona himself who stood beneath her tree.

"If the people do as they are told, then there will be peace in that new world. Everyone will have enough, and nobody will want to take from his neighbor."

"That sounds like a wonderful place," Crying Birch said. "When may I go there?"

"No person may know the time of their passing, but for some they will know at the last moment and they will rejoice. They will dance and sing." And Ma-Ona no longer appeared as a clown but took the form of a great warrior.

"How will they know such a thing?" Crying Birch asked the Great Spirit.

"They will know this because they have already died once and have returned," Ma-Ona said. "They do not know this in their lifetimes, but at the moment of dying and once more leaving this world, they remember the happiness of the world to which their spirits will return, and they are filled with joy."

"Whoo are they who are sent back to this world?" Crying Beech asked.

"They are people of pure soul who have known love instead of hate, friendship instead of anger, and hope instead of fear. They are the heyoka for they know that mankind must laugh at this world in order to know the next."

"But why have they been sent back?" Crying Beech asked.

"To teach the People."

"But what is the lesson they are to teach?"

Ma-Ona laughed at the question. "That is for them to learn," the Great Creator answered.

"Whoo ..." Crying Woman began to ask her next question, but the Great Spirit had gone. Still she perches in that tree and calls her question to the night, "Whoo? Whoo? Whoo?"

ΩΩΩΩΩ

"What does this story mean?" Lonely Cricket asked. "What am I supposed to do?"

"I do not know," Dreaming Woman answered.

They sat inside the midwife's cabin. She sat on a buffalo robe that had been dyed with many colors and designs. The young man sat on a deer hide that had been rubbed bare by the many people who had come to seek Dreaming Woman's wisdom.

"You asked me what you must do. You asked me which father you must follow. You asked me who you truly are. These are not questions that I can answer. I only know that Ma-Ona has a plan for you, or you would not have been given a second life."

Lonely Cricket blinked twice and stared at the woman. "What do you mean a second life?"

"When I was called to the home of the Indian Agent Jones, your mother no longer breathed and your breath had also stopped. My herbs and chants could not revive the woman Josey, but Mother Atina answered my prayer and brought you back to this world. You are one of those of whom Crying Woman was told. It is you who must teach me."

"But what of my father?"

"That, too, I cannot tell you."

"And what am I to do?" He cocked his head to one side to better hear her answer.

"You must do what your heart tells you," Dreaming Woman answered. She took water from the pot that she had placed in the middle of her cooking fire and made a tea from roots and herbs. Handing the cup to Lonely Cricket, she added, "Drink this and sleep. When you wake, you will be ready for your journey."

By the time that Lonely Cricket woke, the sun had left the sky to the fingernail moon and her sister stars. He rose from the deer skin where he had lain. "I dreamed of a place I have not yet seen. My friend Plenty Horses was there, and he showed me a trail. He did not accompany me. 'It is not a place that I may go,' he said to me. I followed the trail and then I awoke."

"And what does this dream tell you?" asked Dreaming Woman who still sat on the buffalo robe.

"I know that the White Man who is my father travelled to the land of the Lakota. That is the tribe of my friend. Am I to go there to seek the White Man?"

"Dreaming Woman did not answer the question. Instead she took a small deerskin pouch from where it lay near to her. The pouch was attached to a thong so it could be worn around the neck. "You will want to take this with you."

"What is it?" The young man started to open the pouch, but it was sewn shut.

"It is not for opening." The medicine woman leaned forward and slipped the thong around Lonely Cricket's neck. "When you were born, the White Woman said I should throw away the afterbirth, but I saved your cord in this pouch so it could be buried in the garden of your home to mark the place you belong. However, when I brought you to Yquili Sparrow she would not allow me to bury it near her cabin.

"'Lame Bear wishes to have a son,' she said to me. 'I will raise him as my own, but this boy will never take the place of Gentle Hawk in my heart.' So, I have kept this pouch for you. You must wear it. You must take it with you. When you find the place in which you are meant to die, there it will be buried to assure that Ma-Ona will know that it is truly you."

Chapter 52 ~ Boys

The clown smiled at the boy sitting opposite him. "You know, Many Fish, it isn't often that a boy your age comes to me seeking understanding."

"My father says that often it is the heyoka who is wisest, Falling Cloud."

"Does Lame Bear know that you have come to see me?"

The boy shook his head. "I just want to understand why my brother Lonely Cricket is no longer ...." He picked up a twig and scratched at the dirt.

"No longer welcome in your father's lodge?"

The boy nodded agreement. "I know that I'm not supposed to talk about him, but I miss him. He was good to me; he taught me the ways of the animals." The man spread his hands before him. "Then I shall tell you the story." And, he continued.

ΩΩΩΩΩ

In the first times before the creatures of all creation had learned to fear and to fight, the birds who sing to us from the treetops and the snakes who glide silently on the ground were friends. This is the story of how that friendship ended.

"You are not yet ready to fly," the brightly colored cardinal said to his chicks. "Your mother and I must find insects and worms to feed you and bring them back to the nest where you wait in comfort." His loud, clear whistle filled the air as he used his red wings to gently push the three hatchlings back from the edge of the twig and grass nest and into the safety of its hollowed-cup interior.

"That isn't fair," the youngest of the three hatchlings declared. "I'm brave and strong and I should be free to explore the world."

"If you were free to explore the world," his fawn-colored mother replied, "you would be eaten before you could discover the bottom of this oak tree." She laughed in a "cheer-cheer-cheer-what" voice and her mate added his "purdy-purdy-wait."

His parents' laughter made the young cardinal all the more determined to leave the nest and find his way in the world. "I will show them," he said to his two sisters, who cheeped their disapproval. "Who will bring you food?" one asked.

"Who will cover you with their feathers when the night becomes cold?" asked the other.

"Or when it rains?" the first one chirped.

"I will feed myself. I will build my own nest. I am not a hatchling. I am not a chick. I am not a fledgling. I am a cardinal. I am a bird and ready to fly."

With that the young bird hopped to the side of the nest and leapt off into the air. He beat his wings as he had seen his parents do, but they were still covered with down and a few scrawny feathers, hardly enough to catch the air. Downward he plummeted. As he fell, the youngster tried ever harder to beat his wings, to fight against the pull of the earth, to save himself. All to no avail.

"Help, help," he cried out. "Father, you were right. Mother, I need you."

Hearing their brother's cries, the two other chicks hopped to the edge of their nest and looked down helplessly as their brother twisted, turned, and bounced through the leaves and branches below.

"This is surely the end of me," the young cardinal thought. "I wish I were back in our comfortable nest. He closed his eyes so that he could not see the ground rushing towards him. "I wish—" His thought was interrupted when something stopped his fall.

Slowly and filled with terror, the youngster opened his eyes to find himself held by a snake. "So, you thought that you would learn to fly," the snake hissed at the young bird.

"Yes, Snake, but I have learned that my parents were right, that I am too young. Will you help me to climb the tree and return to the safety of our nest.

The snake held the young cardinal and started to climb the tree. "This is hard work," the snake thought. "Is it worth the effort to help this foolish young bird?"

Still, he continued to climb. Stopping for a rest, Snake looked down and realized that he had not climbed very far. He looked up and saw that the cardinals' cup-shaped nest was still a long way to go. "I am getting tired," the snake said to himself. "Worse, I am getting very hungry." Perhaps Snake should not have thought it, but hungry as he was, Snake could not help wondering. "I wonder what this bird would taste like? Perhaps I should see." He flicked out his tongue and licked the young bird. "Oh, my, he is delicious. So delicate and sweet."

Just then, the young bird spoke. "Will we get back to my parents' nest in time for lunch? I am getting very hungry. Maybe you can teach me how to fly."

"Teach you how to fly," the snake replied. "If I could fly do you think I would be slithering up this tree. I cannot teach you how to fly, but I will teach you how to slither within a snake." With that, the snake popped the chick into his mouth.

"Help, help," the young cardinal cried. "This snake has eaten me."

Above them, the two other chicks heard their brother and were calling for their parents. "Come rescue our brother," they cried. "Come rescue our brother."

Mother and father cardinal heard their chicks' call and flew as swiftly as they could back to their family nest. Seeing the situation, they quickly flew down and pecked at the snake. Over and over they attacked hoping to cause him to open his mouth so that their son could escape.

The snake, feeling much affronted for had he not tried to rescue the young bird and return him to their nest, fought back lunging at one and then the other of the birds. "Your baby made a good appetizer," he hissed, "but I am still hungry, and a full-grown dinner would be delicious."

His threats did not deter the parents, for they truly loved their son and wanted to rescue him. But, their efforts were to no avail. Finally, they gave up and flew back to the nest where their other chicks waited. "Why have you not rescued our brother?" one of the other chicks asked. "It was more than we could do," the mother explained.

"Never again can there be peace between the birds of the trees and the snakes of the ground," added the father. "Once the world has taken a child," the father said, "there is nothing to do but suffer the loss and to curse the evil in the world that has made it happen. Now, we curse the snake and you know to not leap too quickly into the world. In that way, your brother's loss will help you to be better cardinals."

ΩΩΩΩΩ

"That," continued Falling Cloud is how the birds and the snakes stopped being friends. Now, it is best that you go back to the lodge of Lame Bear and listen to his words. It is a foolish bird indeed that does not listen to his father's counsel."

***

On the way back to his parents' cabin, Many Fish decided to stop by the stream to drink and to refresh himself with the cold, splashing water. The youngster sat with his back against an ash and watched the fish and frogs playing in the stream. "I know that Falling Cloud is right, but still I wish I could talk with Lonely Cricket. Even more, I wish I could again be with Happy Turtle. Once I had a brother and a sister. Now, I only have the memory of a brother who died before I was born and the memories that my parents forbid me of the brother and sister whom I knew."

Many Fish sat and thought. He did not hear the barefooted White boy who came up beside him. Without Lonely Cricket to motivate him, the boy had become bored with cutting grass. After a lunch of two boiled eggs and a piece of bread, he had wandered off. Meandering through the countryside, he saw the copses of trees that ran close to the water and went to investigate. No bored and lonely boy could withstand the attraction of such a stream. Skirmer was fascinated by the darting fish and the kicking frogs. He followed the run of the water stopping occasionally to pick up a stone, throw it with a splash into the stream, and watch the small creatures dart away from the ripples. Suddenly, as if from nowhere, there was the Indian boy, only slightly older, the son of the man who lived next door to them but who would not speak to his pappa.

Many times, Skirmer had wished they might play together. Sometimes, he had watched the other boy doing chores. Sometimes, they would be doing the same tasks. Skirmer was tempted to call out, to say, "Hey, do you like vatering those plants?" or "Does your cow give good milk?" Often, he wondered if the other boy spoke English. "If he does, would he answer me?" He wanted to ask Lonely Cricket about the other boy, but he knew that the topic was förbjuden. Stooping, Skirmer carefully chose a small rock. Then he stood and arced it into the water to get the other boy's attention.

Startled by the splash, Many Fish jumped to his feet and looked around.

"Hallå! I'm Skirmer." The youngster held his hand to his chest as he repeated, "My name is Skirmer."

Many Fish stared at the skinny, blonde headed youngster. He, too, had stolen forbidden looks from his father's allotment to the farm next door. He, too, had thought that they might someday play together. However, now faced with the son of the White Man, the Ho-Chunk boy did not know what to say or do.

Skirmer moved closer. He stopped, bent over, and picked up two more stones, and then again advanced. He took one stone in each hand. Holding one out to Many Fish, he tossed the other high so that it splashed into the stream. Both boys turned their attention to the splash and to the darting creatures. "Here, you throw one," Skirmer said. Many Fish took the stone that he was offered and threw it directly at a large frog that was sunning himself on a mossy rock. The frog leapt into the water just as the stone cracked against the larger rock. "You could have hurt the groda?" Skirmer remonstrated.

"Frog good eat," Many Fish replied.

"Oh, you speak English?"

"Many Fish speak English not good. Not like talk White Man talk."

"I'm Skirmer," Skirmer said once more, again touching his chest.

"What mean Skirmber?"

"No, Skirmer. My name is Skirmer." The boy stomped his foot as he hit his breast once more.

"What name Skirmer? It not White man name."

"I'm Svedish."

"I thought you White Man."

"You live next door to us," Skirmer commented. "I see you help father," Many Fish said.

"I'm called Skirmer."

Once more the boy touched his breast. "I am Many Fish," came the response.

"Oh." Skirmer stooped down and picked up two more stones. Handing one to Many Fish, he threw the other as far as he could. Many Fish's throw was much harder.

"You throw good." It was the Indian boy's turn to find two rocks. He aimed at a tree and threw his stone. Bark fragmented into the air at the impact. Skirmer's stone also hit the tree but not with enough force to chip the bark.

After a few more throws, the boys turned their attention back to the stream. Skirmer found a leaf which he allowed to float away. Soon, they were working together to build a small raft of twigs and leaves.

As the raft floated downstream, Many Fish said, "Time go home." Without a backwards glance, he strode away from the stream.

"It vas good to play med you."

There was no reply. As Skirmer traced his path back up the stream, her heard a voice, "Hey, you, White boy. Many Fish not enemy. Not friend, but not enemy. Only want White Man not steal our life."

The youngster turned back to reply, but when he looked, Many Fish had disappeared into the copse of trees. "I'm not your enemy either," Skirmer called out to the leaves that stirred in the late afternoon breeze.

Chapter 53 ~ The Leaving

"Skadedjur, vhat is the matter. *Varför gråter du*?" Ebba Anderson squatted down and caressed her son's hair. She used a corner of her blue gingham handkerchief to dry away his tears and then wetting another corner of the cloth with her spit, she scrubbed at the dirt streaks that remained. Her efforts forced his head back against the plain boards that sided the back of the cabin.

"You get so dirty here," Ebba mumbled as Skirmer squirmed away from her ministrations. "Hold still, min lilla. Hold still so I can clean you."

Once she had finished his improvised grooming, Ebba took her son by both shoulders and again asked, "Vhy do cry?"

"I don't vant them leave," the boy responded. At his own words, he buried his face against his mother's breast and resumed sobbing.

"Who is leaving? Nobody leaves."

"I heard them. I heard them in the barn ven I go to milk cow. They vas in loft and I heard them talk. Lonely Cricket was yelling med hög röst. I hear Sapphira cry. I not vant to listen so I run avay. Vill Pappa be angry that I not finish milking cow? I not vant Pappa be angry at me, but I not vant listen to Lonely Cricket be angry and Sapphira cry. I not vant they leave."

"Sometimes people med loud voice and not angry." Ebba stood and tugged on her son's arm. "You know some your pappa and I, ve yell but ve not be angry."

Resisting his mother's tug, the boy pulled his hand free and settled himself back against the cabin wall. "No, not that kind yell. Not yell like make baby. Not yell like that."

Ebba blushed. Reached down and again took his hand. "Sometimes, Skadedjur, you talk silly stuff."

"Not silly. I don't vant them leave."

"They not going anyvhere. This their home, too, now. They part of family."

"Lonely Cricket said he had to go, has to find his pappa."

"His pappa live next door." Ebba pointed in the direction of Lame Bear's allotment. "Not that pappa, his real pappa. Pappa vhat live in Dakotas. Sapphira said he was being fool. She said if they go, they should go back to Indiana."

"You know it is not good that you listen to people through door." She yanked the boy to his feet. Clumps of earth and bits of straw dropped from the seat of his overalls as he stood.

"There is no door in barn, Momma. I not try to hear; they talk med hög röst. So hög I get scared. I run avay, and cow not milked." He looked up at Ebba and she could see the worry in his face.

"You go back. Finish chores. I talk med Lonely Cricket and I talk med Sapphira. Do not vorry so. Let your pappa and me do the vorry for family." She smiled and the boy smiled back. To herself, Ebba wondered, "Vhat is going to happen now. This life in Nebraska not so simple as Lars vast think."

***

"How do I know how to be a man if I don't find him?"

Sapphira reached over with her left hand and touched the shaft of Lonely Cricket's semi-erect penis. "I didn't know you had questions about being a man."

At her touch, the young man stirred and hardened.

Sapphira turned sideways, raised her head from the pillow on which it rested, bent sideways, and kissed the young man's foreskin. "For me there is no question."

"Man not about make love." Lonely Cricket took Sapphira's left hand in his right and gently conveyed it to his mouth so that he could suck on her fingers. "Make love not take brave. Not take strength. Not take what supposed to do. It happen between man and woman. It happen between us. It happen with Dinah."

At the mention of Dinah, Sapphira groaned slightly and pulled her hand away.

"Make love happen. Cannot make not happen," Lonely Cricket said. "Dinah woman. I man."

"Yes, I understand. You had sex, but did you love her?"

"What difference?"

"We've talked about this before. The difference is here." She covered her breast with her hand. "Love is here. Sex is … well, sex is here." She moved her hand to cover her genitals. "We've had this talk many times. Sex does not make a man, but a man, a true man, makes love."

Having gently teased Sapphira's right nipple with his tongue, Lonely Cricket whispered, "I love we have sex." With those words he reached his fingers towards her vagina and gently massaged her.

"I love we have sex, too," Sapphira responded, their argument for the moment forgotten.

Soon they were again using loud voices, but this time filled with pleasure.

"Oh god, oh yes, oh yes," Sapphira cried out. Lonely Cricket's words were in Ho-Chunk. "Woman make man good. Man find much pleasure." He had heard Lame Bear say these same words. Even as they passed his lips, he wondered what words Theodore Pirrip had shouted when he had been conceived. "Who father?" The question paused his humped movements, but only for a moment, only for a slight disturbance in their rhythm.

When their coitus was finished, when they lay side-by-side gazing up at the beams and boards of the barn's roof, Sapphira spoke. "I know that you will go."

"Yes, must find father."

"Lame Bear is not father enough?"

"Not know. If Lame Bear welcome back, then maybe it would ... he not want me be son. Talking Mountain not want Shadow Fox. Lame Bear not want me. Send away. Tell White Man take. Say learn be White Man. Not welcome back. No, he not father. Not father now. Once ..." Dinah saw the tears in the corner of her lover's eyes, but she said nothing of them only, "If you must go, I will wait. I will wait here for you. I will wait here as long as Ebba and Lars will allow."

***

The passing breeze whipped the dust of the road into small, dancing frenzies. Crops wilted listlessly in the unrelenting summer's heat. A few puffs of clouds dotted the sky but promised nothing. There was no buoyancy to their steps as Lonely Cricket, Sapphira. Skirmer, and Ebba, Hilda in her arms, made their way to the edge of the Anderson homestead.

"Lars says you must promise to come back," Ebba said as she handed the toddler to Sapphira and hugged the lanky young man. "He says you and Sapphira always velcome here. That this is your home, too." She held Lonely Cricket's shoulders as she gently pushed him away. "You know that this is your home?"

"I know and thank you and Lars." Lonely Cricket pressed his right hand to hers. "You are good friends. You are good family." Pulling back, he turned to Sapphira and repeated the promise he had made many times to her in the past days. "I will come back. We will be together soon. I swear to you, I will come back."

They clutched one another in a tight embrace. "I know you will," Sapphira whispered. "And, you know that I love you."

"Yes, I know Sapphira Cook has always loved me." He took a gulp of breath before adding, "and I have always loved her."

"Can I come with you?" Skirmer asked.

"Only as far as that bush," Ebba instructed. She pointed towards a chokecherry that stood a hundred yards or so along the road. The bush's vermillion fruits not yet quite dark enough for picking.

"Only to bush," Lonely Cricket echoed. "You walk with me that far."

Lonely Cricket heaved his deerskin haversack over his shoulder and took the boy's left hand in his right. Skirmer squirmed his hand free and instead held to Lonely Cricket's pocket.

"I vill miss you so much," Skirmer said as they moved forward. "I will miss you as well. I know your mother says you are a skadedjur, but you are no pest. Skirmer, you are a hard worker and a good boy. Your parents are proud of you, and Sapphira and I are proud to have you as friend."

The boy swelled with pride. Suddenly, Lonely Cricket stopped walking. He turned towards his young companion and bent down so they were eye-to-eye. "Will you do something for me, Skirmer?"

"Of course. Vhat do you vant me to do?"

"Take care of her until I come back. Sapphira is all by herself and she will need you to help her."

"I vill help and I vill study hard vhen she teach me English and to read."

"I know you will." The young man put his hand on the boy's shoulder, and they continued down the road. Neither of them noticed the other youngster who watched them. Hidden in the tall grass, Many Fish watched Lonely Cricket and the White Boy walking, and he felt the missing of his brother. Tears came to his eyes as the two walked past the place where he hid.

When they reached the chokecherry, Lonely Cricket stopped and offered Skirmer his hand. The boy took it and then threw himself against the man. "I will miss you, too," Lonely Cricket said as he gently rubbed the boy's back. Then, releasing himself from Skirmer's arms, he continued towards Pierce and to the adventure that lay ahead. Skirmer stood for a few minutes watching his friend and hero receding in the distance. Finally, knowing that Lonely Cricket would not turn back, the boy turned and walked slowly, head down, towards the two women who waited for him.

As Skirmer passed his hiding place, Many Fish whispered so softly that the younger boy did not hear, "I am not friend, but I am not enemy." He wished that Lonely Cricket could hear his words.

"Have you told him?" Ebba asked Sapphira as they watched Skirmer make his lonely way back towards them.

"Told whom?"

"Have you told Lonely Cricket that you carry his child?"

"How did you—"

The older woman chuckled. "We vomen know things that men do not."

"No. I didn't."

"It will be time enough when he returns."

Part Five ~ Ending and Continuings

Chapter 54 ~ Horse

"Great Horse works hard; that is why we must take good care of him," Lame Bear said as he rubbed the animal's mottled gray withers with a piece of burlap.

"I help care for Great Horse," Lonely Cricket replied. His voice squeaky with childish excitement as he rubbed the giant gelding's sweaty hindquarter. There was little he loved more than helping his father care for the animals, and of all the animals, Great Horse was his favorite.

The only thing the boy enjoyed even more than helping to rub Great Horse down was riding on the giant beast. Precariously perched on that broad, gray back, his legs barely able to bend over the enormous curves of the animal's barrel, his hand twined in the horse's mane, Lonely Cricket's face would light with delight as he urged the beast forward with chortles and tiny kicks. All the while, Lame Bear, one protective hand resting on his son's leg and the other holding the animal's rope bridle, would smile with paternal pleasure.

"Your boy's right good with animals," the Indian's White neighbor and friend Harry Cook observed more than once.

"Good with horse," Lame Bear replied. "Horse love boy and boy love horse."

"Sure takes natural to it."

"Horse is the best animal," Lonely Cricket proclaimed as he reached under Great Horse to rub his belly.

Great Horse whickered with pleasure at the soft scratch of the burlap in the boy's hand. "Where did horse come from, Ate?" the youngster asked his father.

"After our work is finished, I will tell you the story of horse," Lame Bear answered. Later, sitting with their backs to the barn and watching the sun disappear in the melon orange horizon, Lame Bear told his son the story of the first horse.

ΩΩΩΩΩ

When first man came to the top of the great tortoise, he was surprised at how great the world was. It was a journey of many days to go from one village to another, from one hunting ground to another.

One day, Walking Woman, who made the very best rabbit skin moccasins among the people, realized that the weather was changing. The days were getting shorter and the sky was getting colder. At night, when she huddled in her wickiup with her children and her husband, Walking Woman worried that soon they would all freeze. "I must find warm robes so that we can sleep in these cold nights," she thought. "We must learn how to sleep in the cold as does Brother Bear. For that we need thicker fur to cover us. Sister Rabbit is too small. I must take my moccasins and trade them for such sleeping robes."

When Walking Woman decided to trade the rabbit moccasins she had made for buffalo robes to keep her family warm, she filled a pack with moccasins and took pemmican made from the deer and berries gathered from the bushes near her village, and she walked in the direction of the setting sun. For many days, Walking Woman travelled towards the setting sun. She would start walking when Wira spread his first light into the sky and only lay down when He had returned to his wigwam leaving Huhawira to light the night. She walked and walked.

Still, Walking Woman did not find another village with which she could trade her rabbit skin moccasins for sleeping robes. So, she walked on and on.

When Walking Woman had run out of pemmican and her feet had grown very weary, she decided to pray to Ma-Ona and to ask him to help her.

That night, when the sun no longer lit her way, Walking Woman struck a small fire for warmth and companionship, and she sat beside that blaze still shivering from the cold and from hunger, and she spoke aloud to Kabibona'ka, "Kabibona'ka, bringer of great winter, your season is soon upon me. My children lie huddled in my wickiup and I have journeyed far from them to find robes to protect them from your cold. I have brought all that I have to trade, these moccasins. Now, I beg you to take them and give me the robes I need so I can take care of my children. I beg you to give me the warm robes of the buffalo for my children for I am too tired to go farther, and I have nothing left to eat."

Kabibona'ka heard Walking Woman's entreaty. When she had fallen into the world of the dream, Kabibona'ka sent the Trickster to her in the form of a man.

"I will take your moccasins for my people," the Trickster said, "and I will give you these great robes in their place." With those words, a great pile of buffalo hides stood before the woman, enough for her children and for her entire village.

In the morning, when Walking Woman awoke, she saw that her dream had been real, for next to what remained of her campfire was the great pile of hides and the moccasins which she had brought to trade were gone—all except one pair which the Trickster had left behind.

Walking Woman knew that Kabibona'ka had listened to her words and had answered her entreaties. With great excitement, she ran to the pile of buffalo hides and tried to pick them up. They were too heavy for her to lift. She realized that although Kabibona'ka had sent the Trickster to answer her prayers, her problem was not solved. Walking Woman gathered much wood and made a great fire. She readied herself to plunge into those flames and she spoke to Gitchi Manitou saying, "Creator of all. First among the gods of this world, I beg you to take my life as a sacrifice that these buffalo robes may be brought to my children to keep them from the cold of winter."

With those words, Walking Woman threw herself into the flames. But the fire did not consume her. Even as she leapt into the blaze, Gitchi Manitou transformed her into a great horse.

Reaching down from his perch among the clouds, the great creator picked up the pile of buffalo hides as easily as you could pick up a pile of feathers and placed it atop that horse. He tied the hides in place as a fetish bundle might be tied and made sure that the load was even so that Walking Woman, who was now a horse, would not stumble under the weight. Finally, he placed that last pair of shoes on top of the load so that her people would know Walking Woman when she returned.

So it was, that Gitchi Manitou gave us the first horse.

ΩΩΩΩΩ

"Cortés and them other Spaniards was something." The barrel-chested teacher thumped his stick on the desk to emphasize his words. "They took over right fast. Thing is them Indians down in Mexico didn't have no gun powder, no big ships or cannon, nor metal armor. No wonder they was scared of them conquistadors. But you know what really got them?" He paused and waited for one of his pupils to raise a hand.

The students sat rigidly in their wooden bench seats—trying to not squirm against the unfamiliar scratchiness of their uniforms. Metal-nibbed pens held at the ready. Some of the older pupils, already lanky adolescents, their knees crammed under the metal writing desks fixed to the floor in front of them, shared furtive glances. But no hands were raised in response. The youngsters in Amos O'Brian's American history class knew better than to hazard opinions.

"Them Spaniards had themselves horses." The teacher thumped his stick again.

At the mention of horses, Lonely Cricket did something O'Brian's students seldom did; he looked directly at the teacher, cocking his head to one side so he could better hear.

"Now, none of them Indians had ever seen a horse," Amos O'Brian continued, " 'cause these was the first ones ever here in America and that Cortés, he had them. Them soldiers sitting on top of them horses scared the bejesus out of those natives. They started bowing down and carrying on like the Spaniards were gods or something."

O'Brian paused for a moment and rubbed his stubbled chin. "Anyways, them Indians was fighting with some other Redskins they called Aztecs and they wanted Cortés and his horses to help them take those Aztec fellas down. Which he does. Soon as you know it, Cortés is running Mexico. And you see, it was all because of them horses."

O'Brian chuckled and continued, "See, boys and gals, it's all in what you know. Now, them Indians that met Cortés, they didn't know much. If they had, well maybe they'd have fought him off. Maybe they'd have kilt them horses like them ancient Greeks did, so the Trojans won that war. See what I mean?"

Some of the students nodded their heads as if in agreement. They had learned that was what their history teacher expected, especially when it came to his basic message: the Europeans were much smarter than their own ancestors. That was why they had to learn the White Man's ways.

Another thing the young Indians knew was that to disagree with Mr. O'Brian was to guarantee a thrashing. "It's the only way to get any knowing into them dumb heads," the stores-keeper and teacher had argued when Robert Langdon suggested that beating the students interfered with their learning.

"Don't seems to me it helps a whit," Langdon had replied.

"Well, you try teaching them history or even how to count what we got in the storeroom. Course the only thing they count is what they steal. I fought them Paiutes in Neevada with Joe Stewart. Mustered out at Churchill. Worked with them Indians and learned that weren't no way you teach 'em or you trust 'em. You do and you'll end up beating them or banging your head on one of them posts that holds the roof up." Wiping spittle from his lips, O'Brian continued, "Might as well since they're dumb as posts anyways."

"If you feel that way, what the hell are you doing here?" Langdon asked.

"Hell, it ain't a bad job. Easy work. Room and found and money in my pocket, to say nothing of what I can pick up on the side. I sure ain't here to save the world, Langdon. Just want to get by."

"By teaching history?"

"Nah. I was hired to do the stores. The teaching, hell, the Major needed somebody, and I figured a bit extra in my packet wouldn't hurt."

"What do you know about history anyway … or managing stores."

"I was an assistant quartermaster, so don't give me no grief about that. As for the history, I've read a book or two. Remember some from school. Hell, it ain't like these bucks and squaws need to know much 'cept the White Man won."

"The Major's okay with that?"

"I don't recall him ever asking or commenting. Must figure I got the right bumps on my noggin."

"And he thinks these Indians are dumb as posts," Robert Langdon muttered to himself.

***

"Mr. Langdon, we speak to you?"

"Sure, John, what can I do for you fellas?" The man pulled up short and spread his legs slightly. Nodding his head in Lonely Cricket's direction, he added, "How you doing, Harry? You settling in?"

The boy didn't answer, so Langdon turned his attention back to the young Lakota. "What you need, John?" Plenty Horses pointed in the direction of the classroom building. "Teacher say horse brought by Span-yard people. That not true. Horse given to Indian from god."

"Well, boys, I can see how that would bother you. Thing is, I reckon everybody got their own way of lookin' at things. Me, I don't know how horses come to America, but I sure as hell am glad they did because I ain't big on walking." Guffawing at his own joke, it took a moment for Langdon to realize that the two young men didn't understand him. "It's this way," he tried again. "When Mr. O'Brian he asks you in class, why you tell him that the Spaniards brought horses. Then he won't beat on you and yell. Out of class, you just tell yourself whatever you want."

"Not have to believe?" Plenty Horses said. "Nope, just got to agree."

The two Indians nodded their heads. "

Besides, I don't think there's a horse alive that cares about history. All they care about is bein' fed, and rid, and treated right."

"Horse need good care," Lonely Cricket agreed.

"That's true, Harry. That sure is true.

"Hell, boys," the teacher added, "I'd bet a dollar there ain't a horse anywhere cares about history. Bet they don't know any more about it than Amos O'Brian and that ain't saying much." His rough laughter filled the space between them.

"I go barn," Harry said.

"Need repair wagon," Plenty Horses added.

"You run along, boys. If you got work to do, the Major won't want me gabbin' with you."

Chapter 55 ~ Across the Prairie

The young man pulled his coat tighter as much against loneliness as the bite of the northern wind and the spit of impending snow. His blood bay trudged through the brown short grass of the Dakota winter. Lameness in the horse's left flank meant Plenty Horses could not ask him to lope. Already he had ridden two days from his village near Spring Creek. It would be a ride of two more days before he could join his friends at Pine Ridge. He hoped that his horse could last the trip. Plenty Horses was sure that the journey would be worth the time and the bitter cold. He was on his way to the great dance, the dance that would summon the Messiah to come for his children. Soon, they would be lifted to the next level of the world, to a place where the hunting was plentiful and where no man would be forced to give up his spear or his coupstick. Had he not given his black-legged gray to Lonely Cricket, the journey would have been much faster.

Would Lonely Cricket join him at Pine Ridge? That wasn't clear. The young Ho-Chunk had come on a different quest. "My White father mines the yellow metal. I asked Ma-Ona to guide me to him. The Creator sent a dream to show me the way," Lonely Cricket had told him after they had exchanged corn pollen and smoked tobacco.

"What was your dream?" Plenty Horses had asked his school friend.

"In my dream I saw you dancing with many warriors and with many women. I saw horses. Many horses and they were all walking together. I saw great birds flying overhead and everybody looked up and they were happy. When the spirits send this dream, I knew you would help me find my White father so I can learn who I truly am."

"That a good dream," Plenty Horses had replied. "Black Elk has told us of such a dance. Soon the people will gather at Pine Ridge and we will call on the White Man's savior to come for us. He will take us to a better world."

"I cannot go to a better world until I understand my life in this one," Lonely Cricket replied.

"Then perhaps this man you seek is nearby. You can take my horse to search for him."

"I'm glad that I helped my young friend," Plenty Horses told himself as he urged the bay on, "I only hope that I am able to join Red Cloud in time to take part in the great dance." Bending forward, he caressed the horse's red neck. "It's all right, horse," he said aloud. "You are doing the best you can." The animal whickered in response, tried to break into an awkward, hitching trot, and then settled back into a walk.

"When we do the dance, the White Jesus will heal you, too," Plenty Horses assured the animal. "In this new land everyone will be healed."

***

"Now ain't that a joke?" The tall man in a dirt encrusted army coat and slouch-worn Stetson directed his question into the half empty saloon. "This here Injun's looking for TJ, for TJ Pirrip. I guess he must be the only Injun in the world wants getting near TJ."

"Boy, what you lookin' fer TJ on account of?" one of the men at the nearest table to the door where Lonely Cricket and the tall man stood.

"Need talk to him."

"Yeah. Now that ain't gonna happen less you're gonna tell him where some damn goldmine might be. Then he might listen afore he shoots ya. Course, he may just shoot ya anyway," the second man guffawed as he spoke.

"Where Theodore Pirrip? I go talk. He listen. I think he want hear."

"Well, if you're sure you want killin', you sure can go lookin' for him. But, TJ, he took off while back," another man commented.

"Where he go?"

Lonely Cricket moved to enter the saloon, but the tall man barred his way. "No Redskins allowed."

At the same time, one of the men at the table answered Lonely Cricket's question. "He's gone hunting Redskins." The comment brought a round of laughter from all the White Men who were paying attention.

"You want he should take your scalp, too?" another of the men asked. This man—short and dressed fancy—drummed his fingers as he spoke.

"Want find to talk."

"Yeah, well you do that," the fancy-dressed finger drummer continued. "You go find those Hunkpapa Injuns the Seventh Cavalry been hunting. That's where you'll find Old TJ. He give up mining and turned Army Scout. Said to me, 'Lordon, maybe I'll find a claim while I'm out there. Maybe I won't. At least I won't be sitting around that saloon wishing my life away. What the hell, the army pays more than nothing. So, when I get back, the first round's on me.'"

"Now we know you're lying, Lordon. TJ Pirrip ain't never gonna buy the first round for nobody," one of the others commented.

"Anyways, you got your answer," the man in the doorway said. "You find them troopers and them Sioux they're after, and you'll find yourself TJ."

Without saying another word, Lonely Cricket turned toward the black-legged gray horse.

"Hey, Redskin," the man in the doorway called after him.

Lonely Cricket turned back to the man.

"What you doing with that horse?"

"Belong friend, Plenty Horses. He give me to come look for TJ Pirrip."

"Looks to me like he prob'ly stole it or maybe it were you that stole it."

"No steal." Lonely Cricket warily backed away.

"Hey, fellas," the White Man called into the saloon; "I think we got us a horse thief here."

Lonely Cricket mounted with a quick leap, pulled on the bridle, and heeled the animal into a gallop.

Finally, when he felt safe, Lonely Cricket slowed the grey to a lope. "Long way go to Pine Ridge," he said aloud. "Maybe my father there with soldiers."

He remembered Plenty Horses's last words. "Even if you do find your father, what makes you think he'll want to know you?"

"That doesn't matter. When I look into his eyes, I will know the truth of who I am. Then I will know that I am a Ho-Chunk or that I am a White Man."

"Well, when you know, you come meet up with me at Pine Ridge. If you're a Ho-Chunk you'll dance with us and, who knows, maybe we'll go to a new world."

"If I'm not a Ho-Chunk, if I am a White Man?" Lonely Cricket asked.

"Well, at least we'll still be friends."

"Yes," Lonely Cricket said against the cold air, "we'll still be friends."

"You know the funny thing?" Plenty Horses commented. "When we went to the White Man's school, I don't think Major Pratt wanted us to become friends."

"You and me? Why not?"

"No, not just you and me. Any of us. He didn't want us Indians figuring out that we were … I don't think he wanted us knowing that we should matter, not to one another."

"Plenty Horses, we still be friends."

They had embraced one last time before Lonely Cricket rode off.

"See you in Pine Ridge," Plenty Horses had called after him.

***

Bent over the animal's mane, Lonely Cricket would have seemed more apparition than human to anyone foolish enough to also be out in the storm; but there were no others—not man nor beast. The blizzard whipped over them, over the young man wrapped in the White Man's overcoat and over that a gray blanket and over the gray horse that struggled against the wind and the wet snow that pulled at his hooves.

The cold seeped through the layers of cloth, crept into the young man's bones, and clutched at his mind.

"Why does it snow?" he had asked many years before. "Why does my mother cry when the snow comes?"

Lame Bear had told the boy to sit by the fire. Placing his arm around Lonely Cricket's shoulders, he told a story of the first snow.

ΩΩΩΩΩ

When the first people found their way to the top layer of the world, they found that it was a place rich with game and fish and with nuts and berries. They learned how to grow the three sisters and how to use the hides of animals to give them shelter. They learned the ways of the sun and how to follow its path in their dances, and how to sing songs that brought the harvest and brought rain when it was needed. Life was good for the people, but they were not content.

Each man wanted more than his neighbor. Each man wanted to catch the most fish. Each man wanted to kill the most game. Each man wanted to be the strongest and fastest in their games.

Each woman wanted more than her neighbor. Each woman wanted to find the most berries and fruits. Each woman wanted to have the finest cooking fire. Each woman wanted to be the most desirable and beautiful in the village. When a stranger came among them, all the men and women competed to impress him and to win his favor. Since all were equal in the sight of Ma-Ona, it seemed important to them that they should not be equal in the sight of other humans.

Thus, there was much bickering and arguing among the people. Men would exaggerate the number and size of the fish they had caught. They would kill more animals than they needed so they could brag of the waste that remained.

Women would cook more food than their families required. They found berries, barks, and creatures of the water with which they could color their clothes and their skins to appear more beautiful.

So great was the competition among The People that the children of one tipi were not allowed to play with the children from another. Parents told their children that the offspring of other parents would steal from them. The boys of each clan fought against boys from other clans and the children would not play together. The girls of each clan talked and washed clothes by the stream only with the members of their clan.

The creator grew weary of the bickering and arguing among the people. He grew angry that, instead of taking care of the land he had given them, they took more than they needed. He grew tired with their boasting and their posturing.

The creator called the Trickster to him. "Go among the humans and teach them humility," he instructed. "Teach the people that sharing is better than greed."

When the sun next rose from his sleeping mat, a stranger stood outside the circle of lodges of The People and called out, "People, bid me enter for I have brought you a great gift." Three times he said this as was the custom, and he stood outside the circle of the lodges as was also the custom, and he waited for a response.

One of The People called out to him and asked his name, his tribe, his clan, and his business.

The stranger responded, "I am Walker of Miles from among The Strong People. In my tribe we do not speak of clans, for they are sacred, but I am allowed to tell you that I am not of the sky, the land, or the water."

At those words, The People trembled in fear, for if he was not from the sky, the earth, or the water, he must be from a clan of the spirit world and the stranger surely brought death.

The stranger, seeing people tremble in fear, called out to them, "Do not be afraid. I have brought a precious gift to give you."

Immediately upon hearing these words, The People welcomed the stranger into their village. Each man among them wondered if they could get the gift for himself and pondered if it would make them stronger or better hunters. Each woman among them wondered if they could get the precious gift for herself and pondered if it would make her a better cook or more attractive. There was no end of the wishes of The People, each for their own greed.

"What is this gift you bring? "one of the men asked.

"Show us this precious thing, "one of the women demanded.

"Surely, you will feed a stranger and make him welcome before you demand what he has to give," the stranger replied.

After he had eaten, Walker of Miles asked, "Do you people not dance to celebrate when a guest comes among you?"

The men of the village were embarrassed that they had not thought of such a common courtesy. The truth was that they did not trust one another to share their music and their dances. However, what could they say to this bringer of a precious gift? They ran to their tipis to get their drums and their flutes. Soon, music filled the air. The people danced and forgot to envy one another. The small children watched and laughed with happiness. Mothers, seeing their children so happy, began to talk with one another. The silence of envy was broken by the sound of conversation.

As the light from the ceremonial fire dimmed to the glow from its coals, the stranger announced, "I grow tired. Soon I must sleep. But, first, I will teach you a magic dance of my people."

"Is this the gift you have brought us?" one of the men demanded. Immediately, they were all reminded of their greed. Each man eyed his fellow with distrust. Each woman stopped her words. Even the children, who were already quite sleepy, stopped their laughter.

"No, that you will receive in the morning. Tonight, I just want to show you this dance." Walker of Miles took one of the drums and began to beat a rhythm that was not known to The People. When some of the men took up that beat, he took a flute and began to play the melody of the song. Soon, other men were playing it as well. Then he returned that flute to its owner and began to dance.

A few of the men followed his lead. "Come, it is for everyone," Walker of Miles said. "Men, women, even children can do this dance."

It was strong music that brought good energy to the people. Soon, they were all dancing. Again, for the moment their greed and distrust were forgotten.

"I will sleep now. When I wake, I will reveal the gift," Walker of Miles announced. He took his pack into the tipi that the people had offered him. As he closed the flap of the tipi, which faced the direction in which the sun would rise, the stranger said, "I will see you in the morning. Then, when I see you, you will see the magic that this dance I have taught you can make."

Even though it was a warm night, Walker of Miles fastened the flap closed so the people knew that he would not want them coming to him in the night. When the people woke, the village was covered in snow. "What is this stuff we have never seen?" they asked one another.

"It must be the magic of the stranger's dance," the told themselves.

"Where is the stranger?" they wondered. They went to his tipi and the door flap was fastened just as it had been the night before.

"Walker of Miles," The People called out.

"Whooo," a large white owl responded from high in a spruce. When Walker of Miles did not reply, The People unlaced the thongs that held the flap of his tipi in place. When they entered the tipi, the stranger was not there. Spread on the ground of the tipi was the down of a snowy owl.

"Whooo, whooo," called the owl once more.

Then The People understood that Walker of Miles was not a man but the Trickster. "Why did you teach us that dance to bring this white cold?" one of the woman called up to the great bird.

With the soft whoosh of wings, the owl disappeared into the rising sun.

"Come back. Where is our gift?" another of the women yelled. Even as the woman spoke, the children began to play together in the snow. At first, some of the parents tried to pull the children apart. But the joy of playing in the new white powder enticed the children away from their parents' words.

As the laughter of the children filled the air, the adults, too, began to frolic in the snow. Soon everyone was making snowmen and throwing handfuls of soft, fluffy powder at one another. Some of the men tried to build a house of snow. Then the children joined with them, everyone running about and sharing their ideas.

There was much fun that day in the village. People sang happy songs and talked without worrying who was listening. They talked of how to fish and where to hunt and where the best berries were to be found.

When the sun rose higher in the sky, the snow began to melt. It was only then that The People realized that they were cold. "We need to make a good soup to warm us," one of the women suggested.

Some of the men gathered wood for a fire. Meanwhile the woman assembled the ingredients. They heaped snow into the pot so it would melt into their broth.

When The People gathered to share their soup, one of the men asked, "Why did Ma-Ona send the Trickster to us with this white snow?"

Another man asked, "Where is the gift that he promised us? What is so precious about this snow; it only lasts for a short time?"

"Perhaps Ma-Ona sent this snow to remind us that we are one people and that we should share our joy. Perhaps the owl's message is that greed and envy are not good. I think we must give to one another," one of the oldest women suggested.

"Perhaps it is to remind us how it is better to dance together than to hide our instruments," said another.

"Yes," said a third women, "this snow is a way to remind us that we are one people and that we must not become selfish or envious."

"But why did he make it so cold and wet?" asked one of the young men shivering on the edge of the group.

"To remind us that we must work together to make life's joys even when times are hard," answered the woman who had spoken first.

When she spoke, the snowy owl flew once more over the village and then disappeared in the brightness of the day.

After that, The People agreed snow was indeed a precious gift. Each winter, when the sun sleeps, Ma-Ona sends us snow once more to remind us of these things.

ΩΩΩΩΩ

"That's a good story, Father," Lonely Cricket said when Lame Bear had finished, "but, why does my mother cry when it snows?" "Enough stories, Lonely Cricket. We have work to do. The cow needs milking and all the animals need food. On days like this, they need extra. It's hard work keeping warm."

"Yes, Father," Lonely Cricket mumbled to himself. "It is hard work to keep warm."

With that thought, the young man slid from atop the black-legged gray horse and crumpled into a snow-covered mound on the prairie. The horse, too tired to go forward without the young man's prompting, stopped, turned his hindquarters to the wind, closed his eyes, and slipped into sleep.

Three Brulé Indians—trying to reach the nearby mission where they could escape the storm—might well have passed the fallen young man were it not for the larger pile of snow that had accumulated over the dead horse. Seeing the coat and pants Lonely Cricket wore, one of the two Brulé men said, "We should leave this White Man here."

"He is still alive, we cannot leave a human to die," the third Indian, a woman, responded. "The Great Spirit would not approve even if he is a White Man." With a grunt and a nod towards the woman, the third Indian tugged at Lonely Cricket to free him from the snow. Shaking what snow they could from the blanket in which the young man had wrapped himself, they rolled him onto it and pulled him towards the nearby mission.

"He couldn't have ridden another mile?" the second man asked.

"I hope we can drag him that far," the woman replied.

"If we do, he'll probably die anyway," the first of the men commented.

"If he does, at least Ma-Ona will not blame us for his death," the woman answered.

"And if we die trying to save him," the first man said, "will Ma-Ona blame us for our foolishness."

"His weight may hold us back, but our arguing about saving him will give us strength," the woman said. "Save your words if you would have strength," the second man said. In silence they trudged forward.

"Are you sure this is the right direction?" the first man asked. Just then, there was a quieting of the wind. The whirling snow slowed. They could see the mission walls looming dark gray against the unrelenting white of the landscape.

Chapter 56 ~ Endings

Through the haze of cold-induced sleep, Lonely Cricket strained to hear the murmuring voices. "Até." He muttered the word and again, "Father."

"Yes, my son," the black-robed man, sitting beside the cot on which Lonely Cricket lay, replied. Turning to the elderly Lakota woman stirring the large pot of soup set over the nearby fire, the priest whispered, "You hear, Hantaywee, he calls me father. The young man must have been baptized. Soon he will recover, and I can learn more."

"Yes, Father, I hear. Perhaps God wills."

"We must pray."

"Father, if I stop to pray, your dinner will burn."

"Then pray while you stir, and I will take the time."

"Why must I go away, Até? I fear the White Man's iron horse."

The priest bent over to hear the young man's words, but he couldn't make them out. "There will be time for your confession when you are well." Again, he spoke to his housekeeper, "I cannot understand his words and I do not think these are the words of your people."

"No, he is not of our tribe. Must have heard of great dance."

"And, thanks be to God, he must have escaped."

"He should join others. Flee before Buffalo Soldiers come and kill."

"They will not kill him. Not here at the mission. Here he is in my care. He is in the house of God. They will not kill him, and they will not kill you, Hantaywee. Have faith, my child, nobody will die here this day."

"It not matter kill Hantaywee or not, Father. If killed, I go to Jesus. If not, I continue to be your helper. When I die, I still go meet Jesus. Have you not promised?"

"Of course, I have. Your faith is good." He turned his attention back to the young man, took a cloth, dipped it into the nearby bowl of warm water, wrung it out, and then dabbed at Lonely Cricket's temples. "The three people who brought him to us, were they Christians?"

"I don't know, Father."

"They must have been. Why else would they have saved him from the storm?"

"Goodness is not found only among Christians," Hantaywee thought, but she did not dispute the cleric's words. Instead, bobbing her head, she replied, "Good Christian." Lonely Cricket tensed, then cried out. The dream was of long ago. The train on which he rode. The boy Standing Oak sitting next to him. The White Man Frazier. He, looking up into the man's face. The White Man's smirk revealed rotting teeth. The scar running down his left cheek stood out against the grizzled brown of his beard. The eye above that scar drooped. His left hand, missing the little finger and half the ring finger. "Do not hit me."

Even in his dream, Lonely Cricket knew he had not said those words even as he had not pleaded with Lame Bear begging to remain with him, Yquili Sparrow, Happy Turtle and Many Fish. But, in the dream he looked Duke Frazier in the eye and defied him.

As the White Man raised his hand, Plenty Horses grabbed his arm and held him back. "Not hit friend," Plenty Horses said. "Lonely Cricket my friend. Together we find his father."

"Até," Lonely Cricket cried out once more. "Yes, my son, I'm still here."

***

Each step was an effort. Lonely Cricket was glad the Lakota woman Hantaywee had bound his legs with deerskins. He was even glad that the priest had insisted on giving him a walking stick.

"Not old man. Not need stick," the young man had insisted.

"Trust me, Harry, you will be happy to have it when the snow is deep," the Jesus man had insisted.

Reluctantly, Lonely Cricket had accepted the staff. "Why does the White Man not call me Lonely Cricket?" he had asked Hantaywee.

"He want believe you Christian. He want believe we all Christian." The old woman had chuckled. "When he believe we Christian, he give food. He give blanket. He give clothes."

"So you do not believe?" Lonely Cricket stared at the woman's lips to better understand her words.

"I believe we find out in the next world." She busied herself wrapping food in a pack made of burlap for him to carry over his shoulder. "You need to eat when you walk in snow."

"Hau!" Gratefully, he took the pack.

"Take this blanket, too." She handed him the buffalo robe in which she herself had slept the night before. "Hau! You and White Man saved my life. Now, I must find my friend."

"If Plenty Horses lives, will you come back to Drexel Mission?" the priest asked for a second time. Lonely Cricket had not heard him at first.

"If still live, if not dead at Wounded Knee or at White Clay Creek, I ask him return with me."

"And, if he has died?"

"Then Até, I will bury him among our people." At each step the young man's foot would hesitate for a moment on the crust of ice and then, as he shifted his weight forward, would push into the slushy snow beneath. Then he would pull the hind foot free to repeat the process. It was difficult work. Soon he was panting with the exertion. His diaphanous white breathes wreathed upwards. His muscles ached.

"We have no mule to give you," the priest had warned him. "Walking will be very difficult."

"Life difficult. Not living easy. I must find friend."

"Of course. Of course." The priest had drawn on his pipe. "I will pray for you."

"Pray good. White Man pray many good words." That had been Lonely Cricket's last words before he turned his back on the mission and plunged into the hoary landscape.

***

What passed at first glance as friendship was that special relationship shared by men who are pariahs to the rest of the world—a grudging realization that they had no one else. Then, too, they shared some common pleasures: the joy of killing; the pleasure of destruction; the discomfort of women, and greed for gold. Whether it had been the war and the opportunities it gave to hurt others, the hunting of great herds of buffalo to the point of extinction, or the killing of Indians, both men pleasured in the inflicting of pain and especially the shedding of blood. If it filled their pockets and eased their cocks, all the better. Rejected even by the army troops for which they scouted, Teddy and Duke made a pair that only a gambler so down on his luck as to be desperate would have played. That hadn't stopped James Forsyth from signing them on. "Hell, the more they want to kill them savages the better," he'd explained to General Nelson Miles.

"You give me a reason, and I'll send them Redskins to their maker, and I ain't talking about no God in Heaven," he had told the two scouts.

They had done their work and more. The dead at Wounded Knee and White Clay Creek were evidence. The snow had soaked red with the dying. Now, they hunkered down and waited. Who knew if more Sioux would come looking for a fight? Who knew how many more believed in that "ghost dance" that was supposed to protect them from the White Man's bullets?

"Well, the Seventh showed 'em." Duke Frazier opined, ignoring, as was his want, the Black cavalry that had come to the Seventh's rescue at the second fight.

"Killed plenty of them, but I ain't sure it was enough," the other scout replied.

"'Nough fer what?"

"Enough so's we can get at that gold."

"That all you care about, Teddy, getting' your hands on gold?"

"Shit, what else is worth caring about in this godforsaken place? Sure ain't the women."

"Now, that's fer sure. I sure ain't interested in no squaw."

"Well, them whores in Rapid City ain't no better."

"Get yerself a disease from them," Duke replied.

"Or give one to them." Teddy's laugh was filled with spite.

"Hey, what's that?" Duke Frazier pulled his Army-issued glass from its protective leather tube, rubbed away the ice crystals that had formed on the eyepiece and lens, and carefully took in the scene.

"What you see?" Teddy Pirrip asked. "

Over there," Duke pointed. "See that fella? Don't know as he's an Injun or just lookin' to steal."

Teddy reached for Duke's spyglass and squinted into it. "Maybe hundred yards."

"Give or take."

"Yeah, I see him."

"Think we should kill 'im?" Duke asked.

"Not if he's a White Man. The Army don't take kindly to killing White Men."

"Not since the War anyways," Duke said. "Yeah, not since the War."

"Ain't War strange?"

"What does that mean?"

"Nothin', just if we'd met back then we'd be shootin' at each other."

"I suppose."

"Now," Duke continued, "we're on the same side."

"I guess you could say that if the same side is killing Redskins."

"Ain't it?"

"Sure," Teddy replied. Under his breath he added, "leastwise for now."

They turned their attention back to the man wandering among the distant bodies.

***

Tears streamed from Lonely Cricket's eyes as he turned the bodies with the priest's staff. Men, women, children, old people. Some eyes still open in surprise. A mother's body covering her dead infant. An old man clutching his coup stick. A boy holding another's hand.

At first, he looked for Plenty Horses. Then, mind numb with the dead, he just looked because he couldn't look away. The painted buffalo robe dropped unheeded from his shoulders.

Kneeling on a patch of red-stained snow, the young man cradled a girl in his arms. Looking into her face, Lonely Cricket saw Happy Turtle in her eyes.

With his tears came the sounds of choking pain. Distraught, in the agony of the moment, he pulled off his short, black, corduroy coat and the blue cotton shirt that he wore beneath.

He spoke into the cold air and watched the steam of his words dissipate. "I do not want to live as a White Man. I do not want to wear the White Man's clothes." He took his knife from its sheath and cut away the bindings around his legs, pulled the Army issued belt from his trousers, and allowed them to drop to the ground.

Standing only in his rough cotton union suit, Lonely Cricket cried out, "Ma-Ona, why do you allow such things to happen? Where were you when these people were killed?"

Raising his hands above his head—reaching towards the sky—Lonely Cricket began to dance. He danced slowly. He bent to the ground with his hands reaching to the earth, and then stood and again reached upwards and bent again. Stepping on his heel and then shifting his weight to his toe, he danced. He turned in the direction of the sun following the day as he danced. It was a dance he remembered from years before, the dance his people had done when they buried the dead. The dance they did to escort the dead to a new world.

In his head, Lonely Cricket heard the music of that dance. He heard the slow rhythm of the drum and the wail of the flute. He heard the cries of the people who danced. He heard the chant of the women who promised the dead that their souls would return to the place of their home, to the place where their afterbirth had been buried.

The young man didn't feel the cold. He no longer thought of his breath, of its steam. He no longer thought of Plenty Horses or even of himself. Lost in the moment of his dancing, Lonely Cricket had gone to a place far from where he was.

At that moment two, almost simultaneous shots rang out. First, Teddy's Sharps boomed. Within the second, Duke Frazier's Remington rolling block kicked back.

The bullets hit Lonely Cricket as he reached towards the sky. One bullet hit him near his heart, the other in his stomach. He crumpled slowly. He did not cry out.

At the moment of his death, the young man thought, "I will never know who I am."

"Got him," Duke Frazier exalted.

"God damn him to hell," Teddy Pirrip added. "God damn him to fucking hell."

***

An adolescent buffalo, separated from his herd, wandered by. The animal stopped some distance from the carnage. He snuffled the wind, pawed the earth, started as if frightened, and then meandered away.

Two buzzards landed, drawn as they were by the freshness of death. Hopping excitedly, they made their way among the scattered corpses. One stopped for a moment to pull an unseeing eye from its socket. The other hopped onto the face of the girl whom Lonely Cricket had cradled, looked almost lovingly into her innocent visage, and then pecked at her lips.

By the time Plenty Horses arrived on the scene, those first scavengers had been joined by a flock of their brethren. Their hissing, grunting, barking sounds filled the crystal air.

Straining to make his way forward through the snow and trying to shoo the giant birds from their feast, Plenty Horses didn't see his friend's body at first. Perhaps the tears that streamed from his eyes impeded his vision. Perhaps he did not want to see the personal details of the carnage that lay before him.

Had he not stumbled on the priest's walking stick, perhaps Plenty Horses would never have noticed Lonely Cricket's body, the eyes already gone, the nose pecked, the lips pulled free.

With the aid of that stick, Plenty Horses scooped a shallow grave in the snow, rolled Lonely Cricket into that depression, and covered his body. Plenty Horses knew this was but a gesture, but he also knew that sometimes gestures were all that was available. Gestures and tears. As he struggled off in the direction of the Drexel Mission, Plenty Horses heard the howl of wolves in their hunt and then the bellowing cry of a buffalo.

"Life, death, both go on. No Messiah today," he thought.

Chapter 57 ~ Continuings

"Momma, Momma." The boy ran crying up the stairs to the back porch, slammed his way into the kitchen, and screamed again, "Momma, where are you?"

"What's matterin' you, little one," the old man seated at the table asked. "You sounds like you done run into a mess o' hornets."

The boy threw himself into the man's outstretched arms, "Where's my momma, Grandpa Mose?"

"Now, don't you fret yourself so, child, she's upstairs doin' them papers."

Pulling away, the boy started towards the hall door.

"Hold on, child," the Black woman at the sink hollered after him. "You come on back o'er here and let me wash away them tears. No sense you goin' upstairs lookin' like that. No sense 't all." By the time she had finished talking, Esther's arms were around him, dragging him to the sink. Grabbing a cloth, she dunked it into the pan of warm water with which she was about to scald the chicken she had plucked for dinner, wrung the cloth out, and started dabbing at the boy's face. He pulled away.

"I want my momma," he said, this time in more of a whine than a scream. "What ails you so, child?" Mose asked.

"It ain't fair. That's what," the boy yelled. "Jimmy Junior and the other boys were playing cowboys and Injuns and they said I had to be an Injun cause of my being young." With a snarl he added, "I don't want to be no Red Injun. They always lose."

"Now what fool's been sayin' that?" Esther demanded.

"Jimmy Junior says it. He says, that's what his daddy says. He says, 'Them Red Injuns always lose, and that's a fact.' That's his very words."

"Well, him sayin' it don't make nothin' a fact. You hear me young'un?" the black man asked. The boy nodded.

"Now, you want your momma, she's upstairs. You go on up, but don't you make no noise. Miss Abagail ain't doin' so well todays." Mose spoke slowly and softly to emphasize his point.

Despite the black man's words, the youngster ran up the stairs, his footfall made a tympani of his progress.

"Momma, Momma," he called from the hallway. The father and daughter sitting in the kitchen could hear Sapphira's soft response.

***

Before Sapphira Cook sat on the fainting couch, she took time to adjust the shawl that covered the headrest. She took another moment to tuck a few escaping strands of hair beneath her blue and white checked bonnet. "My, my," she said to herself seeing a wisp of gray among the orange. "What on earth is it?" she asked the impatient boy who pulled at her skirt for attention.

The youngster laid out his complaint and ended it with, "I don't want to be no Indian, Momma. They ain't no good at all. All they do is kill folks and steal—"

"You hush. Have you ever met an Indian?"

"No, Momma, course I ain't. There ain't none here in New Albany."

"No there aren't, but they aren't like your playmates say."

"How do you know? Did you ever meet one? Huh? Did you?"

"As a matter of fact I did, and I knew him real well. Would you like to hear his story?"

"Yes, Momma. Would you tell it to me?"

"If you'd like. I tell you what, Little Cricket, you climb up here and I'll tell you all about him."

Bibliography

Below is a list of books consulted while writing this novel. Of course, in no way are these sources or any other sources I may have consulted responsible for this work of fiction or for any inaccuracies, deliberate or accidental, contained within.

Adams, David Wallace (1995) Education for Extinction; University of Kansas Press

Archuleta, Margaret L, Brenda J. Child, and K. Tsianina Lomawaima (eds) (2000) Away From Home: American Indian Boarding School Experiences; Heard Museum

Brown, Joseph Epes (1953) The Sacred Pipe: Black Elk's Account of the Seven Rites of the Oglala Sioux; University of Oklahoma Press

Dunbar-Ortiz, Roxanne (2014) An Indigenous Peoples' History of the United States; Beacon Press

Hungrywolf, Adolf (2008) Tribal Childhood; Native Voices

Hunter, Sally M. and Joe Allen (2006) Four Seasons of Corn; Lerner Publications

Lake-Thom, Bobby (1997) Spirits of the Earth; Plume-Penguin

Maryboy, Nancy C and David Begay (2010) Sharing the Skies: Navajo Astronomy; Rio Nuevo

Mauro, Hayes Peter (2011) The Art of Americanization at the Carlisle Indian School; University of New Mexico Press

Page, Jake (2003) In the Hands of the Great Spirit; Free Press

Pevar, Stephen L. (2012) The Rights of Indians and Tribes; Oxford University Press

Radin, Paul (1990) The Winnebago Tribe; University of Nebraska Press

Smith, David Lee (1997) Folklore of the Winnebago Tribe; University of Oklahoma Press

Trennert, Robert A., Jr. (1988) The Phoenix Indian School; University of Oklahoma Press

Yenne, Bill (2006) Indian Wars; Westholme

About the Author

Ken Weene learned to read at an early age. "I asked my father where baby's come from. When he said that he was too busy to talk, I figured that I'd have to find out a different way," is the explanation Ken gives. "My uncle, who was a doctor then serving in the army during World War II, had left his books in our attic. I figured that if I learned to read them, I would get my answer."

The joke was on Ken; those books were in German. Still, he had found the joy of reading, a joy that has never failed him. In addition to loving books, that early experience gave Ken a fascination with human behavior and how people lie to one another in order to give meaning to their own lives. Lonely Cricket, the protagonist of Red and White, draws on and reflects Ken's fascination with the search for human truth and the connection between that truth and stories.

With a Ph.D. in psychology and a never-ending love for language, writing, and his fellow humans, Ken has devoted the past twenty years of his life to creating stories, poems, essays, novels, and plays. Of these, All Things That Matter Press has published five full length novels and two short books. With each published word, Ken tells himself, "I think that's it." Still new ideas come. Even as *Red and White,* Ken's latest book published by All Things That Matter Press, was being edited he was co-authoring a full-length play, *Ashes* which is being published in Africa.

When asked how he can write about Native Americans, Black Americans, and characters from so many diverse backgrounds, Ken replies, "We're all more nearly human than otherwise." For Ken, writing is a celebration not of one group or one culture but of the human experience. "As long as I have the capacity to empathize, I will have a never-ending source of stories," Ken said about *Red and White*. Then he added, "I think that's it." Of course, we at ATTMPress wonder what will come next.

ALL THINGS THAT MATTER PRESS

FOR MORE INFORMATION ON TITLES AVAILABLE FROM
ALL THINGS THAT MATTER PRESS, GO TO
http://allthingsthatmatterpress.com
or contact us at
allthingsthatmatterpress@gmail.com

If you enjoyed this book, please post a review on Amazon.com and your favorite social media sites.
Thank you!

www.ingramcontent.com/pod-product-compliance
Lightning Source LLC
Chambersburg PA
CBHW060220030726
47499CB00004B/1123

* 9 7 8 1 7 3 2 7 2 3 7 7 1 *